Rose

ALSO BY ELLE CASEY

ROMANCE

Red Hot Love (3-book series)
By Degrees
Rebel Wheels (3-book series)
Just One Night (romantic serial)
Just One Week
Love in New York (3-book series)
Shine Not Burn (2-book series)
Bourbon Street Boys (4-book series)
Desperate Measures
Mismatched

ROMANTIC SUSPENSE

All the Glory
Don't Make Me Beautiful
Wrecked (2-book series)

PARANORMAL

Duality (2-book series)
Pocket Full of Sunshine (short story & screenplay)

CONTEMPORARY URBAN FANTASY

War of the Fae (10-book series)
Ten Things You Should Know About Dragons (short story in
The Dragon Chronicles)
My Vampire Summer
Aces High

DYSTOPIAN

Apocalypse (4-book series)

SCIENCE FICTION

Drifters' Alliance (3-book series)
Winner Takes All (short story prequel to Drifters' Alliance
in Dark Beyond the Stars Anthology)

To keep up-to-date with Elle's latest releases, please visit
www.ElleCasey.com
To get an email when Elle's next book is released, sign up here:
http://www.ElleCasey.com/news

ELLE CASEY

Montlake
Romance

Text copyright © 2018 by Elle Casey
All rights reserved.

Published by Montlake Romance Publishing, Seattle

www.apub.com

Amazon, the Amazon logo, and Montlake Romance Publishing are trademarks of Amazon.com, Inc., or its affiliates.

ISBN-13: 9781542047074
ISBN-10: 1542047072

Cover design by @blacksheep-uk.com

Cover photography by Matthew Hegarty

Printed in the United States of America

For Sandrine, fellow animal lover and friend I can always count on.

CHAPTER ONE

I close the last of the clinic's kennel doors and look down at the wiggling, waggling ball of energy at my feet. "Are you ready to go home for the day, Banana? Is that what you're trying to tell me?"

My three-legged border collie mascot whines in response and looks at the door as his tail wags. His communication skills are the stuff of legend. I could have named him Lassie, except he's not a girl and he's always so crazy-excited and going . . . well . . . *bananas*. Naming him after the fruit seemed more appropriate.

"Fine. Let me get my coat."

Before I can even think about following through on my statement, he runs to the rack in the lobby, grabs the bottom of the jacket with his teeth, and yanks it down, dragging it back over to me. He only trips once. The rack doesn't fall over because I've learned from experience that these kinds of things need to be permanently affixed to the walls in order to remain in one piece. Banana has not yet learned how to be graceful in his approach, but he's still young. Given enough time, I'm sure he'll figure out how to do just about everything around here as my helper, despite the fact that he lacks opposable thumbs.

"Why, thank you very much, kind sir." I bend at the waist to take my coat from him, with an exaggerated smile for his benefit. I scratch the side of his head in gratitude. "Good boy, Mr. Banana. Good boy."

He nearly turns himself inside out with happiness, managing some-how to smile back at me. I wish everyone were as easy to please as my dog is.

My cell phone rings as I head toward the door. When I recognize the caller as the thorn in my side—Betty Beland from the town council—I hit the Ignore button and slide the phone into my coat pocket. I'm too tired to deal with her nonsense right now. She has never respected the fact that I'm running a business here, and that if she wants to talk to me about it she needs to call me during regular hours on the work number, and not on my personal phone at eight p.m. *Some people . . .*

I know very well what she's going to tell me—that there's going to be a meeting soon about the use of my family's former barn as a clinic and that it doesn't look good for me or my patients. Been there, done that, and not worried; I have the law on my side.

I've been battling these small-minded bureaucrats for years, ever since I decided to make my business—a nonprofit animal rescue—official. You'd think they'd be grateful that I cure their sick pets at discount prices and the local injured wildlife at no cost to them, but nope . . . no, a hundred times no. They want to tax me, fine me, and wrap me up in red tape so tight I suffocate, because they cannot stand that all the efforts they've made thus far to control my life have failed.

If it weren't for Betty's personal vendetta against me, I doubt the town would continue to bother with the issue, but hell hath no fury like a woman scorned, and her ex-husband asked me out on a date once. In her eyes, I think it means she was rejected by a man who wanted to be with me instead. He never asked again and I never see him around town, but that doesn't seem to matter to her. Just the fact that he wanted to take me out was enough for her to hate me. It almost makes me want to date him, just so the whole thing would be fair, but I don't go out with guys who have the kind of baggage he's carrying around; Betty always struck me as a potential *Fatal Attraction*/boil-the-bunny-type person.

If it's not one thing, it's another with her, but I'm going to stand strong like I always do. The only things I care about are the animals who need me at the clinic and the family that loves me. Those stiff-necked politicians can go suck a bag of lemons as far as I'm concerned.

I can't help but smile at the image this thought conjures . . . all of them puckered up and cringing. It's not all that different from how they look every day, even without lemons being involved.

After I turn out the lights and lock up, Banana and I make our way up the road to the house. It's getting pretty cold and dark, but the stars are out and bright, lighting our way. My down jacket is keeping me warm tonight, but I'm going to have to add a scarf and mittens to my getup soon. Luckily, we don't have far to go, only about three quarters of a mile.

We're more than halfway home when Banana stops and turns around. His tail goes straight up in the air and stiffens as he leans forward and sniffs the wind.

I pause, looking over my shoulder. I've never been afraid to walk anywhere at night around here, since we own the entire property that our intentional-living community sits on, and there's rarely anybody around this time of year to bother us, but the dog's body language is a little freaky.

"What's the matter, Banana Bread? You smell a deer or something?"

He takes off running, barking like a mad fool, his little black-and-white form quickly disappearing in the dark. Missing a leg doesn't slow him down one bit.

Fear makes it feel like my heart just flipped over in my chest. *Do I follow behind him or go home and get help?*

The decision is easy. If there's anything happening back at the clinic, there's no way I'm going to waste any time getting someone at the house in person. I dial my home number and put the phone to my ear as I turn around and walk rapidly back in the direction I came from.

"Hello," a voice says. I immediately recognize it as belonging to my sister Emerald.

"Hi, Em. It's probably nothing, but Banana just ran back to the clinic barking like mad. I was on my way home, but I need to go find out what's making him act so silly."

"Isn't that what Banana always does? Goes bananas for no reason?"

"Not like this. Maybe it's just a deer or something, but I need to be sure."

"Do you want someone to come with you? Just in case it's not a deer?"

A chill slides over my bones. "Maybe?"

"Okay. I'll have one of the guys come out." She doesn't sound worried, and she shouldn't, because this is probably nothing. I'm ninety-nine percent sure of it. Our farm is the safest place on earth: a hippie commune in the middle of central Maine doesn't have much to offer the darker parts of society.

"Great. Thanks." I don't bother to ask her which guy she's going to summon on my behalf. There are plenty to choose from, since we're still hosting the members of Red Hot—the rock 'n' roll band our mothers have been in love with since they were teenagers. They arrived over a month ago as blasts from the past, and I honestly thought they'd be gone by now.

It's no big deal that they've stayed; I couldn't care less either way. But our moms just secured a permit to build an addition onto the house—a future recording studio—so I suppose I'd better get used to them being around when they're not on tour. They've been using the living room for their jam sessions, and it's been really amazing to see them in action, but, truth be told, I could use a little break from the music. I've been listening to their stuff since I was born because my mothers are such big fans, but it was always the polished version that played on our stereo, and it came with a volume button. Their new stuff is raw and edgy—an update to their old sound—and even though everybody agrees it's awesome, there is no volume button, and they're still working out the kinks.

It's not like I'm a prude or anything, but parts of the creative process—aka the swearing, ranting, and arguing—are a bit much for me. Our lives were so peaceful before they came; now everything is loud and crowded and . . . totally rock 'n' roll. I think I'm more of a Carole King person, really, but I'd never admit that to my mothers. The sun rises and sets on Red Hot for them, and I'm not going to be the one to burst their love-bubbles. Having the band living at our house has made all three of my mothers feel and look twenty years younger. They still do the work and chores that keep our community running, but they do it with a spring in their step and Red Hot songs on their lips. I've never seen them so happy.

I do enjoy the fun part of the band's creative process, where they laugh and joke around. There's a lot of that going on, especially because it's not just the band jamming alone; their three favorite groupies are always hanging around when they're in session. But still . . . I feel like my life has been turned upside down, and I can't seem to get it right side up again. We used to work side by side in our big garden, but now when I'm out there in the early morning, I'm more often alone than with someone. Their new schedules revolve around the band, which means gardening happens when I'm working at the clinic in the middle of the day. My mothers are too tired from staying up all night to wake up early and pull weeds or harvest pumpkins and other fall vegetables.

The clinic appears in the distance. *That's funny* . . . I thought I turned the lights off when we left, but there's a faint glow coming from one of the windows. And then, suddenly it's gone. Maybe I imagined it . . .

The light comes on again and moves.

A chill runs through my entire body from my toes to my nose as I realize that somebody is inside the building with a flashlight. That can't mean anything good. My blood starts to boil. If anything happens to the animals, I'll lose my mind . . . and I'll be kicking some serious butt, too. *Nobody* had better be messing with my patients.

"Bananaaaaaaa!" I scream, panicking now that I'm picturing him running straight into the arms of a criminal.

CHAPTER TWO

I want to sprint to the clinic to commence the ass-kicking, but I'm feeling pretty vulnerable without a weapon. I don't think my rapier wit is going to be very effective in this situation. I slow down and pull my phone from my pocket again. The home line rings several times before someone answers my call.

"Hello, Glenhollow Farms, this is Sally."

"Sally, hi."

"What's wrong, sweetie?"

I don't want to upset my mother and make her freak out about something I may be imagining, so I work to calm my voice. "Oh, nothing. I was just wondering who's coming out to the clinic. Em said she was going to send somebody to walk back with me."

"I think it's Ty. Do you want me to ask? Amber is just in the other room."

"No, don't ask her; it's fine."

"Maybe we should've sent Sam, too. Do you need more muscle?"

I can just imagine the goofy look on her face. She is so proud to have two of her daughters—Em and Amber—paired off with such 'gorgeous hunks'—her words, not mine. Sometimes I think our three mothers view these relationships as their own personal accomplishments. It doesn't matter that our moms only have one biological daughter each; all three of them claim all three of us as their own. One of the consequences of living in a free-loving hippie commune is that we are all family, as close as if Amber, Emerald, and I were born to the same mother when in fact we weren't. I'm not complaining, of course. I wouldn't have it any other way.

"No, it's fine," I say to Sally, the one of us most easily worried about silly things and my actual birth mother. "Leave Sam alone. He's taking care of a girl tortured with morning sickness."

"Boy, you can say that again. Poor Em. I've never seen anybody so sick before."

Footsteps crunch gravel behind me. "I'll be back soon," I say. "I've gotta go." I turn to see my sister's fiancé—Ty—arriving in the dark, his hands shoved into the pockets of his jacket. I slide the phone into my pocket and walk over quickly to meet him. As usual, his hair is sticking out all over the place and his expression is dark. The Stanz brothers definitely know how to get a brooding look on.

"Hey, what's up?" Ty asks. Amber's boyfriend—otherwise known as the lead guitarist for Red Hot—is usually a man of few words when he's around me. She claims he has all kinds of things to say when they're alone, but I'm not sure I believe it. Not only have I not witnessed this personally, but people have reported having a hard time getting a word in edgewise when Amber is around.

"I was headed home when Banana suddenly went on alert and ran off toward the clinic, barking like crazy. When I turned around to figure out what was going on, I'm pretty sure I saw somebody moving around inside the building with a flashlight."

Ty looks toward the clinic. "Why don't you stay here, and I'll go check it out?"

"No, I need to go with you. If any of the animals have been affected . . . I have to be there."

"Fine." We start walking together, the pace much faster than I'm used to, but I'm glad for it. He's taking my concern to heart. "I don't see any lights there now, do you?" he asks.

"No. And I could have been imagining things earlier. When Banana started barking, I got a little nervous."

"All right. Don't worry about it. We'll figure out what's going on."

His assurances soothe my nerves a little, but I won't be able to sleep if I don't see for myself that everything is okay.

The wind picks up, bringing tiny shards of icy rain to prick our faces. I'm going to feel really stupid if we get to the clinic and there's nothing there. Ty is from California; he's not used to this cold, and yet here I am dragging him out in the driving rain in the pitch black of night. "I saw the light for just a couple seconds, and then it was gone. Like I said, I might've imagined it. I haven't been sleeping a lot."

"We'll figure it out."

Banana is barking again, but he's not at the clinic anymore. It sounds like he's headed for the main road. When we get to the front door, I can see why.

"You didn't imagine anything. Somebody broke in," Ty says, pulling the door open and looking at the jamb. The metal plate that covers the lock is dented and doesn't look fixable. The door shuts, but it's not pretty.

"But . . . how did they do it so fast? I was *just* here." My heart sinks, and I feel nauseated when I realize that this person, this *thief,* must have been waiting close by for me to leave. "What the hell." I rush inside, my first thought for the animals and their safety. I'm stopped by Ty's hand on my arm.

"Let me go," I say, annoyed that he's slowing me down. "I have to check on my patients."

"No, you need to stop for a second. What if somebody's in there? You don't know what could be waiting for you."

"Yes, I do. Nobody's here waiting for me, because Banana is chasing whoever it was off the property. You can still hear him." The barks are fading in the distance as the clinic's mascot pursues our burglar. I panic, thinking about him out there all alone with a bad guy. "Could you please make sure he's okay?"

"I'm going to wait here with you first. Let's go check the animals." Ty gestures into the building.

I flip on the lights and run to the back room without another word, Ty following right behind me. The open space is lined on two sides with veterinary kennels, larger ones on the bottom and smaller ones in the middle and on top. Some of the patients who are able to vocalize start barking and meowing at my presence. A couple whine, but many of them remain silent. I take in all types of animals, and the wild ones know it's best to keep quiet when bad things are happening.

I turn on the light, checking each cage to make sure my patients haven't been disturbed. Intravenous lines and bandages all appear to be in place. The kennel that holds the great horned owl still has a sheet over it. I take a peek behind it to ensure that he's still inside and not overly stressed. Thankfully, he seems no worse for wear. I know he'd rather be flying around catching mice and other things right now, but his wing needs another few days of healing before he'll be able to do that. Getting caught in a construction fence did a heck of a number on him. "G'night, Hooters," I whisper.

I turn around to find Ty standing in the doorway. "Everything okay?" he asks.

I nod. "Doesn't look like they were in here for the animals, at least."

"Didn't you have a computer at the front desk?" he asks, looking over his shoulder.

My chest suddenly feels tight. "Yes. Why?"

"I don't see it where it usually is."

He moves out of my way as I rush past him to run down the hallway. My destination: the front desk, otherwise known as Command Central, the nerve center of my operation, where I have spreadsheets that keep track of all the animals who've come in, their care records, donations received from the public, and vet bills paid to the visiting doctor who's contracted to do surgeries and come up with the treatment plans I follow for each animal. When I get there, my heart sinks down into my toes. Sure enough, someone has yanked the laptop from its cables and it's nowhere to be seen.

"Dammit!" I yell out into the lobby. I face the door and shout, "Banana, I hope you tear him a new butthole!"

Ty comes up next to me. "How do you know it was a 'he' who stole your laptop?"

I glare at him. "You know very well it was a man. Girls don't break into buildings and steal computers."

He gives me a charming half grin. "Why, Miss Rose, I do believe that's just a little bit sexist."

I punch him lightly on the arm. "Don't try to make me laugh. I'm not in the mood."

"Just tell me you backed everything up." He picks up the end of one of the cables. "This sucks."

"I did back it up, but that's not the point. I don't have money in the budget for another computer, and even if I did, I'd have to hire an IT guy to come out and do everything for me, like transfer the data and software and all that junk. I don't have money for that either."

Ty drops the cable he was holding and shakes his head. "I don't know what it is with you girls."

I fold my arms over my chest, sensing a lecture coming on. "What's that supposed to mean?"

"You know exactly what it means. All you have to do is say the word, and you'll have ten million bucks of inheritance money dropped into your bank account from the band, but you refuse to do it. I don't understand what the big problem is."

I know a little bit about his history, so this is an easy debate for me to win, and I'm not in the mood to tiptoe around the facts to avoid hurting his feelings. "If *your* father offered you ten million bucks, would you take it?"

He laughs. "Hell yeah, I would."

I raise my eyebrow at him. "Even if taking it meant that you were okay with everything he did to you all your life?"

His good cheer drops away. "Yeah. Even then. People can make you say what they want you to say, but all that really matters is what's in your heart."

"Good. Then we agree."

He frowns. "We do?"

"Yes, we do," I say in a light and airy voice. In his effort to convince me to accept the fortune my mothers' boyfriends tried to bribe me with, he reminded me about what's important: my heart and my soul. And neither of them is for sale.

Not agreeing to take the money offered on behalf of the band by their lawyer, Greg Lister, doesn't make me unreasonable. I appreciate the fact that our mothers lived the way they thought was best and made choices in their pasts based on their limited understanding of the facts—leaving their positions as groupies to the band Red Hot without telling our fathers, the band members, that they were pregnant with us three girls. As a result, my sisters and I had a good life. *But* we also missed out on a lot of things, including having a relationship with our fathers, and it's not just because our mothers left without saying a word. It also happened because those men made it clear pregnant women weren't welcome in their lives, and they never tried to track our mothers down either. We can never get that back, and the money isn't going to change anything. It may make our lives a little easier now, but I'm not convinced that easier is better in the long run.

If I take that money from those men, it means that none of it mattered to me, that their letting our mothers disappear without a trace doesn't mean anything, and that their using our mothers for partying and sex is of no consequence. But it does matter . . . a *lot*. I'm not going to dignify their behavior by accepting their payoff. Just because our mothers are okay with letting bygones be bygones, it doesn't mean

I have to sign up for that plan. I have my own life and my own mind, and I'm not going to just adopt someone else's way of thinking because it would be convenient for everyone.

The band members seem nice enough now, and I know they regret their ways, but it doesn't erase any of the past for me. It doesn't take away the pain. I always wondered what it would be like to have a father who was there for me to talk to, to take walks with . . . to know he was there protecting me, thinking about me, looking out for my best interests, and teaching me what he knew about the world. But because of the decisions those men in the band and our mothers made, my sisters and I didn't get that. Those men were out there, alive and well, but they were too busy being famous and using other women to bother finding out about our mothers and, as a consequence, us. To put it simply: we got shafted.

I try not to be bitter about it, but I always fail. Maybe one day I'll be able to move past it, but today is not that day. And besides . . . Ty is full of crap. I've heard enough of his story from my sister Amber and from Emerald too, since Ty and Sam are brothers. I know these men carry a deep resentment for their father in their hearts, and there's no way they'd take anything from that man, not even a pile of money. Besides, they don't need to take a payoff from a ghost in their past. They're doing pretty well now, being in the employ of Red Hot, the hottest rock 'n' roll band of the last two decades. Sam's songwriting is really coming along, and Ty's role as guitarist has totally been solidified over the past few months.

"You should call the cops," Ty says, pulling me out of my sad little thoughts.

I flop down in the front desk chair, feeling totally dejected. *Why did this happen to me? Is this my karmic punishment for being unforgiving?*

"I know." I sigh loudly. "Could you do me a favor, though?" I look up at him, pleading with my eyes. "Could you go check on Banana? It's possible he has somebody pinned down near the entrance of our property, and I don't want to get sued for that, too." I'd go myself, but I'm worried someone might come back here and mess with the animals. Anyone who'd steal a computer from a nonprofit animal rescue is capable of anything, in my mind.

"What do you mean 'too'?" he asks. "Have you already been sued?"

"Yes." I gesture at the room. "Thanks to this."

Ty looks around. "Because of the animals?"

"The animals. The building. Me."

He leans on the counter with one hand. "I don't get it."

I feel so tired all of a sudden. "It doesn't matter. Suffice to say there will always be people in the world who will try to get you down. You just have to ignore them, and when they sue you, hire a good lawyer."

He smiles. "I take it you have one."

"Oh, yes."

"And you've won these lawsuits?"

"Every single time." I smile faintly at the memory of our last run-in with the town council. They tried to claim I didn't have the proper license to run this business, but they were wrong. They've also tried to claim that I provide veterinary services without a license, and they were wrong on that count too. If they'd even bothered to talk to me before they wasted the town's money on a lawsuit, they would have known that I always hire veterinarians to come in and do all the medical procedures. I'm basically just an assistant and a bookkeeper who also cleans up animal poop and dog vomit in her spare time.

"I'll go check on the dog. Want to call the house and get some of the other guys down here to keep you company?"

"Sure." I'm not going to do that, but it'll make him feel better to think that I will, so I lie. After what happened tonight, I'm not leaving here, and more people means more arguments about it. They'll say it's not safe for me to stay alone, and I'll have to remind them that I've done it hundreds of times before, and they'll disagree . . . It'll just be a mess.

Instead, as Ty leaves the building, I pick up the phone and call the police. The dispatcher is the only one there right now, and after I explain what happened, she tells me somebody will be out in the morning to write up a report. I guess the robbery of an animal clinic doesn't constitute an emergency to anyone but me.

After ending the call, I rest my head down on my folded arms on top of the desk. Everyone keeps telling me I need to put a cot in here somewhere, so I can get a proper night's sleep when I'm with the animals, but I don't have room for it. For years, my bed has been this desk, and my arms have been my pillows. I'm dozing off in no time.

CHAPTER THREE

A strange sound and a blast of cold air pull me out of my sleep. I lift my head from my numb arms and look up to find Ty standing in the doorway, holding Banana in his arms.

I leap to my feet and run over. "Oh my . . . where did you find him?"

"He was in a ditch next to the main road." Ty is grunting with the effort of carrying him. It's no wonder . . . he has to have walked almost a quarter mile. A quick glance at my watch tells me I've been sleeping for almost forty-five minutes.

"Follow me." I lead him into the first exam room, going through the door ahead of them so I can be on the opposite side of the stainless-steel table.

"Lay him down here." I stare at Banana's face, wishing his eyes didn't appear so glassy. My heart feels like it's collapsing in on itself. "Oh, Banana, what happened to you?"

After Ty places him gently on the table, I begin my preliminary examination, checking over his whole body. There's blood on his fur, but I can't tell where it's coming from. He picks up his head and whines at me, which I'm going to take as a good sign. I'd rather him complain than fade away.

"What do you want me to do?" Ty asks. I've never seen him look so angry before, like he wants to punch someone in the face.

"Call the vet, Dr. Masters." I'm pretty sure I'm holding a broken leg in my hand right now. "His number is on the wall behind the front desk."

I lean down and look into the eyes of my baby, Banana. "You're going to be okay, little guy, I promise."

His tongue comes out to lick my chin, and I start to cry. "Please don't leave me," I beg in a whisper.

Thirty minutes later, Sam joins us in the exam room after being called in by his brother. Ty is in the other room, waiting for the vet to show up. Sam isn't saying anything; he's just staring at the dog. Banana licks my hand and whines, making me think he wants me to comfort him some more. Or maybe he's being his typical Banana self and trying to comfort me.

I lean down and kiss him on the head. "You're gonna be okay, buddy. We're going to fix you right up. You'll be as good as new in no time." I'm fighting back the tears and anxiety that threaten to overwhelm me.

"Who would do something like this to an animal?" Sam asks.

I straighten, gently petting Banana on the neck—the one place I know is not injured, thanks to the X-rays I took. "My guess is . . . somebody who would also steal a laptop from a nonprofit animal rescue."

"I want to murder somebody right now." Sam seems surprised at his statement.

"You and me both. And believe me, as soon as I get Banana back on his feet, I'm going to be on a one-woman mission to figure out whose ass is going to get buried in an unmarked grave."

Sam reaches over and squeezes my arm. "Whenever you're ready, just call up a posse. I'll ride with you."

Sam's kind words fill my heart with warmth. He really is a good guy. I glance up at him and catch a strange expression on his face. He's out of his element. Scared. Sad. I get it; I've seen it a thousand times. Injured, innocent animals are hard for some people to cope with.

"You're good people, Sam. I'm glad you're with Em and that you're raising Sadie together and have a baby on the way. You make a beautiful family."

His smile is awkward. "Thanks. I think you're pretty cool too, and Sadie loves you. She really digs being here at the clinic with you and learning about all the animals."

"Thanks." I look down at Banana. He's panting too much, which means he's suffering. His gums are going pale, too. "I need to push some more painkillers into his IV. Could you stay here and keep him calm?"

"Absolutely. Do what you have to do. I'm here."

As I gather the syringe and bottle of pain meds from the other room, I hear voices. Ty is back in the exam room with his brother. I work around them, giving Banana another low dose of painkiller. I can't give him too much or I risk causing problems with the potential surgery he may need to undergo. I've learned so much under the supervision of Dr. Masters. I'm so happy he agreed to work under contract with the clinic years ago.

"You want me to get him some dog chow or something?" Ty stares at Banana, looking almost as helpless as the dog.

"No. No food. He's going to need surgery, I think, and he can't have anything in his stomach."

"What's wrong with him?" Ty asks, looking at me.

"He's got at least a broken leg. Maybe some internal injuries, too." I don't have the equipment to test his blood count here, and none of the labs are open at this time of night, but judging by this leg, I think it's likely that there's more than meets the eye with his injuries.

"Did he get hit by a car?"

"Maybe. It's hard for me to say." I stroke Banana's neck, relieved to see his respirations calming a bit.

Sam looks at his brother. "We're putting together a posse after everything is taken care of here."

"Do we know who did this?" Ty looks from Sam to me.

"No. But we're going to try and find out," Sam says, sounding very sure of himself.

"I'm in." Ty exchanges a high five with his brother. I offer my elbow, not wanting to get anything from the dog's injuries on to their hands.

I stare down at my sweet little Banana Bread, aka Banana Muffin, aka Banana Pie, aka Banana Buns, always a bit small for his breed but so huge in his heart. The poor thing has already gone through so much—at least one car accident where he lost one of his legs. It happened when he was a puppy. Thank goodness a Good Samaritan was there and was kind enough to pick him up and bring him here.

I can't believe this is happening to him again. He deserves so much better. The vet has to fix this leg, because Banana can't afford to lose another one. A tear slips past my defenses, and I wipe it away quickly. Sam and Ty both reach across the table, each of them putting a hand on my shoulders.

"It's gonna be okay," Ty says.

"Yeah. Don't worry," Sam says. "It's going to be fine."

I nod, hoping they're right.

CHAPTER FOUR

It takes the vet much longer than it normally does to get here, and I'm on pins and needles the entire time we're forced to wait. I've worked with John Masters, DVM, for several years, and he's usually quick to respond to my calls. It's getting close to midnight now, and Banana isn't doing well. He's drawing into himself to manage the pain. I've seen animals do this and then just disappear, never recovering. I'm trying not to panic too much. Banana has a strong spirit, no one can deny that. *Please God, send me a miracle.*

When John finally arrives and gets into the exam room to look at Banana, he doesn't look very happy. It's strange, because despite the sometimes grave injuries we've faced together, I've never seen him look even remotely distressed. I get the impression that his dark mood isn't because of his patient.

"Is everything okay, John?" Maybe he's not happy that I've called him in so late. I've done it before, but only for emergencies. This qualifies as one of those, though.

"Why don't we talk about it after we get Banana stabilized?" he suggests, listening to the dog's heart rate.

"Sure." I thought my day couldn't get any worse, but it sounds like it's going to, if the tone of John's voice is any clue. I'm not going to stress out about that now, though, because I have plenty of other things to worry about. Banana is my top priority, followed by recovering my laptop, and then murdering, or at least severely maiming, the person who took it and injured my dog in the process.

John glances up at Sam and Ty, who are standing in the corner of the room, both of them with their arms crossed over their muscular chests. They look like bouncers. "What's going on in here tonight?" John asks, meaning, 'What are two bodyguards doing standing over a three-legged border collie?'

"This is Sam and Ty. They're . . . my brothers." It seems easier to say this than to go through the strange and confusing explanation as to why two rock 'n' roll geniuses are standing in my clinic in the middle of the night.

Neither of the guitarists bats an eyelash, but John stops his exam and stares at me. "Brothers? I didn't know you had any brothers."

"They're . . . new," I say, feeling totally awkward. I point at our patient. "I think Banana has a broken right foreleg. I took X-rays, but you can feel the fracture."

"Let's take a look." John walks over to the light boxes that have the films hanging from them. After he's done, he goes back to Banana and gently palpates his leg. "You're exactly right." John glances at me with pride in his eyes. He's taught me so much over the years.

"Is he going to need surgery?" My heartbeat picks up speed as I wait for his diagnosis.

He sighs, frowning at the dog. "On any other canine, I would say no, just a splint could do it . . ."

"But . . . ?" I prompt.

"But because this is Banana, and because he only has three legs, I'm thinking otherwise."

I nod. "He's special."

"Yes. Special is one way to put it. What are the chances you'll be able to get him to rest for a few days if we don't do the surgery? If we just put a splint on it and see how that goes first?"

I look at him like he's nuts. "None? You know better than anyone that I named him Banana for a reason."

"That's what I thought. Let's prep him for surgery. I've got one hour and that's it."

I look at my newly minted brothers. "Could you just hang here for a minute while I get the operating suite ready?"

Sam gives me a thumbs-up and Ty nods.

I leave the room and go through the process of preparing for my baby's surgery. As I get out equipment and supplies, I try to process what's happening. I can't believe how sick I feel, how panicked, how utterly hopeless. Banana was just fine a few hours ago. We were headed home for dinner and a good night's sleep in a real bed, and then minutes later he was busted up on the side of the road. How did this happen?

Everything was going well in my life up until tonight. Yes, we have a bunch of strangers living in our house who sometimes make me question things about my life; and yes, our mothers are so crazy-in-love and silly over them I don't even recognize them or our lives together anymore; and yes, my two sisters have fallen in love with men who play in a band, who got them pregnant, who make their hearts sing and their lives full, even though they only met mere months ago; and yes, if things keep going the way they're going, they'll get married and have their babies together, and Emerald will have an adopted daughter, Sadie, too; and yes, I will still be alone, working eighteen-hour days in this clinic, trying to save as many animals as I can. But that's all okay, because my sisters and moms are happy and I like my life. I don't mind being alone for the most part . . . as long as being alone means I still have Banana with me. I don't want to be here without him running around, barking like mad, and being my ridiculous assistant.

Tears roll down my cheeks as I make sure the already sterile operating room table is sterilized again.

CHAPTER FIVE

A tongue on my face tugs me from a dreamless sleep. Then the dog breath follows, hot and smelly. I lift my face off my arms and crack open an eye, peering at a slightly sedated but happy three-legged border collie who's wearing a post-surgical cast on his right foreleg. I guess for now I should think of him as my two-legged pup. *Poor thing.*

"Hey, Banana Muffin. How're you feeling?" I stretch my arms above my head to work the kinks out of my back and then focus on checking my patient. His gums are pink, his eyes are mostly bright, and his tail is thumping on the floor. We slept together, him on a pad and me on sleeping bags in the lobby, the floor out here being the only space big enough for both of us and far enough away from the other patients that their sleep wouldn't be disturbed. I couldn't bear the idea of putting him in one of the kennels, even though I know they're comfy and I do it with other animals all the time. I need to be closer to him than those boxes allow.

I stand and look around. Ty is sleeping in one of the waiting room chairs, but otherwise, the clinic looks as it always does at—I check my watch—six in the morning.

"Hi, Ty," I say. "What're you doing here?"

He sits up immediately, startled out of his sleep. "What? Who?" He stares straight ahead, as if he's hypnotized.

I have to smile, seeing for a split second what caught Amber's eye and heart all those months ago when she went off to Manhattan to meet the men who claim to be our fathers and tell them we weren't interested in the inheritance money they were offering. Ty is pretty adorable with his hair sticking out all over the place and his rumpled clothes. "Over here." I wave at him.

He slumps down in his chair and runs his hands through his hair. Then he winces, swiveling his upper body left and then right. "Oh, shit. My back is killing me."

I stretch with a few bends and twists. "Serves you right. Why'd you sleep in the chair?"

"Couldn't leave my girlfriend's sister out here by herself in the middle of the night, now, could I?"

"I've done it plenty." I can't remember the last time I had a full week of sleep at home.

"Yeah, but that was before you had a burglar." He stands and stretches up to the ceiling and then bends over to touch the floor. He and my sister have been doing yoga together, and she's been trying to convince me to do it, too. So far I've resisted, because I've been too busy, but I'm feeling pretty stiff myself. Maybe I should try a couple stretches. I reach up toward the ceiling, looking over at Ty to see if I'm doing it right.

"Are you mocking me right now?" he asks, not looking at me.

I glance at Ty between my arms. "No. I'm stretching. Ohhhmmm . . ." I try not to smile, I really do.

"Sure you are." He drops his yoga stance and sits back down in the chair, yawning and looking at his phone. Amber warned me he was feeling self-conscious about their exercise regimen, worried that somehow the press would find out about it and start running stories about how his relationship with a hippie chick was changing him. He's sensitive about Amber being cast in a bad light by the public, and I appreciate his concerns for her well-being, especially now that she's pregnant. I feel just a tiny bit bad that I ohhhmmm-ed at him.

"When you were out there last night looking for the three-legged wonder . . . ," I'm avoiding saying 'Banana' so my patient won't get too excited and try to stand up, "did you see who broke in, by any chance? A car, maybe?"

"Nope. I didn't find anything but the dog." He looks up at me. "And I walked past him about three times before I finally saw him. Sorry."

"It's no big deal. The police are going to come out later today to write up a report. Hopefully, the thief's fingerprints are in the system." I've watched a few detective shows, and that's the line they always use: 'fingerprints in the system.' It sounds so official.

"Any chance you had one of those 'find-me' apps on your computer?" Ty asks.

"Nope. I figured it was in the safest place it could be out here."

He hisses in disgust. "Nothing is safe anymore. Not even on a hippie commune in the middle of Maine."

It makes me sad to think that crime from the bigger cities is making its way out here to the farm. "It's probably just some teenager from town. I'll let everybody know at the next farmers' market that I'm missing it, and maybe it'll show up outside my door." Just like the litters of kittens and puppies that people dump here.

The sound of a car stops our conversation. Ty stands and walks over to the door, looking through the window. "Cops." He looks over his shoulder at me. "I'm going to head back to the house unless you need me."

"No, go ahead. I'll be fine. Thanks for keeping us company."

"No problem."

Ty leaves, and I glance around the lobby, wishing I could clean up the mess left behind by the stolen laptop but resisting because I know the officer will want to see it. Voices come from outside, and then the door is pushed open. A cool burst of air follows, and I cross my arms over my chest, wishing I had my jacket on. Banana seems fine on his soft bedding with the heater blowing nearby. He doesn't budge.

"Hear you had a break-in last night," the officer says after shutting the door. I recognize the man but cannot recall his name. I think I've seen him at the supermarket a few times.

"Yes," I say, walking over to shake his hand. "As far as I can tell, the only thing they stole was my laptop." The odor of woodsmoke comes from his clothing, making me think I've pulled him away from a warm fire.

"Is that where it was?" He points at the desk.

"Yes." I lead him over to it. "Do you want to dust for fingerprints?"

A slight smile plays across his lips. "You want me to dust for fingerprints, huh?"

He's acting like I said something funny. "Isn't that what you do?" I stare at his badge for emphasis.

He shrugs. "Not really. It's just a laptop. I doubt it was stolen by a criminal who already has his fingerprints in the system. It was probably just a teenager causing trouble."

Fingerprints in the system! Ha! I knew it!

He and I are speaking the same language, but I find his blasé attitude more than a little annoying. "Oh, really? Just a teenager? Do you see some sort of evidence of that?" This guy is a police officer; shouldn't he be taking this *crime* more seriously? My temper begins to rise.

"It's what we typically see."

I resist the urge to plant my hands on my hips, lacing my fingers at my waist instead so as to appear less threatening. "Have you had a rash of laptop thefts lately?"

He gives me a funny look. "I don't know that I'd say we've had a rash of them, but it's not completely uncommon."

"Fine." I guess I'm not getting my fingerprint dusting. *So disappointing.* "I suppose you can just take my statement, then."

He stands there, staring at the desk, moving his jaw back and forth as he rubs his chin. It looks like he's going to tell me no.

"Please tell me that you're going to write up a report." I almost laugh, thinking he's playing some kind of joke on me by doing a great imitation of Rosco P. Coltrane from *The Dukes of Hazzard.*

"Yeah. I suppose I could do a report." He hooks his thumbs into his thick leather belt and rocks back and forth from heel to toe, heel to toe . . .

Maybe I haven't gotten enough sleep, but it sure seems like he doesn't want to help me and that he's trying to figure out how much he can get away with *not* doing. Apparently, I've been transported to another era, to a time when women weren't taken seriously about anything. I open my mouth to say something about how my tax dollars have to be worth something in this town, but he cuts me off at the pass.

"I'll be right back." He leaves the building abruptly, going out to his car. When he doesn't come back in a couple minutes, I walk over and look out the window. He's sitting in his vehicle talking on his cell phone.

"What in the hell are you doing, Officer Whatever-Your-Name-Is?" I mumble to myself. Is he seriously sitting out there chatting away while I wait in here for him to do his damn job? *How rude!*

I'm all set to get steamed up about it, but then I figure, what's the point? I have to get to work, and it's not like I'm going anywhere—I can wait all day. Besides . . . even if he does take my statement and fill out a report, I know very well he's not going to follow up on it. He's going to just dump it in his circular file as soon as he gets back to the station and never look at it again. I've done something to annoy him; either that or he's the laziest officer of the law to ever wear a uniform. Or maybe he's friends with Betty Beland. That would totally be my luck.

I go to the telephone and dial the house number. "Hi, it's me," I say to the male voice who picks up the phone. I have no idea who it is, and I don't really care.

"Hey, Sugar Pop. It's Mooch. What do you need?"

The kind voice of the gray-haired, barrel-chested drummer of Red Hot and the term of endearment he uses threaten to soften me, but I resist the siren call. I'm going to need to stay mad to get stuff done around here today. "Anyone in the mood to bring me some breakfast? I'm starving and I never made it home last night."

"You got it. Just give us about twenty minutes to get it put together, and then we'll drive it up to you."

It sounds like the moms and the band members are working in the kitchen together again; it seems to be their routine now to cook up a big breakfast for whomever is around before they head out to the gardens or groves to weed and harvest. "Perfect. See you then." I hang up the phone and sit in the chair at the front desk, staring at the empty space that used to hold my laptop. I wasn't exaggerating when I told Ty that I don't have the money for a new one. I also wasn't joking about not having the time or the expertise to deal with moving my backed-up data and software onto a new hard drive. I suddenly feel so overwhelmed, I don't know what to do with myself, so I drop my face into my hands and cry.

I don't know how long I sit there like that, but someone clearing his throat pulls me out of my pity party. I lift my head to find the police officer staring at me.

"You have anything to add to what you've already told me?" He shifts from his left foot to his right, making the leather belt holding all of his equipment creak with the movement.

I shake my head, realizing my case isn't that complicated: my laptop was stolen . . . period. No wonder he didn't want to fill out a report. Can a report even qualify as a report if it only has one sentence on it?

"No," I say, feeling monumentally disappointed. "Other than I think they got in through the locked front door. Everything was fine when I left, but now it's broken."

"Yeah, I noted that." He puts a form down on my desk and points to it. "Could you just sign there on the *X*?"

I stare at the form in front of me. It has the name of my business, the address, and a single line: *Front door break-in, laptop stolen.* I cannot for the life of me keep from commenting on it. "It's so great to see my tax dollars at work." I pick up a pen and sign on the dotted line and hand the paper back. I can't even look at his face.

"You have a nice day, now," he says as he walks away. There's a smile in his voice.

I guess it's supposed to be some sort of twisted joke for him to tell me to have a nice day after he basically tells me to screw off . . . simply because I asked him to do his job. Why couldn't he dust for fingerprints? Does the dust cost too much to waste on a nonprofit clinic? Is it *golden* fingerprint dust? *Ugh.* What a jerk. I hate people sometimes. I don't know why it has to be such a battle with some of them. It's probably why I've dedicated myself to working with animals. They're so much easier; they never lie, they never pretend to like you when they don't, and they never intentionally or carelessly break your heart, which is more than I can say for most of the humans I've known.

My mothers moved here twenty-six years ago, and they haven't done anything wrong to anyone, but it still seems like some of the people living in the nearby town would like nothing more than for all of us to disappear. They'd probably love it if we all followed Amber down to New York City. No way would I ever do that, though. Manhattan is not my scene. And it's not Emerald's either. We're here for good, and the people in town just need to live with it.

Amber will head back to New York next month probably, but Em and I aren't going anywhere. And now, since I have to buy a new laptop with money I don't have to spare, I can forget hiring any help through the winter, so I'm really going to be doing everything on my own. I guess that'll make some people in town happy, since they won't see me. I'll be too busy to go to the bar or the grocery store.

I'm just grateful that the veterinarian who does the surgeries and makes up the treatment plans here gives me such a great deal on his services; otherwise, I don't know what I'd do. I can't stand to see the animals suffering, but unfortunately taking care of them isn't free. The donations I get from people who are grateful for my work barely cover my expenses. Any income I have comes from the farm's food production and sales at the farmers' market that we attend every week, not from my work in the clinic.

Rather than continuing to dwell on my problems, I decide to distract myself by cleaning. I do my best to keep my mind off Betty Beland's vendetta against me and the police that don't act like real police by straightening up the desk area. Then, I reorganize my medicine closet, verifying that nothing was taken in the process. Even bandages have to be accounted for because I run on a shoestring budget.

As I put everything back into neat rows, my mind wanders to the person who came in here last night with the intent to do my business harm. If I were a criminal, I would go right for the narcotics, not the bandages. That's where the real money in my budget goes, and that stuff is sellable on the black market. Not that I keep narcotics right here out front where anybody could see them, but still . . .

I feel a little sick to my stomach over that thought and rush to the back room. I can't believe neither I nor that sorry excuse for a police officer thought about the narcotics! What the hell is wrong with me? With him?

The lock hasn't been touched, thank goodness, but I open the cabinet anyway and verify that everything looks okay inside. Maybe the thief was going to take the drugs, but he ran out of time, thanks to Banana.

Banana! Panic grabs me. Why haven't I been worried about him this whole time? I've been so focused on the stupid laptop and that jerk officer, I haven't checked on him in almost thirty minutes.

I walk quickly back to the lobby and find my buddy sound asleep. The painkillers and leftover anesthesia are working their magic, making it possible for him to miss the worst of the pain. He isn't going to be happy later when he tries to move around, but for now, he's okay. I look up at the ceiling, battling tears. *Thank you, God, for saving my puppy.*

The idea of someone saving Banana makes me think of John, the vet. He took off the moment he was done with the surgery, leaving me to finish the stitches. Whatever he wanted to talk to me about went with him. He was bothered when he got here and not any better when he departed, but I'm not going to worry about that now. My plate is already full enough.

CHAPTER SIX

The next three hours pass in a blur. I finally have a chance to breathe and eat the breakfast that has grown cold and hard on my desk. For at least a few moments, I am alone. I can sit and wallow in my bad fortune for a little while before I have to put on a happy face for the world.

John, my trusted veterinary partner of five years, is bailing on me. He called and gave me some lame excuse about his practice growing and the distance becoming too much, but he also mentioned the town council, so I know what the real score is: they got to him. Betty harassed and threatened him enough that he finally bought into her bullshit. He can't take the risk of helping me anymore.

I don't get it. My lawyer has done such a great job all these years coming up with legal support for the fact that I can run this business the way I do using John as a contractor veterinarian. So what's the big deal? Why is Masters now suddenly chickening out? I'll probably never know, because he wouldn't answer any of my questions. Not really. The guy is very good at beating around the bush and playing head games, something I never knew about him before. He reminds me of a guy I dated a few years back in college, who I thought I loved but who was just using me. He was a master at playing head games. I never saw that heartbreak coming.

I lean back in my chair and stare at a ceiling that's stained from several roof leaks. *Why, oh, why must this building suck so much?* My mind drifts a little, fantasizing about what I wish I could have, besides an unstained white ceiling. I dream of a state-of-the-art medical facility with no expense spared and a veterinary school diploma on the wall with my name on it. I could do everything with one of those; I wouldn't need to depend on weak men like John Masters to help heal my patients.

I snort, thinking about that man. *Masters? . . . Please.* Talk about a misnomer. Master of *what*, I'd like to know. Master of nothing, since he lets women like Betty Beland boss him around. *Jerk-head.*

I sit up straight in my seat and sigh. Reality is back, slapping me in the face with her cold, cruel hand. There will be no fancy medical building or vet school diploma on my wall. Graduate school just wasn't in the cards for me, and no amount of dreaming or fantasizing is going to change that. The family and the farm needed me here and then so did the animals who started showing up at our door one after another in a steady stream. It's not like I could abandon them for four years of focusing on my dreams. Doing what I do is good enough.

There's a huge risk in going to vet school, too. There's all the money involved, the pressure, the time spent away from family who depend on me to make ends meet. I would never put them through that, and frankly, after four years at the local college, I didn't think I had four more in me. No way was I going to risk all that money and difficulty for my family just to fail out. Besides . . . I don't need a veterinary diploma to help and heal animals. I do it every single day.

I stare at the door longingly. Sometimes I just want to walk right through it and keep on going . . . never come back. It sure would be easier not having to deal with the stress of unpaid bills and the nonsense brought by Betty Beland. But I'd never do that, of course, because I have all these beautiful little souls counting on me. I hear one of them whining in the back room, demanding my attention. It's a puppy who was abandoned on my doorstep last week. He had an eye infection that was so bad we almost had to remove it, but he's better now, and waiting with two eyeballs for someone to adopt him. If I had my computer, I'd be uploading the pictures I took of him yesterday to the Internet right now. Poor little nugget. He's loaded with love and just needs a person to share it with.

I go into the back room and find him waiting patiently at the door of his kennel for me, his little tail wagging. He's a pitiful mix of basset hound and dachshund, which means he could not be any uglier or more adorable. I take him out of the kennel and cuddle his long, heavy body in my arms. His short, chubby legs and sharp baby nails poke into me as he tries to climb higher, attempting to get nearer to my face.

"What are you doing, Oscar Mayer? Was that you causing all the fuss in here? Don't you see your injured friends in here trying to sleep?"

He pants and licks and wiggles and squirms and barks. He's ridiculously happy to see me, even though I was just in here thirty minutes ago cleaning out his kennel. I can't bear to put him back in there now that I have his warm body melting into mine. "Come on out front with me, little stinker. You can keep me and Banana company."

My two-legged Banana Muffin now has a child gate all the way around him, keeping him from crawling away from his resting spot, and keeping any visitors like Oscar Mayer puppy from getting too curious. Even with painkillers, my patient is in considerable pain and will be for at least the next week. He already tried to stand once today and quickly gave up.

As I'm walking out of the hallway and into the main room, the door to the clinic opens. A hunched-over man wearing what looks like a safari hat and a dark-blue coat comes shuffling in. He comes inside and puts a stack of mail on my desk.

"Hey, Hal." I shift the puppy so he's hanging over my shoulder like a human baby, freeing up my face and attention for the mailman. "How are your knees holding up?"

He shakes his head. "Not good, not good at all." He winces, using acting skills that could have won him an Oscar had he ever been in a film and not just in my life. "This cold weather makes me ache all *over*." His wrinkled face creases as he lays it on thicker. You'd think he had a sword stuck in his gut the way he's folding in on himself.

"I hear you. Did you try rubbing in some of that tea tree oil like I suggested?"

"I did. And it did help. But I ran out." His face is all innocence now, as if he's not here looking for more of the tincture I use for arthritic animal joints.

I sigh and shake my head. "You'd think, being the postman, that you'd know a little bit about ordering things online."

"I do, but you know what? . . . I'm kind of old-fashioned. I don't really like all that online ordering. That's how my knees went bad so fast . . . all those packages. You know, before Amazon came along, everything was fine. People used mail-order catalogs, which took a lot of doing. Took some time. Took some money to pay for the shipping. Christmas was a little busy, but nothing like it is now. But the day *that* company took off, and people could just click-click-click their pay-checks away, my workload quadrupled, and then it quintupled, and then it got a hundred times worse. Seems like every week I'm carrying more and more boxes." He's clearly disgusted with the public's online ordering habits.

"Damn that Amazon," I say. "Knee-destroying bastards." I try not to smile but fail. I don't feel at all guilty about the amount of shopping I do online. It's the only way I can get some things without having to drive an hour on questionable roads.

"Yeah. Bastards."

"And those damn televisions and automobiles too," I say, feigning seriousness with a raised fist. "Grrrr. So annoying."

He opens his mouth to agree, and then stops. His face falls. "Don't sass me, girl." He points at me. "I told you, my knees are sore. I'm not in the mood." He turns to leave, shuffling even more drastically than when he came in.

I walk over to the tall medicine cabinet behind my desk and pull out a small dark-blue jar, hurrying over to give it to him before he reaches the door. I put the puppy down on the floor and hand it over.

"What's this?" Hal asks, as if he doesn't know.

"It's for your knees. Just rub a little bit on both of them in the evening, on the sides and back of the joint."

"Thanks, Doc." He smiles big at me, revealing the large gap between his front teeth.

"Don't call me Doc. You know I'm not a doctor." All I need is the town council thinking I'm telling people I'm a vet. They'd shut me down for sure.

"You're a healer. In my book, that makes you a doctor." He nods his head once, like it's now a fact; I am officially a vet because Hal Warner, the postman, says so.

I hold the door open as he walks out, now with a spring to his step since he no longer needs to wrangle more tea tree oil out of me.

"Stay warm," I say.

"You too. I'll see you tomorrow."

I shut the door quickly, shivering with the chill. I rush back over to my desk and sit down, hoping the space heater at my knees will quickly warm me back up. I hear a noise and look down to find the little stinker, Oscar Mayer, digging through my purse.

"Get out of there, you tiny punk." I grab him and put him in my lap. He's holding a tampon between his teeth.

"What are you doing? You're not supposed to touch those things. That is so rude." I lower my voice and whisper next to his floppy ear, "Those are girl things and they're *not* for *you*."

I try to take it from between his sharp baby teeth, but he's not having it. He wrestles me for it, growling when I try to pull it away.

"Let go of that. How dare you." I can't stop laughing. "No, sir, it is *not* a toy!"

His tail rests over the desk, shuffling my mail around as he wags it. Some of the letters are thrown off to the side, revealing an envelope from the middle of the stack whose return address and logo I know only too well.

I put the puppy down on the floor and let him play with his new non-toy. No one is here but us animals and poo picker-uppers, so what do I need to worry about? Other than this bad news that's arrived in the form of a letter from the town council, that is.

Picking up the envelope, I stare at it, dread filling me. *What do they want now?* I tear it open and find the familiar letterhead—a missive accompanied by a legal document that's several pages thick. My heart deflates like a leaking balloon. "Oh, for poop's sake, what . . . ?" It's all a bunch of legalese, but if I'm reading it correctly, it says I'm being sued. "You have *got* to be kidding me." What am I going to do now?

Suddenly, as if in response to my question, the front door flies open. I look up as the gust of cold air hits me. There's a man standing in the entrance, for a split second looking like some kind of superhero who's come to save the day. I blink a few times before his identity registers. My heart beats just a little bit faster than usual.

"Mr. Lister? What are you doing here?"

CHAPTER SEVEN

I stand, dropping the letter on my desk. I've met Greg Lister a few times now, and I wouldn't say that those meetings were entirely pleasant. I know we're not supposed to shoot the messenger, but he has carried some pretty ridiculous news with him whenever he's come out to the farm. I wish my heart wasn't beating so damn fast. It's going to make me sound breathless when I talk, and he'll think he makes me nervous. And even if he *does* do that, it's not like I want him to know it.

The first time he came to Glenhollow Farms, it was to tell my sisters and me that Red Hot wanted to pay us ten million bucks apiece as some sort of early inheritance or delayed child support. The second time was to announce that Darrell—a former member of Red Hot and now persona non grata—was making claims against the band that might actually hold up in court. I block out all of their gossip whenever they talk about it in my presence because it doesn't affect or involve me, so I really don't know what's going on with that now.

"Hello," he says, coming into the room and shutting the door behind him. "I heard you had some trouble down here last night, and I thought I'd stop by to see if there was anything I could do."

I can't help but stare at him. He's wearing form-fitting, dark-blue jeans that bunch at the ankles, a long-sleeved gray T-shirt, and a dark-green down vest. His boots look brand-new, made of the type of yellow leather worn by men in construction. He looks like he just stepped out of a catalog for L.L.Bean—impeccable to a fault.

Now that I think about it, I don't believe I've ever seen even a speck of dust on the man. He is big-city perfection, more suited to a magazine's pages than to real life. His dark hair is cut in a style well suited for work in a high-rise Manhattan law firm, but today it's ruffled by the wind. His face is all chiseled angles with wide, high cheekbones, a broad chin, and deep-set, steel-gray eyes. In other words, he's completely out of his element here on the farm, *and* he makes me almost drool because he is entirely too handsome for his own good. The wind he let in carries the scent of his cologne over to me, and my eyes drift closed for a fraction of a second as I inhale. *Damn. He even smells good.* My memory of him has not paled in the least since I last saw him, and he's still the handsomest man I've ever met.

He clears his throat.

"Do?" I finally say, jolting myself out of my self-imposed hypnosis once I realize that he expects some sort of reaction from me.

His attention is pulled away from the conversation when Oscar Mayer runs over and jumps onto his feet.

I instantly see the future with a clarity that is normally reserved for women with crystal balls and tarot cards. I know exactly what is about to happen—the disaster that awaits. I'm reaching out my hand to stop it as Lister leans down to greet the puppy.

"No! Wait!" I yell.

Too late.

Oscar Mayer is so excited at the attention he's getting from this great big human, he loses control; in response to Lister's greeting, the puppy pees on the man's brand-new boot. The left one. The next thing he does is drop his new toy on Lister's other boot. The right one. He looks up at the man with his mouth open and his tongue hanging out, panting with happiness.

Oscar Mayer is in love with Lister, and now Lister is picking up the toy his new best friend brought him . . . a dog-drooly, soggy, raggedy old tampon that should be in my purse, in a wrapper, hidden from the view of every single non-female person in the entire world.

Lister stands straight, examining the tampon closely as he turns it around, swiveling it left and then right, frowning as he tries to figure out what it is. The string hangs down and tangles in his fingers.

"Put that *down*!" I yell with way more force than I mean to.

Both the puppy and Lister immediately respond: Lister drops the tampon like it's a hot potato, and Oscar Mayer sits on his chubby rump, looking over at me with his tongue hanging out. He is so very proud of himself.

"What was that?" Lister looks up at me, stricken, his hand frozen in front of him.

I try to smile through my life that is a complete disaster. "Just a dog toy. Ha, ha! No big deal."

I grab some tissues from the nearby box and rush around the desk, running over to pick up the puppy before he can do any more damage. I snag the tampon, too, and slide it into my pocket. "Here." I hand Lister the tissues.

"What am I supposed to do with these?" He stares at them with dread in his eyes.

I look down at his feet, cringing as I answer. "I thought you might want them for your boots."

He looks down and stares at the big stain on his toe. There are a couple little droplets next to the bigger stain, and if I stare at it in just the right way, it looks like Oscar Mayer actually peed a happy face onto the leather.

"I think I just got marked," he says. Believe it or not, he doesn't sound angry.

I can't help but be grateful at Lister's easy acceptance of being urinated on. I'm pretty sure his three-hundred-dollar boots will never be clean again. "He's young. He's still learning to control himself."

Lister sighs and leans down to wipe his boot. "I should've known better."

I have to think about that for a couple seconds before it hits me. "That's right. You have a dog, don't you? If I recall correctly, she's a Yorkie?" The first time Lister arrived at our house, she was in the car with him.

"Yep."

It's a breed famous for peeing on feet when they're young, so I have to agree with him; he should have known better. I've treated exactly three of them here at the clinic, as pets of people in town. One had intestinal problems and the other two needed to be spayed—an operation I paid Dr. Masters to do.

"Where is she now?" I ask.

"She's back at my place. I have someone watching her."

"What's her name?" I ask, trying to keep his mind off the idea of Oscar Mayer's weak bladder.

"Veronica."

"Your dog's name is Veronica?"

"Oh. No. Uh . . . my dog's name is Tinkerbell. Tink for short." He stands up with his dirty tissues and looks around. I take them from him gingerly and walk with the puppy back to my desk, pulling the chewed tampon out of my pocket and dumping it with the tissues into the trash bin.

"Thanks for coming, Lister, but I don't think there's much you can do here."

"You can call me Greg, you know. Lister's my last name."

"Oh. Yeah." I feel silly now and get a little hot under my collar with embarrassment. "Of course it is. Sorry."

"Don't worry about it." He walks over and stops at the baby gate that surrounds Banana, looking down into it. "How's your dog doing? I hear he got injured last night. Looks serious."

"He's okay. Well, he's *going* to be okay." My heart seizes up a little as I say that and look over at Banana's still, sleeping form. He'd normally never let anyone walk into the clinic without at least checking the person out, so the fact that he's dozing through Lister's—*Greg's*—visit says a lot. I'm praying with everything I have in me that I'm telling the truth, that he's going to be fine when this is all over.

"The surgery wasn't easy on him. He was very stressed." I force myself to look away so I don't start bawling like a baby in front of this sexy L.L.Bean wannabe mountain man.

"Got a lot of patients right now?" Greg is looking around the room, taking in the posters on the wall about vaccinating animals, the pamphlets about neutering, and a handmade sign I created on the computer and taped to the desk to remind people that they shouldn't feed wildlife in the area.

"Almost a full house."

He nods, his eyes still roaming. "The guys in the band tell me they don't see you at the house very often."

"I spend most of my time here. I don't like leaving them alone for long. The animals, not the band." I try to laugh at my lame joke, but I can't quite get there, and he gives me no indication that he's even heard me. My smile falls away at the awkwardness. He doesn't want to talk about how I feel uncomfortable in their presence, how they're able to make me feel nervous without even saying a word, or how they make me sometimes feel like they've stolen my family away from me.

He comes over to my desk and glances down at its surface. The letter from the town is in plain view. I can tell he's reading it too. I put the puppy down, and of course the little butthead goes right for my purse. I ignore him so I can get to that letter.

Elle Casey

I try to act like I'm just straightening the desktop and fold the papers up, shoving them back into the envelope, which I put in the paper tray that holds my bills. I move some other papers, too, but I can't concentrate on what I'm doing with Greg so close and staring at me. I'm shuffling my mail the way I used to shuffle cards when I was three years old.

"We've got a great horned owl in the back if you want to see him," I say, hoping to distract Greg from the stuff on my desk.

"Really? A great horned owl?" He stands up straight and makes a funny face, like he's thinking it through and surprising himself with his interest in the subject. "Isn't that an endangered species?"

"Nope. They're protected under the Migratory Bird Treaty Act, but they're not listed as threatened or endangered. They sometimes take over territories of threatened species, in fact."

"Interesting. And you're treating him for injuries?"

"Yep." I nod enthusiastically. "He's really big, too. Super big." *Super owly too. You should go back there and forget what you just saw on my desk.*

"I think I'd like to see that." He raps the top of the desk with his knuckles. Then he smiles. At least, I think he smiles. I've never actually seen the guy looking happy, but I'm pretty sure that's what all those teeth are doing at me right now.

"Come on. He's in the back." I walk away, leaving Oscar Mayer to the trouble he's going to get into in my purse, hoping Greg will follow. I'd rather deal with another soggy tampon than with this man who makes my heart beat way too fast knowing I'm being sued.

The heavy footsteps I hear behind me tell me I've succeeded in getting him away from the legal document, which is probably very titillating stuff for a lawyer. The last thing I need is the band and my mothers getting into my business out here. I'm going to deal with this problem myself. They have enough going on, and I don't like the idea of those men—as nice as they are—getting involved in my life. My family used to be involved in the lawsuits as they came up, but that was before

Red Hot turned our lives upside down. They already have enough of a presence here on the farm . . . I don't need them in my clinic too. It's the one place left that I can go to and be alone.

When I reach the back room, I walk over to the last kennel on the right and lift up the sheet. I turn to see Greg's reaction.

Greg stands a couple feet away, his eyes going wide. "Wow. He is huge; you weren't joking."

"Yeah, he's a big boy." The owl blinks and turns his head, reminding me of a robot with his precise movements.

"How on earth . . ." Greg shakes his head, staring at the bird and then at me.

"How did I get him in there?" I've had that question asked so many times, I expect it at this point. No one can imagine how a girl my size, with no education besides a bachelor's degree in biology, can do the things I do with these creatures.

"Yeah. That was *one* of my questions."

"I've got special gloves." I wiggle my eyebrows, teasing him.

He almost looks embarrassed as he turns to look at the other cages. "You have some dogs and cats, I see." He pauses, bending down. "And . . . what is that? A rabbit?"

"Chinchilla."

He looks up at me with suspicion in his eyes. "A chinchilla? Are you serious?"

"Of course." I shrug. "I get all kinds of animals in here."

He goes back to staring at it, touching the outside of the cage. "Is that a species native to Maine?"

"No." I laugh. "It's somebody's pet."

"Oh. Yeah. That makes more sense. I think." He stands, looking into the other cages.

I'm pleased that he's interested in the animals, but I'm exhausted. I don't want to be rude, but I'm not really in the mood to run a full tour. I take a deep breath and sigh, my hands folded at my waist. He came here for a reason, and it wasn't just to see an owl. I wish he would just get to it, whatever *it* is.

He stands and looks around the room, sliding his hands into his back pockets. "So. You're probably wondering what I'm really doing here."

"The thought did cross my mind." I smile, glad we're getting down to brass tacks. I had enough of the runaround today with Officer I-Never-Did-Learn-His-Name.

"It's band business, actually."

I'm immediately on my guard. Band business has nothing to do with me. "Okaaay."

"I guess they'll be leaving soon," he says.

"So I hear." *So I hope.*

"But they'll be back."

"I heard that too."

"I was just wondering . . . what you think about that settlement . . . or inheritance? Do you have any interest in picking it up?"

"Picking it up?"

"Accepting it. Taking it. Taking the money they've offered." He finally looks at me, no longer feigning interest in my work or in helping me. He's here to get me to take that money so he can say his job is done and go back to his office in Manhattan and stop playing lumberjack model in the sticks with a bunch of hippies.

"No." I shake my head.

He nods. "Okay, good. That's good." He gives me a brief smile and turns around to leave.

I probably should just keep my mouth shut, but I can't help saying one more thing. "Why do you ask?"

He pauses but then he keeps going, walking faster now. "No reason. So, I'll see you at the house? Dinner?"

"Maybe." I follow behind him but stop at the desk while he keeps walking to the front door. I take that moment, while there are no witnesses to catch me doing it, to stare at his rear view and assess his physique. He's tall, but not overly so . . . maybe four inches taller than me. His shoulders are well made, not crazy broad but not narrow either, which is a point in his favor. His butt is amazing—round, tight, and substantial enough that I think he must have been an athlete in college. Or maybe he does a lot of squats. *Gluteus maximus, indeed.*

I giggle in my head, imagining the conversation my sisters and I could have about him. We can seriously gossip when we put our minds to it. We haven't done much of it lately with all of us being so busy, and I miss it. I could totally chitchat about Greg. I wonder if he has a girl-friend. I hear from Amber that he has a niece who works in his office, but other than that and the fact that he has a dog named Tinkerbell—Tink for short—I know nothing about him or his family. Not that I want or need to know anything about the guy, but still . . . it might be fun to get to know him a little. My body goes warm with the idea.

I glance down at my paper tray with the legal document in it, and my feelings toward him chill immediately. I can't help but recall that vision of him looking at my mail and then acting like he was interested in my patients just so he could talk to me about the band's legal issues. He's nosy and sneaky. Why is he so hung up on that damn inheritance, anyway? He should be glad we turned the band down; it leaves more money in their coffer for his fees.

No, I won't be gossiping about Greg with my sisters; nor will I be learning anything more about him or his family. There's no point. He has his final answer now: I'm not taking the money. He can go back to New York, leave behind his misguided wardrobe choices, and forget all about us. I know I'll be forgetting about him about two seconds after he walks out that door.

I meet plenty of men at the clinic when they bring their pets in, but I don't generally date anyone I have contact with through work; I don't want to create conflict, and there are always high emotions where sick or injured pets are concerned. I haven't gone out much at all since college.

I don't have any time for it, and nobody has interested me enough to make me want to put in the effort. My one serious relationship during my junior year ended with me being cheated on and my boyfriend of eleven months telling me I was too *basic* to bring home to his parents, so I'm in no hurry to hand my heart over to another man. Too basic? I don't even know what that means, but I sure didn't like hearing it about myself. I guess living on a hippie commune is basic in a way, but he didn't say it like 'back to basics.' It was more like he was saying I was plain. Boring. Not interesting enough. He was a jackass, but it still hurt. Even thinking about it now makes my heart ache.

Sometimes I'm sad about not having a special someone, but most of the time I'm fine with it. Maybe one day I'll settle down, but then again, maybe not. I often doubt I'll ever find a guy who could put up with my work hours and the animals. If I ever had to choose between a man and my patients, I'd choose the animals every time, so I'm probably doomed in the romance department. No man likes to be second place behind puppies that eat tampons.

Greg stops at the door and turns around before he opens it. "You sure there's nothing I can do for you?"

My mind jumps to the letter on my desk, but I shake my head emphatically. "Nope. I'm all set."

He nods once and leaves, shutting the door behind him. Another burst of cold air hits me, and this time it feels like it's settling into my bones.

CHAPTER EIGHT

I was going to call and ask somebody to bring some dinner down to me, but I have to get out of the clinic for just an hour or two tonight or I'll go insane. Going home for a meal will give me a chance to take a quick shower, change my clothes, and gather some bedding so that I can set up a proper place to sleep tonight. I might even break down and bring a cot to the clinic. Banana and the patients need me to be at my best so I can take care of them, and right now, every cell in my body is crying out for a good night's sleep. But when I have a full house like I do now, and a couple of high-maintenance, critical cases, I really need to be on site as much as possible.

The house is loaded with people and the noise that comes with such a big group. Our seasonal guests have gone, but our new guests— the men who will probably soon become semipermanent fixtures on the farm—are still here. When they first came, they stood around and watched people work, but now they're into the swing of things, all of them lending a hand at mealtimes and otherwise. When I come in the front door, Cash, the band's rhythm guitarist, is walking by with a giant cooking pot in his hands. He reminds me of Chef Boyardee with his big, round belly, pudgy cheeks, and graying hair. All he needs is a chef's hat and he'd be a dead ringer.

I catch a whiff of the pot's contents as he passes. "That smells good."

"Spaghetti. My grandmother's recipe."

I look at him in surprise. "You cook?"

He grins as he puts the heavy pot on the table with a grunt. "Yeah. Maybe. I hope it's edible, or we're going to have to order some pizza."

His bandmates laugh good-naturedly as they help to set the table. My mother, Sally, comes out behind him, carrying a handful of silverware. "It's great. I already tried it, so you're all safe."

I go into the kitchen and find both of my sisters and my other two mothers inside. "Hey, girls." I try to sound chipper and not completely wiped out.

Amber and Emerald turn around and squeal, running at me with their arms open. I'm enveloped in love, my sisters bringing with them the smell of garlic, flowers, and paint.

"Have you been out in your studio?" I ask Em. She smells of acrylics.

"Yep." She's smiling from ear to ear. "Sadie and I have both been out there, painting up a storm."

I reach up and rub some green paint off her earlobe. "I can't wait to see what you're working on."

"Getting ready for Christmas," she says, pulling away and rubbing her hands together with glee.

"Where is the little rascal?" I ask, looking around the room.

"She got so tired, she fell asleep before dinner."

Motherhood looks great on Em. She's just barely pregnant, so that's not what's making her glow; it's Sadie. Em isn't the little girl's mother officially, but she's taken on the role of substitute mom with gusto. At the beginning of her relationship with Sam and his four-year-old daughter, I think Em may have felt that she was being trapped by this ready-made family, with Sam needing to be alone to do his creative songwriting work for Red Hot and his daughter here at the farm needing supervision; but that feeling only lasted about half a day. Sadie can do no wrong in Em's eyes, and Em is the mother that Sadie never had. After Sadie's mom died from a tragic drug overdose, she and Em bonded like glue. I'm happy for them and for Sam. They make a very cute little family.

"What can I do to help?" I ask, pulling out of my sisters' hug circle.

"Everything on that table needs to go out," Barbara says. She gestures at the round work surface in the middle of the room.

"I'll take these," I say, grabbing a huge stack of plates.

"Oh my god," Em says. I look up to see her face going white and her lips pressing together.

"What?" I'm completely mystified, looking down at the plates and then at my chest. *Do I have a booger on me or something? Poo? A tampon chew-toy stuck in my hair?*

Amber points at Em's face. "Don't you dare." She puts her hand to her mouth.

Em shakes her head at Amber, her eyes going wide.

Amber narrows her eyes at Em. "Don't. I'm telling you, *don't.*"

Em dashes from the room with her hand on her stomach, and Amber goes running right after her.

I sigh, realizing there was no personal crisis for me to avert; this is all them. I shake my head. "A couple weirdos is what they are," I mumble, turning to go out the door behind them.

"Oh, I had morning sickness so bad with you," my mom, Sally, says.

"And I had it terrible with Amber," Barbara says.

"They're just feeding off each other's baloney," I say, pretty sure most of this morning sickness is in their heads, since it seems to rise up most often while they're feeding off each other's emotions.

"Oh, it's real. And you'd better be ready for it to happen to you, too," Emerald's mom, Carol, says, walking past and nudging me with her hip. "Karma brings morning sickness to women as a special punishment for doubting other women."

I laugh. "As if." I'm pretty sure I'm not going to have to worry about it, since I'm probably never going to have children. I'd need to find a boyfriend first, and that ain't happening anytime soon. My children are in kennels down the road, and that's good enough for me. The good news? I'll never suffer morning sickness with those kinds of kids.

I carry the dishes from the room and help set the table. Soon we're all seated in a giant circle in front of our plates, holding hands while Carol says a prayer. This is new for us; dinner prayers aren't something we ever did before, but she's feeling particularly grateful now that she's going to be a grandmother and the loves of her life—Red, Mooch, and Cash, the original members of Red Hot—are here in her home. She likes Paul, the bassist, too, but he wasn't with the band when she, Sally, and Barbara were groupies, and he doesn't share their history like the other three men do.

I'm not exactly sure which of these men is *the* love of her life, though, which one is her favorite. When our three moms met the men of Red Hot, they were in the throes of a free-love movement. They never really left that life philosophy behind, and apparently neither did the band. I didn't think it was going to work with the men being here long-term, but so far they've proven me wrong. Everyone seems to be getting along really well. I've seen no jealousy among our mothers, even though all three of them seem to be equally enamored of Red, Cash, and Mooch. And the band members and our mothers all seem genuinely happy to spend most of their days together, whether it means our moms are watching them jam on their instruments or they're all out in the cold harvesting fruits and vegetables. They're also being very discreet. I'm pretty sure these men are getting it on with our moms, if the good moods I'm sensing around me are any clue, but I don't know who's doing what with whom or where. And I'm glad for that, because the last thing I want to be thinking about is middle-aged parents getting busy under the same roof as me. Not that I'm here that often, but still . . .

I glance at Greg and find him staring at me. It happens several more times throughout the meal as the conversation swirls around us. It makes me feel strangely anxious to have his eyes on me. Is he watching me eat and critiquing me? Wondering what I'm thinking? Remembering those legal papers on my desk? Thinking something worse about me that I haven't thought of?

The more I spin my spaghetti and crunch into my garlic bread, the more curious I become about why he's here at the farm. He's talking normally, adding to the conversation once in a while, but not completely here. I mean, he's physically here, okay . . . yes . . . I see him sitting there across the table from me, but he's not *here* here.

There's something about Greg that always seems . . . removed. I don't think I've ever seen all there is to see of Lister. Heck, I don't know that any of these people at the table have. He's a lawyer for the band, and I'm pretty sure he doesn't have any other clients, but it's not like he lives here with them. It's not like anybody would *want* him to live here either. I get the impression that they respect him for the work he does, but he's not exactly anybody's friend. *So why is he at the farm now? Why didn't he go home this afternoon?*

The conversation turns to my work and then to Banana. I smile and nod at everyone sharing their good wishes for his recuperation and recovery. "He's going to be fine," I say, taking another piece of garlic bread. I don't really want to talk about it. It was hard leaving him to come back to the house.

"Where's *your* dog?" Amber asks. I look up and see that she's talking to Greg.

"She's with a friend."

"A *girl*friend?" Amber asks, her eyes twinkling. Apparently, she's over her morning sickness issue, happily eating plain pasta from a big bowl.

I'm tempted to mention the name I heard earlier today: *Veronica.* A flash of something hits me out of nowhere, just thinking her name. I quickly realize what it is. *Jealousy? Really?*

Whoa. I definitely need to get out more, if I'm envying a man's dog sitter. But seriously . . . how easy is that job? Sitting in a Manhattan high-rise watching a Yorkie all day? I could do that in my sleep. I snort just thinking about it and then try to hide the sound by coughing. Mooch, the man sitting next to me, pats me on the back until I calm down. He keeps up a nice, steady beat that almost sounds like the lead-in for a song. It must be all those years of banging on drums that makes him do this like it's second nature.

Greg is in the middle of eating a forkful of spaghetti, but his chewing slows as he looks at Amber. He probably wonders if he heard her question right, but he should know my sister pretty well by now. Amber being the PR manager *and* band manager of Red Hot means that she and Greg are in each other's business every day, with contracts and other paperwork to deal with. Surely he must realize that she's as nosy as a person can be, and she doesn't bother to hide it.

"No, she's not a girlfriend," he says. He sounds . . . cautious. Or guilty. Or . . . I don't know. It's weird how he sounds. He looks at me again for a few seconds before dropping his gaze to his food.

Amber looks at Emerald and they both nod together. "She's a girlfriend," Amber says, going back to her noodles.

"She's *not* a girlfriend," Greg says, glancing at me again.

I look away. What do I care whether some girlfriend named Veronica is watching his dog?

"I know that tone in your voice," Amber says, smiling. "Maybe she's not your actual girlfriend, but you've got the hots for her."

Greg stabs at his pasta over and over again, as if he's trying to force the noodles up onto the fork through sheer determination, but it isn't working; they keep falling off. "I don't have the hots for her. You're wrong."

"Yeah." She snorts, under her breath. "I'm wrong like the day ain't long."

I find myself oddly entertained by my sister's teasing of this man. No one else seems to be paying them much attention. The conversation moves on to a song the band was working on today, and it distracts Amber from her pursuit.

I feel Greg's eyes on me again and look up.

"She's not my girlfriend," he says.

I look to my left and right. My sisters are talking about the song now, completely oblivious to the fact that Greg feels the need to convince someone—anyone who will listen, apparently—that Veronica is not his girlfriend.

"If you say so." I shrug, feeling supremely confused. And something else too . . . I feel . . . happy. On a whim, I wink at Greg . . . And then I feel my entire body flush when he looks down at his spaghetti and smiles.

CHAPTER NINE

When it's time to go back to the clinic, I expect my sisters to accompany me, because they never miss an opportunity to gossip—and surely Greg has given them enough reason to speculate about his personal life with his adamant denial of having a girlfriend named Veronica—but both of them beg off, claiming they're too tired. Normally, it wouldn't bother me to go to the clinic alone after dark, but this time I have a lot to carry, and more hands would make lighter work. I'm staring at the pile of things on the porch that I plan to bring with me, wondering if I can carry all of it by myself in one trip, when a man's voice startles me.

"Need a hand?" Greg asks. He is standing behind me, looking through the screen door.

I contemplate his offer. Saying yes means more potentially awkward moments between us, but saying no means more work for me, and I'm thoroughly exhausted. "Sure. I have to warn you, though . . . It's a bit of a walk."

"We could drive."

I smile at his city-boy solution. "No, it's not far enough to drive." Sure, it would be easier to take the truck, but my mothers have always emphasized the need to keep our environment as clean as possible, and using a vehicle to go less than a mile up the road feels really wasteful to me.

He doesn't respond except to come outside and pick up the cot in its bag, settling the strap over his shoulder. After he fills his arms with a blanket and a pillow, he gestures with the pile toward the stairs. "Lead the way."

"You want me to take one of those things?" I ask, feeling guilty that the only item I'm holding is my overnight bag.

"No, that's all right. This can be my workout today." He flashes me a charming smile.

I guess that solves the mystery of how he stays so fit. I can totally picture him in shorts and no shirt, pumping iron, his chest muscles bulging, sweat dripping down his abs . . .

"What does that look mean?" he asks as he descends the stairs. He glances up at me once he reaches the bottom, waiting for my answer.

Great. He caught me fantasizing about him being half-naked and sweaty. "What look?" I ask innocently, following him down the steps.

"The one you just gave me. When I said this would be my workout."

My efforts to play stupid are not going to fly, so I decide to go the other direction. "Well, to be honest, I was wondering earlier today how you stay in shape when you work in an office all day, and now I have my answer. You work out. That's what I was thinking."

Our shoes crunch over the gravel as we move down the drive and my face slowly burns.

"You don't have to wonder things about me. You can just ask, you know."

I'm surprised to hear him say this, because he doesn't seem like the type of guy who'd be willing to answer personal questions. When my sister was teasing him about Veronica earlier, he sure didn't act like he wanted her in his business. So is the problem the girlfriend issue, or is it Amber?

Because it's late and I'm too tired to convince myself it's a bad idea, I decide to conduct a little test; we'll see if he really means what he says. "So, the lady watching your dog, Veronica . . . ?"

"Yep. That's her name."

Wind blows into my jacket, but it doesn't affect me. The conversation is too interesting for me to worry about the cold. "You said I could ask you questions if I'm curious, so . . . is she or isn't she?"

"Is she or isn't she what?"

I smile sadly and shake my head. He obviously wasn't serious about his offer to divulge his personal information. And our walk was going to be so interesting, too! I actually would've had something to chat about with my sisters later besides animals, for a change. Amber would have cursed the moon to know that I got the information from Greg that she wasn't able to squeeze out of him at dinner. It's so rare that I can get her goat like that, too. *So disappointing . . .*

The conversation goes silent for about fifty yards before Greg speaks again. "Are you going to answer my question?"

"What question?" I'm totally lost.

"You said, 'Is she or isn't she,' but I don't know what you're asking, exactly."

"Oh, I think you do." Aaaand now I know Greg Lister is into head games. But he *is* a lawyer, after all, so I shouldn't be surprised. It's a little disappointing to find out how *much* of a lawyer he is, though. I was kind of hoping he was different from the kind that is currently suing me.

He sighs. "Are you asking me the question your sister was asking me at dinner?"

"Bingo." I look over at him, waiting for his next move. He said all I had to do was ask, so now he either has to follow through on that statement or admit he didn't mean what he said.

"Veronica is not my girlfriend."

Amber and Em are pretty good at reading people, and they saw something in his eyes when he talked about this woman that I didn't. Something that led them to believe she was somebody special. The nosy part of me wants to know more, more, *more*. I really should just let it go, though . . .

"What is she to you?" I ask. "Is she just a dog sitter, or something else?" This is none of my business, but does that stop me from hanging on to every second that ticks by as I wait for his response? Uh, no. Not at all. I think my intense reaction is the result of not getting off the farm more often. I really should get out more.

"You and your sister sure ask a lot of personal questions."

I feel deflated at his response. For a moment, I was thinking that he was going to open up and that we were going to share a connection more personal than I'd normally have with the people who visit the farm. But now I know we aren't, and I'm disappointed enough that I no longer really care what his answer is. I shrug. "You told me all I had to do was ask. I guess I shouldn't have, though. Sorry about that."

"Don't say that," he says, sounding sad.

"It's all right. Having a stranger ask a bunch of personal questions isn't very comfortable; I realize that. I was just testing you, anyway. You don't have to answer."

"Testing me?" He looks over at me. "Did I pass?"

I catch his eye for a moment before I go back to looking at the ground in front of us. "What do you think?" Strangely, I feel like crying. This is the worst case of sleep deprivation I've ever suffered.

"I think I probably failed."

He sounds disappointed in himself, which is completely silly. We're not even friends. We're just . . . acquaintances . . . brought together by shared circumstances. He works for the men who are enamored of my mothers—for now at least—and that's it. There is no other connection between us, and there never will be, especially since I'm not taking that money from the band.

I need to do my best to get along with him and not expect anything in return, so I try to think of something that will lighten the mood. "Well, you get an *A* for effort, anyway. You had good intentions." I think he really wanted to be able to answer my questions; he just wasn't prepared for how intimate they would be. My sisters and I never did learn to follow the socially accepted rules of personal space and privacy. It's not really in the hippie credo.

A minute or so later he speaks. "You're similar to your sister, but not as much like her as I expected you would be."

"Which sister?"

"Amber."

"Amber and I have some similarities, it's true. We've lived together all our lives, so that's not a surprise, is it?"

"No, it's not a surprise, but I'd say you're more different than you are alike."

"I'm not sure whether that's a compliment or not."

He doesn't answer. I don't think small talk is Greg's forte. He seems uncomfortable but at the same time like he's making an effort to be friendly. Maybe this is his apology for not answering my questions.

I'm not going to give him a hard time about how awkwardly this conversation is rolling out. Some people are less gregarious than others— like my sister Em, for example—but it doesn't make them less interesting. The old adage 'Still waters run deep' could be true when it comes to Greg, like it is for my sister. I definitely get the impression that there's a lot more to him than meets the eye. And what meets the eye is pretty darn nice. Too bad he's not staying around so I can find out whether the adage is right where he's concerned.

"Whup, watch out," he says, jumping toward me.

My skin prickles with sensation as he moves sideways around a pot-hole and his arm brushes up against mine. His close physical presence takes over my mind, making it race with thoughts of intimacy, touch-ing, and yes, sex. Before tonight, he was just the band's highly paid, big-city attorney—their messenger in a suit that fit nicely enough that I paid attention. Now I see him as a man—a really attractive one—who's struggling to carry on a conversation with me and pretending he had to jump next to me to avoid a little hole in the ground. It makes him just a little bit adorable in my eyes, imagining how capable he must be in the business world but how not-so-capable he is out here on the farm. Is he trying to flirt with me? It's impossible for me to tell, and I find that I like that about him.

"Amber is definitely more determined," he says, obviously not feeling the same angst I am about our proximity.

I move to the right a little, to put some distance between us. It makes it easier to think. "Determined? I can be pretty determined." I'm feeling inadequate at his description, as if he's comparing Amber to me and I'm coming up short in his eyes.

"No, that didn't come out right. I mean, she's more . . ." He glances at me, concern shading his expression.

"Pushy?" I suggest, trying not to laugh. Both Em and I have accused her of being too bossy on many occasions. She started in the womb, determined to come out first and be the oldest of the three of us, even though my mother's due date was before Barbara's.

I can hear the smile in his voice when he answers. "You said it, not me."

"She's been determined since she was little. She was always the boss of our childhood games."

"Do you think her being first in the birth order has anything to do with that?"

"I don't know, maybe. She's not older by a lot."

"No, she's not," he agrees.

"Oh, that's right. You know all our birthdays, don't you?" I say this with a touch of bitterness. The day he showed up at our house for the first time, bringing news of legal settlements, he recited all of our birthdays to prove that he knew who we were. I will never forget that day—the day everything started to change. For the worse or better, I'm still not sure. Amber's permanent address is in Manhattan now, and both she and Em are up to their eyeballs in new relationships with rock 'n' roll stars and their pregnancy side effects. It's been a heck of a whirlwind these past several months, and even just standing on the periphery of it can be overwhelming sometimes.

"Yep," he says.

More time passes with just the sound of wind in the trees before he speaks again. "So . . . Amber is the determined, business-savvy one, and Emerald is the shy, creative one . . . What about you? How would you describe yourself?"

I can't answer him right away. Never having thought about myself or my sisters like that, I have to ruminate on it for a bit first. The only label that pops into my head, though, is one I don't want to say out loud: Rose Lancaster, The Boring One Who's More Comfortable With Animals Than People.

"I don't know," I say. "I guess I don't really have a label for myself." I look over at him, barely making out his features in the starlight. "What do you think?" I could be asking for a compliment, but so what? It's dark out and he can't see my burning-red face. Besides, he'll be gone tomorrow.

"I don't think I know you well enough yet to make that call."

It's the 'yet' that gets me. Does that mean he wants to spend more time with me? "Well, you have about another ten minutes to figure me out," I say, smiling at him.

"Ten minutes?"

"Yeah. That's how long it'll take us to get to the clinic from here. You're leaving tomorrow, right?"

"Yes. How did you know?"

"You came out here to ask me about that money again, for whatever reason, and you don't have any other pressing business with the band right now, so why would you stay?"

"Who says I came out here just to ask about the settlements?"

"Because that's the only business-related thing I've seen you do while you've been here."

"Yes, but you've been at the clinic almost the entire time."

"True, but my sources haven't reported any other business being conducted in my absence."

He chuckles. "Oh, your *sources*."

I try to remain serious. "Yes. They're very well placed."

"I'll bet they are."

We walk the rest of the way in silence. It's not far, and soon I'm opening the door of the clinic to the sound of Banana whining.

CHAPTER TEN

I drop my overnight bag on the floor in the entrance after I turn on the lights, going right over and taking the baby fence from around Banana's sleeping area so I can kneel at his side. He obviously tried to move while I was gone, and he's made a mess.

"Is he okay?" Greg asks, setting the cot down, along with the pillow and blanket, before walking over to join us.

"Yes, but I need to clean him up. I also need to get him standing just a little bit."

"What can I do to help?"

"For right now, nothing. But when I'm ready to get him up, I might need your muscles."

"You've got it."

I busy myself with cleaning Banana and giving him lots of kisses to help calm him. I sense anxiety in his vocalizations and struggles, and I need to get rid of as much of it as possible or it'll interfere with his healing. Animals can be so sensitive, even the crazy ones like Banana, and stress is never good for them. I find a bedsheet in the back room and hold it out at my pup so he can give it a good sniff before I use it on him.

"What are you going to do with that?" Greg asks.

"I'm going to put this under his armpits so that I can stand over him and use it as a sling to hold up his front end while we walk. That way, if he slips with that cast on, he won't go down and neither will I."

"Can I help get him up on his feet?"

"Yes, you absolutely can. Let him sniff your hands first so he can get to know you a little bit." I'm so glad Greg decided to walk me down here. I don't know if my sisters would've had the strength to do what needs to be done.

I thread the sheet under my patient's legs and spread out the material to make sure it doesn't cut into him anywhere. Scratching him behind his ears, I speak softly. "Banana, you need to get up and walk around a little bit, okay?"

He wags his tail weakly.

"I'm going to help you. I need you to trust me, okay?" Normally, Banana would never bite anyone, but stress and fear can change a dog's temperament in a flash.

He licks my hand. I nod at Greg, who positions himself behind the dog after letting him lick his fingers. "I think we're ready."

Greg reaches down and very gently lifts Banana's chest and belly. I stand too, holding the sheet in either hand, supporting Banana's front end. Together, Greg and I get him on his feet.

Banana immediately starts getting excited and tries to move too fast.

"Just calm down, sweetie." I grunt with the effort of holding up twenty-five pounds of excited, two-and-a-half-legged border collie. "Banana Bread, *calm down.*"

"You want me to let him go?" Greg is leaning over, nearly bent in two.

"Sure, we can try it. But be ready to grab him, in case he falls."

Greg switches his attention to my patient. "Okay, little guy. We're gonna do this. You ready?"

Banana looks up at him and smiles, his tongue hanging out of his mouth as his tail sways slowly from side to side.

Greg's gray eyes catch mine. "I think he just said yes."

Greg's grin is so charming, I have to look away. I need to focus on my dog, not on the cute guy who's so close I can smell his citrusy shampoo.

"Yep. He's ready and so am I. Let's do this." I put some tension on the sheet as Greg slowly releases his hold. Banana is standing on his three legs, the one in a cast held stiffly out to the side. He stops wagging his tail and looks unsure of himself.

"Just take one step toward me, sweetie." I back up half a step.

Banana follows me, his little cast thumping on the ground when he uses that leg.

"Good boy!" Greg says. He sounds genuinely excited. "That's awesome. You're a champ, you know that?"

"You *are* a champ, Banana Muffin," I say, pride and relief nearly overwhelming me. Tears rush to my eyes, but I ignore them. "Now let's take another step. Come on. Follow me."

I take a step back and Banana follows, cheered on by Greg's excitement at his progress. Greg is hunched over, walking with his hands out on either side of the dog, just in case.

"Look at him go," Greg says enthusiastically. "The three-legged dog turned two-legged dog, walking like a superstar. He should be on television."

"He is a superstar," I say, my heart filled with love and pride for my little fighter. A tear slips out and runs down my cheek. I use my shoulder to wipe it off.

"How did he lose his leg?" Greg asks in a quieter tone as we take another step forward together.

The memory hits me like a punch in the gut. It still burns me up just to think about it. "Somebody threw him out of a car window." I'll never be able to tell Banana's story without feeling sick with anger.

Greg looks up at me sharply. "Are you kidding me?"

I shake my head. "Sadly, no. There are some pretty horrible people out there in the world."

"I know, but . . . I guess I've never really seen this kind of abuse up close, or the evidence of it up close."

"No, I can't imagine you would have, sitting in a high-rise office in Manhattan. Lucky you." I don't mean for my response to be rude, but by the way his jaw tenses, I know he's taken my comment the wrong way.

I open my mouth to apologize, but then Banana takes a couple of quick steps and pulls my attention back to him. I need to focus so I don't injure him, so I let it go. I worry my patient will overdo it, so I gather the sheet into one hand and reach over to grab the counter.

"Let me help you," Greg says, reaching a hand toward me. "What are we doing?"

"I think we need to bring him back. I don't want him to do too much on his first try. He'll get sore and then he won't be able to go again later."

"Gotcha." Greg lifts the dog from underneath, holding my baby as though he's made of glass. He brings him over to his sleeping pad, which I've cleaned and replaced, and I use the support from the sheet to help him lower Banana.

"Do you want him standing up or lying down?"

"Lying down, but maybe he can do it himself. Let's give him a chance to try."

"Sure, no problem." Greg slowly releases his hands after putting Banana on three legs, but keeps a close watch.

"Lie down, Banana," I say authoritatively. This is a command he knows well. Being the mascot of the clinic, it's imperative that he know when to chill out and take a spot on the floor. He learned this when he was three months old, before he'd even recovered from his amputation surgery.

He moves in awkward circles on three legs and looks around, stressed when he realizes that nothing on his body is working like it should. He wants to do what I'm telling him to, but he can't. It's heart-breaking to watch him become disappointed in himself.

"You want me to help him?" Greg asks.

I don't have the heart to push Greg aside and do it all myself. He sounds like he really wants to help. "Yes, please. Just be gentle and put him on his left side."

Greg picks him up and gently places him down. He looks like a pro who's been treating sick animals all his life. Banana thanks him with lots of licks while Greg scratches the dog's neck, ears, and muzzle. Even if I'd never seen this man with his Yorkie, I'd know from his actions this evening that he's a dog person. He knows all the things they love—scratches and encouraging words—and he delivers them expertly. I find myself feeling a little jealous of my pup. I wish there were someone out there who knew how to touch me in all the right places and make me feel so loved.

Greg looks up at me and freezes. "What? Am I doing something wrong?"

I hurriedly shake my head. "No. I was just thinking how jealous I am that you're such a good . . . uhh . . . dog scratcher." I try to laugh it off, like I didn't just say something totally weird.

"Oh . . . well . . . you know I like dogs." He stands and swings his arms like a small boy would do. Then he slides his hands into his back pockets, his elbows jutting out behind him. He looks around the room. "So, what's next?"

I sigh, petting Banana a few more times before I stand and put the baby gate around his sleeping area. "What's next is I try to get some sleep. Good luck with that, right?" I laugh without humor as I look down at my little buddy.

"Maybe I can help you set up the cot?"

I nod. "Sure. That would be great. While you do that, I'll check on my other patients."

I go into the back room and make sure that everybody's tucked in for the night. Oscar Mayer is curled up in a ball in his kennel, sleeping on the fluffy little bed that someone from the farmers' market donated to the clinic. I slowly back out of the room, trying not to wake him. Once he gets going, it's hard to get him to stop, and it's too late for him to be awake now. Whoever adopts him will want to have a dog who sleeps during the night, not plays.

When I return to the lobby, my cot is set up and ready for me. There's a sheet on it, and the blanket is tucked in around it, the top of it folded back as if inviting me to slide in between the covers and go to sleep. I can almost believe it will be comfortable, too.

"Wow. That's impressive." Greg went to a lot of trouble to make my bed seem welcoming, and I could kiss him for it.

"What?" he asks. "The bed?"

"Yes, the bed. This is the most comfortable-looking cot I've ever seen." I hope he can tell from my tone how grateful I am for his help, because I'm not really going to kiss him just for making my bed, even though the idea has merit. He sure looks like he'd be a good kisser with those full lips of his.

"I was in the military." He shrugs. "I can't help myself."

"You were? What branch?"

"Air force. I was in the JAG Corps."

"What's that?" I'm imagining a guy with a sniper rifle perched on a ridge, seeking out the enemy while wearing camouflage gear and face paint. In my vision there are lots of muscles involved and primitive-looking tattoos.

"Basically, I was a lawyer for people serving in the air force."

"Oh. That makes sense." Way more sense than what I was thinking. I couldn't really picture him sniping anyone . . . not after seeing him with Banana and that tiny dog of his.

An awkward silence settles around us. I need to brush my teeth and go to bed, but he's been such a great help to me, I feel bad kicking him out.

"Do you sleep here often?" he asks. He rubs his hands together, making me think he's as uncomfortable as I am. He looks at me, cringing. "That just sounded like a pickup line, didn't it?"

I play it back in my head and have to smile. "Now that I think about it, maybe."

"Do you come here often? Do you sleep here often?" He's mocking himself, taking the pressure off both of us.

"To answer your question, yes, I do sleep here often."

"Then why is your cot up at the house?"

"Because I usually don't bother with it."

"Were you in the military too?"

"No, why?"

"Because the only people I know who can sleep on a hard floor on a regular basis are marines."

I look behind him. "I usually sleep there."

He frowns, looking over his shoulder at the reception area. "Where? Behind the desk?"

"Yes."

"On the floor? It doesn't look like there's much room back there."

"No, sitting in the chair."

He frowns and walks over to the desk, pulling out the chair to examine it more closely. "Okay . . . well . . . that's just nuts."

I laugh at his incredulity. "Why?"

He looks up at me. "You spend how many nights a week out here?"

"I don't know . . . Two? Three? It depends on how many patients I have and how serious their conditions are."

"And you sleep sitting up in a chair?"

"No. I put my head on the desk."

"Oh, of course. Your head is on the desk. That's completely different."

I shrug at his sarcasm. "What can I say? After doing it so many times, I don't really think about it anymore. I just sit in the chair, put my head down on the desk, and fall asleep."

He nods, staring at me. It's unnerving.

"Why are you looking at me like that?"

"Because I've just learned something interesting about you."

"What's that?"

"Well . . . I've learned that you're pretty crazy," he says, looking at my desk. His smile fades quickly.

"Oh, you have, have you?"

"Yes, I definitely have." He lifts his brows and looks away, shaking his head slowly.

I get the impression that he's not just talking about me sleeping in the chair now. I lose a little bit of my smile. He means me not taking the settlement also makes me crazy; I know he does. He saw that letter, he knows I'm being sued, and he thinks I'm nuts because all that money could make my problems go away.

"What's the matter?" he asks, clearly catching the expression on my face. "You know I'm only kidding, right?"

"Yes, I know."

"But you're not smiling anymore. I said something that bothers you."

I shake my head. "It doesn't matter. I'm just tired." I look at the door, hoping he'll take the hint.

"You're not going to tell me what it was that I did?"

"It really doesn't matter. I promise." We had a nice couple of moments together, but he's leaving tomorrow, and I have work to do. And I'm exhausted. *And* I'm not taking that damn money, no matter how desperate I am.

"Okay. Well, I guess I should let you get to sleep." He points at the cot. "There . . . ," he points to the chair behind the desk, "not there."

I nod, holding back my smile. He can be a nice guy when he wants to be. "Thanks. I appreciate your help . . . carrying all that stuff down here and helping with Banana, too."

"Are you going to walk him again tonight?"

I look over at my patient, who is, thankfully, sleeping. "No, not tonight. In the morning, after he's had a good night's sleep."

"I can come back and help out if you want."

"Don't you have a plane to catch?"

"Yeah, but it's leaving later in the day."

I shrug. "Okay, sure, if you have time before you go, feel free to come back and help." I never turn down offers of assistance at the clinic, even when they come from a man who makes me feel funny inside, who makes me smile one moment and frown the next.

"Great." His face lights up. "I guess I'll see you tomorrow, then."

"That'll be nice." I'm not lying when I say that. It beats doing everything out here alone. Talking to him for the past forty-five minutes or so has reminded me how much I miss having male company. It's been too long.

A flash of brilliance hits me. Why on earth am I just sitting in this clinic every single night instead of getting out into the world a little? I'm not an old maid; I'm a young, nice, intelligent person. I deserve to have some fun, don't I? Yes, I do.

So . . . I've decided . . . *That's it.* After Greg leaves and I get Banana back on his feet, I'm going to go to the bar in town and have a beer with someone cute. Maybe we'll go out on a date. Or several dates. Heck . . . maybe we'll have hot, sexy sex too! I've been single and celibate for too long. My inability to have a simple, easy conversation with a man like Greg Lister is proof of that.

"I'll bring you breakfast," he says, oblivious to my internal declaration of future sexual liberation.

"Perfect." I walk over to the door and pull it open for him.

Greg pauses in the entrance. He's so close, I can feel his warmth. It's almost as if I'm absorbing his heat into my body, making it so the air sneaking through the door can't touch me, despite its freezing temperature.

I lift my hand and wave it a little, hoping to get past the awkward moment of saying goodbye.

"I'll see you tomorrow," he says, his voice soft and low. His eyes search mine, for what I do not know. Truth? Proof of mutual sexual desire? It's impossible for me to discern. Pulses of energy flow between us. He leans forward just the slightest bit. His eyes are so beautiful, his stare intense. His lips are full. I could so easily kiss him, but . . .

I drop my gaze as I step back. "If you come down here, you will see me for sure." My heart is hammering in my chest. I just came so close to making a big mistake . . . starting something with a man who will do nothing but take what I have to offer and then leave me the next day. I know I said I'm going to go to a bar and pick up some cute guy after Banana is all healed, but I'm full of crap. That's not me. I can't be with a man who will touch my body intimately one night and then leave me the next. I'm not the kind of girl who can turn off her feelings so easily like that.

He reaches up and pats me on the shoulder for a couple seconds before his face goes blank. When he pulls his hand away, he stares at it in confusion. "Okay, yeah. Well . . . bye." He steps out the door and is soon jogging up the road to the house.

I shut out the cold and lock the newly repaired door behind him. Looking through the window, I see nothing, but I continue staring out into the darkness as I think about what just happened between Greg and me. For a second, I thought he was going to kiss me. I moved away before he could, but I don't regret it. I'm glad I did that. Nothing good could come of me kissing the man charged with getting me to accept a legal settlement that I want nothing to do with. Maybe he felt the awkwardness too . . . realized that it would be a mistake. That's why he patted me on the shoulder instead of trying harder.

I should be satisfied with how we ended our evening together, but I'm not. I feel . . . anxious. Unsettled. If I hadn't pulled back, would he have kissed me? Would I have kissed him back? It bugs me that I don't know the answers to these questions. I should be sure of myself, like I am every other day of the week, with every other person who stands in front of me, but I'm not. Even after I brush my teeth and crawl under the blanket on my cot, I'm still wondering what I would have done if Greg had leaned in and touched his lips to mine. I fall asleep before I can come up with an answer.

CHAPTER ELEVEN

I'm up before the sun taking care of the animals, cleaning wounds and replacing bandages as I wait for my breakfast. Normally, I miss the first meal of the day because I'm so busy, and usually by the time I realize I'm hungry, it's already lunchtime. But knowing that Greg will be bringing the food today changes things.

I dreamed about him last night. In my sleeping fantasy, he didn't just put his hand on my shoulder at the door as he left last night; he kissed me, and it was incredible. And we didn't stop at a kiss either. Just thinking about how far we went makes me hot all over again. After feeling these sensations and seeing this dream-version of Greg—enigmatic, seductive, passionate—I'm starting to think there are parts of him that could be very interesting, even though he does a pretty good job of being nearly invisible when he's standing in a group of people. My subconscious has picked up on it and is nagging at me to uncover his hidden personality traits.

He loves animals, he's kind and gentle with the wounded, and he served in the military—three things that always impress me. And he's a lawyer, so he must believe in justice. When you add to that the fact that he's hot as hell and gainfully employed, well . . . let's just say it makes the idea of this breakfast a little more exciting than usual.

When I hear the front door open, I rush over to the mirror that hangs on the wall in the back room so I can check my teeth for anything that shouldn't be there. I brush the loose blond hairs away from the sides of my face and smooth the rest of it back into the clip that keeps it out of the way when I'm working. I take a deep breath to calm my racing heart before I step out into the hallway with a big smile.

Amber is standing in the lobby with a picnic basket in her hand. "Well, don't you look bright and cheery," she says, walking farther into the room. She goes over to Banana and reaches down to give him a scratch behind the ears. "Hey there, little guy. How are you feeling this morning?"

Banana whines as his tail brushes the floor.

"He needs to get up and move around a little bit," I say, walking out and trying to hide my disappointment behind a brisk, businesslike tone. I have a job to do and I'm going to get it done, even if I'm way more affected by Greg's no-show than I want to admit.

"What's the matter?" Amber asks. "Were you expecting someone else to bring you your breakfast, by any chance?"

I can hear the sly tone in her voice, but I don't react to it. With Amber, I'm always better off pretending nothing's going on. Nobody can dig into a personal situation deeper and faster than she can.

"No. I'm not very hungry, is all."

"I saw that big smile on your face when I walked in the door. You thought I was Lister."

I sigh as I look down at Banana. "His name is Greg."

"Oh, is that so? We're on a first-name basis now?"

I glare at her with my hands on my hips. "Don't you think *you* should be on a first-name basis with him? You work with him every day."

She snorts. "Believe me, if you had to work with him every day, you would *not* be on a first-name basis with him; you wouldn't *want* to be."

I let my arms fall to my sides. Maybe I was wrong about him. "What are you talking about?"

She waves her hand in the air between us, brushing off my question. "Never mind. Forget I said anything. Are you okay? I can't believe someone broke in here the night before last."

"I'm fine. Really. Totally fine."

She frowns. "You sure?"

"Absolutely." The last thing I need is my sister freaking out over my problems while pregnant, so I work hard to convince her with my expression. The smile is hard work.

"Are you hungry?" She holds up the picnic basket. "This stuff isn't going to eat itself, you know."

I take it from her, setting it down on a nearby chair and opening it up. There's a warm muffin, a breakfast burrito, and an apple. My appetite comes back as I smell the delicious scents wafting up from inside. "This looks yummy."

"You can thank your buddy *Greg* for that apple," Amber says, sitting down in the chair next to the basket.

"Excuse me?"

"You heard me. He made me put that apple in there."

"He's still here?"

"Yes, he's still here." She tilts her head. "Are you going to tell me what's going on?"

I take a chair on the opposite side of the basket from Amber and reach inside it. I select the muffin because I'm disappointed at Greg's no-show, and I know the blueberries inside it will cheer me up. "There's nothing going on."

"Baloney. He stayed here forever last night. I thought you guys were probably getting it on, but then he came back and he was all grouchy, so I knew that didn't happen."

I nearly choke on my muffin. When I recover, I bug my eyes out at her. "Are you serious? Getting it on? Here in the *clinic*?"

She smiles. "Why not? He's hot. You're hot. You guys could start a fire with the sparks that fly between you two."

"I don't even know the guy." Crumbs come flying out of my mouth with every word. I slap my hand over my mouth to stop the disaster from getting worse.

"So what? Both Em and I are proof you don't need to spend a lot of time with a guy to totally fall for him. What were you two doing in here all night, anyway?"

I chew my muffin and shake my head, answering her after I've swallowed. "He was only here for, like, a half hour. We didn't do anything. We walked Banana; that's it."

"So . . . the big smile of pleasure I saw on your face this morning . . . Was that for me? No, it couldn't have been because you didn't know I was coming. Could it have been for him, perhaps?"

I shrug, pulling more of the paper off my muffin. I can't look my sister in the eye. "Maybe."

"Yeah, I figured." She nods sagely.

I look over at her, unable to resist the pull. "How? Why?"

"I could see it at dinner. He's into you."

I frown, disappointed in her obviously bogus interpretation. "Don't be ridiculous."

She grabs the edge of the basket in her enthusiasm. "No, he is. He totally is. Every time he's here, you're the one he wants to talk to."

"So? I'm easy to talk to, and we don't talk about anything more exciting than the weather, except when he's hounding me about that money."

"Maybe it's because you're easy. Maybe not. He definitely makes the effort where you're concerned."

"I didn't say I'm easy." I reach over and slap her arm. "I said I'm easy *to talk to*. Big difference."

"Whatever." She grins big.

"You and Emerald are spoken for and dating his clients. Maybe he's worried about Sam or Ty getting jealous if he talks to you. That's why he's always stuck talking to me."

"Bull-ony. Come on, don't deny it. There's something going on between you two. Admit it."

"No."

"Not even one little spark?" She leans toward me with a ridiculous expression on her face.

I open my mouth to answer but then close it. She'll know if I lie, so I'm better off saying nothing. At least, that's my theory.

"See?" She points at my face. "I knew it."

So much for my theory. Amber is too good at reading people. "Regardless, it doesn't matter." I take a big bite of my muffin and chew it, smiling. I'm not going to let this silliness get me down, because in a couple weeks I am going to start dating someone. Anyone. Whoever at the bar asks me first gets me. I don't care what he looks like, I will say yes. Senior citizens are *not* off the table. All this angst proves that getting out into the dating world a little will do me good. I definitely need more practice talking to men, and I could use some time away from the clinic.

"Of course it matters," she says, scooting to the edge of her chair and turning to face me. Her hands start moving as she uses her own strange version of sign language while she speaks animatedly. "He's into you. You could go on a date. Then you guys could do *stuff* together." She winks about ten times.

I laugh. "How old are you?"

She points at me. "Do not mock me. I am pregnant and no longer on the market. I live vicariously through you."

"Since when? You haven't missed out on anything. You don't need to live through me."

"Maybe I have missed stuff. You don't know. I'm only twenty-five."

I put my muffin down and reach over to take her hand. "Are you serious? Are you regretting your relationship with Ty?"

She shoves me away. "No. Don't be silly."

"You promise there's nothing wrong?"

She sighs and rolls her eyes to the ceiling. "Heaven save me from dense people."

I laugh, picking up my muffin and eating another bite. "Excuse me very much."

She faces me again. "Do you ever think that maybe you're wasting your life living in this leaky barn all day and all night, every single day of the year?"

I stop chewing as my temperature rises. "No." The word comes out muffled, filtered by crumbs. I hate that Amber is thinking the same thing about me that I'm feeling about myself: that I'm awkward and socially inept.

"You never regret the fact that you have no free time and that you can't ever go out and meet people?"

"I meet plenty of people," I say, painfully swallowing my very dry lump of suddenly tasteless food.

"Tell me the last time you went out on a date. *If* you can remember."

My mind frantically searches for the information she's requested. The answer comes back and it ain't pretty. *Dammit.* I think the last time was eight months ago, and it didn't go anywhere. One date to a movie, and he never called me back. *What was his name?* I can't even remember. "That's none of your business."

She laughs loudly. "Since when?"

I shrug, popping the last bite of muffin into my mouth. I don't bother trying to finish chewing it before I talk. "Since you decided to shack up with Ty."

She raises an eyebrow at me. "Shack up? Are you kidding?"

This could turn into a full-blown argument, and I don't want to go there. I have to take care of Banana, and I don't have the energy for it. I let out a long sigh that deflates my entire body. "Can we just stop this for right now?"

Amber's expression softens. "Of course we can. As soon as you admit that I am right."

I roll my eyes and throw up my hands, sending muffin crumbs out onto the floor. "Fine. You're right. You're right about everything."

She grins. "I am right about Greg being into you."

"If you say so."

"Thank you, because I do say so. And I'm right about *you* being into *him*."

I glare at her.

She points at me. "Don't try to argue that it's not true, because I can go all day."

I shake my head and close my eyes. "Fine. I think he's cute. I think he's nice, and he likes dogs."

"Perfect. So he's into you and you're into him. So why is he not here delivering this breakfast, I wonder?"

I open one eye to look at her while she pretends to be seriously flummoxed.

"Because he's not into me and you're wrong?"

She reaches over blindly and taps my face, trying to cover my mouth. "No. Shush. I'm thinking."

I push her hand away and stand. "It doesn't matter. He's leaving today, and I'm staying here. End of story."

She rises and walks over with me to stand next to Banana. "Since when is a little distance the end of the story?" she asks softly.

"Since the beginning of time."

"But you're forgetting . . . ," she starts counting off her fingers, "Sam and Em, me and Ty, Cash and Mooch and Red and our mothers . . ."

I reach over and put my hand over her mouth. "That's enough. Help me with Banana." I release her so I can gather up the sheet I'm going to use to support his front end again.

"This looks like it needs somebody with some muscle," Amber says. She pulls her phone out of her pocket and starts tapping away at it.

"Not really. You should be fine."

"Okay, but if I'm going to do this, I need to go pee first." She leaves me standing there with the sheet in my hand.

I roll my eyes at her weak bladder and squat down to give my baby some attention. His former IV site is looking good, but he had his last bag of fluids yesterday, so he's going to want some water soon. I check my watch just to be sure it's okay to let him drink now. *Yep. Should be good.* I don't see him relapsing or having any other problems, so I get him a bowl of water and a small serving of dog food and rice mixed together. I pause outside the bathroom door when I'm walking by to yell in to my sister.

"You building a log cabin in there?"

Amber shrieks from inside. "Would you guys stop saying that to me! Ty's going to hear you one day!"

"I'll bet he already did." When Emerald told me the story about how she accidentally told Ty's brother, Sam, that Amber was building a log cabin before she even met him for the first time, I nearly peed myself laughing. My sweet, creative, and very shy sister sometimes says the exact wrong thing at the exact right time. I just wish I had been there to witness it with my own eyes and ears.

"Shut up," Amber barks. "Just shut up and leave me alone. I'll be out in a minute."

I deliver the food to Banana and help him get up so he can eat it. He also drinks some of the water, and I take it as a sign that he's on the road to recovery. If only he had one more leg, this would be so much easier.

"Aren't you done yet?" I shout toward the bathroom. I get no answer.

The front door opens behind me, sending a gust of air through the lobby. Greg is standing in the entrance, his cheeks pink and his hair disheveled. He's breathing hard enough to make me think he ran all the way from the house.

CHAPTER TWELVE

W ell," is all I can think to say as I take in the vision before me. Talk about sexy. Greg looks like he just went for a roll in the hay. I wish I had been there with him.

"I heard there's an emergency and you need my help." He slams the door behind him and walks over.

It takes a few seconds for his words to sink in before I roll my eyes and sigh, picturing Amber texting on her phone. "I'm really sorry about that. That was probably Amber sending you a false alarm." She's match-making. I'm going to kill her. *With* pain. I don't care if she's pregnant; it doesn't grant her immunity from humiliating me.

"Where is she?" he asks, looking around.

I smile evilly. "She's busy building a log cabin right now."

He frowns. "She's building a log cabin? Is that a good idea in her condition?"

The look on his face is classic lost guy. I start laughing so hard I can't contain it. I hold my stomach and bend over so I don't accidentally vomit up the blueberry muffin I just ate.

"Okay, I'm not sure I understand. Do you still need my help or not?"

I gesture for him to follow me over to Banana as I work to control myself. "Yeah. Since you're here anyway, do you want to help me walk him a little bit?"

"Sure. No problem." Greg takes up his position near the dog and I get the sheet in place. Together we get the enthusiastic pup walking around the lobby. He definitely has more energy and balance than he did last night. I'm finally able to control my mirth over Amber's log-cabin-building career when I realize it takes too much energy to hold the dog up and laugh at the same time.

"Listen," Greg says, the muscles in his arms straining as he helps Banana steady himself, "I'm sorry I didn't bring your breakfast like I said I would."

"That's all right. Amber brought it."

"Yeah, I know. I just . . ." He doesn't finish his sentence.

"Thanks for the apple."

He looks up at me. "The apple?"

"Amber told me you insisted there be an apple in there."

"Yeah, well . . . an apple a day keeps the lawyer away, right?"

The insecurity in his voice makes my heart go out to him. "I thought the apple was for keeping the doctor away."

"Oh, yeah. That's right."

"I think if you wanted to keep the lawyer away, you'd put something else in the basket," I say in a teasing tone.

"Oh, yeah? What would that be?"

"I don't know. A Taser?"

He barks out a hearty laugh, and his face wrinkles up on the sides with the strength of his smile. He looks up at me with his eyes twinkling, his bright white teeth shining at me. "That was a good one."

I can't help but smile back. "Thanks. I just came up with that on my own."

Banana starts wagging his tail as he looks at the door. I glance over my shoulder, concerned we're not going to be able to make it outside where he wants to go.

"What's the matter?" Greg asks.

"I think he wants to go out."

"Let's do it."

Thunder rumbles.

"Okay. But we probably shouldn't go too far. I think it's about to rain."

We make our way over to the door and outside. Banana does his best to relieve himself without making a mess. He's partially successful.

"Good boy." Just as the words are out of my mouth, the rain starts. First, it's just a couple of droplets, but then . . . not so much.

"Okay! Back in we go," I say enthusiastically as the water starts running down my back. Banana, unfortunately, is happy in the rain. He sticks his tongue out and smiles, panting happily at the puddles forming around us. I don't think he's very happy being cooped up in the clinic, poor thing.

"You want me to carry him?" Greg is ready to act on my command.

"Go for it. Just watch that leg."

"Sure." Greg lifts my pup as easily as he would a feather pillow. Banana takes advantage of the situation and gives Greg a serious lick-bath on the way to the door. Greg winces. "Thank you. Oh, thank you so much, Banana. That's great. I'll just grab another shower when I get back to the house. Oh, man, that's great."

I can't help but giggle as I assist Greg with settling the dog back onto his makeshift bed. Banana can't stop wagging his tail and lunging for Greg's face to give him more kisses. Greg is being a seriously good sport, wincing and laughing. If I had a tail, I'd be wagging it too. Greg can be very charming when he wants to be. It's sad to say that I'm jealous of my dog's ability to so easily and demonstratively share his feelings.

Greg stands up and rubs his face with his sleeve, trying to remove some of the dog saliva. "I've never felt so appreciated," he says as his face is pulled out of shape by the force of his shirt wiping down his cheek.

"I'd offer you the bathroom, but Amber is camping out in there."

"I thought you said she was building a log cabin." He pauses and frowns in confusion.

I just shake my head at him. Poor guy. It takes everything I have in me not to burst out laughing at his naïveté. Or his class. I can't figure out which is keeping him from understanding what a log cabin is. "Yeah. Well, anyway, don't you have a plane to catch?"

The awkward feeling between us is back. I know he was trying to tell me something earlier about why he didn't bring my breakfast, but I don't understand it and I'm not even sure I want to. After talking to Amber, I realize one thing about Greg: he could seriously complicate my life, and my life is already complicated enough.

"I could . . . catch a later flight."

I have a hard time swallowing. *What is he saying?* I can literally feel the blood drain from my face as my entire body goes cold. "What?"

"If you need any help here or whatever. I have a little free time in my schedule."

I find myself shaking my head, and I don't even know what I'm saying no to. *Do I need the extra help? What would that extra help mean? Does he feel sorry for me, or is he into me like Amber said he is?*

"Or not," he says hurriedly. "I can still catch the flight I have." He looks at his watch, his eyes opening wide in surprise. "Wow, I didn't realize how late it was. I need to take off." He reaches his hand out toward me.

I look at it, slowly raising my arm and putting my palm against his. His grip is firm and businesslike as he shakes my hand up and down a couple times. "It was nice talking to you and seeing you again," he says. "Take care."

"Yeah, you too," I say in a daze. This feels so weird. And I'm pretty sure this would be weird to *anybody*, not just a girl who never gets off the farm and who hasn't had a date in eight months. What the heck just happened? We went from friendly and easygoing to suddenly . . . what? Lawyer and client?

He pulls his hand from mine and walks to the front door, turning around as he holds on to the doorframe. He looks like he's going to say something else, but then he drops his eyes and lifts his hand in a silent goodbye and walks out, shutting the door behind him.

Not two seconds later, Amber emerges from the bathroom. "Well? How did it go?"

I shake my head at her, supremely disappointed in her shenanigans and how it all worked out. "Please don't ever do that again."

"What? All I did was go to the bathroom."

I leave her there, going into the back room to nurse my patients' wounds along with the new ones I just inflicted on myself by starting to fall for a guy who is wholly inappropriate and not at all interested in me.

CHAPTER THIRTEEN

T wo weeks go by, and I find myself thinking about Greg a lot more than I should. Of course I haven't heard a word from him. Why would I? That stuff Amber said about us having a spark between us was just her imagination. Hers and mine. He was just being a nice guy, helping out a woman in need. He's a dog lover after all, like I am. I would do the same thing if I saw somebody else's dog needing a hand. It meant nothing.

I wish that was the only sad news I have going on, but it's not. Banana is doing great, but the rest of my life . . . not so much. The legal document that was sitting on my desk when Greg dropped by has now become a huge problem for me. Normally, I'd just send that stuff off to my lawyer, but this time it's not going to work.

"He loved you guys so much," my lawyer's secretary says, sniffing over the phone. "He said it always brought him so much peace to spend time out at the farm. You really made a difference in his life. He probably would have had a heart attack a lot sooner if he hadn't spent a month every year with your family, decompressing from the stress at work."

"That's really nice to hear. I'm so sorry for your loss. I know you two worked together for a long time."

She sighs, her voice quavering when she responds. "Yes. Twenty-two years we worked side by side. He was a great boss. He really cared, you know? That's pretty rare these days."

"Yeah. I do know." I can think of at least one lawyer who seems like he cares, but the rest of them? Nope. All they think about is money and making me pay it. "Thanks, Winifred. Let me know if we can do anything from over here."

"You did a lot for Robert. Thank you for that. Have a good day. Give my love to your family."

"Will do." I hang up the phone and stare at the stupid lawsuit that has both my name and my business name on it. They're not just suing the clinic; they're going after me personally. According to them, I'm violating some rules against running a certain type of business on our land, and I don't have the proper license—and can't have one—to do what I do. I know for a fact that they're incorrect about this, because we've already gone around and around this issue with them, but now I don't have a lawyer anymore, and I don't know what the heck I'm doing when it comes to the law. It's almost as if they knew Robert was ill and waited until he was a goner before they filed this suit.

The only other lawyer I know who isn't in the town council's pocket is Greg Lister, but there's no way I'm calling him. Besides, he probably isn't even licensed in Maine. He won't be able to help me, and I'll put him in the awful position of having to tell me that to my face, or over the phone, which is almost as bad. No, I have to solve this problem another way. I chew my lip as I consider my options:

Option One: I could contact a lawyer in another town. An appointment with an out-of-town lawyer would cost me a fortune, at least two hundred bucks just for the privilege of sitting down with him or her to talk about my case. And it wouldn't be a short conversation either. I have a box full of documents that pertain to my relationship with the town that would take hours to go through.

Option Two: I could talk to my moms and see what they say. I immediately cross this idea off my list because I know exactly what would happen if I did that: they'd get the band involved, and then all of them would start yammering on and on about that damn settlement and giving me their opinions about how I should be living my life and what I should be doing with it. Yes, the settlement would solve my money problem—easy peasy, lemon squeezy, as my sister would say. But I can't take the easy way out. Like my mothers have always said: the easy way is never the best way, and down the easy path lies misery. Aren't I miserable enough? That money has come to represent shattered dreams for me, and those are things I'd rather bury than keep alive.

Banana is recovering, but my love life is as crappy as ever. I'm too chickenshit to go to the bar and pick someone up to kick-start anything. And after spending that evening with Greg, the only guy I can think about in that way is him. He's ruined me, at least for the time being. It's this lawsuit that's messing with my mind. I need to find an answer . . . a solution that won't send me to the poorhouse or require that I bend my morals in order to make it work.

Option Three: I could pray. Praying is free and it certainly couldn't hurt. I look up at the ceiling and send out my silent petition. *Universe . . . God . . . Almighty One . . . Mother Nature . . . Zeus . . . if you're listening . . . please send me a sign.*

The phone on the desk rings, making me jump. A shiver runs through me. "Whoa. Talk about the power of prayer." I pick up the handset and put it to my ear. I notch up the cheer in my voice because I could actually be receiving a call thanks to Jesus. "Hello, animal clinic, Rose speaking."

There's no one there at first, but then I hear breathing.

"Hello?" I frown at the phone. The caller ID is showing me nothing, and no one is responding. It's more than a little disappointing that I'm getting static after asking God for a sign. I'm afraid it means I'm sunk and out of options.

"Hello?" I swear I can hear someone there. It's a man, I know it is. He's blowing man-breath all over the phone. God sure has a sick sense of humor. "I can hear you breathing, you know. Not cool to call here and not say anything."

There's a really long exhale that feels like it's creeping through the phone lines and going right into my ear . . . and then the line clicks and goes dead. I put the handset in the cradle and push the chair away from the desk, staring at the phone that until this moment never looked scary to me. Goose bumps stand out on my skin.

What the hell was that? Definitely not a sign from above. Below, maybe, but not above. It's nothing. Of course it's nothing. Crank callers are rarely evil, dangerous stalkers, right? *Naahhhh . . .* My brain quickly searches for an alternate, less alarming explanation for the call and the breathing.

Maybe it's because I was thinking about Greg before the call came through, but the first thought that jumps into my head is: *It's him!* Perhaps Greg called me but chickened out at the last minute when he heard my voice, just like I chickened out about going to the bar and executing my amazing pick-up-any-guy-that's-breathing plan. Greg is shy. He's probably having a hard time settling down after our magnetic encounters, just like I am. He can't possibly be unaffected. We have chemistry. Amber says so, and Emerald has backed her up. That makes it practically a fact.

There's only one way to find out whether my theory is correct, and I could kill two birds with one stone by following through on this idea.

Option Four: I could call Greg at his office. I'll find out if he was my anonymous caller *and* I'll also ask him for some legal advice. I won't hire him or anything, but surely he can point me in the right direction. He's a friend of the family, right? Amber might not agree with that, but Emerald would.

I feel energized over Option Four as I surf the Internet, using the iPad Amber left at my desk to find his number and dial it. This is totally going to work. After reaching the receptionist and being passed around to several other people at his firm, he finally picks up the line.

"Lister."

He sounds so cold. I smile when the image of him being licked to death by a rambunctious border collie forces that sensation away. Greg couldn't be cold if he tried.

"I thought your name was Greg," I say teasingly.

"It's Greg Lister. Can I help you?" The chill is still there, full force. It throws me off. I'm instantly battling with myself over the wisdom of executing Option Four. Should I hang up or push through to the end? The end is not looking good . . .

"Hello?" he prompts, sounding annoyed.

Now who's the heavy breather? "Yeah. Sorry. Um . . . this is Rose. Rose Lancaster? From Glenhollow Farms?"

"Oh." I hear shuffling and then silence. "Rose."

"Yes. Hi. How have you been?" I'd say anything to melt the ice that's coating his voice. This is the best I can come up with. I'm doomed. We are over before we even got started.

"Fine. Thank you. What can I do for you?"

Any trace of warmth he might have had toward me is clearly gone. I feel like a complete fool for calling him, but what's done is done. I need to get this over with as soon as possible.

"Um . . . did you by any chance just call here?" I ask.

"Call where? The farm?"

"No. The clinic." I already know his answer will be in the negative. I can tell by the annoyed tone in his voice. *Why did I call him?* I should have known he wouldn't call just to breathe in my ear. He's a New York City attorney who makes fifteen hundred bucks an hour. He's got way better things to do than play stalker, and if he ever bothered to call, I'm sure he'd have no problem saying whatever it is he wanted to say.

"No, I did not."

"Oh. Okay. Well, bye." I have the phone halfway to the cradle when I hear his voice.

"Wait."

I put the phone back to my ear. "Yes?"

"Why did you just ask me that question?"

I instantly fall into panic mode. There is no way I can get out of this without sounding like a complete ding-a-ling. If I say there was some weirdo calling me, he'll wonder why I thought it was him. He might even become alarmed and call my mothers. Or Amber. I'm not sure which of these options would be worse, so I fall back on the only plan I have left.

"Oh, shoot. Animal emergency just walked in. Gotta go!" I quickly hang up before either he or I can say another word.

I sit there panting, sounding like a freight train chugging down the line. My face is hot, and I can feel my pulse pounding at my neck. I'm embarrassed, afraid, and feeling totally out of my element. *What was I thinking?* I acted like a foolish woman desperate enough for a man that she makes up silly excuses to call him. I should have known it wasn't him on the line; he would never be weird enough to call a woman just to breathe in her ear. I convinced myself it was possible because I wanted to hear his voice . . . and that makes me an idiot. A man like Greg Lister would never be interested in a hippie chick like me. Like my old boyfriend said: I'm basic, and guys like Greg never go for basic. They go for high-end, classy women who spend as much money on makeup and clothing in a week as I spend on this entire clinic in a year.

The phone rings and I literally jump in my seat. Looking down at it, I can see the caller's number. It has a Manhattan area code. I stand and walk into the back room without touching it. There's no way in hell I'm answering that call. *Noooo way.* I open up Oscar Mayer's kennel and let him run out. Soon, Banana is hobbling into the room after me, and the two of them play for a little while. Even with only two fully functioning legs, my Banana holds his own against this very energetic puppy. Their antics help me to forget the heavy breather and the humiliation of having exposed myself to the band's lawyer as a complete goober.

CHAPTER FOURTEEN

Three days pass, giving me enough time to forget how stupid I was to call Greg, and then I have to play the remorse game all over again when he shows up at the farm while the family is eating lunch together in the dining room.

"Greg, we weren't expecting you," Red says, standing as Greg knocks on and then walks through the door. I frown as Red walks over to greet our visitor with a handshake, giving the impression that he's the man of the house. It's true he has a natural charisma that pretty much everyone, including me, responds to, but I still don't think it's appropriate for him to take on an actual authoritarian role here. That's not how we've ever operated before, anyway, but I can see from the bland expressions on my mothers' faces that they don't have a problem with this change.

Before I can completely remove the expression of disapproval from my face, I catch Emerald looking at me. She gives me a small shrug, letting me know she's also put off by it. It's nice to know I'm not the only one who's a little bit annoyed by his presumptuous behavior. I look over at Amber, but she's oblivious. She's smiling at Greg as she stands.

"Well, look what the cat dragged in," she says. "Did I forget to finish some paperwork or something? Did you come here to scold me in person?"

Greg lifts his hand in greeting to the group. His unsmiling gaze doesn't include me. "Hello, everybody." He shifts his focus to Amber and the band members. "No, I just had some documents to discuss with a few of you. I figured it would be easier to come out here and do it in person rather than trying to do it long-distance."

"That's *funny* . . ." Amber looks directly at me, her expression going sly. "Doing everything long-distance was working out fine before."

"Yeah, sure. But this situation is a little more complicated."

Barbara stands. "Come on in and have a seat. We were just having lunch. You're more than welcome to join us. We have plenty."

Sam gets up and walks toward the kitchen. "I'll grab another chair."

Amber starts waving her hands at people around the table. "Move over. Move to your right. Make a space there, next to Rose."

I really wish I could glare at her and send her silent promises of future revenge, but she's not looking at me. I'd bet a hundred bucks I don't have that she's avoiding me on purpose. She's playing matchmaker, trying to set me up with Greg, and not being at all discreet about it. I really wish I could keep my face from flaming up red, but it's getting really warm and there's nothing I can do about it other than drape my napkin over it, and that wouldn't be obvious at all.

Sam puts a chair down next to me, as ordered. Greg takes a seat, and I hand him the plates and utensils Emerald has retrieved from the sideboard and passed to me.

"Thanks," he says. His fingers brush against mine when I give him a napkin. They're cold from being outside. This tiny bit of contact sends a thrill through me, which is completely sad. I really should've gone out the other night to the bar when Sam and Em invited me. Maybe if I'd had sex with some random guy, I wouldn't be so sensitive to a man's simple touch.

"So, what's up?" Red asks. "Must be something pretty urgent if it dragged you out here."

Greg helps himself to some leftover turkey. "It can wait until after lunch. This looks really delicious."

"Thank you," Sally says. "I hope you don't mind leftovers. We had a big turkey dinner last night."

Greg pauses and looks at his watch. "Did I miss Thanksgiving?"

"No," I say, when no one else seems ready to explain. "But it was Tom's time to go." Several eyes around the table drop in respect.

"Tom?" He looks around for an explanation, but nobody wants to answer him.

I sigh, the duty falling to me. "Tom the turkey. On your plate."

Greg is about to ladle some gravy onto his meat, but he stops. "Excuse me?"

Em picks up the story. "The meat we eat is from animals we raise here on the farm. Last night and today, we are eating Tom the turkey, may he rest in peace."

He puts the gravy boat down and looks at his plate for a few seconds in quiet contemplation. "Okay, then. Thank you, Tom. I appreciate your sacrifice."

I'm relieved that this hasn't put him off dining with our family. Most people appreciate what we're trying to do, but not everyone does. We've had some interesting meals with newcomers who suddenly lose their appetites when they realize their dinner has a name.

Greg picks up the gravy boat and pours a healthy serving over his meat. "What did Tom do to deserve such a fate—death a month before Thanksgiving?"

"He started getting really aggressive with the other birds," Em says softly. "I was afraid if I let him go for too much longer, he was going to kill one of them. His ending was peaceful. He felt no pain."

"Gotcha." He drops some mashed potatoes next to the turkey and follows up with some green beans. He doesn't seem at all bothered by the fact that he's eating food with a name on it. I imagined a lawyer like him at least making a face, but he's as cool as he ever is.

"I guess what they say about lawyers is true," says Mooch, grinning behind his fork.

Greg starts cutting into his meat as everyone resumes eating. "Oh, yeah? What's that?" He takes a big bite of the turkey and chews it while he looks at Mooch and waits for his answer.

"Heartless." Mooch winks at him to take some of the sting out of his words.

Greg points his knife at Mooch's plate. "I see you're helping yourself."

Mooch shrugs. "He went after me the other day, so there was no love lost between Tom and me."

Everyone around the table chuckles.

Mooch raises his arm to show us the cut on his elbow. "Look. I'm still injured."

"Oh, you big baby," Carol says, nudging him. "That's no worse than a paper cut."

"What? Paper cuts are the *worst*," he says, pretending to be offended. He cups his arm and pouts.

"Lord have mercy," she says, smiling and eating away, not falling for his act for even a second.

He grins at her before going back to his food. He holds up a slice of turkey and stares at it. "Sorry, Tom, but you messed with the wrong guy."

I look over at Em, the one responsible for raising the animals, and she's not laughing. I need to change the subject quickly. "So, how's the big city?" I ask Greg.

"Good. Loud."

"I don't miss that," Sam says.

"I do," Amber says. "I miss the activity and all the things going on." She looks wistful.

"When are you going back?" Greg asks.

"I don't know. Better ask the boss." She looks over at Ty.

Emerald snorts but doesn't say anything. I know what she's laughing at, though. *As if Ty is the boss in that relationship. Yeah, right.*

"I can go back whenever," Ty says, looking around the table. "Just depends on what everybody else wants to do."

"I'm in no hurry to leave," says Red. "We're getting a lot of good things done up here."

"Excellent. Good news," Greg says, taking another big bite of his turkey. I'm surprised by his answer. I can't imagine how it makes his job easier to have them all the way out here, a plane ride instead of a taxi ride away.

The conversation moves to the band's latest material, and I tune it out. I focus on my food, trying not to go all giddy over the fact that my arm keeps brushing up against Greg's. We're both wearing long sleeves, but it doesn't stop me from feeling the heat coming off his skin. Every once in a while his leg bumps into mine, too. I can't believe it's entirely unintentional. Is he thinking the same thing I am? That it feels good to be touching each other? Or am I fooling myself all over again?

"How's Banana doing?" Greg asks me in a low tone, keeping our conversation somewhat private. He digs into his mashed potatoes as he waits for my answer.

"He's doing much better. His cast is off now, and he's walking around on the leg. I had to keep his wound collar cone on, though. You know, the lampshade thingy?" I wait for Greg to nod before I finish. "He still wants to fuss with the surgical site, so it's the only way to keep it clean."

"I'll bet he loves that." Greg glances at me and smiles, charming me to my toes.

"No, not at all, actually. It really cramps his style."

"I can imagine. Tink had to wear one once. She was not a fan."

"How is she doing?"

"She's doing really well."

"Who's taking care of her while you're gone?" I wait a couple seconds before I finish my sentence. "Veronica again?"

Greg's face falls into a mask of seriousness. "Yeah."

That's all he says, making me think the conversation is now over. I hope I didn't say something wrong. "Does it bother you that I asked you about her? I don't mean to pry."

He shakes his head as he takes another bite of food. "Nope." He stabs more turkey onto his fork and shoves it into his mouth.

He's not convincing at all. It makes me smile. "I don't know how well you can possibly do in the courtroom when you're such a terrible liar."

He stops chewing and rests his silverware on the plate as he looks at me. "Come again?" His food is a wad bulging out the side of his mouth.

I smile hard to let him know I'm kidding around. "Aren't you supposed to have a poker face when you go into the courtroom?"

He swallows his food and wipes his mouth with his napkin, resting his forearm next to his plate and turning his head to look at me. "I don't go into court that often, but when I do, I always tell the truth, so there's no need to have a poker face." His gaze rests on me for several intense seconds before he turns his attention back to his food and picks up his fork again.

"I actually believe you." I can't stop grinning as I spear a little pile of green beans with my fork. He's fun to tease; it's easy to get him worked up over little things and then—*damn*—he is so sexy when he gets serious like that. No wonder Amber does it so much. I wonder if he turns her on like he does me. I'm going to have to ask her that. A tiny spark of jealousy lights up in the back of my brain.

"Thank you," he says. "I think."

He's smiling again, the charm of it instantly banishing any negative feelings I have toward my sister. She has her man and she's perfectly happy with him; besides, she's told me several times she doesn't think Greg is all that good-looking. My sister obviously has vision problems.

Greg is incredibly hot, and he's charming to boot. I like it when he and I are getting along like this and he lets his hair down a little. It feels a heck of a lot better than that disastrous phone conversation we had a few days ago. This guy sitting next to me is almost a different person.

Conversation swirls around us, but I don't care about any of it. I just want to know more about Greg. Now that he's not being so cold toward me, anyway. After that last phone call, I didn't think I'd ever see this side of him again. It's such a relief to find out I was wrong about that.

"Sorry about that weird phone call the other day," I say in a low voice, praying my sisters won't hear me.

"Yeah . . . what was that all about?" He wipes his mouth with his napkin and then turns his head to look at me. He's done with his meal and focuses so much attention on me, it's unnerving.

I grab the bowl of potatoes and hold it up at him. "Seconds?"

He shakes his head. "No, thanks. I'm still waiting to hear your answer to my question."

I put the potatoes down and sigh. He may not have much in the way of a poker face, but he gets serious points for persistence. Amber's too busy arguing about a tour stop with Red to worry about what Greg and I are doing, which means I can't count on her interruption anytime soon; I'm going to have to explain myself right here at the dinner table.

"It was . . . nothing. Can we just forget it happened?"

He shrugs and picks up his water glass. "Maybe. That depends."

His tone makes it sound like he's flirting, but I can't be sure I'm reading him right. "Depends on what?" I take a sip of my drink, hoping it will help cool me down.

"On whether it has anything to do with that lawsuit you're dealing with."

Without thinking, I kick him under the table, making him jump. I speak in a low tone, my eyes darting around, making sure no one is listening. "Don't say anything about that here."

He nods slowly but says nothing. The rest of the meal goes by without another word between us. He eats a big piece of pie and I decline dessert, getting up to help clear the table. As soon as I can politely leave without dumping all the work of cleaning up on everybody else, I smile and wave at everyone standing around the table. "I'm off to the clinic. Thanks for a delicious lunch. I'll see you guys later." I need to get away from Greg as soon as I can. Once again, I've ended up in an embarrassing situation with him, and I'm not interested in dealing with the fallout. I can't claim there's an animal emergency and hang up to get rid of him, but I sure can skedaddle out of here.

"I'll walk you out," says Greg, getting up and grabbing his jacket off the hook by the door.

I walk past him frowning, knowing I'm being trapped into a conversation I really, *really* don't want to have.

CHAPTER FIFTEEN

"Are you mad at me?" Greg asks as we walk down the front porch stairs.

I try not to sound annoyed, but it's not easy. "Why would I be angry with you?"

"I take it your family doesn't know about the lawsuit."

"The question is, how do *you* know about the lawsuit?" I jam my hands into my pockets and stride toward the clinic. He's got longer legs than I do, so he easily keeps up.

"I thought I saw something on your desk when I was in your office last time I was here, so I went online to check the public records to confirm."

"Now, why would you do something like that?" I halt in the drive-way to stare at him. I find his intrusiveness both curious and highly annoying.

He stops too and stares back at me, no readable emotion on his face. "I was concerned about you."

It makes me crazy that he can say something that makes my heart stop with the same tone he'd use to say, 'I bought two potatoes at the grocery store today.' I was wrong about him not having a poker face. He not only has a poker *face*, he has a poker *voice*. He could win millions in Vegas. He'd probably make a great con man.

"I can handle it myself." I start walking toward the clinic again, trying to outpace him.

"I'm sure you can," he says, easily keeping up with me. "My looking into it isn't the same thing as me saying I don't think you can handle it."

As we continue down the lane, I slowly let go of my anger, hearing the truth of his words. He's just being a nice person, even if he's a nosy one. Heck, with the family I have, I'm used to that kind of behavior. And he can't help the fact that he has lawyer-face and lawyer-voice. There's a reason he's paid the big bucks; he's more than good at what he does. He was born to do it, just like I was born to do what I do. Besides . . . I can't be mad at him for giving a hoot. My heart is telling me it's time for a confession.

I trudge along, kicking up gravel and slowing my pace because I need time to get this out before we arrive at the clinic. I don't want to sully my place of work with all this negativity. "The truth of it is, the lawyer who usually handles these things for me died. So I'm not dealing with it as well as I normally would be."

"He died? That's terrible. I'm sorry about that."

"Yes, it is terrible. He was a great guy I'll miss as a friend, but his death puts me in a bad spot as his client, since I counted on him to help me with any legal issues I had."

"Do you have new representation?"

"No, but I'm working on it." *Kind of.*

We walk for a while in silence before Greg speaks again. "It's possible I could help you out."

My heart melts a little. Even though I know it's not going to happen, just knowing he'd offer eases some of my burden. A girl can never have too many lawyer friends. "That's really nice . . . seriously. But I'm pretty sure I can't afford you."

"How do you know? I haven't given you a proposal yet."

"I know how much the band pays you. My sister told me."

"Maybe I have a special rate for nonprofits."

I smile sadly at him. "That would be nice. But unless your rate is discounted a hundred percent, I still can't afford you."

He looks at me, his face an unreadable mask. "Maybe it is."

I come to a complete stop, while he keeps going. I'm waiting for him to realize I'm no longer with him and turn around. When he doesn't, I lift my voice. "Greg? What's going on?" Total exhaustion is fueling this conversation now. Normally, I would just play the game with him, flirt, do whatever it is we're doing here, but today I'm too tired from everything that's been happening in my life to keep up the charade.

He pauses and turns around. "What do you mean?"

"Why did you come out here? Is it because of that stupid phone call I made to you?" I knew I was going to regret doing that. I asked the universe to send me a sign, and I got a heavy breather. Most women would have understood that to mean it's time to get professional help, yet somehow I interpreted it to mean I should call Greg up like some desperate loser, begging him to give me special favors—free legal advice from one of the more expensive lawyers in the country. What is wrong with me? Why is my vision so skewed where he's concerned? I never act like this with other men. I'm usually the coolest chick in the room, not caring about any particular guy enough to get nervous.

I glare at the man I'm holding responsible for my lack of control. It's that damn L.L.Bean catalog that's messing me up. He needs to stop wearing jeans and flannel shirts that fit like they were custom made and start wearing puffy, pleated corduroys. That'd do the trick of cooling things down and getting him out of my head. I'm going to suggest it as soon as the opportunity arises.

He slowly walks over to where I'm standing, takes me by the elbow, and leads me up the street toward the clinic. "Am I here because of that phone call? Yes and no."

I wait for him to elaborate, but he doesn't. I'm not going to push. Not yet, anyway. I need time to gather my thoughts. Sometimes it feels like there's something going on between us, but he was so cold when we last spoke, it hurt. He temporarily became this heartless guy I never would have called if I'd known he would make an appearance. After the few great moments we had together at the clinic, and after he was so tender with Banana, I expected something different. Something warmer, at least. Clearly, I don't have what it takes to play head games with this guy. And when I think about how much I have to lose—namely my heart—I find myself wishing he had just stayed away. The distance makes things so much easier . . . as long as I stay away from the phone, anyway.

"Are you keeping Banana at the clinic?" he asks.

I'm good with the complete subject change. The Banana topic could keep me busy all day. "Yes. I'm trying to contain him somewhat so he doesn't overdo it. It's easy for him to go too far on that leg that's still healing."

"I'm guessing he's a ball of energy."

"Yes, he definitely is."

"I'm relieved to hear he's doing better. I kept tabs on him through your sister, you know."

"Really? That's nice." It is nice, but it's also not nice. It's bumming me out to hear that he went through Amber to do that. He could've called me to find out about Banana, but he was obviously either not interested enough in the details or didn't want to talk to me directly. He probably didn't want to lead me on. And then—*oh, God, help me*—I called him at his office accusing him of crank-calling me. *Good Lord, I think I need an intervention.*

"I was going to call you, you know," he says.

"But you didn't." Now I know what it means when people say their heart sank. Mine feels like it just lodged itself in my small intestine.

"No, I didn't," he admits.

I've already been through that scenario where I think I'm getting along great with a guy and then he stops calling . . . and I'm left to wonder what the heck I did wrong. I don't want to go through it again, especially not with Greg. Too many members of my family could get involved in the mess it would create. So rather than call him out for playing games, I keep my mouth shut.

The rest of our trip to the clinic passes in silence, which is fine by me. I cannot recall participating in a more uncomfortable conversation, and I'm happy to be done with it. I just wish my head would stop replaying it over and over and over . . .

CHAPTER SIXTEEN

We finally get to the clinic, and I open the door to find a pile of shredded paper in the center of the lobby and Banana sitting in the middle of it. He's made a nest and he's proud of it. He looks up at me in greeting and doesn't even have the decency to appear guilty. As soon as he sees Greg come in behind me, though, he leaps to his feet and half-runs, half-limps over to greet him, passing right by me. I get it; I'm the mean lady who makes him do his physical therapy every day, and no good deed ever goes unpunished. I said the same thing when Hooters, the owl, bit me right as I was releasing him last week.

Greg bends down and allows himself to be licked as he pets Banana and congratulates him on his amazing recovery. I ignore them and walk into the back room, taking off my jacket and checking my hair and face in the mirror. I want to lock the door and never come out when I find a large piece of salad stuck in one of my front teeth. I seem to recall smiling at least once between lunch and now. *Why didn't he say something? Argh, how embarrassing!* I shake my head. There is no hope for me. For us. What man would want to be stuck with this mess? I'm wearing clothes covered in stains from work, I'm often seen with animal poo somewhere on my person, and I walk around with lunch in my teeth. *Lovely!*

I join Greg and Banana in the other room, bringing Oscar Mayer with me. Hopefully, the pudgy dog's cuteness will help Greg forget that I had a mouth like Swamp Thing just a few minutes ago.

"And who is this?" Greg asks when the little tubber runs over to him. "Oh, wait a minute . . . I know you." Greg starts dancing out of the way.

"This is Oscar Mayer. You know, the one who peed a smiley face on your boots the last time you were here."

"Oh, I remember well." He bends down to pet the puppy, keeping him well away from his shoes. He's wearing what look like brand-new hiking boots in rich brown leather. They go perfectly with the darker denim of his jeans and the forest-green-and-navy-blue flannel shirt he's wearing over a gray thermal. His hair is longer than the last time I saw it. I would love to run my hands through the gentle waves to see if they're as soft as they look . . . There's something about a hot guy playing with a puppy that gets to me.

I have to put some distance between us so I can think properly, so I go over to my desk and sit down. I shuffle papers, trying to act busy. *Bills, bills, bills . . . busy, busy, busy. I do not want to run my fingers through your hair, I really don't. I swear I don't. Maybe only a little.*

"Do you want to show me that complaint?" Greg asks, standing and encouraging Oscar to run over to wrestle with Banana; he pushes on the puppy's little butt, scooting him across the floor in that direction, but Oscar turns around and comes right back, determined to sit on Greg's feet.

"Complaint?" Rose is my name and playing dumb is my game.

"The legal document I saw on your desk the last time I was here. The lawsuit?"

I shake my head, shuffling more papers aimlessly. "No, that's all right. I've got it under control."

He walks over and leans his elbows on the counter, staring at me. He's entirely too close. I can smell his shampoo again. *Citrus and cedar* . . . "What's going on with you?" he asks.

I look up at him. "What do you mean?"

"I thought everything was cool with us."

I shrug, ignoring the thrill that runs through me. "Everything is cool with us. I don't know what you're talking about."

He sighs. "Maybe if I apologize it'll help."

My heart leaps. "Apologize? For what?"

"For that phone call."

My ears are burning like they're on fire. I shake my head a little, hoping my hair will cover them. "Why should you apologize for me calling you?" I wish that heavy breather would call me back right now . . . Anything to stop this conversation from happening would be nice. I should have trained Oscar Mayer to pee on command.

"Because I didn't handle it well," he says.

I can't keep eye contact with him, so I focus on alphabetizing my bills. I shuffle through the stack, pulling papers out and putting them back in. It helps to draw my focus away from how incredibly uncomfortable this is. He actually feels like *he* should be the one apologizing for not knowing how to handle my complete lack of social skills where he's concerned. I wish I could act normal around him, but I just can't seem to get there.

"It was fine," I say, picking up the stack of bills and banging them down on the desk about ten times, trying to get the individual sheets of paper to all line up. "I called you at your office, and you did exactly what you should've done. You were very professional."

"No, I was rude. You caught me off guard."

"That's fine." It doesn't *feel* fine, but what's the point in making a big deal out of it? It's not like he's my boyfriend who hurt my feelings and now needs to make up for it. He has every right to turn me down when I reach out for a favor. He's not a family friend, and he's not a man who comes here once a year to escape the crazy world and work for us in exchange. He's a very expensive lawyer who works for men I hardly know. That's it. The end. Game over.

"There was somebody else in the room when you called."

"Sure. Of course. It's your office, right? I get that."

"I tried to call you back."

I look up at him. "I know. I ignored the call."

"Why?"

"Are you seriously asking me that question?" I look up, trying without success to read his expression. Does he actually believe I wanted another heaping helping of embarrassment?

He shakes his head. "No. I know why you didn't pick up. I was a bit of an asshole."

"A bit of an asshole?" I have to smile at that. "No, I don't think so. I think you were just saying what needed to be said." *Which was, essentially, that you, Rose Lancaster, have no reason to contact Greg Lister when he's not here at the farm. There is nothing between you two, and there never will be, neither professionally nor personally.*

He reaches over the desk, grabs my hand, and shakes my fingers a couple times before he lets go. "Don't say that. I was a hundred percent asshole, not just a bit of one. It's just . . . There are complications."

He's not making any sense. I look up at him and sigh. "Honestly, Greg . . . I really don't understand how me making a simple phone call to your office to ask you if you just called me creates complications for you." I'm starting to think I'm not the only one in the room feeling out of sorts. He's making about as much sense as I am.

He sighs and turns around, walking over to one of the lobby chairs and dropping down into it. He folds his hands over his outstretched legs and twiddles his thumbs while staring at them. "Remember I told you that a woman named Veronica has been watching my dog for me?"

"Yes."

"She works with me. She's an associate at the firm."

"Really? That's interesting." No, it's not really interesting at all, but I feel the need to help him along. He's clearly uncomfortable sharing this information.

"She offered to watch my dog for me and has been really helpful with all this stuff going on with the band, so I took her up on it a couple times."

There's obviously more to the story. He looks very tortured. I'm just not sure that I should hear it, but does that stop me? "And?" *No, it does not.*

"She took it to mean something more than it did." He looks up, staring at me meaningfully.

"Oh." My heart drops into my shoes. He's telling me that I've done the same thing as this Veronica person. I've read more into our interactions than he intended. How embarrassing. So how in the heck do I extricate myself from this mess I've created? The answer comes to me like a bolt of lightning landing right in the center of my brain: *Fake it.* I will say whatever I need to in order to get out of this. I'll pretend it never happened. Some girl was crushing on you and assumed too much? Phew! Glad that wasn't me.

"Well, that's unfortunate," I say. "I hate when that happens. I hope you get it worked out." I stand and turn toward the back room. "If you'll excuse me, I have to go clean out some kennels."

"Don't you want to hear the rest of it?"

I turn around to face him. "I thought that was the end of the story." I pray he's not about to lecture me about how I've done the same thing and really need to get my shit together. I can't think of anything that would be more humiliating.

"You remember how Amber said that she thought Veronica was my girlfriend?"

"Yes . . ."

"Well, I guess that was what she was shooting for. And I didn't figure that out until it was too late."

"Oh. That sucks for her." Now I'm not sure what he's trying to tell me.

"It kinda sucks for me, too," he says, laughing but without humor.

"Why is that?"

"Because she's not really taking no for an answer."

I have to smile at that. "Being that she's a lawyer and all."

"I don't know that it's the lawyer thing. It's more like she's a little nuts, and unfortunately, we work together, so I can't avoid her." He shakes his head in what looks like disappointment. "Anyway, I know it's not an excuse for how I treated you, but when you called, she and I were in the middle of a conversation where I was telling her *again* that I wasn't interested in going out for drinks or dinner or anything else. She'd just asked me for the fifth time."

"Poor you." I have a really hard time believing that he hated the attention so much—seeing as how he's a man and all—but I'm glad to know he's not telling me this story just to lecture me about my inappropriate phone call. I think I'm out of those woods, at least.

He looks up with a slight grin. "Why do I get the impression you're mocking me?"

I shrug. "Maybe because I've never met a man who hates the attention of a persistent woman, assuming she's pretty."

"Yes, you have, actually." He leans over and pets the dogs, who have given up on wrestling and are now lying by his feet. "Met one, I mean."

Now I feel bad for the girl. For Veronica. If Greg looked right at me and told me to get lost, after I put myself out there and asked him out on a date, I'd be devastated. Embarrassed. Humiliated. Pick your adjective. From what I've seen, Greg is a good catch . . . maybe even a great one. To imagine there could be something there between us and then have him crush my feelings . . . I don't even want to think about it; it makes my heart hurt. I need to *not* get attached to this guy. He could really do some damage.

"I hope you were kind to her about it. It's probably not easy putting yourself out there like that only to be rejected."

"She's pretty tough. She can handle it."

He sounds like every other clueless guy I've ever talked to. Emerald's ex-boyfriend, Smitty, comes to mind. He took her out on a couple dates and then apparently things went downhill quick when they slept together, and now she spends any moment he's on the farm avoiding him. He's a super-great guy to have as a friend or pseudo-big-brother—which is essentially what he is after having grown up just down the road from us most of our lives—but apparently he's not Em's type. Too bad he doesn't get it; to this day, he still flirts with her, even though she's pregnant with Sam's baby. Guys can be so oblivious sometimes. "Didn't you say she's watching your dog again?" I ask.

"Yes." He pauses and looks up to see me rolling my eyes. "Are you saying that was a bad call on my part?"

"Well, duh. Of course it was." I'm so disappointed. I thought he was more sensitive than this.

"But she's a great dog sitter. It's hard to find a good one in the city who isn't already watching ten other dogs. I don't want Tink going out on one of those group walks. She'll get crushed."

"I understand that, but still . . . Veronica has every right to keep asking you out if you keep using her for pet sitting." I'm really not sure how a guy as smart as Greg could be so dense.

"Using her? That sounds bad."

I shrug. "If the shoe fits . . ."

He rubs his hands together slowly, staring at them. "You really don't have a very good opinion of me, do you?"

I go back to my pretend organizing. "It's not my place to judge you . . . but if you must know, I don't think you're such a bad guy."

"Well, that's good news." I hear a smile in his voice. He leans over and messes with the dogs some more. They're more than happy to keep him entertained, crawling all over each other to get to him.

"You know," I say, trying to sound tempting, "Oscar Mayer is looking for a new home. Maybe Tinkerbell would appreciate having a friend around to keep her company."

He points at the dog. "*This* Oscar Mayer? The pisser?"

I have to laugh. "Yes. The pisser. He'll grow out of it, I promise."

"I don't know . . ."

"No pressure. It's my job to find him a home, so I had to ask. I put his pictures up on the website several days ago, but I haven't had any lookers yet." I stand, moving toward the back room. "Listen, I have to get some work done. Thanks for walking me down here."

He stands. "I'll help. You can tell me about the lawsuit while I assist."

I fold my arms over my chest, feeling defensive. *Why is he trying so hard? Does he pity me?* I hate to think that could be true. "You seriously don't need to do that."

"I know." He walks over and stops close to me, his presence nearly swallowing me up, it's so intense.

Sweat breaks out between my shoulder blades. "You do realize that this work I have to do involves cleaning up poop."

"I've never been one to shy away from getting my hands dirty." He rolls up the sleeves of his flannel shirt. "Let's do this."

"If you insist . . ." I smile all the way to the back room. I have a very strong feeling he's going to change his mind when we get to the possum cage.

CHAPTER SEVENTEEN

S o, this is what the life of an animal shelter vet is all about . . ." Greg sprays some antiseptic on the tray I slide out from underneath one of the kennels. This is the third one we've done together, but it's not the worst. I'm saving that one for last so he won't quit early. I have a lot of experience with enthusiastic volunteers who suddenly lose their mojo after smelling possum poo.

"No, this is the life of an animal rescue *worker*," I say, scrubbing the edge of the tray, trying not to breathe through my nose. "The beauty of being a vet is you don't have to clean out the kennel trays. That's peon work."

"Tell me again why you're not a vet." Greg twists his arm around so he can get into the tray's nooks and crannies. He's actually very good at cleaning up poop. I might even give him a sticker when we're done.

"Because there wasn't time," I say, tamping down the feelings of regret that always haunt me when the subject comes up.

"What do you mean?"

"After I finished college, I pretty much started up the rescue the next day. And then I had animals coming in left and right and couldn't imagine myself walking away from them. Many of them are wild, and regular vet clinics won't take them in, so the animals die, often after suffering a great deal of pain over a long period of time. I just couldn't do it." I shrug. There's more to the story than that, but I don't want to invite him into my personal life so completely. He doesn't need to know that I was still hurting from being dumped and rejected by my boyfriend of nearly a year, that my family seemed to be struggling to get all the work done on the farm, and that my sisters and I really missed one another. I'd been occupied with my schoolwork for so long, I needed to reconnect. My family is my rock. They are what keep me grounded in life, and after being so hurt I wasn't feeling like a part of anything.

"Sooo, you just woke up in the morning after you graduated college and said, 'I'm going to start an animal rescue'? Have you always been into animals?"

"I've always been into animals, yes . . . but no, I didn't just wake up and decide to do this. Somebody left a box of kittens at the end of our driveway the day after I finished school, and I'm the one who found them. I was so mad that somebody would do that, but I was also instantly busy with feeding them and making sure they survived."

"There are some pretty crappy people out there, that's for sure." He sprays more disinfectant in one of the corners. I don't think my kennel trays have been this clean since they arrived brand-new. "Lucky for the kittens you're a good person."

"Word got around that I was able to get all of them healthy and then adopted out, so more animals started coming in. At first it was just cats and dogs, but then people would bring in squirrels and birds, too."

"What's the strangest animal you've ever treated?"

"I would have to say . . . a caiman."

"A caiman?" He pauses and looks at me. "Please tell me that's not the reptile I'm picturing in my mind."

I smile big. "It is a reptile. A seriously cool one. They look like alligators or mini dinosaurs."

He drops his arms to his sides. "Who in the heck would have a caiman way up here outside of Glenhollow Farms . . . let alone in the entire state of Maine?"

"We have a couple reptile lovers who come to the clinic. One guy drives several hours to come here with his boa. Not a lot of vets around here handle reptiles . . . or they do and they're not . . . I don't know." I shrug. I don't want to brag, but the guy who brings me his boa says they're not nearly as good with his pet as I am, so he's willing to travel to keep his snake happy.

Greg shivers and then goes back to his cleaning. "No, thank you. You can keep the snakes."

"They're not my favorite either, but I'm not afraid of them like I used to be."

His scrubbing slows as he stares at me. "You're afraid of snakes and yet you treat snakes?"

"I used to be. I also used to be afraid of pretty much every other animal that came in here, besides dogs and cats."

"But you treated them anyway."

"Yes, of course. What else was I going to do? Turn them away? I would never do that to a sick animal. Besides . . . I wouldn't be much of a wildlife rescue operation if I only rescued canines and felines."

He shakes his head slowly as he goes back to his cleaning work. "You're a good person, Rose. I admire you."

My heart fills with warmth. "Thank you." We slide the clean tray back in and move on to the one below it. This kennel has the chinchilla inside it. He's almost ready to go home, his injured leg healing nicely.

"Hello there, Chinchilla. How are you feeling today?" Greg asks, sticking his finger in the cage.

"I wouldn't do that if I were you."

He jerks his hand back, his eyes widening. "Are they dangerous?"

"They can bite. But the reason I warned you this time is we should clean the cage before you put your finger on it. It's probably dirty."

Greg inspects his finger and frowns. "Oh, yeah. Good call." He sprays some disinfectant on his fingertip and scrubs at it with a paper towel.

I can't help but giggle. Now I'm seeing the lawyer emerge. I'll bet he's never had to clean anything in his office.

"Maybe I should be wearing gloves." He's squinting at his hand, as if he'd be able to identify microbes sitting there if he looked close enough.

"Feel free. They're in the other room."

He looks at my hands. "You're not wearing any."

"I'm washable. I don't worry about it unless I have an open wound of some sort." Maybe I should wear gloves, but I've been doing this so long and have been covered in poo too many times to count . . . it doesn't even faze me anymore.

He thinks about it for a couple seconds and then sprays the next tray.

I think I just gave his ego some kind of challenge. "You can go get some gloves if you want. I promise I won't make fun of you."

"No, that's cool. I can handle it. I've gotten my hands a lot dirtier than this, believe me."

"I find that hard to believe. I've never been in your office, but Amber tells me it's pretty swanky."

"Who says I got my hands dirty in that office?" He winks at me.

"Okay, I'll bite. What are we talking about here?" I grab a wad of paper towels and start doing my half of the tray.

"I wasn't always a lawyer, you know."

"Really? I thought you were born wearing a suit." I can totally picture it too—a newborn baby in loafers and a tie.

"I was born in a *birthday* suit, yes. It's a little different from the one I wear to work now, though."

"Ha, ha. Very funny." *Do not think about him naked . . . do NOT think about him naked!*

"Actually, I was born in that birthday suit in Upstate New York on a farm. I didn't even get to the hospital before I hit the cold air."

My hand stops in midwipe, and I look up at him with my jaw dropping open. Words fail me.

"You don't believe me?"

I shake my head. "No. I really don't." I can't see it at all. His manicure and his two-hundred-dollar haircut are getting in the way.

"I have pictures." He pauses before finishing. "Maybe you could come and see them sometime."

My mind races. I wonder where he keeps those pictures. Would it be in his office or his apartment? Is he suggesting I might be there someday? No. It's just an expression. He's being silly. Cleaning poop trays with a person always brings you closer together; my sisters can attest to this fact.

"What kind of farm was it?" I ask, trying to direct myself away from the subject of his personal space and me being in it.

"Apples. We had a pretty decent-sized orchard."

"No shit." The words are out of my mouth before I can stop them.

He chuckles. "Yeah. No shit. And speaking of shit, we used some of the neighbor's horse manure to fertilize our grove, so, like I said . . . I've gotten my hands pretty dirty in the past."

"How does an apple farmer end up as a lawyer in a Manhattan high-rise?"

His mood downshifts into neutral again. "When I was a teenager, my parents had some financial troubles. They took out a loan with some shady characters, and when they were unable to pay the note when it came due, the farm was taken away from them. Foreclosure."

"Oh my god, that's horrible. Who would take away somebody's farm?"

"The company that wanted to build a housing development on their land."

I feel sick to my stomach. "No. That's horrible." I could imagine how it would feel if someone did that to us. Our family would be crushed under the weight of sadness. I don't think we'd ever survive it.

Where would we go? This is the only home I've ever known, and unlike Amber, I have no interest in leaving.

"Yes, it was. It was pretty devastating for a couple years, actually."

"What did you do?" I seriously want to hug him right now. He can't be okay with this, but he doesn't look sad.

"We moved to the city. My dad got a job as a cab driver, and my mom worked as a housekeeper at a hotel."

"So, the country boy became a city boy, but not by choice."

"No, not in the beginning. But I ended up liking it. My parents are retired now, and they're happy."

"Do they regret losing the farm?"

"I think they do. We don't talk about it much. It was a long time ago."

"Is that why you became a lawyer? To try to right the wrongs in the world?"

"As a matter of fact, it is. I started out in environmental law, but my first internship out of school was with a big firm downtown, and they put me in with the corporate law group, so I quickly shifted focus."

"Found your true calling, is that it?"

He shrugs. "It pays the bills."

Interesting. He doesn't sound like he's in love with his job. "So, is Red Hot your only client? Or am I not allowed to ask that question?"

"You can ask it. You can ask me anything you want, and I'll answer as long as it doesn't fall under confidentiality rules. They're my only client; you are correct about that."

"That must make your life easier. You don't have to juggle too many accounts."

He shrugs but doesn't say anything. His expression speaks volumes, though.

"Don't tell me, let me guess . . . Your job was a lot easier before Amber was in the picture."

I can tell he's trying not to smile. "No comment."

"I can talk to her for you, you know. She doesn't have to be difficult. Sometimes she just does it for fun." My nutty sister . . . I wouldn't change her for the world, but then again, I don't have to work with her.

He shakes his head. "No, don't say anything. She's not that bad."

"Baloney. I grew up with her. I know she can be a real pain in the butt when she wants to be."

"She's really smart, your sister. She picks stuff up lightning quick. I like that about her."

"Yeah, she is smart. She was wasted out here on the farm." I sigh, knowing she'll be leaving again soon. It's so much quieter without her here, but I don't enjoy that part of her leaving. Sometimes it's *too* quiet.

He pauses and looks up at me. "You're really smart too. But I'm sure you don't feel like you're wasted out here on the farm. You make a big difference in the lives of all these animals." He gestures at the cages.

I shrug, agreeing with him but also feeling a little sad about it. "No, I don't feel like I'm wasting my life. Sometimes I'm frustrated that I'm limited in what I can do, but I definitely feel like my work is worthwhile."

"Why don't you go to vet school? It would only take you four years."

I hate that a tiny light of hope glows in my heart at his words. I tamp it down immediately, like I always do when the subject of me going back to school comes up. "I can't. Who would take care of the animals while I was gone?" I look at the chinchilla, proud that I brought him back from the brink of death. He was too young to go, and his owner was so sad when she came in with him.

"I'm sure you could find somebody to take over. Some volunteers, maybe?"

"Believe it or not, people are not banging down the door to work at an animal rescue in the middle of central Maine."

We both chuckle over that. "Do you get a lot of donations?" he asks.

"Not really. When people are grateful for what I do for their animals, they usually give me what they can afford. Every once in a while a local business will give me something. But I pretty much make just enough to keep the lights on. I don't get a salary or anything. Whatever personal income I have comes from the farm. I participate in planting and harvesting and going to the market to sell things, and I get a portion of the income that comes from that. We all share in everything equally here. My sisters and I started getting our shares of the farm's income when we turned sixteen and could really help out in a significant way."

"If you got more charitable donations, you could hire some employees and then maybe go off to vet school, right?"

I feel a burning sensation in my stomach. It's stress. I always freak out trying to put together the puzzle of me leaving here. "In theory, maybe. But that's a *big* maybe. Running a business from a distance is difficult enough, but when it involves live animals—and people who may or may not be qualified to deal with them—that's a different story. Plus, I'm needed here on the farm. It's a lot of work doing all the chores and stuff, especially now that Amber is mostly gone."

"What about hiring a vet?"

I smile sadly. "That's a joke. Do you have any idea what kind of salary a vet would demand to live out here in the middle of nowhere and work full time?" I shake my head. "I love your ideas, believe me, but it's just not going to happen for me. That ship has sailed."

We slide the newly cleaned tray in and pull out the next dirty one. Both of our noses wrinkle as the odor comes wafting up. Raccoons are not the nicest animals to clean up after. Greg gives the tray a liberal spraying before we even begin.

"I'm just trying to bring the stench level down," he says, talking with his nose plugged.

"I get it. Believe me."

"Nobody can say you're not completely dedicated." He sprays some more.

"No, they can't."

Greg sits back on his heels, trying to gather some fresh air from over his shoulder. "So what about that lawsuit? Do you want to talk to me about it? Maybe I can give you some ideas on how to handle it."

"I guess we could talk about it." After chatting with him for the last hour, I feel really at ease. There's no doubt in my mind that Greg Lister is one of the good guys. Not only does he clean up animal poo at no charge—when he normally works for over a thousand bucks an hour—but he also used to be a farmer . . . or the son of a farmer, which is just as good in my book. Once I found out about that, it kind of sealed the deal for me. Every farmer I've ever met has been a salt-of-the-earth kind of person. Maybe that's why Greg is so good at putting together his country-boy outfits. He knows the look from his childhood and not just a magazine.

"I noticed in the public record there've been a few lawsuits between you and the town," he says.

"Yes. They've had a bug up their butts about shutting me down for years."

"Why is that?"

"Well, there are a few theories out there, but the one that seems most likely in my mind is the one that involves Betty Beland."

"Betty Beland. She sounds sinister," he says, smiling.

"No, she doesn't. I know she doesn't. She *sounds* like a wonderful kindergarten teacher or a pastor's wife, but she's not, believe me. Betty—who's kind of in charge over there—got divorced, and about a month later her ex asked me out on a date."

"Ouch. So, we're talking a woman scorned?"

"Yeah. And I didn't even say yes to him, which is the kicker."

"I'm guessing it didn't matter whether you said yes or no. It was the idea that this guy liked you that bugged her."

"Exactly. But there's also the theory that some well-placed people in town don't really like that there's what they consider a hippie commune out here, so they do whatever they can to encourage us to relocate. We're too close to their precious suburban lives, maybe. I think they're worried their kids will start smelling like patchouli oil or something."

"You guys running around naked and dancing under the moon bothers them?"

I smile, enjoying the vision. "Something like that."

"I hear you have a good reputation out at the farmers' market."

"We do. We've been there since it started. Our mothers were three of the founders, actually. But the snobs on the town council are not the kind of people who have booths at the farmers' market. They'll shop there because they think it's quaint, but they won't mingle with the merchants, if you know what I mean."

"Tell me exactly what it is they're claiming is the problem."

"I don't know *exactly* exactly; you can read the document if you need details. I think it's pretty much that the land-use rules have changed recently, and now this building is not in the right zone. And I'm not supposed to be using this barn as a place to shelter animals. And then there's the same old nonsense about me doing the work of a veterinarian when I'm not licensed."

"Are you?"

"No, of course not. I used to have a contracted veterinarian named John Masters who would come in and do whatever surgeries were necessary and put together the treatment plans, but he backed out on me after Banana's surgery. I'm pretty sure the town council got to him. They may have threatened him with causing trouble with his license if he didn't stop working with me. I wouldn't put it past them to tattle on him to the licensing board or whatever."

"Do you have proof of that? Did he tell you that?"

"No. But he was acting really cagey when he was here last time, when he told me he had to quit, and it was the same day I got the lawsuit notice in the mail."

"Who's doing your surgeries now?"

"No one. Luckily, I haven't had anybody walk in needing anything, but if I did, I'd have to call the local vet and ask if I can send them over to him."

"That could be a problem if somebody has an urgent injury, couldn't it?"

"Yes, it could. But I did put a notice out at the last farmers' market and, as you probably saw, one on the door . . . telling people that we no longer have veterinary services here. So I hope anybody who has an injured animal will go right to the town vet instead."

"Okay. Do you mind if I go take a look at that document now and see what I can do to help you?"

"Are you kidding?" I point at the kennels next me, hoping to sell him on the idea of staying. Not only am I *not* in any hurry to have him read that document—it's embarrassing to be sued—but I'm also having too much fun with him to stop yet. "We have five more cages to go. You expect me to do these all by myself?"

"Don't you usually do them by yourself?"

Busted. "Maybe." I wilt. My plan is not working.

He smiles and crouches down next to me again. "I guess I can help you finish."

"Awesome. And if you do a really good job, you'll get a sticker." I grin big.

"A sticker?" he asks, confused.

"I give them out for good behavior."

"Oh, I get it." He grins. "My niece Linny used to love getting those at the dentist."

"Your niece?" All I know about her from Amber is that she's spunky and works at Greg's office sometimes.

"Yeah. She works at my office doing filing and things." Greg picks up the bottle of disinfectant.

"Are you close?"

"You could say that." He grabs a few paper towels and sprays them, getting ready for the next tray.

He doesn't elaborate on his relationship with Linny, and I don't want to push him.

"What does a guy have to do to earn a sticker from you?" he asks, pulling out the next tray.

"He's got to clean every cage without stopping and without complaining about the smell the entire time."

"Man . . . Anyone ever tell you you're a harsh taskmaster?" He starts scrubbing as he watches me and waits for my answer.

"Who, me? Don't be silly." I kind of love the idea of bossing him around a little. I point to a corner. "You missed a spot."

He grins, moving his towels over to clean where I indicated.

Should I feel guilty about making this high-priced lawyer help me clean out dirty kennels? Maybe. But I'm not going to let myself do that, because I cannot remember the last time I enjoyed being a poop picker-upper.

CHAPTER EIGHTEEN

After we finish our cleanup, we take the two dogs for a walk through the woods. Greg is proudly wearing the sticker he earned for perfect kennel cleaning on his collar. It's an orange with arms and legs, wearing white gloves and giving a thumbs-up.

"It's really beautiful out here," Greg says. "Like heaven on earth." He's walking next to me with his hands in his pockets, his heavy boots crunching twigs and kicking up dried leaves.

"It is. I haven't traveled much, but it's the prettiest place I know."

"I heard you make maple syrup from your own trees out here."

"We do. It's pretty good too, if I do say so myself. You've had it on your pancakes."

"Any chance I can get some to take back with me? I should probably give Veronica a gift for watching Tinkerbell."

Hearing her name takes some of the joy out of the moment for me. She likes him and she's watching his dog. They have a connection I wish I had with him in a way. I know it's not smart to want to be involved with him, but I can't seem to help how I feel. I work to ease the slight tension my weird emotions have created. "Sure. We sell it to friends and family at a discount," I say, teasing. I'd never charge him for our syrup, especially since he's being nice enough to look over my legal papers and scrub poo stains off trays for me.

"Sweet," he says.

"No pun intended?"

He chuckles. "Yeah. I'm not really one for puns."

"You know, my sister Amber thinks you're a real stick-in-the-mud." I look over, hoping I didn't offend him. I wish they could get along better. Maybe I can help that happen.

He loses his smile. "Yeah, I know she does."

"How come you don't talk to her like you're talking to me?" I know for a fact that he doesn't open up with her, because Amber has pretty much filled me in on every conversation they've ever had. Her descriptions of interacting with Greg always include her trying to be friendly and him shutting her down.

"I need to keep a professional distance between myself and my clients."

"Is she your client?"

"No. But she works for them."

"Back when she first met you, she wasn't." I keep pushing because I want to know the whole story. Is the problem Amber, or is it something else?

"That's true. Maybe I just feel more comfortable talking to you than I do her."

"Because I'm a dog person?" I laugh to ease the tension I'm creating with my interrogation.

"Yeah, maybe that. And maybe it's . . . I don't know."

My heart starts beating more rapidly. There's a connection between us, even though we're not touching, and I don't want to ruin it by pushing him into a place he doesn't want to be. "I think you're easy to talk to, too. And it definitely helps that you have a tiny dog named Tinkerbell."

"Did I tell you the story of how I got her?"

"No. Not yet." I zip up my jacket, trying to maintain whatever heat I have left.

"One of my colleagues at the office received her as a gift from a client. But he's allergic to dogs, so he was going to bring her to a shelter."

"Are you kidding me? She's a purebred Yorkie, right?"

"Yeah, and I'm sure she wasn't cheap. She was really tiny, barking a lot . . . I don't know if he actually is allergic, but he's definitely not a dog person. It would have been a mistake to let him take her home."

"So, you stepped in and scooped her up? Animal rescue 9-1-1?"

"Not exactly. She escaped his office, and everybody was looking all over the place for her. I wouldn't let anybody look in my office, though, because I was busy working on some contracts."

"Don't tell me, let me guess . . . She was in your office the whole time."

"Hey, don't skip to the end." He shakes a finger at me, and I hold up my hands in apology. "By the time I was ready to leave for the day, everybody else was gone; the offices were empty. I went to grab my running shoes to take to the gym, and there was this tiny ball of fur curled up inside one of them."

"She went to sleep in your shoe? Aw, how adorable." I can totally picture it.

"What can I say? The girl likes foot odor. She has very peculiar tastes."

I laugh really hard at that. "She must be really special."

"I decided right there that if she liked my feet that much, I probably should just take her home with me."

"Who knows when you'll find *another* girl who likes that, right?"

"Exactly."

We're both grinning from ear to ear. My face starts to cramp with happiness. "That's a cute story. I guess she decided that you belonged to her." I can see why she did it. Greg is pretty cute, and he does wear nice shoes. Knowing how fastidious he is, they probably don't even stink.

"Yeah, she did. And I do. She's got me wrapped around her tiny little paw."

"I love that." I sound like I'm dreaming out loud.

"What do you love?" He stops walking as he waits for my answer.

I turn and face him, taking a slow step back. "I love that you're a big tough guy who adores his tiny little dog. It's pretty stinking adorable, if you want to know the truth."

He takes a step toward me, his hands coming out of his pockets. "I'm not really a tough guy. I just have to keep up a façade."

I stop and tilt my head so I can look up into his steel-gray eyes. His hair has fallen onto his forehead, and I really want to slide my fingers through it and move it over to the side where it belongs. I fold my arms over my chest because I don't trust myself not to reach for him. "Why the façade, Greg? Do you think clients won't take you seriously if you show them any vulnerability?"

"Maybe. Or maybe it's just not my style to be . . . open."

We continue to stare into each other's eyes as a chilly wind blows through the trees. I run my hands up and down my arms, trying to create some warm friction.

"Are you cold?" He reaches out and rubs my arms for me. The movement brings us closer; we're almost within hugging distance. It's intimate and nerve-racking, but in a good way.

"A little bit." I look around, my teeth starting to chatter. "Where did those dogs get to?"

"They're over there." Greg gestures with his chin at a spot over my shoulder. His eyes never leave mine. "Listen, maybe this is none of my business, but I'd really like to help you with your legal problem."

His hands are so warm on my arms, I don't want him to let go. I shift my weight from one foot to the other. "Are you licensed in Maine?"

"No, but someone in my office is, and he owes me a favor."

I'm almost afraid to hope. He's offering me a lifeline, but what will it cost me in the end? "I wasn't kidding when I said I can't afford your fees."

"Consider it a donation to your nonprofit. Our firm is always looking for pro bono work."

"Are you sure? I don't want to take advantage of you because you work for my family members."

He gets a funny expression on his face, but then it quickly disappears as he shakes his head. "Don't worry about it. You won't owe me a thing."

"Well, I *will* owe you one huge favor, at least. I can't agree that I won't owe you anything."

Half of his mouth lifts in a smile. It looks almost devilish. "A huge favor? Hmmm. I think I could work with that. I could get used to the idea of you owing me *something*."

I lift an eyebrow. "Don't get ahead of yourself, buddy."

He tips his head back and laughs loud enough that it echoes out into the woods. "Love it." He turns around, guiding me along with him as he rests his arm across my shoulders. "You make me laugh." We walk back toward the clinic side by side.

I keep my arms folded across my chest because if I don't, I may be tempted to wrap them around his waist. This thing he's doing, putting his arm across my shoulders, it doesn't mean anything. We're just two adults who are getting along and having a nice afternoon together. I have to keep reminding myself of that with every step. It feels so nice to have the side of my body pressing into his. It's both intimate and friendly, hot and cool. I could read so much into this, but I know I shouldn't.

Oscar Mayer and Banana come running by, throwing up leaves in their wake. It helps to keep the mood light, to see them acting so goofy. *Thank God for dogs.* I giggle with happiness.

"Your house is full of laughter," he says.

I nod. "That's true, it is."

"How do you feel about your mothers coming out here before you were born?"

I stop walking but he continues. His arm falls away and he turns around. We're facing each other again, but the mood has changed. The bruising on my heart comes to the forefront, and I lose my smile and those happy feelings I had when we were touching. I don't want to get into the decisions my mothers made way back then. I refuse to be angry with the women who raised me with nothing but love. They did what they thought they had to do, and I'm good with that. And the parts I'm not good with . . . well . . . we don't need to get into those. Not now and not ever.

He's waiting for an answer, and I don't want to shut him out, so I do my best to come up with a bland response that doesn't encourage further conversation on that topic. "I have mixed feelings about it."

"Am I being too intrusive, asking you these questions about your family?"

I can't look at him anymore, disappointed that he so easily ruined the mood. I guess he wasn't feeling what I was. I stare at the ground and shrug again. "No, not really." It's not like my thoughts on the matter are a big secret. And he was willing to answer my questions, so maybe I should answer his. He shouldn't be faulted for not having silly, touchy-feely emotions toward me like I have toward him.

"You can tell me to mind my own business if you want."

I look up at him, catching a vulnerable expression on his face. It instantly makes me want to throw caution to the wind. What could be the harm in opening up a little? Now that Emerald seems to be on board with the men of Red Hot insinuating themselves into our lives more completely, I haven't really talked about this stuff with anyone. Maybe it would be good to get some things off my chest. I take in and let out a deep breath before I start.

"I have a really great life here as a result of the decisions my mothers made, but there's a big piece of me that's angry about it, too."

He nods slowly, his eyebrows pulling together. He doesn't say anything as he waits for me to continue.

"When I found out that I had a father out there somewhere, and that he was able to find me so easily, I got really angry."

"Why?"

"Because." I can't believe I have to explain this to him. "You have a father. Surely you could imagine what your life would've been like if he'd missed your whole childhood and then appeared out of nowhere when you turned twenty-five."

Greg stares off into the distance for a little while and then slowly starts to nod. "I guess I might be a little bitter about it."

"Bitter, yes. But also really disappointed. And sad. When I was a little girl growing up, I always wondered who my dad was . . . where he was. Our mothers never told us the story of their lives with the band. They always managed to change the subject or shift the focus away from the questions of our origins and their shared history prior to our births. They claimed their pasts weren't important. And I understand why they made the decision they made, to leave without saying anything; they were young and they had a lot of people influencing them who had their own interests in mind. But still, I can't help but be angry at Red and the rest of them for the role they played in everything."

"What exactly are you angry at them for? What role did they play?"

I put my hands on my hips, a little upset that he doesn't get it without me having to explain it in such painful detail. "I'm upset that they used our mothers for sex and companionship for years, and then did nothing when they disappeared. I mean, that sounds really selfish to me. Really self-centered. You'd think they would have at least wondered where our moms went. They should've tried to find them. It was the decent thing to do, and they didn't do it."

Greg steps closer and rubs my upper arms a few times before sliding his hands down to my wrists and pulling my hands off my hips. We're standing face-to-face. My fingers curl around his, and it sparks the warmth between us again.

"Thank you for telling me that. I guess I never really thought of it that way, but I can see now why you'd be so upset with them. Is this why you're not taking the settlement?"

The warmth turns instantly to chill and I yank my hands away from his, stepping back. "Please tell me that isn't what this is about."

He looks at me quizzically. "What *what* is about? I don't understand."

I throw my arms out to my sides, glancing around us. "This walk! You helping me with the kennels! Please tell me you're not here doing all this because you're still trying to talk to me about that damn settlement!" I'm halfway to blowing my top at him. One wrong word and it's all over. I will verbally tear him a new butthole. It's one thing to make me wonder about his personal feelings toward me, but it's totally another to deliberately manipulate me just so he can get his business done.

He steps forward in a hurry and puts his hands on my shoulders. "No. No, no, no. Please don't think that." He looks up at the sky and then down at me, his expression more serious than I've ever seen it. "I'm glad you're not taking the settlement. Believe me. I think you're *way* better off walking away from it. Way better."

Now I'm the one who's confused. I tilt my head. "What?"

He releases me and turns around, gesturing for me to follow him back toward the clinic. "Listen, you're not my client, so I can't give you my opinion on this stuff. I've already said too much. Would you mind if we changed the subject?"

I let out a long sigh. "I would *love* to change the subject away from the settlement. That's a great idea. Super. Super duper."

He sighs too. I'm pretty sure it's in relief. He puts his arm across my shoulders again, and we walk together once more, me taking one and a half steps for each of his. I glance over at him, but he's staring down at the ground, deep in thought. I enjoy the last fifty yards of our stroll, the wind burning my cheeks and pulling bits of my hair from the clip it's supposed to be in. It's chilly out here, but I'm getting warmer by the second.

Every moment I spend in Greg's presence brings us closer. Closer to what? I have no idea. Maybe a friendship. Maybe an affair. Would

I sleep with him if he were interested? I might. I definitely might. The more I get to know him, the more I wonder what he'll look like without all that L.L.Bean gear on. *Naked.* I wonder if he'll be as good in bed as he is at work.

Oh, what a rumor mill we would start with that kind of relationship. I smile briefly at the thought but slowly let the fantasy go. There's no way it'll ever happen between us. He lives there, and I live here. He's a lawyer, and I'm an animal caretaker/poo picker-upper. I'm never going to Manhattan, and he's never coming into my bedroom at the farm. Not only are we living in two different worlds, the only privacy we could ever get is out here at the clinic.

I fear I'm doomed to a life of being single because I just don't have the resources to set myself up in my own place where I could have my own adult life. Sure, I could hook up with a guy from time to time, but a real relationship? Not likely. For the first time ever, I'm regretting the fact that I said no to that stupid legal settlement, even though the lawyer standing next to me just told me that it would be a mistake to accept it.

CHAPTER NINETEEN

Ten minutes after Greg leaves to go back to the house, the door opens and Smitty walks through it. I grin at him as he approaches the desk.

Good old Smitty. He never fails to cheer me up with that smile of his. He's been like a brother to Amber, Em, and me since we were small. I can still remember the first day he came to the farm on his tiny bike, covered in dirt. "My name is Jacob Hendersson Smith the third, but you can call me Smitty." And so we did.

The roads weren't paved back then, and he wanted to meet the girls he'd heard about from his mother, so he braved the dust and the potholes and the scary wildlife to get to our place five miles away. Since that day, he's pretty much been a fixture here on the farm. First he was just a playmate, happy to let us dress him up in our clothes and play with his hair. Then he showed us the joys of horseback riding, hide-and-seek, tag, and all the other games country kids play. When he was big and strong enough, he started earning money by helping us with chores around the property. Now he's as close to a farm manager as we'll ever have, splitting his working hours between Glenhollow and his parents' place. He has a younger brother named Brian, but he's only seventeen and a total handful, often in trouble with the law for various things. We've only seen him a few times over the years. He told Smitty he hates our farm, and none of us has any idea why. Smitty says he's jealous, but I have no idea what he's jealous of.

"Hey there, you," I say. "What are you doing out this way?"

He leans over the desk and reaches out to give me a fist bump, bringing the smell of cold outdoors, sweat, and motor oil with him. "Just coming over to check the hives. Making sure they don't need any sugar water from me."

"You're still taking care of them even though Amber is here?"

"Yeah, I'm still helping out. I have a feeling she's not gonna stay here for too much longer."

"Did she tell you that?"

He shrugs. "Not in so many words." He taps the counter with his thumbs, looking around.

"Is everything cool between you and Emerald?" She mentioned a while back that he seemed bummed she was with Sam. I wonder if he's gotten over that.

He gives me a funny look. "Yeah. We're cool. She's got a boyfriend and her little girl now, so I guess that's lights-out for me."

"I heard you were dating somebody, though, right? That's exciting."

"It didn't work out." He turns around and twists the baseball hat on his head left and right a few times before he faces me again. "What're you doing tonight?"

"Going to dinner at the house. You want to come?"

"Yeah, I might do that. What about after?"

I look around. "You know me. I'll be back here."

"And what about after *that*?" He's looking at me funny again.

"I don't know. Probably go back home like I always do."

"You feel like going out and getting some beers?"

"Oh, I doubt it. I'm usually pretty tired by the time I leave here at night."

"Aw, come on. I saw that guy in here with you. Wasn't he helping you out? Maybe you won't be as tired tonight after getting all that help."

This strikes me as a very strange thing to say, coming from Smitty. He's usually not at all interested in what I do. "What guy? When did you see him?"

"That guy who just left here. He was going out when I was coming in."

Weird. I could have sworn a lot more time than that passed before Smitty came in. "You mean Greg?"

"Yeah, that lawyer guy."

"Yeah, he did actually help a little bit." I smile at the memory. My kennels have never been so clean.

"See? You're not going to be too tired. You could have *a* beer."

"Well, I'll ask around and see if anybody's up for it."

"Or you could just come yourself." He lifts his brows high and smiles a little too hard.

I sit back in my chair and stare at him. "Smitty, are you asking me out on a date?" I can't believe I have to ask him this question, but he's acting so strangely, and it sure seems like that's what he's suggesting.

He loses the smile. "Would that be such a crazy thing?"

I frown. "Uh, yes. You slept with my sister."

"So? She's dating that other guy now, and she's really happy. She's probably going to marry him. Isn't she pregnant?"

"Yes, but that doesn't mean you didn't sleep with her."

"We slept together *one* time. And I'm pretty sure she regrets it because she's avoided me completely ever since."

I smile, feeling sorry for the guy. "She's not avoiding you. You know she's just shy."

He rolls his eyes. "Whatever. I don't understand how that means I can't go out with one of her sisters."

"It's a rule we have, Smitty. You have Brian, right?"

"Yeah, but we don't have that rule."

"Well, I appreciate you asking. It was very sweet of you to do that, but no. It's not going to happen."

He leans in closely. "If I hadn't slept with your sister, would you go out with me?"

I have to laugh at that. "I would seriously consider it." Smitty is definitely easy on the eyes. He's one of those good old boys with big muscles, a nice butt, and a special kind of charm with the ladies. I think he could be fun. Emerald always said he was, but he's just a little too brash for her. She prefers the strong, silent type like Sam.

He looks down at the desk. "I see you haven't found a replacement for your stolen laptop yet."

"Who told you about my laptop?"

"I don't remember. I heard in town somewhere."

"So, the word is out, but still nobody has returned it." I shake my head in disappointment. "What is this world coming to?"

"There are a lot of strangers coming in and out of town these days. I'm sure it wasn't anybody from around here who took it. We have nice neighbors; you know that."

"Yeah, I know that. But still, it's really frustrating. I don't have the money for a new one."

"You don't? I thought you got some money for taking care of these animals."

"Some, yeah . . . but believe me, it doesn't last very long." I smile bitterly. "I'm broke. Most people hardly pay me anything. I'm not a vet, remember?"

He nods, looking disappointed. "Yeah, I know. That really sucks. Maybe I can help you out." He turns on his heel and starts walking to the door.

"What are you talking about?" Now I'm a little worried.

"You'll see." He leaves, closing the door behind him. I have no idea if he'll be back.

I lean back in my chair and sigh, propping my feet up on the desk. I can't believe Smitty just asked me out. I'm going home early, before dinner, so I have time to gossip with my sisters about it. Emerald's going to pee her pants. I wonder if she'll be mad. I know what Amber's going to say. I'm hereby mentally betting myself five dollars that she is going to talk about what a backwoods hick he is for thinking he could date two sisters in the same family. I smile just imagining the expression on her face. She's so protective of us.

My watch says I have two more hours before I'm outta here. I look down at the little doggy digging in my purse again. Banana is in the back, sleeping behind a closed door so that he can get a break from his little buddy. He still needs some time to recuperate before he's a hundred percent again. I'm going to take Oscar Mayer and Banana home with me tonight. The puppy needs to get out into the world more, and his brother needs some running time. I lean my head back, remove my hair clip, and let my hair flow over the back of the chair. My mind replays my walk with Greg.

He put his arm around me. *Twice*. He *could* be interested in me romantically. Or maybe he sees me as some kind of sweet sister who he wants to take care of. *Ugh*. That would be totally frustrating. No, that won't work at all. I don't want to be the sweet sister, I've decided. I want to kiss him, at least. I've been staring at his lips and wondering how they'd feel for too long. He's too gorgeous to not at least try, right? I could totally lay one on him and solve the mystery once and for all. And then he'll be gone back to Manhattan, and I won't have to face him anymore. Do I dare?

My mind really starts to wander at this point. I'm really warming to the idea, the more I think about it. It could be perfect, actually. If the kiss works out, we could have an affair—a secret one that nobody but us knows about. I would only have to see him once a month—or even less frequently than that once the band is back in Manhattan. Geez, if I played this right, I could have my cake and eat it too; I could have my work that keeps me busy all day, and every once in a great while I could have awesome sex with a gorgeous guy who makes me laugh. Talk about perfect. I don't need to have what my sisters have—a man by my side all the time, raising a family with me. I could be content with a wild, sexy affair with a beautiful man who used to live on an apple orchard. Oh, yes, ma'am, I could. If I were bold and fearless and not at all worried about being rejected. *Good luck with that.*

I get up and go into the back room. I need to check on my patients so that when I leave later this afternoon I can spend some quality time with my family and enjoy every minute of it. I miss being with them. I've been spending more time than ever out here at the clinic, but it's time I stopped avoiding all the Red Hot drama and became more engaged with what's happening with my moms and sisters. I'm definitely looking forward to seeing Greg at the dinner table. Maybe I'll even get the chance to hint at this affair idea, if I'm feeling particularly bold. I could just imagine the look on his face . . . the point where serious Lawyer-Greg becomes loosened-up, sexy Greg. And I'm the only woman who ever gets to see that side of him. I think I might be a little bit addicted to that idea.

CHAPTER TWENTY

The three of us—Amber, Emerald, and I—are sitting on Emerald's bed with the door locked. So far we've already had three people try the handle in an attempt to enter, but we've sent them away. It's our sister time—our chance to reconnect and gossip about everything and everyone under the sun.

"So, *what* is going on with you and Greg?" Amber asks, rubbing her hands together like an evil genius. "He was down there at the clinic with you for ages today."

"What's he even doing here on the farm?" Emerald asks. She looks at Amber. "Were you expecting him to fly in?"

Amber shakes her head while wearing a big grin. "Nope. He's here for Rose."

I feel my face going pink. "No, he's not. He has work for you guys." I'm afraid to hope that she's right, or that she's right but that he's here because of that silly phone call. I still can't totally get rid of the idea in my head that he's just being nice and trying to let me down easy . . . like he mentioned he's doing with Veronica.

"Ha, ha. *Work.* Please. You should've seen what he brought with him. A five-page document he could've easily emailed me."

"Really?" My face gets so hot I have to put my palms on it to try and cool it down. I want more information, but I don't want to seem too obvious or desperate.

"That is so romantic," Emerald says, sighing and looking at me with googly eyes.

"Cut it out. You have no proof of anything." I don't want to get my hopes up. It's too hard to believe that a guy like Greg would make a special trip up here just to see me. I'm basic. Basic Rose. Nothing special. Not to a guy like him, anyway. I'm more suited to someone like Smitty, someone who grew up just off a dirt road. I probably shouldn't have been so quick to turn him down. He could be my last hope.

"What did he do with you today?" Amber asks. "Tell us everything. We want a total play by play. Did you touch his junk yet?"

I burst out laughing and slap her on the arm. "Are you kidding me? Nothing even close to that."

"Tell us," Emerald urges. "Seriously. We're excited for you."

I shake my head and roll my eyes at their desperation on my behalf. "There's nothing to be excited about. He helped me clean out the kennels, and then we took a walk with the dogs. That's it."

I can't tell them about how he's helping me with the lawsuit because I don't intend for them to ever find out about that damn thing. Both of them are pregnant, and they don't need the stress, and they'd for sure tell our mothers. The last thing I need is them freaking out about something like this. Then the band would get involved, and everyone would have an opinion about what I should or shouldn't be doing with my life. Plus, it would fuel Amber's theory that there is something going on between Greg and me. For sure she'd put her nose into our business and do something to embarrass me.

"He cleaned out those nasty kennels?" Emerald asks. She looks over at Amber. "He likes her."

"Seriously." Amber reaches over and squeezes my arm. "Not even the people who love you most in the world want to do that crap."

"I might have guilted him into it."

"Guilt trips do not work on kennel cleaning," Amber says. She looks over at Emerald. "Am I right?"

Emerald nods. "You are so right. That is my least favorite job on the entire farm."

Amber starts waving her hand in front of her nose. "Possum poo? No thank *you*."

"We only have one possum right now, first of all. And second of all, Greg lived on a farm, so he's used to that kind of stuff."

Amber's eyes go wide. "No shit?"

"I can see it," Emerald says, nodding. "He looks good in those flannel shirts."

"Hey, I forgot to tell you this," Amber says, grabbing me by the hand and squeezing. "I was there when his L.L.Bean order came in."

"I knew it!" I squeeze her back. "I knew he was wearing L.L.Bean." *Totally called it.*

"All brand-new. He practically bought an entire wardrobe. I asked him what he was doing with all that stuff, but he just shoved the boxes aside and changed the subject. I *knew* he got it to come up here." She shakes her head slowly, grinning from ear to ear.

"I wonder why he would do that?" Em asks, trying to be sly.

I shove her. "Be quiet. It's not because of me. It's because of you guys."

"What's that supposed to mean?" Amber asks.

"He's just trying to fit in. He's doing the farm-boy thing so he doesn't stick out like a sore thumb."

"What kind of farm did he live on?" Emerald asks.

"His family had an apple orchard. But he moved to the city when he was a teenager, after they lost the farm. Don't tell him I told you, though." I'm feeling a little guilty that I shared his secret. Is it a secret? He didn't say I was supposed to keep it to myself. Surely he knows sisters tell each other stuff, though. "He didn't say it was a secret, but I don't think he'd want everyone to know."

"I don't think the guys in the band know," Amber says, sounding impressed. "How did you get that out of him?"

"I didn't get it out of him; he just told me."

"It sounds like you talked about some pretty intimate things," Emerald says, wiggling her eyebrows at me.

I suddenly feel like I should be keeping more of my interactions with Greg to myself. Some of the moments between us were very nice and almost . . . private. I don't recall ever feeling that way about a man before. I've always shared everything with my sisters.

"Smitty stopped by today," I say, hoping a change of subject will make this weird feeling I have go away.

"What did he want?" Emerald asks, frowning.

"You're probably not going to be happy about what he wanted." Both my sisters stare at me, waiting. "Believe it or not, he asked me out on a date." I cringe.

Emerald gasps.

"Are you *kidding* me?" Amber shouts.

I hold out my hands like two stop signs. "Shhh . . . geez . . . I didn't say I was going out with him; calm down."

"But . . . ," Emerald says, stopping when she can't find her next words.

"I told him no, obviously, but isn't that weird? That he'd even ask?"

"Of course it's weird," Amber says. She pats Em on the hand. "Don't be upset, sweetie."

Em pulls her hand away. "I'm not upset. He's just a big doofus."

I nod. "He is a big doofus. A doofus with a nice butt, but still . . . I told him we have a rule; we don't date each other's exes."

Emerald sighs and glares at me. "He's not my ex. We went out *two* times. We had sex *one* time. That does not make him my ex-boyfriend."

I raise an eyebrow at her. "Are you telling me I could go out with him if I wanted to?"

She shakes her head rapidly. "Don't. You'll regret it. He's seriously strange."

"He's not strange; he's harmless," Amber says, scolding our sister.

Em sticks her tongue out at Amber. "You're just saying that because he watches your bees for you. But trust me, he's weird."

"I've known Smitty practically his whole life, and I've never seen him act strange, other than this one time," I say, looking at Amber for confirmation.

She shakes her head at me. I think we're silently deciding together that Emerald is hurt that they didn't go out on another date, and this is what's behind her opinion of him.

"Okay, whatever you guys say," Em says. "But you didn't sleep with him, so maybe you should consider that you don't know him as well as I do."

Amber puts her hands on her hips, pretending to be offended. "Are you trying to tell us that you did *not* give us all the details of that encounter? Did you fail to tell us about Smitty's perversions? Because that would violate the terms of our sister contract."

Em shoves Amber until she falls over on the bed. "We don't have a contract. But I told you everything. Almost everything." She casts her eyes down.

I wave my hands and close my eyes. "I do not want to know any more details than I already do. Please. Let's just leave the past in the past."

"Yes, let's. What else did you and Greg talk about?" Emerald asks.

I'm glad for the subject change, so I answer her question, even though it's not exactly going to lighten the mood. "He asked about the stupid settlement again."

"Why would he do that?" Emerald sounds annoyed.

I shrug. "I have no idea. He's brought it up, like, four times so far."

"He hasn't asked me," Emerald says. "Not beyond that one time when he first showed up."

"Me neither," Amber adds. "Why is he so hung up on you and *your* settlement?"

"I don't know." I look at both of them in turn, waiting to hear their theories.

"I think he's just using it as an excuse to talk to her," Emerald says.

Amber's smile turns sly. "I agree. It's quite the conversation opener, isn't it?"

"All it does is make me mad. I don't know why he keeps bringing it up, but whenever he does, I tell him I'm not interested and change the subject." *Usually.* Today during our walk I gave him my rationale for saying no, which will hopefully stop that conversation from ever happening again.

Emerald and Amber share a secret look that makes me instantly suspicious. "What?"

"Nothing," Amber says, trying to look as innocent as possible. Unfortunately, I know her way better than this. I also know Em better than this. I turn to give her a sad look. "Em, are you keeping secrets from me? That hurts my feelings."

"Don't say anything, Em," Amber warns. "She's trying to trick you."

"I think we should tell her." She gives Amber a pleading look.

"Tell me what?" I glare at both of them. "You guys had better not be keeping secrets from me. Now, *that* is a violation of the sister contract."

Em puts her hand on mine and strokes my fingers gently. "We've just been talking about it . . . and we were thinking maybe you should take the settlement."

I pull my hand away from hers. "Why? Are you?"

"I'm thinking about it." She cringes.

I look over at Amber. "What about you? Are you thinking about it?"

She shrugs casually. "I am. I don't think it's such a big deal anymore."

"What happened to change your feelings about all this?" They're wearing guilty looks, but their chins are looking pretty stubborn too.

"We've just gotten to know them better," Em says. "They're nice guys, you can't deny that."

"I agree they've been nice since they've been here." That's about as much as I'm going to concede. Regardless, it doesn't change the past.

"You haven't spent much time with them yet, but if you did, I think you'd see what I see now," Em suggests.

"I work with them and now I've been living with them," says Amber. "They *are* good people. I think they were just young and stupid and full of themselves back when our mothers first knew them."

"I think you're probably right about that," I say, lifting my chin. She's not changing my mind.

"We've all done stupid things in our youth, and I'm sure I'm going to do more stupid things before I become old and wise like our mothers," Amber says, shrugging. "I don't think people should hold that against us in the future. And to be honest, I could do a lot of good with ten million bucks."

I fold my arms over my chest. "Oh yeah? What're you going to do with it? Buy another condo?"

"Actually, I was thinking about donating some of it to a homeless shelter so my friend Ray has a place to sleep at night."

The guilt threatens to drown me. "Oh. Well. That's nice."

"And I was thinking about opening up an art school," Emerald says. Her face turns pink, and she drops her gaze to the bed. "But maybe I wouldn't be a very good teacher. But if I had money, I could hire one."

I reach out and take her hand. "I know for a fact that you would be a *wonderful* teacher. Look at how much you've taught Sadie already." It's true; the little girl is very young, but her drawings show promise, and there's a definite difference between what she's doing now compared to what she was doing when she first arrived here. My sister is one of those rare artists who can not only create but who can also teach others to create.

"What would you do with ten million dollars if you had it?" Amber says. "Just pretend it's not coming from the band. Pretend it's coming from an anonymous donor and you can do anything you want with it."

Emboldened by my sisters' selfless ideas of helping others, I let my mind go to the place I wouldn't let it go before and dream. Greg's voice comes back to me. "I'd hire somebody to watch over the shelter while I went to vet school."

It makes my heart hurt to imagine that this could have been an option for me if things had happened differently in our past. But since that's not my reality, this daydreaming is pointless; it's all just a tease. "But I'm not getting ten million dollars from an anonymous donor, and I'm not taking that settlement." I extricate myself from our sister circle and stand at the foot of the bed. I've never felt so apart from them as I do now, even when we were all going to college in different places. "I think we should get downstairs and help with dinner."

"I think so too," Emerald says, joining me.

Amber scoots over and jumps off the mattress, coming over to be with us. Pulled into a group hug, I inhale the scent of my sisters. I love them so much. I can't let myself be angry with them for wanting to take their settlements. I have to be bigger than that. More adult about the situation. They're going to do great things with the money, and they deserve to have that choice. We're not tied to one another except through love. They make their choices, and I make mine. I just wish growing up wasn't so painful sometimes.

"Are you going to sit next to Greg?" Emerald asks.

"You'd better," Amber says, not waiting for my answer.

The idea of sitting next to him excites me. It's such a simple thing, but just being near him makes me happy. "I'd like to. We'll see if it works out that way."

"Oh, it'll work out that way. Trust me," Amber says.

Emerald giggles. "Uh-oh. The matchmaker is on the case."

"God help me," I say. But secretly, I'm glad for it. I'm ready to admit that I wouldn't mind being matched with Greg. That secret affair is sounding better and better the more I think about it.

CHAPTER TWENTY-ONE

A knock comes at the front door while we're sitting down to eat, and Smitty sticks his head in. "Hey, everybody. Is it time for dinner?"

I stand. "Oh, shoot; I forgot. I invited Smitty over. I'm sorry. Let me go grab another chair."

"I'll help you," Smitty says, following me into the kitchen.

As soon as the door closes behind us, I turn to face him. "I'm so sorry, Smitty. I've just been so busy with work, it slipped my mind that I invited you."

He smiles, pulling his hat off and dropping it on the counter. "That's all right. I know it was just a casual invite. And I didn't have any better plans, so I thought I'd take you up on it." He grins at me, his slightly crooked teeth making his smile that much more charming. I turn to grab the chair, but his hand on my shoulder stops me. I look up at him.

"Did you talk to your sister about you going out for a beer with me, by any chance?"

"I did. And we all agreed it would be a bad idea."

His face falls and his hand slides off my shoulder. "Oh."

"Please don't be mad at me. It's nothing personal. It's just this policy we have."

He nods stiffly. "I get it. It's cool. It's that sister thing." He rolls his eyes a little. "Let me grab that for you." He takes the chair from me and walks to the door.

I watch him go, admiring his broad, muscular back that leads down to a trim waist. Maybe in another lifetime I would've said yes to that beer. Maybe even the fact that he dated Emerald once wouldn't have stopped me. But I've met Greg, and he's the only guy I can think about. I'm sure my crush will pass as he moves on with his life and I don't see him anymore, but while he's here, I'm going to indulge myself. It's been a long time since I've been so excited about a guy.

I follow Smitty out of the kitchen and help him get set up at the table. He's on my right while Greg is on my left. I've sat next to Smitty during meals countless times, and I thought I'd be okay with it tonight too, but as soon as the food is served, it starts to get a little awkward.

"So, Greg, how long are you going to be in town?" Smitty asks, unbuttoning his sleeves and rolling them up as he leans in to see around me. His voice is especially loud, causing other conversations around the table to pause.

Greg glances up at the table before taking a dish that Carol is handing him. "I should be headed out tomorrow, probably."

I poke at my spinach, sad to hear that his visit will be so short.

"Oh, that's too bad. You need a lift to the airport?"

Greg glances at me. "Actually, I was going to ask Rose if she could take me because we have a couple things we need to talk about. About a dog she wants me to adopt."

I look up at him in surprise and catch him staring at me funny. I decide to run with it. "Yeah. Maybe Oscar Mayer will find a new home soon." I grin at everyone around the table.

Emerald claps. "Yay!"

"You really do like those yappy little dogs, don't you?" Cash asks.

"I prefer small dogs, yes," Greg says, cutting his meat. He doesn't look up, and his face is expressionless. He's back to being the lawyer again and not the man I met at the clinic.

"I hope you got tile in your place," Mooch says. "That mutt pisses on everything."

"Be quiet," I say, softening my voice when I realize how rude that just sounded. "Don't mess this up for them."

"I didn't know you were looking for a home for that little guy. Maybe I could adopt him," Smitty says. The tone of his voice makes me extremely uncomfortable. He's acting like this is some sort of competition between him and Greg.

I butter my bread while I speak. "If you're ready to adopt a dog, Smitty, you should let me know, because I'm sure I'll have another puppy very soon."

"Yeah, but Oscar Mayer's pretty darn cute."

"He sure is." I leave it at that, and thankfully Amber speaks up.

"Smitty, what happened to your arm?"

I look over and notice for the first time that he has a bandage wrapped around his forearm. The gauze is pretty thick, too.

I put my knife down. "Geez, yeah, what happened?"

"Oh, nothing. Just cut myself doing some gardening at my place."

"Looks pretty serious," I say, reaching out for it. "Want me to take a look at it?"

He pulls his arm out of my reach. "Nah, that's all right. I got it under control."

"Is it one of those man boo-boos?" Amber asks, lifting her eyebrow toward her hairline.

"What's a man boo-boo?" Cash asks.

"It's where you have a small cut that could do with a Band-Aid but you wrap it up like you almost lost your arm," Carol says, hiding a smirk behind her fork.

"No, it's not a man boo-boo. It's the real deal." Smitty shakes his head at us and digs into his food, mumbling, "Crazy women," under his breath.

"How're the bees doing, Smitty?" Amber asks. "Did you give them some food?"

"I did." He looks up at her. "I think we're going to need to prop them up over the winter."

"Okay. You're the boss."

He smiles and nods slowly. "Well, all right. I like the sound of that."

"What do we have for dessert tonight?" Red asks.

"We have a choice tonight," Barbara says, sounding very pleased. "Pecan pie or blueberry pie."

"You all will have to decide which one you like best," Carol says. She and Barbara exchange a glance, and Sally claps her hands.

"It's a contest," Sally exclaims. "You have to pick your favorite."

"Oh, no," Cash says, shaking his head. "I'm not going to choose a favorite between *those* two pies. I know what this is; this is a setup."

Everybody laughs and starts talking at the same time. Apparently, two of our mothers have been bragging about who makes the best pie, and now they're asking the band to settle the matter. Talk about trouble.

"I'll be taking my dessert back to the clinic," I say. I'm not getting involved in this nonsense.

"I'll join you," Greg says quietly in my ear.

I nod. "I'd like that."

"What'd you say?" Smitty asks, leaning in toward me, his arm resting against mine.

I move away just the slightest bit to give us some distance. "I said that I'm going to try both pies, but I'm not going to say which is my favorite." What I say to Greg in private is none of Smitty's beeswax.

"Yeah, me too." He leans in close and whispers in my ear, "But you're my favorite. Don't tell anyone."

I try to smile. He's acting so strangely, though, it's hard to take what he's saying as a compliment.

The rest of dinner passes quickly, and then the pies are brought out. I put pieces for Greg and me in two Tupperware containers. When I'm in the kitchen with Amber, I pull her off to the side. "Could you please keep Smitty busy so he doesn't see me leaving with Greg?"

"You got it, sister." She hugs me and kisses me on the cheek. "I'm happy for you. I think you should go for it."

"Go for what?" I can't stop smiling.

"*It.* You know . . . touch his junk. Not Smitty's . . . Greg's."

I smack her on the butt and move away. "You are so bad. Remind me not to take any advice from you ever again."

"Why? It totally works. Trust me."

I shake my head. "I do not want to know."

I go back into the other room with our Tupperware boxes full of dessert and signal Greg with a tilt of my head. He gets up and pulls his jacket off the coatrack.

"Smitty!" Amber yells from the kitchen. "Would you get in here, please? I need your help."

"Coming!" he says, striding into the kitchen.

As soon as the door swings closed behind him, Greg and I head to the front door.

"Where're you going?" Carol says way too loudly. "Aren't you staying to eat with us?"

"I can't," I say, handing Greg the containers so I can put my jacket on. "I need to take care of a couple urgent cases."

"Are you going to walk her down there?" Red asks Greg.

"Yes, sir."

"Good man." He turns his attention to Barbara, and I open the front door, tamping down my annoyance at Red's assumption of protective duties and my mother's obliviousness. After Greg joins me out on the porch, I close the door behind us as quietly as I can, not wanting to alert Smitty that we're leaving.

"I feel like we're sneaking out," Greg says in a near-whisper as we head across the porch to the stairs.

"We are. I'm afraid Smitty is going to follow us if he knows we're out here."

"Is he your boyfriend?"

"Are you kidding me?" I scowl at the idea. "No, he's definitely not my boyfriend. He's been a family friend for about twenty years, but that's it, as far as I'm concerned."

"I think he wants to be more than that."

"I think you're right." I really wish we could drop the subject, so I'm not going to elaborate.

"He's from around here then, huh?"

Our feet touch the gravel and immediately start crunching away. The ground has started to freeze. "Yes, he is. It feels like I've known him forever. He's been like a brother to me all these years, but for some reason, today he asked me out for the first time ever. Of course, I told him no."

"Why 'of course'?"

"Because . . . he went out with my sister Em, for one thing. Only twice, but still . . ."

"Oh. I get it."

"You know about the sister code?"

"Is that the code that says you can't date your sister's ex-boyfriend?"

"That's exactly what it is. How'd you know?"

"I'm a lawyer; I'm familiar with all kinds of contracts."

I chuckle.

"That was a great dinner. Your moms sure can cook," Greg says.

I'm happy for the change of subject. "Yes, they can, I agree. I'm glad the clinic is a bit of a walk from the house. It's the only way I keep from gaining too much weight."

153

"You look great. If all you're doing is walking, you must have a really great metabolism."

I smile at his compliment. *He's been checking me out!* "Walking and taking care of the animals is part of it, but believe me, it can be pretty physically demanding. I also do quite a bit of gardening."

"I know it's a lot of work to do what you do at the clinic. I saw that big owl, remember?"

"Oh, that's right."

"I noticed he's not there anymore. Did his release go okay?"

"As well as can be expected. I just got a small nick." I show him my wrist.

He stops and touches the skin around it, examining it closely. "Wow, he really got you."

I pull my arm back, worried he'll see how excited I'm getting at his simple touch. "It's a hazard of the job."

"Have you ever been seriously injured by one of the animals?"

"I get injured all the time, but nothing serious. Knock on wood."

"That's good. I don't want to have to worry about you when I'm not here."

I glance over at him. He's staring at the ground as he walks. "You'd worry about me?"

"Of course."

My heart feels like it's swelling inside my chest. "That's very sweet."

We don't say anything for a while. The wind in the trees makes beautiful music I don't want to miss. I can also hear my heart beating in my ears. I feel flushed all over. He's definitely flirting with me, and I'm flirting back and having a ball doing it.

"So what's on the agenda for this evening?" Greg asks.

"I'll do one last check of the animals, clean up a little bit, and then I'll go back home and go to bed. Oh, and I'll eat dessert with my new assistant, Greg Lister."

I can hear the smile in his voice when he responds. "Sounds good to me. What do you guys do in the evening for entertainment? Or do you always go straight to bed after work?"

"Every once in a great while we go out to a local bar and have a drink, or we'll stay home and play cards, but usually we just read or go to bed."

"You're probably pretty tired when you're done, huh?"

"Yes."

"Me too. I rarely get home before ten at night."

"That's crazy. Why do you work so many hours?"

He shrugs. "That's the job."

"When you get home at a reasonable hour, what do you do for fun?"

"Occasionally, I'll go out for drinks with somebody from work or with somebody I'm networking with. I go to dinner from time to time. I date sometimes. Or I just stay home."

"Are you dating someone now?" I try to frame it as a casual question, just a part of this friendly conversation, but I'm hanging on every second waiting for his answer.

"No. I'm single and looking."

He's looking! Now I have to wonder if he told me this because he's giving me a big fat hint that he's interested or if he's telling me because he doesn't consider me a candidate and we're having one of those buddy-buddy conversations. Time to dig a little deeper; I sure as heck don't want to be flirting with a guy who's giving me signals that he's not into me.

"Oh, really?" I ask, trying to sound cool. "Are you on any of the dating sites?"

"No. I'm just keeping my eyes open . . . waiting for the universe to send someone across my path."

"That's a good attitude. Let the universe decide for you." Greg and I seem to have the same ideas about work and finding love. It's encouraging to know how alike we are. We might actually be compatible, except for the fact that we live hundreds of miles apart and neither of us has any free time. I wonder if he sees that about us too.

"My rule is to keep my eyes open and look for signals," Greg says.

If I were bold like Amber, I'd ask him if he's seen any signals lately. But I'm not. I can see the little porch light that I left on glowing ahead, so our time for conversation is almost over, anyway. Work always has to come first for me, even when I'm crushing on a guy standing right next to me.

"Are you dating anyone?" he asks.

"No, I'm like you—single and looking. But I also work crazy hours, so the universe doesn't send anyone into my path very often."

"I hear ya."

I try to keep my breathing measured, when what I really want to do is pant like Banana does so I can get enough oxygen into my brain. It feels like the world is spinning, and it's making me dizzy. This is such an exciting conversation. It's more stimulating than any I've had in a long time. I just wish I knew exactly what he was thinking.

"Here's a crazy idea," he says.

I wait and wait, but he doesn't finish.

"Yes . . . ?"

"You're single and looking . . . I'm single and looking . . . and we both believe in crossing paths . . ."

"Yes, we do . . ." I feel like sprinting toward the door; I have way too much energy building up inside me as I wait for him to continue.

"Maybe you and I should go out for a beer tonight."

I want to believe he's asking me out on a date, but there's a veeerrry slight possibility that he's suggesting we go to a bar and look for *other* people. I need to play along until I know for sure. I wouldn't want to assume he's into me and then be totally embarrassed when he has to bring me back to reality.

"We could do that," I say, trying to sound cool. "If you're not too tired."

"I'm not too tired. Are you?"

"I told Smitty that I would be when he asked me out, but I'm not. If you want to go, I'll go with you."

"Cool."

Great. I still don't know if this is a date or not.

We get to the clinic and I unlock the door so we can step inside and get out of the cold. We stop in the lobby after I close up behind us and stare at each other. My mind is racing. I really need to know what's going on here, otherwise I'm going to be on pins and needles all night. And I can't be like that around the animals; they'll sense something is off with me, and it'll freak them out. Then I risk either getting one of them or one of us injured.

I try not to fidget. "Can I ask you a question?"

"Of course," Greg says. "Ask away."

"When we go to the bar tonight, are we going there to be *together*, or are we going there to look for *other* people?"

His eyebrows draw together in confusion. "What?"

I feel my face going red hot. This is so embarrassing, but I have to know. I can't walk into that bar thinking he's going to kiss me and then watch him pick up another woman and kiss *her*.

"You said that you wait for the universe to put someone in your path. Are we going to the bar so that the universe can put someone in your path?"

He gives me a goofy grin. "Ah. I see. Actually . . . I was thinking the universe already did."

CHAPTER TWENTY-TWO

We never get to the bar. The dessert starts innocently enough, each of us trying a bite of pecan pie and then the blueberry pie. But then there's the whipped cream . . .

He holds up a forkful of it and examines it closely. "I really love this stuff," he says.

"Really?" I reach out in a flash and swipe at it with my finger, successfully grabbing some of the whipped cream and sticking it in my mouth.

His jaw drops open and he inhales sharply, feigning shock. "How dare you."

I grin. "I love whipped cream too."

He reaches over with his fork and steals some off my pie and quickly eats it before I can stop him.

"Hey! Thief!"

He takes his Tupperware container and twists away from me so I can't reach it. He gives me a fake mean look over his hunched shoulder. "This is my pie. Grrrr . . ." He reminds me of Oscar Mayer claiming rights to his favorite dog toy.

"You got more than I did," I say, reaching around him with my fork. "Gimme some."

He continues to evade me. "I'm bigger than you are. I need more calories. Get back." He pretends he's going to poke me with his fork in self-defense.

"No fair." I lean back in my chair, pretending to pout.

"It's perfectly fair." He turns toward me a little bit. "But I may be open to some negotiation on this whipped cream issue."

I reach out to him with my fork. "Give me some of it and we'll talk . . ."

He holds the pie just out of my reach. "I might be willing to share . . . but you'll have to give me something in return."

My heart is at it again, racing away from me. "I might say yes. Depends on what it is." I stare at my fork first and then at him.

He moves his pie closer. "What's it worth to you?"

We lock eyes. I try to read what's going on behind his, but it's impossible. He's flirting, but he's a mystery. *Is he just goofing around, or does he mean it?*

"I'm not sure," I say, chickening out.

"How about a kiss?" he suggests, lifting an eyebrow in challenge.

I pull my fork back a little. "A kiss? I don't know . . . I'm not sure it's worth it."

His eyes go wide in exaggerated disbelief. "Are you telling me your kisses are *better* than whipped cream?"

I give him a haughty look. "Absolutely."

He moves his pie closer to me. "All right then . . . How about *all* of my whipped cream for *one* kiss. Just one."

"Are we talking tongue or no tongue here?" I'm feeling bold, now that I know he wants the same thing from me that I want from him. My heart is hammering away in my chest as I wait for his answer.

"How about we see where the mood takes us?"

I sigh as if this whole kissing thing is a big chore. "Okay, fine. I'm a slave to the whipped cream. Take your kiss and hand over the goods."

He extends his Tupperware toward me and shoves all of his whipped cream onto my pie and then puts the container down on the desk. He wheels his chair closer.

"Not so fast," I say, putting off the inevitable because I'm suddenly embarrassed and feeling shy. "I haven't even eaten my whipped cream yet."

"Go ahead. I'll wait."

He sits there staring at me, watching the fork move from the pie to my mouth. I know what he's thinking now, and it's making me hot all over. I take another bite, hoping I'm looking sexy placing the whipped cream on my tongue . . . but then I accidentally stab myself in the lip with one of the tines and grimace.

"Ow."

He laughs and backs up a little. "Too much pressure?"

I shove the fork between my lips and pull the cream off. "Yesh," I say. Or *try* to say. Some of the whipped cream flies out of my mouth, and a big blob of it lands on his pant leg. *Oh, God! What is wrong with me?*

He looks down and uses his finger to squeegee it off. He holds it up between us and says in an accusatory tone, "What is this?"

I shake my head, trying to appear innocent. "It wasn't me."

"I know your game, but it's not going to work," he says, licking the whipped cream off his finger.

"What game?"

"Don't try to claim later that you didn't get the full benefit of our bargain just because you're flinging cream all over the room." He moves closer again. "A deal is a deal; I gave you what you wanted, and now you have to give me what I want. It's time for you to pay the piper."

I feel myself growing warm down there, between my legs. Maybe he didn't mean to be sexy, but damn . . .

"Pay the piper?" I say in a near-whisper. I'm mesmerized by his mouth. There's just the tiniest bit of whipped cream on it. I reach over to wipe it away. I contemplate cleaning my finger off on my pants, but instead I stick my tongue out and lick it instead.

"You are causing me all kinds of trouble," he says in a low voice, watching my every move.

"I am?" His statement makes me feel powerful. "How's that?"

"Do you know how far Manhattan is from central Maine?"

I shake my head silently. I do know, but I don't want him to stop talking. Every sentence that comes out of his mouth is turning my insides to goo.

"It's far."

"What's that got to do with the price of whipped cream in China?" I ask, feeling light-headed over all this delightful flirting.

"Not much," he says, reaching out and putting his hand behind my head. He slowly pulls me toward him, and I go without fighting. I lower my pie to keep it out of the way as our lips come together.

CHAPTER TWENTY-THREE

His lips are soft, and he smells of blueberries and cooked sugar. At first, our kiss is innocent and sweet, but then his tongue is there, warm and wet. His hand slides down to my shoulder as his mouth moves against mine, his gentle touch making me break out in goose bumps. We fit together so perfectly. His tongue is in synch with mine as it slides around, going in and out, making me think of other things that we could do together that involve sliding and wetness. Excitement builds inside me. I can't believe we're doing this.

The sounds of growling and barking off in the distance pull me out of my mesmerized state. Greg and I pull apart instantly and stand. I realize as I come back to reality that the noises I'm hearing aren't far away; they're right here in the lobby. Banana is going nuts, staring at the door.

I drop my pie on the desk, watching my sweet little Banana turn into some kind of crazy were-hound. He's acting like he wants to kill whatever is on the other side of the front door. During the entire time I've known him, I've never seen him do this.

Greg looks at me. "Were you expecting someone?"

I shake my head. "No." My entire body has gone cold. The memory of Greg's kisses fades quickly, my happy emotions replaced by stark fear.

"Why don't you wait right here while I go see who it is?" Greg suggests. "Maybe you're getting a late-night visitor."

"It's possible, but I've never seen Banana act like this toward some-body with an injured animal." His sense of smell is so sharp, he can tell who's outside before they've even left their vehicle. "Banana, come."

Banana obeys, but I can tell he's not happy about it. He keeps looking back as he runs to my side. Oscar Mayer follows him, confused about what's happening. I hold Banana's collar to make sure he doesn't take off once the door is opened. His body is quaking with anger or worry, I can't tell which. A growl rumbles low in his throat.

Greg strides over to the door and unlocks it, pulling it open.

For a few seconds, my breath catches in my throat. What if there's someone dangerous out there? Maybe the person who stole my laptop has come back to cause more trouble. I don't want Greg to be injured. Banana growls louder.

"Who's out there?" Greg demands. Gone is the sweet, flirty man I was just fooling around with, and in his place is a man who could command a courtroom, using the voice of an avenging angel. It's pretty impressive, actually. I don't feel nearly as frightened as I did five seconds ago.

I hear feet on gravel and then a voice. "Hey, yeah. It's me. Who's that? Is that Greg?"

It's Smitty. I let out all my breath as my body deflates. *Stupid Smitty.* Banana starts barking like mad, acting like he's going to tear our neigh-bor a new one. I walk the dogs into one of the exam rooms and shut them inside. Banana is obviously reading my emotions toward Smitty and is acting out against him as a protective gesture. I sure do love that dog, but right now his devotion is a little too much to handle. Smitty does a lot around our farm for not much in return; I can't afford to let my silly, overreactive canine scare him away.

I go back to the front room and see Smitty in the glow cast by the entrance light over the door. He pulls his hat off and shakes Greg's hand. "Thought I'd come by and see if you guys needed any help in here. I'm headed home after this."

Greg looks over his shoulder at me and moves his hand off the door so Smitty can enter. "Do you need any help?" He closes the door.

I shake my head vigorously. "No. We're all done here. I was just getting ready to go back to the house."

"You need a lift?" Smitty asks. He looks hopeful.

"No, I think Greg is going to walk me back, right, Greg?"

He nods. "Yes. I'm staying up at the house too, so it's no problem."

I wave at Smitty, hoping he'll take the hint. "Have a great night. Thanks for helping with the bees and everything."

Smitty smiles as he opens the door and steps out, waving his hat at me before slapping it onto his head. "Sure, sure, no problem. And thanks for the dinner. It was delicious, as usual." He lifts his hand in farewell. "Later."

Banana is still growling in the back room, punctuating his distress with sharp barks every few seconds. Greg glances down the hallway as he shuts and locks the door. "I don't think Banana likes that guy very much."

"I don't know what's going on with him. He normally likes him a lot." I shake my head, going to the exam room to open the door. "Banana, come out here." When he hears me, it switches off the growl button in his brain. His tail wags and he trots over, happy to see me. He and Oscar follow me back to my desk. I scratch his neck and give him a blueberry from my pie when he sits at my feet. "You're a good boy, Banana Bread. Thanks for looking out for us."

Oscar Mayer sits down next to his buddy and looks up at me expectantly. I give him a blueberry too because he's doing such a good job of mimicking Banana's good behavior. "That's the only one you're getting, so don't look at me like that."

Greg comes over and leans on the counter, looking down at the dogs. "You know, I said that adoption thing at the table tonight just to move things along."

"I know. I'm not holding you to that statement, don't worry."

"I didn't mean it when I said it, but the more time I spend with him, the more I start to like him. He's kind of adorable." He's staring at the pudgy puppy, who's trying to capture Banana's wagging tail and failing very comically.

"He is, that's for sure. But I'm honestly not sure if I can adopt him out now. Look at him and Mr. B. They're like brothers."

The two of them are playing a game I call Bite Club, where they pretend to be biting each other like two giant killer beasts, but they never actually make serious contact or do any harm.

"If you change your mind, let me know. Tink might like to have some company since I work so late sometimes. But if you're going to keep him, that's cool too. Maybe we can visit."

I look up at him, the memory of our kisses coming back. "You should . . . visit, I mean. And you could bring Tinkerbell next time so she can hang with the boys."

His smile is slow and sexy. "I think I might just do that."

I'd really like to do more of that kissing stuff, but two seconds after the thought crosses my mind, a raccoon in the back starts banging on her kennel door and I have to go take care of her. Once I get her settled, I come out and Greg has packed up the rest of our pie and is getting the dogs on leashes.

"You ready to head out?" he asks.

"Yeah. Are you too tired to go to the bar?" Personally, I could go either way. I'm exhausted, but I wouldn't mind doing some more flirting and kissing.

"Yes, I'm afraid so. I have an early flight out. I'm sorry about that. I wish I'd booked a later one."

"That's fine." One of us has to be a responsible adult; I'm glad it's not me. "I'm sure you have work you need to get back to." I slide into my jacket and hold the leashes as he gets into his.

"I had a really great time out here this trip," he says, moving closer. He adjusts the collar of my jacket for me.

"I did too." I can't stop smiling about how happy he makes me. "I'm glad the universe put you on my path."

"Me too." He draws me to him using the lapels of my coat and leans down to give me a tender kiss. It lasts just a few seconds and then he's pulling away. "You taste like blueberries," he says.

"So do you."

"To be continued?" he asks, letting go of my jacket and brushing a stray bit of hair off my face.

I nod, not capable of words. I'm overwhelmed by the idea that this is a version of Greg that my sisters and his employers have never seen. He's sharing his secret self with me, and I know that's a big deal for him. I'm very, very lucky.

He takes my hand and opens the door. "After you."

We walk out into the night with the two dogs, and he shuts the door behind us. I make sure the clinic is locked up tight before we head back to the house, hand in hand, the dogs trotting out in front of us. I wish I could let them off the leads to run free, but I'm feeling a little paranoid about the break-in and worry they'll take off on me and get hurt. They don't seem to mind, staying close to our feet and not pulling much.

The stars are bright and the air is crisp. I'm holding hands with a gorgeous guy who makes my heart feel as full as the moon looks tonight. I wonder when Greg will come back to the farm again, but I'm not going to ask him about it. I don't want to put pressure on this thing, whatever it is. He'll be back here when he can be, and I can only hope that we'll pick up where we left off.

I know one thing for sure; his being gone for extended periods is going to make the days drag. But for the first time in weeks, the doom and gloom of that lawsuit and my uncertain future has lifted, and in its place is this feeling of warmth and light. I'm so glad the universe is on my side, taking care of me and sending this guy my way. I don't know that this thing between us is a forever situation, but I'm going to enjoy it while it lasts.

CHAPTER TWENTY-FOUR

A week passes, and I hear nothing from Greg. I'm a little disappointed, but not too surprised. After mulling it over, I've determined that when he goes to New York he becomes this other person—lawyer-Greg. Lawyer-Greg is focused, putting all his energy into his work and his dog. Maybe he even temporarily forgets about me and the kisses we shared. But I believe he'll come back to the farm, and when he gets here, he'll remember how well we get along and how much fun we have hanging out, and then we'll pick up where we left off.

There's a connection between us, no doubt about it. I just have to be patient and let things work out the way they will. Besides, I have plenty here to keep me busy. I'm in the back room feeding three baby birds who fell out of their nest, when the phone rings. Emerald just left, so there's nobody out front to answer it, and I'm waiting on a call from the insurance company, who may or may not be paying for a replacement laptop. I quickly drop a blob of food into a baby's mouth before I run to the desk to grab the phone before it stops ringing.

"Hello, animal clinic, this is Rose."

I'm waiting impatiently, hoping whoever it is will hurry up and speak so that I can get back to the birds. I hate leaving them in the middle of a meal.

No answer. There's nothing but a dead line.

"Hello? I can't hear you. Are you there? Hello?"

Then the heavy breathing starts. Again.

My heart stops beating for a couple seconds, and I feel sick to my stomach. The panic that instantly takes over makes me angry; I'm furious that this person—whoever the sick bastard is—can get me so worked up by doing absolutely nothing but dialing and breathing. He has *way* too much power over me.

"Are you kidding me?!" I yell into the phone. And then I hang up and run back to be with the birds. I fill the eyedropper and start with the first baby. As I feed the next and the next, my mind calms with the monotonous task, and I can think clearly again without anger or fear.

There must be a reason someone would crank call me over and over. To scare me? Make me angry? To get his rocks off? This is the fourth anonymous call I've gotten in the last week. Every single time, it's the same thing. He—I'm almost positive it's a man—stays on the line for a few seconds being totally silent, and then he starts breathing like a weirdo until I hang up. You'd think he'd be bored with this game by now. I know I certainly am.

If he does it again, I'm going to call the police and tell them what's going on. I don't have a lot of hope that they'll do anything, since a stolen laptop and a break-in don't seem to rate any official follow-up, but I have to do something. I can't just sit here and let someone harass me like that.

Ten minutes later, the baby birds are full enough that they stop their squawking. I put them back in their nest of shredded paper and blankets inside their kennel box and adjust the heat lamp in the corner to make sure it'll create the right temperature before I leave them and go back to the front room. I hate that I feel a trickle of fear seep into my body when I step into the lobby.

Of course, there's no one there. Banana would let me know if some-body had approached, but still . . . That stupid telephone stalker has cast a cold shadow over the whole area.

I'm seriously considering burning some sage when the front door opens. Banana jumps to his feet and starts growling and barking. I have to grab him by the collar to stop him from lunging at my visitor—Smitty.

"Hey, what's going on?" he says. "Damn, your dog is seriously agitated right now." He frowns at him. "Banana, what's wrong with you?" He bends over and holds out his hand toward him.

Worried Banana is crazy enough right now to bite him, I pull the very unhappy dog away by his collar and shut him into the hallway that leads to the back room. I push Oscar Mayer in after him. I wouldn't put it past Banana to teach himself how to turn the door handle and let himself back in, so I block the door with my chair.

"He's been like this since his accident," I say by way of apology. "I don't know what's going on with him." I don't want to hurt Smitty's feelings by telling him Banana is only like this with *him*. No one else seems to bother my dog, except maybe Oscar Mayer, but that's just because he's an annoying puppy.

"You mean when he got hit by a car a few weeks ago?"

"Yeah. He's been kind of aggressive ever since. I don't know what to do about it." After seeing Banana doing this again, I worry he has some neurological damage from his accident. I wish Dr. Masters hadn't quit on me. Maybe I could call him later. There's a chance he'd still give me a consultation over the phone as a personal favor.

"You should get a dog trainer for him."

"Yeah. Maybe." I sit down in the chair at the desk, not really interested in talking about how my dog needs training with someone who knows nothing about canines.

Smitty looks around. "This place is empty today."

"It's empty a lot these days. I have to send all of my hard cases into town now."

"Why?"

"Because Dr. Masters quit. I thought you knew."

"Yeah, I might've heard something about that." He removes his hat and scratches his head. "That's too bad." He puts his hat back on and smiles at me. "But I have some good news for you." He rubs his hands together.

"What is it? I could do with some good news."

"Stay here; I'll be right back." He turns and jogs out the door, leaving it open. The lobby fills with cold air. I lean down and adjust my heater.

Smitty's carrying a bundle under his arm when he returns. "I have a gift for you." He shuts the door behind him and walks over, placing a large box on the counter.

"What's that?" I ask, hoping it's not an injured animal. It doesn't matter how many I see, I always get sad when another one arrives. And Smitty is acting so strangely these days, I wouldn't put it past him to think that an injured animal would cheer me up. He knows I love my work . . .

He turns the box around so I can see the label.

I read what it says and my eyes bulge out. "Is that what I think it is?"

He grins big over the top of the box. "It's a new computer."

I put my hand over my heart, shocked that he'd do something like this for me. "Smitty. You can't do that."

He frowns. "Why not? It's a donation."

"But . . . it's expensive."

"So? You need one for work, right?"

I look down at my desk, the dangling cords still where they were left by the thief. "Yeah, but . . . it's too much. I can't accept it."

"Of course you can. You accept donations from people all the time." He takes the box off the counter and puts it on the ground. The sound of ripping cardboard follows. "The guy at the store told me it's a really good one. It's got a lot of memory and power. It should hold all of your records and whatever else you need to put on it."

I walk over and watch him pull it out. It's definitely nicer than the one I had before. "Smitty, I don't know what to say. This is really, really thoughtful of you." I'm both thrilled to be back in business and afraid he's going to expect something in return. It makes me feel a little sick to my stomach. I hate turning people down, especially people who don't take no for an answer very well.

"It's no problem at all. Believe me. I'm just real proud of you. You work really hard out here, and people don't give you the respect you deserve. But I respect you, and I want you to know that." He straightens and puts his hand on my shoulder, leaning down to look me directly in the eyes. His gaze is intense. "You're a good person, Rose. You deserve good things."

"Thanks, Smitty. That's a very nice thing to say." I step away to put some distance between us. He's big . . . an imposing figure; not unfriendly, of course, but . . . intense. At my desk, I hold up the cords that are supposed to attach to the computer. "I don't really know how to connect all these things."

"I can probably figure it out." He pulls the packing material off the ends of the laptop. "Give me a few minutes and I can usually figure out pretty much anything."

The sense of relief that flows over me is incredible. I love Smitty; he's been in my life forever. He's like a brother to me, which is why his being suddenly interested in me romantically is so strange. I hope I haven't hurt his feelings by turning him down, because I do appreciate his friendship and his help. I smile at him, hoping he knows how much I care. "This is so nice of you. Really, I'm just blown away. Are you sure you want to do this?"

"It's no problem at all. I'm sure." He comes over, and I go to the other side of the counter to watch him hook things up. He does seem to know what he's doing.

"You wouldn't happen to know how to get my data off the cloud and onto the laptop, would you?"

"I probably do. I've done a little bit of computer work in my time." He looks up at me and winks. "I'll just need your username and password."

"You never cease to amaze me, Smitty. You're a handyman, you take care of the bees . . . Now I find out that you're a computer whiz too? What other secrets are you hiding?"

He pauses for a moment and looks up at me, his expression unreadable. "I'm full of secrets. You should get to know me better and then you'll see." The smile that follows is crooked.

I laugh as he goes back to his computer stuff. Talk about not taking no for an answer. "I'm still not going out with you. This computer doesn't change anything."

He pauses and puts his hand on his chest. "Ouch. You just sent an arrow right into my heart."

I roll my eyes and sigh. "Please. As if."

He takes a pad of paper and a pen from my desk and puts them on the counter. "Write your username and password down and the name of your cloud service. I'll see what I can do about getting your data and software downloaded."

He goes back to squinting at the computer cords, so I write down the info and leave him alone to do the work. It feels wrong to accept this gift from him, but I'm too desperate to do the right thing. I need a laptop to do my work efficiently and safely. I'm not able to update the animals' care plans without one, and writing everything down is turning into a disaster, even with the smaller group of patients I'm caring for now. I'm not organized enough to run this place old-school style.

While Smitty works his magic, I go to the narcotics cabinet in the back room to do an inventory as the dogs play nearby. Banana has stopped worrying about Smitty being in the building, acting like his old self, but just in case, I'm keeping him here with me. My mind drifts to Greg and conjures an image of him in a business suit sitting at his desk, doing his work. I wonder if I'll ever see him there in his environment, and I wonder when I'll hear from him again. I want to ask Amber what he's been up to, but I don't want her or Em to get involved in our relationship at this stage. It feels too new, too vulnerable. I could just imagine Greg deciding that being with me isn't worth the hassle of having my sisters' noses in his business. Amber and Greg have a somewhat antagonistic relationship, and I don't want any of that rubbing off on what he and I have. She doesn't see the things in him that I do, but she doesn't know him the way I do either, so that's understandable. If this thing between us has any chance of surviving, we need to keep it between us, at least for now.

"I think you're ready to rock and roll," Smitty shouts about a half hour later.

I walk out to the front room, leaving the dogs in the back, and see the computer's welcome screen on.

"Got your data *and* your software on here," he says, grinning.

I can't keep my enthusiasm from taking over; I jump up and down and clap like a crazed cheerleader. "Yay! I'm so happy!"

Smitty stands up and holds his arms out. "How about a hug?"

I happily walk into his embrace and squeeze him around his waist. He's really strong, his body like a big tree. "You are such a sweetheart, Smitty. Thank you so much. I don't know what I'd do without you."

"Well, you wouldn't have any honey and you wouldn't have a computer, I can say that much." He kisses the top of my head before letting me go.

I step left so he can go around to the other side of the counter. I sit down and stare at the screen, letting my fingers hover over the brand-new keyboard. "This is really nice. You spent way too much money, I know you did."

He reaches over and pokes the end of my nose. "You deserve it." He grips the edge of the counter as he looks around for a few seconds. His eyes roam the walls, the ceiling, the waiting area . . . and then he lets go and claps his hands together. "Welp, I gotta go."

I stand. "Thanks so much. For everything. You are a champion."

"Nah, I'm just a regular guy trying to fix things . . . I mean . . . do the right thing. Whatever. I'll catch you later." He waves at me over his shoulder as he strides out and shuts the door behind him. It seems like Smitty doesn't move anywhere at a slow pace anymore. It must be because he's always either working several jobs here on the farm or chasing after his younger brother. I seriously don't think that man has any free time, which makes this gift even more special.

I walk over to the back door and open it, looking down at Banana. Oscar Mayer is nowhere to be seen. Banana just sits there, staring and growling softly at the front door.

"Banana, what is wrong with you? You know Smitty's a nice guy."

Banana runs out of the hallway and gets busy sniffing every place Smitty had been standing or sitting. He stops at the front door, lowers his head, and lets out a big huff of air.

Is it possible that Banana knows Smitty is trying to violate the sister bond? That he feels my inner conflict over accepting this generous gift? That he senses my concern that Smitty is going to expect something from me in return? I wouldn't put anything past this dog. He's smarter than any human I know.

"Banana Muffin, come over here."

My baby comes over and sits in front of me, waiting expectantly for my next command. I need to get his mind off whatever is making him act so crazy. "Where's Oscar?"

Banana turns to the side and looks down the hallway.

"Is he sleeping back there?"

Banana looks again. I think this is his version of a nod.

"Okay, let's let him sleep. He's still a baby." I take his head and aim it at me so he has to look me in the eye. "I need you to do me a favor."

Banana looks to the side and puts his foot up on my knee, leaving him only two legs to balance on. It's a big gesture. He's listening and acknowledging me as his pack leader.

"You need to give Smitty a break. He means well. I know he's acting a little weird, but he's a good guy."

Banana turns his whole head away and puts his ears down.

"Just do your best. That's all I ask." I lean down and kiss him all over his face until his tail starts wagging.

The phone rings, pulling my attention away. Banana walks off to the back room as I stare at the caller ID. The area code tells me my caller is from Manhattan. I can't stop grinning as I pick up the phone.

CHAPTER TWENTY-FIVE

Hello, this is Rose."

"Rose. Hi. It's Greg."

My heart sinks when I hear the tone of his voice. I was so sure our first conversation after the other week would be great, but this one already ranks up there as awful.

"What's up? You sound upset."

"I am. I'm really upset. I need your help, I think." He sounds like he's either about to cry or he's already got tears running down his face. I can't even picture a guy like him that broken down; this must be serious.

"What's going on? Talk to me. I'll do whatever I can."

"It's Tink. Something's happened."

I grab pen and paper and get ready to take notes. "Tell me what's going on. Details."

"Everything was fine with her when I got back from the farm last week. She was acting completely normal. But then a couple days later she got real tired, and then a couple days after that she stopped eating."

"Was she vomiting?"

"Kind of. Nothing was coming up, but she was trying. She kept twisting her head funny, too. Her bark sounded weird, but the worst part is she can't walk anymore. The vet thinks maybe she was injured somehow, but he can't find anything wrong with her. Her X-rays are completely clear."

"Is there anything else you can tell me that the vet said?" I'm racking my brain trying to come up with an answer for him. An inability to walk makes me think there was some sort of spinal injury or injury to the legs too, but if the X-rays are clear . . .

"No. Her blood tests are all mostly normal other than some levels being off, but nothing drastic, he said. No obvious signs of something he'd expect. All of her legs are fine; there's nothing broken. I don't know what to do." He sounds close to tears again.

"You said Veronica was taking care of her while you were here, right?"

A few seconds pass by before he answers. "You don't think she did something, do you?"

"No, not at all. I was just wondering if you know what her routine with Tinkerbell was when she was watching her."

"I don't. Do you think that has any significance?"

"It could. If she exposed the dog inadvertently to some sort of parasite or toxin. If the vet doesn't know what to look for, it could interfere with his diagnosis. Veronica's routine could be very pertinent."

"Let me ask her. Could you hold on?"

"Of course. Take all the time you need." While I listen to classical music coming from the law firm's phone system, I mess around on my new laptop. I have several weeks' worth of paperwork backlog to enter into it. I guess that's one good thing about not having a vet here right now; there are fewer surgeries to document.

Greg comes back on the phone sounding breathless. "Veronica said that she would get up in the morning, feed the dog, and then they'd go for a walk. She'd come to work for half the day and then go back to my place to walk the dog again, and then she'd go back to work until dinnertime. When she got home at night, she'd feed the dog and then go for one last walk."

"Where did she take these walks?"

"Central Park at lunchtime, and just the sidewalks around my place in the morning and evening. That's what I always do, too."

"Did she by any chance let the dog go in any long grass?" There's a diagnosis tickling the back of my mind, but I find it very hard to believe a dog could pick this up in New York City.

A muffled version of Greg's voice speaks to someone there with him. "Did you walk her in long grass?"

I hear a female voice, but I can't tell what her answer is. Greg comes back on the line, his voice excited. "Yes, she did. She said at one point Tink got away from her and went running into some grass with some other dogs."

"Okay." My pulse is picking up speed. I don't know if I can help him, but I want to very badly. "I need you to do me a favor. Write this down."

"I'm ready."

"Tick paralysis. It requires treatment using a medication called TAS and other necessary support like high-dose, soluble cortisol, and rapid fluid loading in case of anaphylactic shock. This is a really rare thing, and the chances of it being her problem are very, very slim, so I don't want you to get too excited about it, but you should definitely mention it to your vet."

"What is it?"

"It's caused by a toxin released by ticks. Like I said, it's very rare, and I find it hard to believe she has this problem, but you should check for it, at least."

"What do we do? Is there a test?"

"You have to search the dog all over from head to tail for ticks. Check in her ears, between her toes, under her tail, in her private areas . . . in addition to everywhere else. They like to hide. If I'm correct, she'll have a tick or more than one tick somewhere, or evidence that she had one."

"What does the evidence look like?"

"A crater in her skin. If the tick is there, it might be so tiny, it'll be very difficult to see. You need to remove that tick, and once it's removed, sometimes within just a couple of hours, a dog will recover or at least be able to walk again. In her case, since the tick has been there for a while, it might take longer . . . *if* this is her problem. In addition to the other treatment I mentioned, she'll need IV support for a day or two, but if this is the correct diagnosis, she should fully recover within a week if the doctor gets to it quick enough."

"Have you told me everything I need to know?"

"Yes. Just make sure you check every square inch of her body. If you miss any tick, you might miss the one that's causing the problems. There could be more than one."

"Rose, thank you so much. I have to go, but I'll call you back later."

"Please do. I'm going to be worried about both of you until I hear from you again."

"Take care," he says breathlessly, and then the line goes dead.

I hang up the phone and sit back in my chair. I have to take a few deep breaths to release the stress that built up during our call. I can't believe how fast my heart is racing. I've never done a diagnosis long-distance like that. I look up at the ceiling with my hand on my chest. *Please, God, let this solve Tinkerbell's problem. Let her be okay.* Having recently experienced a near-death experience with my little Banana, I know what Greg is going through. But I see death every day, so it's possible this is harder on him than Banana's accident was on me. I wish I could be there for him, and not just over the telephone.

I'm tempted to hop on a plane or into a car and get myself to Manhattan, but then I imagine myself showing up at his door, smiling and waving, and saying, "Hello, remember me?" He'd think I was a lunatic. Nope. Can't do it. I'm going to have to sit here and wait to hear from him, hoping for good news. Not that I could go on that crazy adventure anyway. Who would watch the animals? I ignore the nagging thought telling me I don't have that many patients these days, because

I never know when another one will show up and people expect me to be here for them. I'd never forgive myself if an injured animal came in with no one here to help them.

For the first time in my life I feel tied down by my job. It's a lot different from voluntarily being here and giving up on having any kind of life by choice. It makes me sad. I love my work so much, but it does interfere with me joining the rest of the world sometimes. My mind drifts over to my last conversation with Greg about the settlement. He seemed to agree that it would be a really bad idea for me to take it, but like my sisters were saying, I could do so much good with it.

I let the fantasy conjure in my mind . . . I could build a facility in a commercial area in town. It wouldn't be as convenient, but it would be totally legal and there would be nothing the town council could do about it. I'd have more modern X-ray machines hooked to computers, MRI machines, and ultrasound units. I'd have several operating suites and tons of exam rooms. I'd hire veterinarians who have experience in all kinds of animal care. Heck, I could even go to vet school myself and start doing all the surgeries I know I'm already qualified to do. I've watched Dr. Masters do enough of them over the last few years, and I've assisted in almost every single one of them. He used to let me do a lot of the stitching, too, and I've gotten pretty good at it. Vet school would be so amazing . . .

The phone rings again, and I grab it without looking at the caller ID. "Hello, this is Rose." I forget to add the rest of my normal greeting, expecting to hear Greg on the other end of the line.

There's silence for a few seconds, and then the breathing starts.

A fury builds in me, spreading like wildfire, and the anger takes over. "I don't know who you are, but this is getting ridiculous!" I shout. "I've got much better things to do with my time than listen to your stupid, sorry, loser breath in my ear, do you hear me?! I'm calling the cops on you right now! They're going to trace this call, and you're going to be in a *load* of trouble, buster. A whole *shitload* of it."

The phone clicks dead.

I hang up too and rub my arms, the goose bumps coming out in force to cover my body. Banana trots over and sits at my feet, looking up at me and whining.

I pet his head and scratch behind his ears, allowing his concern for me to calm my nerves. There's no need to get him all anxious too. He needs all of his energy to finish healing his body. "Thanks, Banana. I needed that." I get on my computer and find a telephone number for the local police department. The dispatcher tells me a police officer will call me back soon. I hang up the phone and frown. "Yeah, right. It'll probably be Officer What's-His-Name again, and this time I doubt I'll be able to convince him to fill out a police report."

I spend the next hour cleaning the already spick-and-span lobby. I even do the windows, knowing they will soon be dirtied again. It's that time of year—not quite cold enough for moisture to freeze every day—so it's thunderstorms and mud splatters for us.

The phone rings again, and fear makes me freeze up. I look across the lobby at my desk. I want it to be Greg, but it could be that crank caller again. I'm breathing heavily, trying to manage the stress. Fear is a powerful thing, and I hate that it's ruling my emotions.

Banana nudges me on the leg, distracting me. I smile down at him, realizing that he knows me better than most people. This panic is just plain silly. I can't let my fear win. I go over to the phone, but this time I'm smarter and check the caller ID. It's a Manhattan area code, so I grab the handset and throw it up to my ear without hesitation.

CHAPTER TWENTY-SIX

H i. It's me again."
I sigh with relief. "It's so good to hear your voice. What's going on? Do you have an update yet?"

"Well, they did find two ticks on her. You were right about that." Greg sounds exhausted. "My dog has never had a tick in her life. I can't believe it. They found *two*."

"Anything else?"

"They were impressed with your diagnosis. They don't see that very often in Manhattan, I guess. Or ever, actually. The doctor told me this is a first for them."

"I don't imagine they would see it." I'm filled with relief. This feels right. I pray my intuition has worked this time.

"They said they'll know more in a couple hours, but they also said they were encouraged by the first signs. Now the blood results they had make more sense too."

"Okay, so we're going to be cautiously optimistic, then."

"Yes. That's what I'm going to do . . . or be . . . whatever." He lets out a long, ragged sigh. "I don't know what I'm going to do if she doesn't make it." He goes silent, and I'm pretty sure he's shedding some tears.

"Why don't we worry about that when and if the time comes? We're not there yet, right?" I can't tell him it's going to be okay and give him false hope. I've been around enough sick animals to know this could go either way really quickly.

"Yeah. Let's talk about something else."

"What do you want to talk about? I'm totally free for at least the next half hour."

"How about we talk about your lawsuit?"

"Do we have to?" Here I was hoping we'd talk about his next visit. *Major bummer.*

"No, we don't have to. Would you rather talk about something else?"

"No, you might as well tell me what you know. It's not going to help me to stick my head in the sand and pretend my problem doesn't exist."

"You don't need to sound so sad about it; it's not all bad news."

Hope? There's hope? I sit up straighter in my chair. "Okay. I'm listening."

"I told you about the guy in my office who owes me a favor, right?"

"Yes, you did. I hope it's a big favor that he owes you."

"It is, but I don't have to call the entire favor in, actually."

"You don't?"

"Nope." I can hear the smile in his voice now. "I don't have to be licensed in Maine to do legal research, so I did a little digging, and it's pretty clear what's going on here."

"What's that?" My heart fills with real, honest-to-goodness hope. *Hallelujah!*

"Shenanigans, is what."

His answer takes me aback. *Is he joking?* "Shenanigans? Is that an official legal term?"

"In my office it is. Some court districts would call it 'illegal maneuvering,' though."

"Tell me." I am getting all fired up over the idea that the people in town are trying to pull a fast one on me. Oh, they are going to be *so* sorry. If I took that settlement money, I could sic a whole army of lawyers on their butts. The idea is more than tempting.

"Your town council recently made a change in the local laws that seems to be directly designed to impact you."

"What do you mean?"

"They changed the language in a couple of their town ordinances. I went back into the other lawsuits they filed against you—got copies of them from the clerk—and these are the same ordinances they used to sue you before. The problem for them back then was, the way the language was structured in the past, your lawyer was able to prove that the rules didn't apply to you or your situation. However, they recently changed the language of those ordinances, and it appears as if they tailored them specifically so that they could get around your lawyer's arguments, and then they basically refiled the same lawsuits. They tried to tweak them enough to get around defeat by a motion to dismiss, but I'm not sure they were successful with it."

"Those dirty bastards." I swear, if steam could come out of a person's ears like it does in the cartoons, I'd be screaming like a teakettle right now.

"Exactly. It's dirty pool and not permitted in any jurisdiction. I'm pretty sure we're going to be able to get this lawsuit thrown out. Now the question is, how aggressive do you want to get over this?"

"What do you mean?" I'm thinking about putting together a posse. *Would that be aggressive enough?* I'm pretty sure I could get Ty and Sam to ride with me.

"We could countersue them for harassment. It's pretty clear what they're up to. I'm looking at it as an outsider, and I really haven't done that much digging yet, but it's pretty obvious. If you want, we can go after *them* for going after *you*. It would put them on notice that you're not somebody they should be messing with."

I chew my lip as I think about it. This sounds like something that would need an army of lawyers and therefore be very expensive. "What would you advise me to do if you were my lawyer?"

"I don't know at this point. There's a lot that goes into these decisions; it's not purely a legal thing."

"I trust you to give me advice that isn't just legal."

"You do?"

"Yeah, of course." My heart warms. "I think you get me. I feel like . . . we get along."

"Me too."

I don't know what to say to his mutual feelings. All I know is that they make me happy.

"I've been thinking about you a lot this week," Greg says, his voice softer. He doesn't sound like a lawyer anymore; he sounds like the man who was standing in my lobby wearing a flannel shirt and playing with my dogs.

"You have?"

"Yeah."

Heart flutter. "I hope they were good thoughts."

"Absolutely. Really good."

I feel like a schoolgirl experiencing her first crush. "Well, I have a confession."

"You do, huh?"

"Yes. I've been thinking about you a lot, too."

"Good thoughts?"

I nod like a bobblehead doll on the dashboard of a car driving down a potholed country road. "Yes. For sure. All good thoughts."

"Sooo . . . I guess that means you haven't talked to your sister lately."

I frown. "My sister? Do you mean Amber?"

He chuckles. "Yeah. She's mad at me right now."

"She hasn't said a word, but I haven't seen much of her. I've been kind of lying low." I don't want to tell him why—that I'm keeping my sisters out of my business until this thing with Greg is more defined . . . more certain.

"Are you really busy at the clinic?"

Now I either have to lie or tell him the truth and expose myself. *Dammit.* "Not really. I still don't have a vet here, so I've had to turn a lot of people away."

"What have you been busy with if not the clinic?"

I run my fingers across the keyboard of the laptop. I could tell him it's my new computer that's been taking up all my time, but that wouldn't be true. "I don't know. I've just been spending more time away from the house. I guess I'm not ready for the interrogation that I know is waiting for me." *There. I confessed.* I thought I'd feel better saying this out loud to him, but now I'm worse off. Talk about nervous. I'm halfway to telling him I have a crush on him.

"Interrogation? About the lawsuit?"

I sigh. "No, not about the lawsuit. About *you.*"

"About me? Did something happen?"

"No, nothing other than the fact that you and I spent some time together and it put us on Amber's radar."

There's a long pause before he responds. "Oh. I gotcha. She wants to talk to you about why we spent so much time together, is that it?"

"Yes. That and other things."

"And you don't want to talk to her about it?"

"It's not that I don't want to do that, exactly. We talk to each other about everything. It's just . . ."

"You don't want to tell me, do you?"

"Not really?" I chuckle, relieved that he doesn't sound mad. In fact, he sounds like he might be teasing me.

"You know, I'm hundreds of miles away." Yeah, he's definitely teasing me; I can tell by the tone of his voice.

"So?"

"You could pretty much say anything you want and not be embarrassed or be worried about what I think."

"Because of the distance?"

"Sure. Isn't it easier to talk to somebody when you can't see them looking at you?"

"I guess."

"Sure it is. So go ahead. Say what you have to say."

"I'm not sure I have anything to say." I laugh again, feeling giddy about how sweet he's being and how close I am to telling him all of my secrets.

"Come on. Help keep my mind off my problems. Talk to me about your life."

I roll my eyes and sigh loudly, acting as though I'm being put out. Secretly, I'm thrilled to have somebody pushing me toward speaking the truth, the whole truth, and nothing but the truth. I might as well tell him how I'm feeling. What's the worst that could happen? I could go too far and he could decide not to visit me anymore. Like Amber said, they can do all of their business long-distance. I'd never have to see him again if I embarrass myself too much.

"The more I get to know you, the closer I feel to you," I say. "And I like spending time with you. You're a cool guy." *Phew.* That wasn't so bad . . .

"I like spending time with you too," he says tenderly.

"I was thinking after that kiss . . ." Oh, this is so hard! I can't finish. I can't . . .

"Yes? Go on."

I take a breath and dive in. *Nothing ventured, nothing gained.* "I thought maybe we would do more of it. Or something." I'm sweating from nervous energy.

He chuckles. "Or *something.* I like the sound of that." His tone is devious. Sexy. *Wow.*

My nipples go hard as my whole body shivers. Greg makes this happen with a simple statement. This guy has so much sexual power over me, I can't even imagine what it would be like to actually feel his hands on my skin.

"So, yeah," I say, letting out my stress in one long sigh. "Things are kind of crazy or could be crazy between us, and I don't want to mess it up by getting Amber involved."

"She does have a tendency to dive right in and make things a little nuts," he says.

"Yeah. She's a bit of a rabble-rouser, my sister."

"She's good at shaking things up, for sure, but that's not necessarily a bad thing."

"I hear it's been good for the band."

"It has. I have to give her credit for that. It's making my life more difficult, but it's making theirs more successful, so I can't complain. The better off they are, the better off the firm is."

"I'll bet it makes Veronica happy," I say, jealousy temporarily taking over my tongue. I can imagine her standing at his side, assisting him with all of his work. I wonder if she's the woman Amber told me about who always wears see-through blouses and leans over his desk to show him her cleavage.

"What do you mean?"

"Doesn't she help you with your work?" I try to sound innocent, but I'm not sure I'm pulling it off. The jealousy monster has this woman looking like a supermodel in my head.

"Yes. Some of it."

I stop myself from saying anything else. It's totally not my place to be involved in his work life. Somebody must have put a crazy pill in my breakfast muffin this morning.

"You sound upset. Are you worried about me working with her?"

"No, no, no. Please don't think that. It's none of my business."

"I'd still like to know your opinion about it."

"I don't know that I *have* an opinion about it." I'm lying. Of course I have an opinion; I'm a woman, after all. I don't know this Veronica person other than the fact that she voluntarily watches his dog when he's out of town, which is really convenient for him and for me. I wouldn't want her to be in a bad situation because of something I said that was totally out of line.

"Come on, you must have some thoughts on the matter," he prompts.

"What do you care? Why does my opinion matter to you so much?" I'm trying to change the subject and fish for a compliment at the same time. Is this skilled conversational work or me being pitiful? I do not know.

"Because. You're different." He makes a noise that signals either frustration or humor; it's hard for me to tell long-distance. "I don't know, to be honest with you. This whole thing . . . It's throwing me for a bit of a loop."

"What whole thing?"

"You. Me. Me going out there to the farm just to see you."

He said *just* . . . He said *just to see me!* "You come out here for me?" *Amber was right!*

"Pretty much every time I've been out there, with the exception of the first trip."

I will never doubt my sister again! I'm shocked. Shocked *and* pleased. My whole body goes warm. I could probably stand outside without a jacket and not even feel the cold. "Really?" I sound so needy it's ridiculous.

"Really." His voice is so soft and tender. And sexy. Again. "It's why I haven't called you as much as I should have or as much as I've wanted to. I'm trying not to get ahead of myself."

I have to be cool. I can't blow this. What would a cool person say? Very little. *Keep it short and sweet, Rose. You can do this.* "That's very flattering."

"It's not too much?"

I shake my head, even though he can't see me doing it. "No. Not too much."

He lets out a long sigh. "Thank God. I felt like I was standing on the edge of a cliff getting ready to jump off. Now I know how it feels to experience acrophobia."

I laugh. "Believe me, I know what you mean."

"I guess this means we're both into each other," he says matter-of-factly.

I have to rest my hand on my cheek to try to cool it down. "I can't believe you just said that." I have to stand up. I have too much energy to remain seated. I do a dance, throwing out my free arm and kicking out my legs, nodding my head to an internal rhythm only I can hear and feel. I'm so happy I want to sing like Maria in *The Sound of Music*.

The clinic is aliiiive with the sound of muusiiiic!

Banana comes over and starts dancing around me, and then Oscar Mayer joins the fun. We're having a silent dance party in the office, celebrating the fact that I could be about to enter into an official relationship with a guy who is amazingly smart, gorgeous, sexy, and kind.

"I take measured risks," he says, oblivious to the existence of my silent dance-off. "I figured laying it out there was worth it."

I stop dancing and smooth my shirt down, trying to collect myself. "Hey, it's cool. I take risks too sometimes."

"You sound like you're out of breath," he says, sounding confused.

"Uh, yeah." Great. Now who's the heavy breather? *Quick! Think of something to say!* "Just . . . you know . . . lifting heavy things and stuff. Makes me lose my breath sometimes."

"You're doing heavy lifting while you're on the phone?"

Oh, Lord, why can't this part of the conversation be over already? "Yeah. Don't you?"

"No," he chuckles. "Not in my office, anyway."

"Yeah, okay. That makes sense." I cringe, wondering if he knows my secret: that I am so excited over a potential relationship with him that I'm losing my mind right here on the spot. I walk back to my desk, trying to calm myself by taking a seat and breathing slowly and deliberately. No more dancing. Not until I'm off the phone, at least.

"So, when am I going to see you again?" he asks.

"Whenever you get the itch to come to Maine, I guess." I start randomly pressing the space bar on my laptop to keep my hands busy. I'm on pins and needles, waiting to hear when I'll see him again. *Please say tomorrow!*

"Would you ever consider coming here to see me?" he asks.

I spin a pencil on the desk. "Maybe. But it would be pretty difficult with my patients here needing me."

"Yeah," he says, sounding disappointed, "I understand."

I hear a voice in the background of his office and then some muffled sounds on the phone. He comes back on the line sounding completely different. "Listen, I've got to go. I'm sorry. Can I call you later?"

"Sure. I'll be here, and if no one answers, you can try the house phone."

"Why don't you give me your cell phone number?"

I cringe. "Because I don't have one?"

"You don't?" He sounds shocked.

"There really isn't a need for me to. I'm always either at the clinic or the house." I don't mention the fact that a cell phone is an expense I can't afford.

"Oh. Okay. I'll try one of those numbers, then."

"Okay, great. Talk to you soon, I hope." I pray that didn't sound too desperate.

"Sure will. Bye."

I hang up the phone and then spend the next five minutes dancing like a crazy fool around the lobby. Banana and Oscar Mayer join me, barking like mad. I probably could have gone on for another ten minutes, but the phone rings again and puts a stop to the silliness. Running over to the desk, I go to grab the handset, but then I stop when I see this call is coming from an unknown number. *It's the stalker.* Fury fills me, even seeping into my bones.

I take the handset in a grip of iron and yank it off the cradle. I don't even give him time to start his nasty breathing before I hit him with both barrels. "Listen here, you pervert! This is the *last* time I'm going to answer your telephone calls! You need to *stop* calling me and *stop* breathing in my ear, do you hear me?! You are going to get arrested! This is deviant behavior, do you understand me? You are a *deviant*. You are ill! You need to get *help!*" I pause to catch my breath.

"Is this Rose Lancaster?" says a deep male voice.

I feel the blood draining from my face and become instantly dizzy. He's talking to me now. My stalker is a man. A big one. A scary one. Maybe a killer. And he knows my name. I fall into my seat and grab the edge of the desk. "Yes. It is. And this is . . . ?"

"This is Officer Brownlee. I understand you have some sort of crank caller problem?"

I let out all my air and lower my head to the desk, banging it a few times for good measure. I cannot believe I just went off on a police officer. He's going to think I'm a complete nutcase. "Yes. I do."

"Sounds like he's got you pretty stressed-out over it."

"You could say that." I can't believe the emotional roller coaster I've been riding over the last few hours. I need a nap.

"How about I stop by in a little bit and take your statement?"

I sit up, a trickle of relief making its way into my heart. "That would be really, *really* awesome. I would seriously appreciate that."

"Can I bring my dog?"

His question throws me for a moment. "Your dog?"

"Yeah. He's limping. Maybe you could take a look at him for me?"

"Sure. Absolutely. Bring your dog; I'd love to see him."

"Great. I'll see you in a little while."

I hang up the phone and allow a small smile to play along my lips. This is very unlike what I was expecting from the police department. Maybe they're actually going to take me seriously this time. Or maybe this guy just wants free medical care. But what the hell . . . I'm not above using that as leverage. Anything I need to do to get rid of this weirdo, I'm going to do. *Bring on the free medical treatment!*

And I'm not going to let all this nonsense get me down. My phone call with Greg has the power to keep me riding high for days. Maybe weeks. Maybe months. Who knows, it could last a lifetime. But I can't get ahead of myself. For right now, all Greg and I have is an acknowledged mutual attraction. We both want to see where this is going and whether we're interested in pushing forward beyond where we are right now. That's all good, right? And it sounds like my lawsuit is going to be a thing of the past soon. Everything is going my way for the first time in a while.

Banana looks at me with his ears perked up.

"You want to dance again, don't you?"

His mouth drops open and his tail starts wagging as he smiles at me. Oscar Mayer does the same. My heart fills with joy at all the wonderful things I have in my life. "Let's go then, boys! Puppy dance-off! Woo hoo!" I jump up from my seat and go back to the lobby and dance until I'm too exhausted to bust a single other move.

CHAPTER TWENTY-SEVEN

The puppies are down for their nap and I've just finished putting new bandages on the few patients I have when the phone rings. I pull off my gloves and walk into the front room, dropping them in the wastebasket on the way. It's Greg calling; I recognize his number now.

"Hi. What's the news?" I have my fingers crossed, praying he won't be crying.

"I have great news. You were right. It was the tick thing."

I sigh with relief. "That is *amazing*. I am *so* happy for you."

"It's a miracle. She's actually up and walking around, like nothing ever happened."

"That toxin is pretty nasty stuff."

"It really is a miracle how you figured that out. I mean, I was dealing with the top vet in New York City, who had my dog right there on his table, and the fact that he didn't know what was going on with her and *you* did—and you didn't even have to see her? It's just incredible to me. Unbelievable."

I feel a little pit develop in my stomach. If he were talking to another vet right now, he'd be happy but not this impressed. It makes me feel like he considers me to be . . . less. "Yeah. Sure. I get it. It's amazing. Totally."

He pauses. "I said something wrong, didn't I?"

"No, I get it. He's a veterinarian and I'm not. I can see why you'd be so shocked."

"But I didn't mean it like that. I just meant . . ." He hisses out a sigh, his tone dropping its enthusiasm. "That was a poor way to say what I was thinking. I know you have a ton of experience and you're just as qualified as the vets here in the city. What I meant to say is that you have a gift. You're born to do this stuff. You know more than the people who've been to school to become experts."

"No, that's not true. I don't have their level of education."

"But you're experienced. And you obviously have seen things in the field that they haven't. Seriously, why don't you go to vet school?" He sounds like he's begging me to do it.

I have to laugh at that. "You know why I can't go. I have a busy animal clinic here. And I can even afford a cell phone, so unless they've started giving education away for free . . ." I stop right there because this idea of not being able to do something that could be very tempting is too difficult for me. Vet school is a dream, not a reality. I don't have the luxury of putting myself first. I have a family business to support with my labor hours, and I have a community I already provide services to, and they all need me to keep doing what I've been doing for the past few years.

"Yeah. I get it."

I expect him to say something else, but he doesn't. I wait several long seconds but then decide it's up to me to pick up the conversation. "Do you have Tinkerbell home with you yet?"

"No. They want to keep her overnight for observation. Do you agree with that idea?"

"Absolutely."

"You don't think they're milking me for more money? They're charging me an arm and a leg for this. I don't mind paying for it, if it's what she needs, but I don't want to be taken advantage of."

"Not at all. If she were my patient, I'd want to keep her at least one night, maybe two, just to be sure."

"Then I'll do it. I'll do whatever you tell me to do with my animals."

"Do you have more than one?"

"Not exactly . . . but I was thinking about Oscar . . ."

"And?"

"I think you're right; Tinkerbell could use a companion. I'm not out of town very often, but it would be nice for her to not be too alone when I am."

"You can always bring her here, you know."

"I was thinking about that. Maybe next time I come she could come with me."

"We'll put a tick collar on her."

"Heck yeah, we will."

I play with the pencil on my desk as I wait for him to speak again. I want to talk more about this budding relationship we have, but I'm not going to be the first one to do it.

"I think I need to come up there to have you sign an engagement letter."

I'm seized by a case of sudden-onset tinnitus, and my eyeballs nearly fall out of my head. "An engagement letter?" Is he asking me to marry him in a really lawyer-like way?

"Yes. In order for my colleague to do that legal work for you, he has to have an official contract with you as his client. It's called an engagement letter."

I let out a long, shaky breath. "Oh. Yeah. That makes a lot of sense."

"Why do you sound strange right now? Did I say something wrong again? You're not changing your mind about my firm's representation, are you?"

I fan myself with a stack of papers. "No, no, not at all. I'm just tired." No way in hell am I telling him the real reason for my panic attack. *I thought you wanted to marry me, ha, ha!*

"Are you free in the next couple days?"

I pretend to look at a calendar. "Let me check . . . Umm . . . absolutely. I'm wide open."

"Great. Once Tinkerbell has recovered, I think I can move some things around and come out that way, if you think you'll have time to discuss this legal matter."

"Yes. The legal matter. Sure."

He lowers his voice. "And maybe you'll have time for another one of those kisses?"

I can't stop smiling. "I could probably work that into my schedule too." I reach over to my desk calendar and write *KISSES* on one of the squares.

"Great. Looking forward to it."

"Me too. Talk to you later?"

"Yep. Absolutely."

"Bye."

"Bye."

I hang up the phone and allow myself a few moments to imagine us getting together again. Will we hold hands? Walk with our arms around each other? Kiss? Make love? Anything could happen. I'm going to let it, too. There will be no rules and no expectations. I don't want anything getting in the way of the fun we could have together.

CHAPTER TWENTY-EIGHT

The past two days have been the longest of my life. I don't have a large wardrobe, but does that stop me from putting together every possible outfit and trying them on twice? No. Of course not. I even used the iron, which is something I do only once a year at Christmas. And even though it's not Christmas, it feels like it is. Greg is due here any minute. Smitty is picking him up from the airport.

There's a knock at my door, and Em sticks her head in. "What're you doing in here?" She steps inside and closes the door behind her.

My bed is covered in clothing. I'm totally busted. "Getting ready for a Goodwill run?"

She sits down and smiles. "No, you're not. You're trying on clothes because Greg is coming."

I'm standing in front of her holding a shirt over my chest. "Is it that obvious?"

"Only to every single person on the farm. People in town probably don't know, though, if that makes you feel any better."

I sag, drop the shirt on the floor, and flop onto my stomach on the bed. "Why am I like this?" I say into my comforter. "Why can't I be cool?"

She rubs my back. "You are cool. You're the coolest one of the three of us."

I turn my head to look at her. "But you said everybody knows that I have a crush on Greg."

She gives me a pity frown. "There's nothing wrong with that. Amber and I both fell in love in front of everyone; you know that."

"Who said anything about love?" I prop myself up on my elbow so I can scowl at her.

"You know what I mean. You can say 'like' if you want, but I think you guys are really compatible, and it probably wouldn't take much for you to fall in love."

"You just want everybody to be like you are." I stick my tongue out at her. Sometimes she and Sam are so cute together it's annoying. Or maybe I'm just acting like a brat because I'm so stressed about Greg's arrival. It feels like there's a lot riding on this visit.

"I do want that for you, you're right." She stands and starts pulling clothing off the bed, holding up different combinations. "What about this one? I always thought it looked especially good on you."

I sit up and think about it. What would Greg think? Would he think it was sexy or frumpy? "I don't know. I don't really know what his taste is."

"Who cares what his taste in shirts is? His taste is *you*. You just need to feel comfortable and pretty, and the rest will take care of itself."

"I guess that outfit could work." I fall back onto the bed and stare up at the ceiling. "What if he changes his mind, though?"

"What if he doesn't?"

I twist my head to glare at her. "You need to answer my question first."

"If he changes his mind, that's life. You let it go and move on." She shrugs.

"I know." I sigh. "Sometimes I wish I could look into a crystal ball and see the future so I'd know what to expect."

"You don't need a crystal ball to do that. I can tell you exactly what to expect."

I roll onto my side and put my hands in prayer position. "Please, Madam Zelda, tell me what my future holds."

She lies down next to me and wraps her hands around mine. Her eyes are super sparkly, and her face is so beautiful. I love her so much. I listen with everything I have, believing she has the answer for me.

"Your future will hold passion and love, anxiety and worry, adventure and loneliness, togetherness and family. You will be impressed and disappointed. You will be excited and sad. You will have triumphs and defeats. But through it all, one thing will remain the same."

I feel tears building in my eyes. "What's that?"

"You will have the love of this family surrounding you, and it will never quit on you and it will never dim, no matter what."

I throw my arms around her and pull her up to me. "How did I get so lucky to have you as a sister?"

"Karma. Something you did in a past life." She hugs me back fiercely.

I let go of her and wipe the tears from under my eyes. "I must've been a really good person in a past life."

She pinches my cheek. "I'm sure you were. You sure are in this life." We both stand up slowly and then spend some time pushing my clothes around, arranging them into different outfits.

"Do you think Amber will be upset about this . . . relationship . . . or whatever it is?" I ask.

"No, why would she be mad?"

"Because she and Greg don't get along very well."

"That's just Amber; you know her. She wants you to be happy. I know she respects Greg. She says he's a good lawyer and he always has the band's best interests at heart."

"Are you sure? Sometimes I wonder."

"I'm sure. She told me just the other day how cool it was that he comes all the way out here to see you."

"I'm nervous about this visit," I admit.

"Why?"

Maybe I shouldn't tell her, because it means for sure that Amber will find out within minutes, but I can't keep this all to myself anymore. "Because we've both acknowledged that we're into each other and that something is going to happen."

Em grabs my hands and squeezes. "That is so cool! I'm so excited for you." She drops her voice to a whisper. "You're finally going to touch his junk."

We both start laughing at her imitation of Amber.

The door opens and Amber sticks her head in. "What are you laughing at?"

Em and I look at each other and burst out laughing again.

Amber comes in and shuts the door behind her. "If you're laughing at me, you're both dead."

She comes over and jumps onto the bed, ruining the outfit I was thinking about wearing.

I push her off it. "Move, pregnant lady, you're wrinkling my stuff."

"Getting ready for your hot date?" she asks, wiggling her eyebrows at me.

"It's official," Em says, her eyes gleaming. "They are *officially* into each other."

Amber smirks. "I knew it. Greg was acting totally squirrelly on the phone a minute ago."

"You talked to him?" My heart starts going crazy again.

"Yeah. He's on his way over right now. You have about ten minutes before you have to do the big reveal."

I jump off the bed, immediately throwing things all over the place. Maybe that outfit I picked isn't the right one. Maybe I should wear something else. Something more subtle. Something less subtle. Something crazy, something normal, something colorful, something bland . . .

Emerald holds up two articles of clothing. "This is what you're going to wear. Calm down."

I take the white peasant blouse and dark-blue jeans with flowers embroidered on the back pockets from her and hold them up against my body. "Are you sure?" I've never really given a hoot about what I wear. Today is a first for me—being nervous about how I look, worrying about what a man might think of me.

"It's perfect," Amber says. "It totally shows off your boobs."

I look up at my sisters, stricken. "Is it too much? Am I being too obvious?"

"You wear that shirt all the time," Em says, laughing. "Why do you think he fell for you in the first place?"

I reach out and hit her with the hanger. "Shut up. You act like I intentionally tried to snag him or something."

"Nobody's saying anything of the sort," Amber says, folding her arms over her chest. "But my question is, where is this going?"

The tone of her voice and her question work like a two-by-four banging me over the head, knocking some sense into me. "What do you mean?"

"Have either of you talked about where this might go? I mean, he lives in Manhattan and he has a job there that he's not going to leave, and you live out here in the sticks, and I know very well you're not leaving either."

My face falls.

"Wow, talk about a downer," Emerald says, scowling at our sister.

Amber shrugs. "I'm just being realistic. I don't want Rose getting hurt. Am I a bad guy because of that?"

Em doesn't say anything. She looks at me, waiting for my response.

"No, you're not a bad guy." Reality sucks. I throw the clothes onto the bed and walk over to the mirror. What does it matter what I'm wearing? This is going to be over before it even begins.

Amber comes up behind me and puts her hand on my back. "I'm sorry. I shouldn't have said that. That was me being way too nosy and way too bitchy. Can we blame it on the hormones?"

I rub under my eyes, hoping there are no traces of my earlier tears there. "No, you're just being honest, saying what needs to be said."

"What do I know? If you had sat here a few months ago and told me that things with Ty would never work, I would've agreed with you. But look at us now."

"Yeah, but you were willing to move. I'm not and neither is Greg. You were right about that. It's an impossible situation." Depression looms. I knew going into this it was just going to be an affair, but what if I want it to go beyond that? I can't. Am I setting myself up for future heartache? Would it be better to just never go down that road at all? People say it's better to have loved and lost than to have never loved at all, but I'm not sure I'd agree. But I can only guess, since no one but my mothers and sisters have ever loved me back. One-sided love doesn't count.

"No, it's not impossible," Em says, coming up behind me. In the mirror there's one sister on my left and the other on my right. I've been looking at their faces for twenty-five years, but today everything feels different, like I'm about to take a step toward the rest of my life. I'm so grateful that they're standing here next to me for this.

"Anything is possible," Em says. "Love can surmount any obstacle."

Amber frowns at Emerald. "Who says they're in love?"

She scowls back. "Who says they're not?"

I turn around and put one hand on Amber's shoulder and one hand on Em's. "Please don't fight. I do like him and I *could* love him one day. Maybe this is all a big mistake, I don't know. But how about if I just take this one day at a time and let the universe figure it out for me?"

My sisters nod at each other and then hug me. "I think that's a fantastic idea," Amber says.

"I second that," Emerald says.

I have to wipe tears from under my eyes again. "Damn, I am so emotional right now. What is wrong with me?" I try to laugh it off.

"You might be in love," Amber says, looking at me closer. She turns to Em. "You could be right about her."

"Stop. You guys are being silly." I try to wave them off, going back to look at my hair in the mirror.

"Have you two noticed how easily we fall in love?" Emerald asks. Her expression is serious. "It started with our mothers falling for the band, but we're no different. We meet a guy who rocks our world, and then suddenly there's nobody else for us. We're done looking and the search is over."

"It's a good thing we fell in love with guys who fall easy too," Amber says. "Could you imagine falling for somebody who didn't return the feeling?"

Pain and fear strike my heart like a lightning bolt. I could imagine it very easily because I've lived it. And I pray it doesn't happen to me again, because I think my sisters might be right . . . I think I could fall in love with this man very easily, and I don't think I could manage having my heart broken like that again. Not by him. And he's not with the band. He's not an artist who gives freely to the world. He's a man who stays locked up in a tower, working his fingers to the bone, rarely going out and rarely spending time with anyone but his dog.

Oh my goodness, what have I gotten myself into?

CHAPTER TWENTY-NINE

I hear Greg arrive downstairs, but I'm too much of a lily-livered coward to go down there and greet him. I've put my wardrobe away, and I'm wearing the outfit my sisters and I decided is my best approach, but now I actually have to leave my bedroom and go downstairs to face the man who has agreed that we're going to start what might be termed an affair.

I'm twenty-five years old. I *should* be perfectly capable of doing this, but fear has my feet frozen to the floor. I'm staring in the mirror, looking at the image before me. My blond hair is falling in waves past my shoulders. I've put on a little mascara for the occasion to highlight my light-blue eyes, but that's it. Normally, I don't wear any. My face is freshly scrubbed and slightly pink from my heightened emotions. I put a dab of perfume on my wrists and behind my ears. Greg might have a hard time recognizing me. This is the first time he'll see me with my hair down. I wonder what he'll think.

There's a slight knock at the door, and I turn to face it. "Come in." I expect one of my sisters or mothers to be there, but it's Greg's head coming around the frame.

"Can I come in?"

My heart lurches and then races. I break out in a cold sweat. "Sure. Come on in." I rub my hands together. My palms are clammy. I can't believe how quickly my body is reacting to seeing him here. *In my bedroom!*

He closes the door behind him and stands there looking around. "So, this is the inner sanctum, eh?"

His joke instantly puts me at ease. "Yep, this is it." I gesture with my hand. "This is where the magic happens."

The way he looks at me is incredibly sexy. "The magic?"

I suddenly realize what I've said. "The sleep magic. This is where I *sleep*." I really would love to open a window and let in the cold autumn air—anything to keep me from sweating more than I already am. *Why is it so stuffy in here all of a sudden?*

"I get it. Sleep does feel like magic after a long day."

I need to do something with my hands, but it's not like I can pick up my brush and start stroking my hair with it. That would be too intimate. I fold my fingers at my waist and twiddle my thumbs instead. "Did you have a nice trip?"

"I did. I left Tinkerbell downstairs, but I'm worried about leaving her alone for too long. I just wanted to come up and tell you something in private because I wasn't sure when we would have another chance with the family around."

"Sure. What's up?"

"I brought that engagement letter, but because we were getting close to the deadline to respond to their complaint, I had my colleague go ahead and file a motion to dismiss. I hope that's okay."

"It's totally fine. What does it mean, exactly?"

Greg takes a couple steps closer to me and adopts his lawyer face and tone. "Essentially, we're saying that they lack the legal elements necessary to bring a lawsuit in the first place. I assume it will fail, but it's worth a try."

"It's going to fail?" The panic over my predicament instantly returns.

"Don't worry about it. This is just the standard process we go through. We first try the easiest route, which is to get the whole thing thrown out on a technicality, and if that doesn't work, we take the next step."

"And the next step would be?"

"The next step will be some discovery, where we ask them for some information and documents. We'll also probably send over some interrogatories, which are questions they'll have to answer in writing. And if what we find through those avenues is encouraging, we'll file a motion for summary judgment."

"And what will that do?"

"If we win, it will throw the case out without a trial. If we lose, then we'll move forward to the next step, which is settlement talks."

"Settlement? I don't know what I could do to settle. They'll want me to close down, and I don't want to do that." *What would I do then? Go to vet school? Ha, ha. As if.* The very idea sends me into a panic.

"There's always a way to settle a dispute, but we're getting ahead of ourselves. I really think we could defeat this on a motion for summary judgment, if not with the motion to dismiss, so I don't want you to worry."

I think about that for a few seconds and nod, forcing myself to calm down. "If you tell me not to worry, then I'm going to stop worrying right now."

He smiles, his lawyer façade falling away. "I like that." He takes a step closer. "You mean I can just tell you to do something, and you'll do it?"

I shrug, suddenly feeling a little saucy. "I guess that depends on what it is you're telling me to do."

He walks even closer and reaches out, taking my elbows in his hands and pulling me to him. Mere inches separate us, and I can feel the warmth from his hands seeping through my shirtsleeves into my skin. "What if I told you to kiss me right now?" he asks. "Would you do it?"

"I don't know. Why don't you give it a shot and see what happens?"

"Rose Lancaster." He moves in closer. I can smell his cologne. It's a sophisticated and sexy scent. Maybe even a little bit dangerous with the way it makes my body respond. He warms me to my toes as our thighs touch.

"Yes?" I ask.

"I want you . . . to kiss me." He leans toward me, his eyes falling shut.

My hands slide up his arms to his shoulders, and my eyes close too as our mouths come together. The memory of how it felt to be touched by him comes back. I love how full his lips are and how warm and soft his tongue is. I've never experienced kisses like this before, replete with both tenderness and passion. His hands roam my body, and I grow warmer by the second.

"I've been thinking about this for days. Weeks," he says against my mouth. His hands slide up and down my back, kneading my muscles and sending shivers through my body.

"Mmm, me too," I say, my hands going up into his hair. It's as thick and soft as I imagined it would be.

"How much time do we have before we have to go downstairs?" he whispers.

"That's up to you," I say. "You didn't want to leave Tinkerbell down there too long, right?"

He backs up, breaking off the kiss. "Damn. I can't believe I forgot about her." He looks stricken.

I put my hands on his cheeks and smile. "Don't feel guilty. I have pretty powerful kisses."

He grins charmingly, looking relieved. "That you do." He leans in and gives me three sweet kisses before pulling away again. "Are you coming down with me?"

"Yes." Part of me wants us to stay up here in my room and hide because I know I'm going to be wearing a goofy grin when I go downstairs that everyone is going to see. But I'm afraid if I stay up here

I'll never come down again; my fear and anxiety over potential heartbreak will grow to the point that it defeats me. And I don't want to be defeated. I want to enjoy this while it lasts, even if that means there's the pain of loss waiting for me down the line. I'm going to believe my sister Emerald when she tells me that anything is possible. Until the universe shows me otherwise, I'm going with that theory.

CHAPTER THIRTY

Greg and I share lunch together. Surprisingly, we're dining alone. My moms are with the band, and they're all in town together shopping. Emerald and Sam are at the clinic keeping an eye on the front desk and the animals for me, and Amber and Ty have taken Sadie and all the dogs, including Tinkerbell, on a hike. It's the first day we've been without rain in a while, and Sadie loves hunting for mushrooms. She's learning about them from Barbara, and Emerald has been showing her how to draw them in a little notebook that she carries everywhere. We're guaranteed at least an hour of complete privacy. It's a miracle. We even received Amber's assurances that if Tinkerbell starts to tire, they'll carry her. She only weighs four pounds, so it shouldn't be too difficult.

"Is this normal?" Greg asks, looking around. "I've never been here when it's been this quiet before."

I shake my head, taking a sip of my lemonade before answering. "No. This is not normal at all. I'm pretty sure this was manufactured to give us some alone time."

He pauses with the sandwich halfway to his mouth. "Seriously?"

I nod, taking the tiniest bite of my sandwich. I have a very nervous stomach right now.

He slowly lowers the food to his plate as he stares at me. His gaze goes very intense after it drops to my lips.

"What are you thinking right now?" I ask. I'm pretty sure I know the answer to my question, but I need to hear him say it.

"I was thinking that we've been given a rare gift and we really shouldn't squander it."

I lower my sandwich to my plate too. "What did you have in mind?"

He reaches over and holds my fingers. "You're going to think I'm rude if I say what's in my head right now."

I have to smile at his naïveté. "I doubt it. I live on a hippie commune, remember? We're what you'd call 'free thinkers' around here."

He smiles somewhat shyly. "I don't want to screw anything up between us."

"The only way you could screw something up between us is to not be honest."

His grip on my hand tightens, and his expression slips. The sexual intensity disappears, replaced by something I don't recognize. He lets go of my hand and grabs his sandwich. "That's fair." He takes a huge bite.

I pick up my sandwich too, wondering what I said wrong. Maybe I just misinterpreted that earlier expression he was wearing.

He takes another bite of his food and then a drink. I watch his throat move as he swallows and then his jaw muscles bulge out over and over again as he chews his food. Is it possible for a man to be handsome when he's eating? Before this moment I would've said no. Now I'd say yes. *Definitely.* He's literally turning me on by eating a sandwich. I am so desperate it's ridiculous. I really wish he'd said what I was imagining he was going to say earlier: *Let's go up to the bedroom and get naked.*

I use two hands to hold my sandwich and bite off a corner. I try to remember to chew with my mouth closed so I don't gross him out. I've never been so conscious of how I eat. He takes another huge bite of his sandwich too. We're staring at each other as we chew. His gaze is focused on my mouth.

"What?" I wipe my lips with my napkin. "Do I have food on my face again?"

"Again?" He uses his napkin too.

I sigh. "Don't pretend you didn't see that giant leaf on my tooth the last time you were here. After lunch. I had, like, an entire head of lettuce on there."

He tries not to smile. "I don't know what you're talking about."

I point my sandwich at him. "Honesty. Remember?"

He puts his sandwich down and takes my hand. "Okay, I saw the lettuce leaf. But it did not diminish your beauty one iota."

I pull my hand from his and slap him gently on the arm. "Oh, shut up. You are such a liar."

He takes my sandwich from me and puts it on my plate. He places his hands on either side of my face and leans in close to stare at me. "You could have an entire head of broccoli in your teeth and I'd still think you're beautiful."

My face flushes under his hands. "Well, there's obviously something wrong with you. Broccoli?"

"There's nothing wrong with me." He leans in and kisses me, the scent of his ham sandwich and lemonade making me feel like I'm falling into summer, which is really nice considering how cold it is outside. On a whim, I throw my arms around his neck and pull him toward me, thrilled to have him here in my house and telling me I'm beautiful.

"You want to know what I was thinking earlier?" he asks, moving his lips down my jawline to my neck so he can kiss me there.

"Yes." Goose bumps come out on my arm near where he's kissing.

"I was thinking we should take advantage of this alone time and go upstairs."

I scoot closer to him, feeling a thrill and then warmth between my legs. "That sounds interesting."

He pulls away to look at me. "Interesting? Does that mean it's a good idea or a strange, rude idea?"

"Could be a good idea, could be a bad idea. We won't know until we try it."

He stands immediately, his chair making a scraping sound as it slides along the floor. He holds his hand out. "I'm willing to give it a shot if you are."

I stand, another thrill running through me. I am so ready for him; my body is already responding, and he hasn't even really touched it yet. I place my hand in his. "Okay. I am too."

We race up the stairs together, both of us realizing that this is one of those stolen moments that only come around once in a while in busy lives like ours. Who knows when we'll have this kind of time together again? We reach my room, both of us breathing heavily and laughing as we trip over our own feet trying to get in the door. As soon as I lock it behind us, Greg grabs me, pulling me against him.

"How much time do we have?" he asks.

"We have as much time as we need. It doesn't matter if people come back before we're done."

"No, we need to be back downstairs when they get here."

I stop snuggling against him and pull away. "Why?" I'm trying not to be offended. *Is he embarrassed to be with me?*

"Because. I work for those guys. I need to stay professional around them."

I nod, my worries fading away instantly. "I get it. That's fair."

He lunges toward me and grabs me around the waist, making me squeal in surprise. "Get over here, girl. We don't have enough time to be messing around."

I throw my arms around his neck and pull him down to me. "But I thought we were *supposed* to be messing around."

He spanks me on the butt. "No, we're fooling around, not messing around. Why do you have all these clothes on?"

I step away and pull them off in mere seconds. My shirt goes flying and my jeans follow right behind. My bra and panties are gone, dropped at my feet. I'm standing in front of him, naked as the day I was born, waiting for him to follow suit.

He stands there staring at me. "Damn, girl. Look what you were hiding under all that fabric. Mmm, mmm, mmm . . ."

I look down at myself. "What?" I shaved and trimmed, so I hope he's not making a comment about my personal hygiene.

He's shaking his head slowly. "You are . . . incredible." He reaches down to squeeze his crotch. He's growing hard and it's getting uncomfortable. Or he just needs to touch himself because I'm turning him on. Either way, it makes me feel like the champion of sex, and I like that a *lot*.

I gesture at his jeans and shirt. "Well? Let's see what you've got."

He grins dangerously and starts pulling his clothes off. He goes slower than I did. My breath stops for a few moments as I take in the physique that's slowly being revealed. He must spend a *lot* of time at the gym. Every single muscle in his body is sculpted and visible.

"Look what *you've* been hiding under all those clothes," I say breathlessly.

"What? You like this?" He actually flexes for me.

I slap my hand over my mouth to stifle the giggle that erupts. "Yes. Do it again."

He presses his hands together near his waist, causing his chest muscles to flex.

I reach over to touch one of his pecs, and he makes it bounce all of a sudden. It scares me enough that I jerk my hand back and shriek with laughter.

"You like that?" He makes his left pec bounce and then his right, then his left and right. They're dancing in front of me. It's hilarious and gross and sexy, all rolled into one.

I throw my hands over my eyes. "Stop. That is so silly."

"How about this?" he asks.

I move my hand away from one eye and open it. He's got one arm shooting up diagonally to the sky and the other one doing a bicep curl. He stares up at his straight arm like he's Superman and says, "Fi-yah pow-ah!"

I really start laughing then. I can't get control of myself. *Firepower, indeed.* "You have to stop . . . you're killing me . . ." I had no idea Greg was so funny. And sexy. His body is incredible. It's intoxicating.

He drops his arms to his sides. "You're supposed to be getting turned on by this pose-down, not thrown into hysterics."

The look on his face is priceless—totally dejected man-boy. I snort, I'm laughing so hard.

He comes storming over, pretending to be mad, and throws his arms around my waist. He lifts me up and throws me onto the bed. I shriek with laughter as I bounce up and send pillows flying. He leaps toward me, wearing only his boxer shorts. He lands right next to me and then closes the space between us by pulling me toward him. Our legs and arms tangle together, and I no longer feel the cold temperature in the room. I love having his soft body hair against and tickling my skin.

He kisses me and then presses his lips along my neck as he slowly works his way down to my collarbone. "I'm an idiot," he says. "I left my protection downstairs."

"I have some in that drawer over there," I say, pointing to the bed-side table. My sisters were kind enough to fill it up for me, but I'm not going to tell him that.

"Good." He makes his way down to my breasts, and I arch my body against his lips, wanting more of what he's giving me. His hands roam and slide to my thigh. We're both getting hotter and hotter, a sense of urgency taking over. "You smell so good," he says. "Like flowers."

"It's my perfume," I say, my eyes closed so I can feel every sensation he's creating.

"No, it's just you. It's your skin, your natural scent. You remind me of spring. Everything new and fresh and beautiful . . . the promise of sun and warmth . . ." He runs his tongue across my chest and then moves over to my breast to make lazy circles around my nipples.

I moan in response, my hand dragging up his back to his head. I grip his hair, loving the feeling of him being there, his head moving as he sets me ablaze with heat and emotion. It's not going to take me very long to reach orgasm. He's already got me halfway there with this simple foreplay.

"What can I do for you?" I ask, wanting to please him like he's pleasing me.

He lifts his head and sits up quickly to remove his boxers and put a condom on. "You can stay right there and let me have my way with you," he says as he works the protection down over his erection.

He doesn't have to tell me twice. I position myself in the middle of the mattress, watching his muscular back as he moves his arms. He's even gorgeous from behind. He finishes his task and comes back to me. We draw together again, his warm body sparking me up again right away.

"Are you sure you want to do this?" he asks.

"I'm sure. What about you? No regrets?"

He shakes his head. "No regrets." He positions himself above me and slowly enters me. It sends a shock through me as we become one, our bodies melding together. I slide my hands down his back to his rear end, helping guide him. It feels *so* incredible. We fit together like two pieces of a puzzle. I'm so glad we decided to jump into the deep end together.

"Does it feel good for you?" he whispers right next to my ear, moving in and out, setting a slow but deliberate pace.

"Perfect," I say, practically purring.

Moments later he speaks softly in my ear again. "I'm going to have a hard time holding back," he says, moving faster. His breath is coming more rapidly, his muscles tensing all over. I love the feel of him under my hands and over my legs.

I meet his pace, my hips moving naturally with his rhythm. "You don't need to hold back for me. I'm already so close." I'm not just saying that to stroke his ego. I can feel my orgasm coming already, building to the point of no return. It's been so long for me, and I've been thinking about him day and night for weeks now. And even though I've pictured this in my mind many times, it was never as good as this reality.

Sweat drips down from his chest onto mine and our stomachs slide together with the salty wetness we've created. The heat builds inside me and I hear myself whimpering, preparing for the emotional and physical sensations that are looming.

"Come for me, baby," he growls in my ear. He sounds dangerous, someone to be obeyed.

I can't hold back any longer. I hang on to him as I start crying out in ecstasy. He joins me, panting, thrusting faster and harder, his body a wall of solid muscle.

"Greg," I cry, holding on to him for dear life. *Is it really him? Are we really here together? Doing this? Feeling this? How can this be real?*

"Rose . . . babe . . . ," he answers, arching his back then jerking in seizures as he finishes.

I cry out as waves of an orgasm crash into me with every thrust. I ride higher and higher and then, slowly, fall to the depths when it's over. My vision fades to black for a few seconds before my brain comes back online.

For a few moments we lie in one another's arms, covered in sweat. Our hearts are beating loud like thunder. I can hardly breathe. My abdominal muscles ache from the workout they just got.

"Thank you," he says, kissing me gently on the cheek.

I have to smile at that. "No, thank *you*."

He drops off to the side and looks at me, smoothing sweaty hair away from my face. "I *was* pretty incredible," he says, lifting his eyebrows at me a couple times.

I smile up at him, emotions flooding my heart as I take in his rugged face and adorable smile. "You were. I agree. And so was I."

"You're damn right you were," he says, leaning in for a slow kiss.

"You think we'll try this again sometime? Take another risk?" he asks. He attempts to hide his vulnerability behind a teasing grin, but I see it hiding there.

I nod, reaching up to stroke his sculpted cheek with my finger. "It would be criminal for us not to, really."

His grin is slow but so beautiful. He leans down and kisses me on the end of the nose. "I think we'd better get dressed and go downstairs before your moms get home."

I nod and pull away, sliding over to the edge of the bed. I'm ready to stand, but suddenly he grabs me from behind and pulls me back. I look up at him in surprise.

He grins devilishly down at me. "Ooor . . . maybe we've got time for one more round before they get here?"

I can't stop smiling as I snake my arms around his neck and bring him down to my mouth. "We've got all the time in the world."

CHAPTER THIRTY-ONE

We're just putting on our clothing when the doorbell rings downstairs. The only people who ever ring our bell are strangers who pull off the road to buy our products. I rush to pull my shirt over my head and run a brush through my hair. "I'll go see who it is," I say to Greg, who's putting on his jeans. "Take your time."

"I'll be down in just a minute," he says. "I need to clean up around here first." He grabs the garbage on the side table and wraps it in a tissue.

I leave him to it and dash down the stairs. Banana is waiting patiently at the front door with his tail wagging. At least I know it's not Smitty out there, which is a relief, because it would be weird for him to maybe find out I was just being intimate with Greg after turning him down so recently. I wonder where Amber and Ty are, though. Banana was supposed to be with them. He could have broken off their walk and used the doggie door, I suppose.

I open the door and smile at the woman standing on the doorstep. She's wearing a very fancy and expensive-looking trench coat, heels, and black stockings. She's absolutely beautiful, and she reminds me of how Amber looks when she's staying in Manhattan. I stand there with my mouth open, staring.

She gives me a tight smile. "Hello? I assume this is Glenhollow Farms?" She points down the drive toward the main road. "I saw a sign."

"Oh! Yes, of course. Yes. You're in the right place." Great sex kills brain cells, I guess. That's a bummer. Does it mean I'll stop sleeping with Greg? Definitely not. Hopefully, I won't be completely brain-dead by the time this affair is over. I pull the door open enough for her to come inside. "Please. Come in out of the cold. Have a seat."

"Thanks," she says, stepping inside. She stands just inside the entrance as I shut the door. She's looking around as she slips her satchel from her shoulder and sets it down on a nearby chair.

I step back to give her some space, and smile. "Are you interested in purchasing some honey, by any chance?"

She gives me a funny look. "That would be . . . nice, I guess."

Her answer seems a little stiff, so I don't go right into the kitchen to get it. "Maybe you're looking for some preserves? We have jams and jellies; you can take your pick."

Her smile is pained. "That would be nice also."

"Maple syrup?" Surely she came here for *something*. I feel like I'm forcing the jam and honey on her. We have advertisements for several products out by the road. I wish she would just tell me which one she wants.

"Sure. Why not." She throws her hands up. "Get me one of those, too."

"Which flavor of jam do you prefer? And how much do you want?"

She reaches into her shoulder bag and starts hunting around inside it. "I don't know. Surprise me."

"Okay." I walk into the kitchen, headed to the pantry without another word. I've sold our products to tons of people out here on the farm and probably thousands at the market over the years, but this has to rank up there as one of the strangest customer experiences I've had. I pull out one of our bags, made of recyclable material, of course, and put in a jar of our strawberry jam—the most popular flavor and one of my personal favorites—a small bottle of maple syrup, and a small jar of honey. If she wants to upgrade to larger sizes, I'll let her tell me. She's kind of an odd customer, and I don't want her accusing me of trying to charge her too much. I throw in one of our business cards and a free sample of our lavender oil for good measure. You never can tell who your next number-one customer will be, so we always put our best foot forward. As I'm headed out of the kitchen, I hear voices in the dining room. Somebody must've come home.

I walk through the door and find Greg standing in front of the woman with a very angry look on his face. I stop just outside the kitchen door, holding the bag in one hand and supporting it underneath with the other. "What's going on?"

The woman is holding her satchel against her, almost like a shield against his verbal attack. I look from her to Greg and can't figure out what I'm seeing. She seems worried at first, but then when she sees me, her expression morphs into something else. *Satisfied, maybe?*

Greg looks pissed. All I can think is that he really shouldn't be treating our customers that way. "I see you've met Veronica," he says, before I can intervene.

My jaw falls open, and I almost drop the bag. I catch it before I completely lose my grip. "Heh, heh . . . not officially."

She lowers her satchel to her side and walks over to me, holding her hand out. She looks very lawyerly now. "Nice to meet you."

I shift the bag of products to my left arm so I can free myself up to do the handshake thing. "I'm Rose."

She backs up and looks me up and down. She's not even trying to be cool about it. "Nice to meet you, too."

I'm at a loss. I look to Greg, silently asking him to take over.

"Veronica was just telling me why she came all the way out here without calling me first." He's offering me an explanation and also telling me he's not happy that she's taken it upon herself to do this.

Now the picture is starting to come together for me. This woman is looking at me with a very competitive expression on her face. It's like she knows Greg and I have been intimate, but she's staking her claim anyway. She's come out here to pee on her territory and to let me know that she's not giving up on him so easily. I wonder if Greg knows how sneaky she is. Or how determined. I guess he does now. Surely he doesn't believe that she's here for work purposes any more than I do.

"You said this case was really important to you, so I thought you'd want an update and to see all the data I've put together." She opens her satchel, pulling out a thick file. She hands it to him and smiles. "I knew you were still upset about Tinkerbell, and I wanted to help you out as much as I could."

I walk over slowly and place the bag of items on the dining room table. I feel ten kinds of foolish having brought these products out to her. She didn't come here to buy anything from us; she came here to take Greg back to where he belongs.

"I don't need to see this right now." He drops it on the table. "Do you have anything else for me? Anything urgent?"

For the first time since she arrived, she looks like she's lost a little bit of her confidence. She glances nervously down at the folder and then over at me. "No, that's it. But when you left, you told me to keep an eye on this case and let you know what was going on."

"An email would've sufficed."

I stare at him, the transformation shocking. Not five minutes ago he was a funny, sexy, warm, incredibly tender man performing silly pose-downs and making love to me. Now he's a hard-nosed, angry attorney, dressing down his employee.

"I'm sorry. I thought I was just doing my job," she stammers.

I narrow my eyes at her, taking in all the evidence before me. I don't believe her act for a second. I don't think she's as innocent as she's trying to pretend she is, and I don't think she's going to stop at this little road-block either. But I feel sorry for her anyway, despite all these negative feelings her attitude is stirring in me. She came all the way out here to the farm to fight for Greg, obviously expecting a different result from what she's getting. She took a risk, but it doesn't look like it's going to pay off. I took a risk with another man that didn't pay off, and I still remember how it feels. *Not good at all.*

My heart goes out to her. I totally understand how she feels about this man; he really is a good catch. And I don't know if she's slept with him yet, but if she has, no *wonder* she traveled hundreds of miles and made a surprise entrance. At this point, I'd probably follow him to the ends of the earth, if only to get more of that action I just got upstairs. He really knows what he's doing in the bedroom, *and* he's a kind man. A gentle man. A very capable man. In my experience, they are in short supply out here in central Maine. Maybe they are in Manhattan too.

I walk over and pull the strawberry jam out of the bag and hold it up to her. "This is our most popular flavor. I know you really didn't come here to buy anything, but I want you to try it anyway. Are you hungry? Have you had lunch yet?"

She slowly reaches her hand out and takes the jam from me, looking sadly at the label. "I haven't, actually."

I grin. "Perfect." I take the jar back from her. "How about if I make you a slice of toast to start with? You can try the jam, and if you're still hungry, we can make you a ham sandwich, too."

"That would be nice." She looks at me a little confused, maybe doubting my motives.

I turn to Greg. "You want to help me in the kitchen?"

He nods. "Sure."

We leave together and whisper once we're past the closed door.

"I'm really sorry about this, Rose. I did *not* tell her to come out here. I hope you believe me."

"Of course you didn't." I put a piece of bread into the toaster and lean on the counter, facing Greg. "She's trying to stake her claim. I get it."

"What do you mean?"

"She wants you in her bed. And she obviously knows you have something going on out here besides legal work, so she came out to pee on her territory. I get it."

"I'm not sure about that." He looks doubtful.

"I am. Listen, it's a girl thing. You have to admire her determination, at least."

"I don't think I have to admire it at all. I actually find it quite irritating. She's gone way over the line here."

"She has. But you're a good catch. I don't blame her for taking a risk. I took one today myself. It's just turning out better for me than it did for her. I feel bad for her."

I turn my back to him so I can monitor the bread. He comes up behind me and puts his arms around my waist, leaning over to kiss me on the neck. "You think I'm a great catch?"

"I do." I can't stop smiling. I'm getting warm again and my nipples are going hard.

He reaches up and cups my breast. "Maybe I'm not. Maybe I'm just trouble."

"Well, you're definitely trouble. I'm not going to argue that point." I turn and put my arms around his neck, staring into his beautiful gray eyes. "But I think you're worth the risk. Veronica and I have that in common."

"It's the *only* thing you have in common, believe me."

"She is awfully pretty." For the first time in my life I feel a little insecure. Compared to her, I look like Oscar Mayer.

He reaches down and grabs me in a hug so tight, my feet leave the floor. I almost lose my breath before he puts me down again. "You're the most beautiful woman I know," he says, leaning down to kiss me tenderly. He stops and frowns. "I think the toast is burning."

I squeak and quickly turn around to pop the button. A perfect piece of toast flies out of the toaster and lands on the plate. "It's not burned, it's perfect." I frown at him over my shoulder, pretending to be mad.

He spanks me lightly on the butt. "I'm going out there to tell her she has to go back to the office immediately."

I reach out and grab his hand as he begins to walk away. "Don't. Don't be mean."

"I'm not being mean. I'm going to be honest. She stepped over the line, and she's here to cause trouble. I'm not going to put up with it. It's unprofessional."

"Sometimes honesty is not the best policy," I say. I let go of him and turn my back so I can spread jam on the toast.

He says nothing. I turn around to see what he's doing and find him staring at me with such intensity it's almost scary.

"What? What did I say?"

He shakes his head, almost like he's bringing himself back to reality. "Nothing. I'll be out there. Don't worry, I won't be mean."

He leaves me standing in the kitchen with the toast half-finished. I go back to my task, thinking about what just happened. His mood swings are a little jarring. I write it off as us still getting to know one another and the pressure we're under with trying to conduct a secret affair among the nosiest group of people who ever walked the earth. We may have slept together twice already today, but we've only known each other in any meaningful way for a grand total of a few days.

I guess my sisters were right; we hippie chicks sure do fall fast and easy. I grin as I finish putting jam on the bread. I totally do not care. I'm not going to live my life through the eyes of other people, and I refuse to allow anyone's judgment to affect my choices. I'm a grown woman, and I'm going to follow my heart. If it leads me into pain, so be it. At least I'll enjoy the ride on the way there.

CHAPTER THIRTY-TWO

G reg sits down and looks at the legal file Veronica brought as she munches on her toast. I go into the kitchen to give them some privacy, but I'm only there for five minutes before several voices and a cacophony rise up from outside. It's the sound of many footsteps running up the front porch stairs and several voices talking at once. I come out of the kitchen to see what's going on.

The door bursts open, and a group of people comes in. My mothers are first, followed by Sam and Emerald, and then the entire band. Greg and Veronica look up in surprise. Greg stands.

"What's going on?" I ask, when I see the stricken look on my mothers' faces.

"Some jackass defaced the clinic," Carol blurts out. She's clearly upset.

"What?" I stare at her like she's lost her mind. She's making no sense. I was there not that long ago, and it was perfectly fine.

"I'm so sorry," Emerald says, rushing over and taking me by the hands. "I can't believe we didn't hear it happening. We must be deaf or something."

Sam joins her, stopping in front of me. "We're seriously sorry."

I pull away from my sister and move so that I can see the group better. Almost everyone has taken a seat around the dining room table. Veronica looks from one person to the next. I think she's as confused as I am.

"Does somebody want to explain to me what the heck is going on here?" I'm quickly losing patience.

Greg comes over to be next to me. I'm glad he isn't touching me and blowing our cover, but I'm also happy that he's there lending moral support. It feels good to have a strong presence backing me up.

"We were coming home from the market, and as we were driving past the clinic, we noticed something was wrong," Barbara says.

"Like I said, some jackass spray-painted the outside of the building," Carol says.

Mooch taps her on the shoulder and pulls her in for a hug. She starts to cry.

I feel sad too, but I'm also angry. "Somebody actually spray-painted the clinic while you were *inside* it?" I look at Emerald and Sam for an explanation.

Emerald nods as Sam answers. "I don't know how we didn't hear the hissing of the paint coming out of the can, and I swear to God it wasn't on there when we went in."

"It's pretty windy out there," Veronica says. She looks to her left and right. "With all the trees around here, it kind of sounds like somebody spray-painting all the time, doesn't it?"

After a few seconds, almost everyone nods in agreement.

"Maybe," Sam agrees. He looks at me. "It doesn't change the fact that we're real sorry. It was our responsibility to keep an eye on things, and we blew it. We'll help clean it off."

"But why would someone do that?" Sally asks. She looks like she's about to cry too.

I shake my head. It's got to be my crank caller, who has now elevated himself to being my stalker. It's probably the person who stole my laptop, too. It's not like I'm going to tell my family this theory, though. They're already upset enough. "It doesn't matter. It's probably just kids from town who are bored and looking to cause trouble. I'll take care of it."

"We'll help," Greg says.

"We absolutely will," Cash says. He stands. "We can go right now, as far as I'm concerned."

"Why don't we call the police first?" Red says, holding out his hand to slow his bandmate down. "We need to file a report, and they'll want to see what it looks like before we clean it up."

"Don't bother," I say. "They're totally useless."

"Why do you say that?" Barbara asks.

"Because . . . they've done nothing about my stolen laptop." Not to mention my crank caller. "You think they care about spray paint on a building way out here?" A building the town is trying to get rid of? I wish I could share everything I know. Heck, maybe it's Betty Beland herself coming out here being a delinquent. Scorned women have been known to do some batpoo-crazy things.

"They're gonna care if I have anything to say about it," Red says. His expression turns dark.

Here he goes again, acting like the big man of the family. I look up at Greg, silently begging him to understand. He meets my eyes, and I swear I feel a connection between us that goes beyond simple understanding. He gets me.

He looks up and surveys the group. "How about you guys let me handle this one?"

Red shrugs as he looks at my mothers and me. "If you think that's the best course of action."

"I do." Greg nods for emphasis. He shifts his gaze over to me. "I do think we should contact the police. You want me to make the call?"

I nod wordlessly. I trust him to do the right thing. And if I say no, my mothers are going to start asking a lot of questions I don't want to answer, and it won't be worth the trouble trying to fend them off.

Greg goes off into the living room with his cell phone to make the call. I turn my attention back to my family. "I'm sorry you guys got mixed up in this garbage."

"Hey, don't apologize," Red says, coming over to stand next to me. He puts his hand on my shoulder. "We're here for you. Whatever you need."

I glance up at him and then down at the floor. "Thanks." I feel bad for thinking negative thoughts about him acting like the man of the family. He's just one of those take-charge people. A natural-born leader. He reminds me so much of Amber. I look up at him again and focus on his eyes. His kind eyes. Are these the same ones that have been staring back at me for twenty-five years? Bossing me around almost every day of my life? It's hard to say, but it sure seems that it could be possible. I break my gaze to look at everyone else around the table, the people I love so much. They're worried about me. Even these men I really don't know all that well feel a strong connection to me through my mothers. It annoyed me before, but now I'm starting to get used to the idea.

Life is so strange. Sometimes I think I have it all figured out, and then the universe throws me a curveball and I realize I really don't know a damn thing. All our lives, my mothers have been telling my sisters and me that there's really only one reason for us to be here on this earth: to love one another and to love ourselves. Love is why they stayed with the band and enjoyed their time with them so much, and it's also why they left. And then love welcomed these men back into their lives two and a half decades later. As long as I've known these women who raised me, they have always been happy. Maybe their simple philosophy about being on this planet simply to love one another isn't such a bad idea after all.

I look over my shoulder at the man nodding and hanging up his cell phone. Is he doing his lawyer thing and taking charge to please his clients, or is he calling the police for me because he cares about me and is worried about my welfare? I think it's a little bit the former, but much more the latter. I'm feeling very lucky, even though there's somebody out there in the world who is coming after me for a reason I don't understand.

CHAPTER THIRTY-THREE

Veronica is headed back to the airport, courtesy of Smitty's personal taxi service, and the rest of us are hanging around waiting for the police to show up, when the doorbell rings. Banana barks once and trots over to the door, waiting for one of the humans to open it for him.

I lean on the couch as Red goes to the door and opens it. He greets someone who sounds like a man. When he walks in, I recognize him as the officer who wrote up my last two police reports and who has a golden retriever with a sweet itch problem that I treated last time I saw him. I walk over to greet him.

"Hello, Ms. Lancaster," he says, shaking my hand.

"Hello, Officer Brownlee. Thanks for coming so quickly."

"Somebody made a very convincing case for a speedy response, telling my dispatcher that we'd better get out here before there's more trouble," he says, looking around the room. I think he's trying to find the bossy attorney who put the fear of the law into him, the man who also may have pointed out that the officer's last two responses to our address weren't really in keeping with that whole 'protect and serve' motto they have written on the backs of their squad cars.

"Would you like a cup of coffee?" Carol asks.

"Sure. And I wouldn't mind one of those muffins either." He grins at my mother. "My wife buys 'em every week at the farmers' market." He rubs his belly. "This spare tire is here thanks to you all."

Barbara and Sally both stand, pulling out a chair together.

"Have a seat," Barbara says, grinning.

"We're so happy you're here," Sally adds. They exchange glances that can only be described as competitive. "So . . . which is your favorite kind?" Sally asks.

I roll my eyes because I know exactly where this is going.

Officer Brownlee walks over to the proffered chair and puts his clipboard on the table. "That's kind of hard to say, actually. They're all so delicious." He looks up at the women flanking him.

"Is it the blueberry ones?" Sally asks.

"Or is it the maple pecan?" Barbara prompts.

Emerald comes from the kitchen with his cup of coffee and puts it down in front of him. There's a plate with two different kinds of muffins on it. *Aaaand the competition is on.*

"Before you answer their questions," Cash says, "know that the two women who baked those muffins are sitting on either side of you, and they take a lot of pride in their recipes."

The cop stops reaching for a muffin, his hand freezing halfway across the table. He looks to his left and then to his right, understanding dawning. His other hand slowly joins the first, and he reaches out to take both muffins at the same time.

Everyone laughs, and Paul, the bassist, claps him on the shoulder. "Smart move."

Sally and Barbara wander off toward the living room, feigning disgust at the fact that everyone's kidding around. "We'll leave you to your work," Carol says, joining them.

The officer looks down sadly at the confections in his hands. "I really love these muffins."

I grab a knife from the sideboard and walk over to sit down across from him. I gesture for him to put the muffins back on the plate and then pull it toward me. I unwrap each of them and cut them into smaller bites, mixing them up with the knife before pushing the plate back over to him. "They'll never know which one you tried first," I say quietly so the moms won't hear me.

He glances over into the other room suspiciously and then grabs a piece of the blueberry muffin and pops it into his mouth. Two seconds later, he chooses one with the pecans and does the same thing.

I wink at him. Maybe he's not such a bad guy after all.

He takes a sip of his coffee and opens up his clipboard. "So . . . talk to me about what's going on here." He looks up expectantly.

I glance over at Em and Sam, silently asking for them to contribute. They come over to sit down, and Em speaks first. "Sam and I were in the clinic while my sister had lunch. We were there for about an hour. When we went in, there was nothing on the door, but when we came out, there was spray paint there."

"I noticed the paint. Does the message mean anything in particular?"

"What message?" I ask. I scan the faces around me. Everyone looks guilty. "What does it say?"

Greg comes over to stand behind me and puts his hand on my shoulder. "It says 'bitch.'"

I'm taken aback as hurt feelings assail me. "'Bitch'? Do you think it means me? Am I the bitch?"

Emerald shakes her head but hunches forward. I can tell by her body language that she does think it's about me.

"Of course it's not you," Carol says, coming into the room. "Nobody in the world who knows you would ever call you that word. It's the *last* word anybody would use to describe you. You're a saint."

I roll my eyes. She's not biased at all.

"Maybe they're just talking about one of your patients. A female dog you have in one of the kennels," Mooch says, trying to make a joke.

Nobody laughs, but I appreciate him trying to make light of such an ugly thing.

"Do you have any enemies?" asks the officer. "Anyone who would like to do harm to your business or to you personally?"

"That sounds pretty serious," Red says. "It's just a little spray paint, right? There're graffiti artists all over the place who apparently have nothing better to do than deface people's property."

"But it's not just the spray paint, is it?" the officer asks, his question going out to the group.

I glare at him and slowly shake my head, hoping he'll take the hint, but he just keeps on digging my grave. He ticks items off his mental list using his fingers. "First, we had the laptop being stolen, then we had all the crank calls and hang-ups, and now we've got the spray-painted profanity. My guess is there's somebody out there who thinks he's got a bone to pick with you." He looks at me and raises an eyebrow, as if waiting for me to confess.

"Crank calls? What crank calls?" Sally asks, coming into the dining area again. She looks around the room. "Did I miss something?"

"I think we all missed something," Carol says, giving me the mother-guilt-trip stare-down. Barbara and Sally join us, both looking concerned.

Greg sits down in the chair to my left and faces me. "You've been getting phone calls?"

I wish I could disappear into thin air. Why is everybody gawking at me like I'm the bad guy?

"You haven't told them?" the officer asks.

I look around at my family and friends, an apology in my eyes. "I didn't want you guys to worry."

Greg's voice goes very soft. "That's why you called me, isn't it? You thought it was me."

I put my hand on his. "Can we talk about this later?"

He pulls his hand back. "Sure."

233

My heart lurches at the cold look on his face. Did I hurt his feelings somehow, or is this him keeping our relationship secret? I'm so confused.

"Honey, you need to come clean," Barbara says. She walks over to stand at the head of the table. "Tell us everything that's going on. We can't help you if we don't know what's happening."

I take a deep breath and let it out, closing my eyes. I really wish I didn't have to be here, but this is what I must put up with in order to have what I have—a big family and all the love its members bring. Love doesn't come without cost, and that cost is being open and honest about things I'd rather keep to myself. God, I hate this part.

I open my eyes. "After my laptop was stolen, I started getting phone calls. It was just somebody who was breathing heavy on the other end of the line. I'm pretty sure it was a man, but he never spoke; I never heard his voice or anything. He called, like, five times."

"Why didn't you tell us?" Carol asks.

"I didn't want you guys to worry about something that was probably just some kid messing around."

"What made you think it was a kid?" Greg asks. He sounds like a lawyer.

"It was something a kid would do. It's not a very grown-up thing to call somebody and breathe in the phone all the time, right?"

· "On the contrary," Officer Brownlee says. "I've seen full-grown adults do some very immature things."

Sounds outside the front door announce visitors. First there are footsteps on the porch and laughter; then the door opens and a rush of cold air comes in followed by Amber, Ty, Sadie, Tinkerbell, and Oscar Mayer. They close the door behind them, but Amber and Ty stop in their tracks and stare at everybody in surprise. "What's going on?" Amber asks.

"Just have a seat and we'll fill you in, in just a minute," Red says.

Surprisingly, Amber does exactly what she's told without complaining. She ushers Sadie into the living room and sits with her on the couch. Ty perches on the arm of the sofa next to her, and they wait for us to continue in louder voices so they can hear from the adjoining room. I appreciate Red taking charge this time. Without his steady, commanding presence, this house would probably erupt in chaos. I'm not going to question right now why I'm thinking this way. I have bigger fish to fry. My reprieve is over, so I go back to my explanation.

"The last crank phone call I got was yesterday, and I yelled at the guy and threatened him; I told him I'd trace the call. I didn't hear from him after, so maybe he's done harassing me."

"I doubt it," the police officer says. "This stuff often escalates."

He writes something down on his paper. "It could be that this is the same person who spray-painted your door. Maybe they weren't happy with how you dealt with the last phone call."

"Oh, so we're going to blame the victim, is that it? Great. Perfect." I glare at the man sitting across from me. "What was I supposed to do? Be nice? Thank him and tell him to have a nice day? Offer him a free spay or neuter for his pet?"

"On the contrary; my advice to you is to not engage," the police officer says, not reacting at all to my emotional outburst. "If you get another call, just disconnect without saying anything. Eventually, he'll get bored."

"I would've thought he'd be bored already," I mumble.

"Can we trace the calls?" Greg asks.

"It depends. We can make a call over to the phone company and see if it's a possibility, but I don't have high hopes that that'll be the case." He closes up his clipboard book and slides it close to him, helping himself to another few bites of muffin and some of his coffee.

"What do we do next?" Red asks.

"I'll look into a few things and get back to you." The officer takes another sip of his coffee and more muffin before standing. "I should probably get going. If anything else comes up, let me know."

"Aren't you going to check for fingerprints or anything?" Emerald asks.

"We don't generally get fingerprints off graffiti. The perpetrators rarely touch anything but their paint cans," the police officer says. He tucks his clipboard under his arm and pulls a business card out of his pocket, putting it on the table. "Give me a call if anything comes up. Don't hesitate. I'll be in touch." He walks away from the table, and everybody stares at him.

Barbara stands. "Would you like a muffin to go?"

He grins like he was just waiting for someone to ask. "Sure."

"What do you prefer? Blueberry or pecan?"

Emerald stands. "I'll go get him one of each." She rolls her eyes as she walks past our mother.

Foiled again, Barbara turns around, frustrated.

I can't help but smile. Our mothers are goofy, but I love them so much. And because I do, I don't want them to worry about me. So somebody thinks I'm a bitch? Big deal; I can handle it. I lift my hand in a wave of goodbye as Officer Brownlee leaves. Red walks him to the door and shuts it behind him.

"So . . . are we putting together a posse or what?" Ty asks.

Sam nods. "I'm in."

Red shakes his head. "I don't think we need a posse, but I sure as heck don't feel like Rose should be going down to the clinic by herself anymore."

"I agree," Mooch says. "It's not safe."

I stand, irritated with these well-meaning fatherly types. "Hey! I've been going down to that clinic by myself for years. I'm not going to stop taking care of my animals because some jerk has decided to be rude to me."

"Nobody's telling you that you need to stop going down there," Amber says. "We just want you to be safe."

"What are you going to do? Hire me a bodyguard?" They're being ridiculous, treating me like a frail flower. Just because I'm named after one doesn't mean I am one.

"No, but we can keep you company," Red says. "Right?" He walks over and stops in front of me. "Would it be so awful to have somebody help you out down there once in a while?"

"Not necessarily." I look up at this tall man who I know has my safety at heart when he acts all bossy and controlling. I can't fault him for that. If I did, I'd probably deserve that spray-painted moniker on the clinic's door. "But I think you guys are pretty busy doing your own thing, aren't you?" All I need is for my work to get in the way of their next album. I'd have a fan base of millions hating me. Having one guy think I'm a bitch is enough for me. More than enough.

"We're never too busy to help out family, right?" Red surveys the group, seeking support for his statement, and everyone nods.

"Never too busy," Cash says, putting his arm around my shoulders. "Especially for somebody as cute as you, Bugaboo."

I try not to smile. I try really hard, but it's just not happening. They care about me, and I know I'd be stupid to hold that against them.

"I'm happy to take a shift once a day," Paul says. His gaze moves to the ceiling as he thinks about his offer. "Yeah . . . it might actually be nice. Quiet. I could get some reading done."

"I'm in," Mooch says. "I can sleep there, right? You have a couch?"

"I don't, actually."

"Fine. I'll get you one." He smiles like he's just solved all my problems. His cute expression makes me think that maybe it wouldn't be so awful to have somebody else around.

"You can't sleep," Cash says, frowning at his bandmate. "The idea is to be *vigilant*. You can't be vigilant if you're staring at the inside of your own eyelids."

I chuckle. "Trust me, you don't need to be vigilant when Banana is around." My little dog comes running over after hearing his name. I scratch the scruff of his neck. "He's a great watchdog."

"It's settled, then," Greg says. "For the time being, when you're down at the clinic, you will have someone to keep you company . . . in addition to Banana."

I stand, knowing there's going to be no arguing this point today. At least for now, I'm stuck with having a chaperone at work. "I need to get going, so if somebody wants to come with me, they need to be able to leave now." I walk over to the door and grab my jacket. Part of me wants Greg to come, but then again maybe not; he's acting funny. I think I offended him, but I don't know how it happened. Maybe it's better if we spend some time apart. Not a lot of time, but enough that I can get my head on straight and not be so emotional when we talk about it.

"I'll go first," Red says. He takes his jacket off the hook. It's black leather with silver zippers on it.

I turn around and face the room, but my words are for Greg. "If anybody needs me, you can call me at the clinic."

Amber gets up and comes over, taking my hand. "You okay?" she asks softly, so only I will hear her.

I nod. "I'm fine. Totally fine." Other than the fact that my heart is hurting. Greg is looking at me, but I can't read his expression, and it's making me so sad and confused. I wish I could get inside his head and figure out what he's thinking. Then again . . . maybe I don't want to do that.

"Call me if you need me." Amber kisses me on the cheek. I give her a quick hug and turn around to go. Greg still has a chance to stop me, but he doesn't. I walk out the door with Red at my side. The cold rips right through my jacket and chills me to the bone, and now my skin matches the temperature of my heart.

CHAPTER THIRTY-FOUR

Red and I walk to the clinic together with Banana and Oscar Mayer trailing behind, the two of them smelling every scent there is on the ground between the house and our destination. Several times the pups get tangled up in each other's paths and they pause to wrestle in the dirt. It's the perfect balm for my aching heart to see them acting so silly.

Most of the conversation between Red and me centers on the weather and the season that's coming. He's never spent the colder part of the year with us, so he doesn't know how much work is involved. I wonder, as I explain some of it to him, if he'll decide he prefers Manhattan winters to Maine ones. He doesn't say either way. I'm not sure how I feel about it now. Two weeks ago, I was sure, but now . . . not so much. Life is so confusing sometimes.

As we arrive at the clinic, the conversation stops and my heart sinks. The letters *B-I-T-C-H* are scrawled across the front door in bright-red paint. It makes me want to cry. Or vomit. Or cry *and* vomit. Who could possibly hate me this much? All I ever do is try to be nice to people and help their animals.

"Don't pay any attention to that garbage," Red says. "It's gonna be gone by the end of the day." He pulls out his cell phone and sends off a text.

I lift my chin, trying to put on a brave face and force the hurt feelings to go away. The asshole who did this doesn't deserve my emotions. "It doesn't bother me. People can say whatever they want. I know who I am."

I try to fit the key into the lock, but I'm shaking too much to make it work. Red silently takes it from me and gets the job done, opening the door for me and then closing it behind us once we and the dogs are inside. The warmth is very inviting and so are the sounds of restless animals coming from the back room. This is where I belong, and there's nowhere I'd rather be, *B-I-T-C-H* or not.

"I need to check my patients. I'll be back in a minute."

"Sure, no problem. I'll wait for you out here."

I make short work of checking everyone's bandages, pain meds, and IV fluids, and then I'm back in the lobby with Red. I take a seat at the desk and ease myself out of my jacket, draping it over the back of my chair behind me.

"I'm glad I'm getting the opportunity to spend some time here with you," Red says, looking around the lobby. "The circumstances aren't the best, but I've been wanting to get some alone time with you for quite a while now."

I place my hands on the desk, a little uncomfortable with his revelation. I feel trapped. "Really? How come?"

He hooks his thumbs into his waistband, his legs spread out in front of him. He looks like the quintessential rocker with his leather jacket, black motorcycle boots, and beat-up jeans. There's a black T-shirt on underneath his jacket that has writing I can't read because it's so faded, but I do recognize the image on it; it's one of his album covers.

I never used to think much of him when I'd see his face on the dust jackets of my moms' vinyl records, but looking at him now, I can almost imagine what drew my mothers to him; his personality is powerful—enigmatic while also being charismatic. And he's taking time out of his day to watch over me while I work, to make sure I'm safe and protected from whoever is out there with something against me. How could I not be impressed with that? It engenders a patience in me that allows me to hear him out.

"I've had ample time to chat with Amber, and a little bit with Emerald, too, but you're always so busy." He looks over at me. "You're a hard worker. I really admire that about you."

"Thank you."

He smiles, his charm coming through easily.

As I stare at him, I wonder what it is specifically that my mother saw in him besides that smile and his rock 'n' roll exterior. Was it his take-charge attitude? His natural charisma? His musical talent? The fact that he's adored by millions of women all over the world? It's hard to say. But underneath that hard rock 'n' roll exterior, there does seem to be a very interesting person. I guess I can't blame her for being drawn to him, for even falling in love. Heck, I'm halfway there with a man I hardly know. I guess the girls in my family do fall fast and hard.

"You put this whole thing together yourself," he says, gesturing out at the clinic. "Your mother told me."

"I did." There's no point in denying the truth.

"It must be really hard to see somebody trying to hurt it, like that asshole who painted on your door."

A dull ache settles into my chest. "It is hard." I pick up a pencil, doodling on a pad of paper that's on my desk, trying to force the images of that painted message out of my head.

"Ever thought about doing any upgrading around here?" Red is looking at the ceiling, at a water stain above his head.

"Many times." My smile is sad.

"What stopped you?"

"Money, mostly." I squirm as the contradiction overtakes me. He's offering me a fortune—exactly what I say I need—and I'm walking away from it.

He frowns. "You're a nonprofit, right?"

"Yep."

"Do you actively solicit donations?"

I sigh, knowing a lot of my problems are self-created. "Not really. Everybody knows that I'm a charity. I put up notices around town, and it's on my business card. But I guess I'm not really good at the money-raising part of this job."

"That's normal. The person who does the actual *doing* is often not the best at the promotion. That's why charities often hire someone to do that part of it." He shrugs. "That's how it works in my business, and we're not even a nonprofit. Right now your sister is out there every day making the business end of things happen for us, and before her, there were others. If it were up to me or any of the guys in the band to make things happen, we would have been done a long time ago. We wouldn't know how to promote ourselves if our lives depended on it. Everything we do is scripted by someone else. Everything but the music, of course."

I have to smile sadly at that. Twenty-six years ago, someone wrote our mothers out of his script, and now here we are.

"Our money managers are there too, making sure nothing gets wasted and everything's accounted for. We learned pretty late in the game that you can't blindly trust someone with your money, or one day you'll wake up and someone will have robbed you blind and used your own money to destroy your life."

It makes sense on more than one level that the band has money managers. I've gotten the impression from the stories I've heard from Amber that Red and the other guys don't really know how much money they have; they just spend it. I wish I had so much money that I could have the same cavalier attitude. Instead, I watch every single penny and agonize over every expense.

"I probably should've paid better attention from the very beginning," he says, sounding supremely disappointed. "Maybe if I had, none of this mess would've ever happened."

I look up at him, confused about the topic. "What mess?" Is he talking about the writing on my door? I don't understand the connection.

"The one with your moms. With you and your sisters."

My heart sinks. I'm being dragged into a conversation I've been avoiding for months. I'm so not in the mood for this.

He looks up at me, his expression as vulnerable as I've ever seen it. "I know you're upset about what's going on with your business here, but would you allow me to talk to you about a few things that have been on my mind for a while?"

I feel my face starting to burn. My emotions are a mix of embarrassment and anger. Now I know how a wild animal feels being pushed into a corner. The beasts in my care usually react by attacking when put in this position. But every once in a while, one of them surrenders. And I'm so tired of fighting . . .

"Go ahead. I'm listening."

CHAPTER THIRTY-FIVE

Red leans forward and rests his forearms on his thighs as he stares alternately at the floor and at me. "This was many years ago, you've got to remember. It was before I had all these wrinkles and these aches in my back."

He's trying to be charming so I give him a smile, even though I'm not really feeling it.

He plays with the rings on his fingers as he speaks. "We were so young. Darrell was with the band then. He was a great guy when we were younger. He was so full of life, so excited about our future. He knew exactly where we were going before any of the rest of us did."

I look up, surprised to hear him speaking of Darrell in such glowing terms.

Red seems lost in the past, staring off into the distance as he turns the rings on his hands. "We played for two years before we could get anybody but our friends to listen to us. And then things just happened. It went really fast. One day we were playing in our moms' basements, and the next we were playing in arenas . . . zero to sixty in two seconds flat." He shakes his head in disbelief. "It was like a fairy tale, and your moms were there almost from the start." He grins at me. "Your mom, Sally, actually sat in my mom's basement for one of our shows."

"She did?"

"Yeah. She saw us at a local show first, but then we did this party at my mom's place and I invited her, and she showed up. It was crazy."

"I never heard that story." Red has genuinely surprised me. I thought my mom had told me everything by now.

"We had this manager. You know him . . . Ted. Anyway, he was young too. We were a bunch of dumbasses. We had no idea what we were doing."

"Seems like you figured it out."

"We did. We made a lot of mistakes along the way, though. A *lot* of mistakes." His smile disappears. "Success didn't happen overnight, but it sure felt like it. We never stopped. We hardly ever slept. It was just go, go, go, all the time. And in the middle of it, we were writing music . . ."

"I hear it was your most productive time."

"It was." He shakes his head, lost in the memories. "A lot of that was Darrell. He was kind of the motor . . . the engine in front of the whole thing. He wanted it more than any of us."

"So if that's true, why did you kick him out of the band?" It seems like a really cruel thing to do to the guy who made everything happen.

Red's face morphs into something that looks like anger . . . or maybe it's regret. "It was a combination of things. We'd been going full blast for a couple years by then. We had your moms with us, and everything was pretty great. But the pressure started to get to us. Other people started getting involved in making decisions for us—people from the record label who had more experience than we did. They were the money guys. They started calling the shots. And Darrell didn't get along with them."

"I hear he's kind of pushy."

"Pushy? That's one way of putting it. I'd say he's an asshole, but that's just me."

I have to smile at that. I think Red would describe any man who didn't agree with him in that way.

"Anyway, we were so wrapped up in ourselves and the music, we didn't see what was going on with your moms. I mean we didn't get it *at all.*" He looks surprised at his own memory. "One minute they were there, having a ball, kicking back with us, and the next they were gone." The look on his face says it all. Red and his bandmates were lost. Confused. Totally in the dark. Kids trying to live the lives of grown-ups.

"I remember the day they left like it was yesterday. I woke up and went looking for them, but I couldn't find them anywhere. It was crazy." He shakes his head, pressing his hands together. "At first I thought they were out shopping. I thought maybe they were getting their hair done or something. They didn't usually do that, but I was trying to find reasons for their absence. Where were they?"

I can see the stress building in him as the memories wash over his mind. He rubs his hands harder and gets up, pacing the floor. "I asked Ted where they were and Darrell too, but nobody had any answers. Cash, Mooch, and Keith were just as upset as I was, but Darrell wasn't. He just had this look on his face." Red looks like he wants to punch something. Or someone. "It was like he was happy they were gone."

"Was he?"

"He was behind the whole thing. I don't know when he got pulled into the scheme, though . . . whether he initiated it or joined in after. Nobody's given me a straight answer yet, but it doesn't matter."

"Maybe it does."

He looks up at me, coming back to the present. "I want you to know that I went straight to Ted and asked him what was going on, and he looked me right in the eyes and lied to me. He told me he had no idea, but he's the one who arranged for your moms to leave. He's the one who gave them the money for it. He stole money from us to do it."

I really want to believe him, to believe he was so young and so clueless that all of this made sense to him. But it seems so far-fetched. "What I don't understand is how you didn't know. How is that possible?"

"We had no clue. I told you before, I'm terrible with money. It comes in somewhere, and I spend it with the credit cards I'm given by our accountants. I don't know how much money I have. I never do. When I need something I can't buy with a card, I ask for the money and they give it to me. I pay people to watch it for me and make sure no one steals it, but I didn't have the checks and balances in place for the first five years. That's how Ted got away with it."

"What about the others?"

"They're just as bad as I am." He winces. "I know this is going to sound terrible, but when you have as much money as I do, you don't worry about it. You just spend it on whatever makes you happy."

I shrug, not taking offense and not connecting with his statement in any way. I've had the exact opposite experience. I have almost no money, and all I do is think about how I don't have enough to pay for the things I need.

"It was crazy. When your mothers left, it was a really dark time for us. You can hear it in the music."

"You didn't look for them." My heart is still hard. He's making a convincing case for being a dumb kid, but not for letting our mothers walk away or for using them. Dumb is one thing; being heartless is another.

"We had a full tour, completely booked. We needed to be in twenty cities over thirty days, and that was just the first month. It went on like that for two solid years, *and* we had to write new material at the same time. We had no time to do anything but play the music and try to survive."

I can't put myself in his shoes exactly, but I do know what it means to have so much work that I don't have time to think about anything but eating, breathing, and taking care of business. It's possible I've let some important things slip when I was too busy working.

"I guess that made Darrell happy."

"It did make Darrell happy. And Darrell being that happy over something that was breaking us apart inside just pissed me off." Red is back to being furious again. "I nailed him one day. Right in the face. I gave him a black eye. I'll never forget that day. It was glorious. I'll never forgive him for what he did."

This is also a story I've never heard before. "What happened?"

"He said something that I still can't get out of my head." He looks up at me. "He said we were better off without them. Without your mothers in our lives."

My heart hurts for the pain expressed plainly on his face.

"He was wrong. He was wrong then, he was wrong for twenty-five years, and he's still wrong. We are not better off without your mothers."

Tears well up in my eyes, and I shake my head. "How do you know that? After all the time that has passed and all your success without them?"

His expression is pure anguish. "Because we missed out on our daughters." His voice breaks. "How could that possibly *not* be wrong? No amount of success will ever make up for that."

I have to look away. I grab some tissues out of the box on my desk and press them to my eyes. My heart is aching; I think it's breaking in half. "This is really not a good time for me to be talking about this."

He gets up and comes over, crouching down next to me. He puts his hand on my knee. "I know it's not, and I'm real sorry. I know this is hard for you, but you have to understand that it's really hard for me, too. It's hard for all of us. We missed out on so much."

He sighs, his breath shaky. "You're not a parent, so maybe you can't understand what I'm trying to say here, but please believe me when I say that our hearts are torn in two. All these years we've had three little girls—three beautiful little girls who grew into amazing women—living their lives out here on a farm, sometimes struggling to get by, and there we were, out in the world with all the money we could possibly need, and we were oblivious to it all. You struggled, and we could have helped, but we didn't. We could have shared our lives and our successes with you. We could've helped you along. We could've made your lives easier. And had we been given the chance, that's exactly what we would have done, but we weren't. It was stolen from us. *You* were stolen from us, but not by your mothers. They did what they thought was best. We were stolen from you by Ted. By Darrell. By everyone at our label who had a hand in squirreling you away and sending you out here to the farm."

I lower the tissues from my face and stare at him. His words are overwhelming. Sad. But they miss the most important point entirely. "We don't care about the money. Don't you get that?"

"I'm starting to get that impression," he says.

I don't appreciate his humor. "You could've been dirt-poor. It didn't matter. All you had to do was show up at the front door and everything would've been fine. But you never showed up." Now I'm really crying. "You never came. You were out there living your lives, and we were here, living ours. You never knew you were missing out on anything until now, but we knew all our lives that we were missing out on having fathers."

"I know," he says, taking my hand. His hands are warm but mine are ice-cold. "That's what I'm trying to say. We didn't even get the opportunity to know what we had . . . the most precious thing a person could have . . . a child. Maybe I should be mad at your mothers for taking that opportunity away from us, but I just can't be. I love them too much. I've always loved them. Twenty-five years have gone by and I *still* love them. That's why I never married. It's why none of us ever married. Your moms were always there in our hearts, even if they weren't physically present."

I want to believe him, but common sense keeps pushing back in my head. "You never bothered to try to find them, for twenty-five years. That doesn't sound like love to me."

"When somebody who loves you says, 'I don't want to see you anymore and you need to stay away,' that's what you do. Their actions and the messages they left behind with Ted told us very clearly that we were to leave them alone. And so we did. With love comes respect. And we respected your mothers."

I laugh bitterly at that. "I don't think so." Respect has nothing to do with drug-filled orgies, which is pretty much how our mothers have described their relationship with the band. Not in my book, anyway.

Red lets go of my hand. "I know you're angry. I get it, believe me. I'm angry at me, too. But please don't accuse me of not respecting your mothers. I do." He puts his hand on his heart. "I truly do. That's why I haven't pushed you guys to take the money. Your mothers asked us to let you decide how to handle this situation, and out of our respect for them and you, we have agreed to those terms. But I sure do wish that you'd give us a chance." He strokes the back of my hand. "Like it or not, I'm your dad. So is Mooch, so is Cash, so is Paul . . ."

"So is Darrell?" I ask. I mean, if he's going to include a guy who wasn't even there during the sexy parts, he at least needs to include a guy who *was* there.

Red's nostrils flare, but he answers. "Yeah, maybe. He was around then. It's possible he was . . . involved."

"I don't know what you want me to say." I'm finally able to look into his eyes. They're swollen and red-rimmed. Mine are probably worse.

"I just want you to tell me that you'll give us a chance," he pleads. "Let us try to make up for everything we missed. I know it's not possible, but we'd like to try. Let us get to know you. Make an effort to get to know us. I promise, you won't regret it." He tries to smile. "We're good guys. We made some big mistakes in the past, but we're doing our best to make up for that now." He puts his hand on his chest. "I personally am going to work the rest of my life to be a good man and a good father to anybody in this family who will let me. I think Amber is considering it, and maybe Emerald is too. I'd love it if you would join them. But there's no pressure. If you decide it's too much, I get it. Some mistakes are unforgivable, and you're the one who has to decide that. I can't do it for you."

I nod, almost feeling relieved at his request. I think this is something I can do. I can try, at least. "Fair enough."

"I know you have a lot on your mind and that this is going to take some time for you to figure out, but can I just say one more thing?"

I nod, sniffing and wiping under my eyes with a tissue. "You might as well." I have no more resistance in me, too emotionally exhausted to fight him off anymore.

"You could do an awful lot of good with that settlement the band has offered you. And it's a no-strings-attached deal. If you take it, it doesn't mean that you accept me or any of the other guys as your father, and it doesn't mean you forgive us for what we did or didn't do. It's just a way for you to make your dreams come true, whatever they are." He smiles. "You could rebuild the clinic as it was or make it bigger and better. You could hire people to help you. Or you could do something completely different. Give it all away, for all I care. I just want you to have it."

"Why?"

"Because you're the daughter of people I love. And you're the only family I've got. My money and my music are my legacies. Let me share my legacy with you. Please, Rose."

Tears pour out of his eyes and trail down his wrinkled, weathered cheeks. He makes no effort to wipe them away.

I think about what he's said, and it doesn't take me long to come to a conclusion. We are his only family, and this is a man who's spent the last almost thirty years of his life moving from town to town and country to country. How lonely that must be. My life is all about roots and belonging and family. I could not imagine living *his* life. I'm the lucky one, not him. I actually feel sorry for him, for the first time ever. And I feel sad that I'm the one thing standing between him and his happiness . . . between my mothers and true happiness. They love these men.

What could possibly be so wrong with a love that has lasted more than two decades? How selfish can I be? My mothers and my sisters *and* the band are my family, and the world would be a big, scary place without them in it. Red is sitting here offering me his heart. I would have to be a bitter fool to walk away. I reach over and grab some tissues from the box and hand them to him.

"Thanks," he says, dabbing at his face.

Without another thought, I reach over and put my arms around him and pull him toward me. The leather of his jacket makes creaking sounds as his arms move to return the gesture. The hug is awkward, but it's a great start.

"I promise to try to be more accepting. To work on accepting all of you into my life as family," I say. And as soon as the words are out of my mouth, it feels like all of the weight that has been pressing down on me takes flight and departs for places unknown.

"That's all I can ask," he says.

We pull apart and stand. "I'm going to go wash my face," I say. I need a little space after that heavy moment.

"I'll hold down the fort," he says.

I walk into the back room, my feet barely touching the ground. It feels amazing, and I feel zero regrets over my decision to let the band into my heart.

CHAPTER THIRTY-SIX

I'm lying in bed staring at the ceiling when there's a slight tap at my door. It's ten o'clock at night and I should already be asleep, but my mind won't stop racing; I've been checking the time on my bedside clock for the last hour.

I sit up and face the door. "Come in."

I expect it to be Amber, but it's not; it's Greg, and I'm shocked to see him. He acted so removed at dinner and then went to sleep early in another part of the house without saying anything but 'Goodnight' to me. I did not expect to see him until tomorrow at breakfast, but even then, I know he's scheduled to leave for his office soon after. I was actually starting to wonder if this whole affair thing was already a bust.

He shuts the door very quietly behind him and walks over to the edge of the bed. "Hi," he says. He's fully dressed.

"Hi," I say, pulling the sheets up to my neck. I feel very vulnerable in my T-shirt and shorts when he's standing there in jeans and a sweater.

"Can we talk?"

I nod.

"Thanks." He sits on the bed, arranging a pillow behind his back so he can lean against the headboard comfortably. His legs extend in front of him, crossed at the ankles. He folds his hands in his lap and stares at them. "I'm sorry about everything that's going on."

"What are you talking about?" There are so many things happening, I can't even begin to know which one he's referring to.

"Stuff that happened at the clinic, the way the police department is handling things." He shakes his head, looking supremely disappointed in himself.

"It's a lot to take in, but it's not your fault. I don't know why you're apologizing for things other people have done."

He looks over at me. "There're some things I haven't told you that make it difficult for me to just let it go."

"Like what?" I'm afraid that this is the part where he tells me we can't continue to be together. He lives there and I live here . . . it's an impossible situation.

"You know I have a niece named Linny, right?"

I nod dumbly, thrown by this curveball.

"She's my sister's daughter. My sister has a lot of problems, which means I end up taking care of Linny a lot of the time."

I try to imagine him raising a teenage girl, but it doesn't match up with my earlier impressions of his life. "I thought you said you don't get home from work until ten."

"When I don't have Linny overnight, that's true. But I often have her with me, and in those cases, she comes to my office after school, and then we leave for my place together. It's the reason I took the job in corporate law instead of environmental law and agreed to work exclusively with the band as my only client. I don't have the time to take on other clients when I also have a teenager at home."

I'm a little shocked hearing this. I can't believe I haven't already been fully informed by Amber. "Does my sister know this?"

"No. Nobody knows except the partners at my firm."

"Not even Red?"

"Not really. He knows that she spends quite a bit of time with me, but he doesn't know the details."

"Why are you telling me?" I'm afraid to hope that it means I'm special to him.

"Because. I thought it was important that you know."

I suddenly feel very sad as doubt creeps in and takes over the hope. "Are you giving me the reason why this relationship isn't going to work?"

"No, not intentionally. Why would you think that?"

"What else am I supposed to think? It sounds like you're about to tell me that you have a lot of responsibilities and no free time."

He sighs. "I guess on paper that's what it looks like."

"And you are a lawyer, after all." In other words, a paper chaser.

"I am." He looks up at me, something like sadness filling his eyes. "But I'm also a guy who really likes you."

"I like you too."

"You do?" he asks, sounding like he doesn't believe me. "Even after . . . the way I've acted?"

"Yes, I do. Even after that. But sometimes it feels like we're . . . I don't know . . . doomed, maybe."

He gives me a sad smile. "Star-crossed lovers who can't get the timing or circumstances right."

"Exactly."

"So where does that leave us?"

I shrug. "It's up to you."

"No, it's up to both of us."

"How so?"

He looks down at his hands again. "I believe everything is negotiable. Anything can be settled, one way or another."

"You know this because you're a lawyer."

"Yes. I see it all the time. Two people who are arguing and don't agree on anything can always find a way to compromise and come to a conclusion they can both live with."

"But we aren't arguing, and to be honest, 'living with' something doesn't sound all that romantic." Am I wrong to want it all?

"You're right, we're not arguing, but we are in a somewhat untenable situation with complicated logistics that require some sacrifice to work. And romance has nothing to do with logistics."

His words are cold. Businesslike. The *least* romantic words a man could say to me. I feel like he's going to serve me with a subpoena any second. I slide down into the bed and put my head on the pillow, rolling away from him. "I'm really tired." I can't deal with this right now. It's too much sadness. First I have Red tugging at my heartstrings, and now this. The one good thing I had going on in my life was this affair with Greg, but now it's over. It's over before it even started.

The bed jiggles around, and I think he's getting up to leave, but then I feel him behind me. His body presses against mine as he lowers his head to share my pillow. His hand comes up to rest on my waist. "I don't want to leave."

I shrug, the shared pain of regret and hope lancing my heart. "So don't leave."

"It's not that easy."

"No, it's not." The sadness is almost overwhelming.

"Do you think you'd ever consider moving to the city?"

Part of me wants to lie so that we can continue this love affair for as long as the lie will hold out, but I know that wouldn't be fair to either of us. "No. I would never consider that. I would never be happy in that city. I'm sorry."

His warm breath tickles my neck. "I understand. It's what I expected you to say."

The devil inside me decides I need to drive the knifepoint deeper into my own heart. "Would you ever think about moving out here?" I just need to hear him say the word: *No.* Then I'll know this is finally over.

There's a long pause before he responds. "Maybe."

I twist my head around to look at his face, to check and see if he's lying. His expression is blank.

"Seriously?" I will be so mad at him if he's messing with me right now.

"It's a possibility. I've thought about it."

I fully turn over to face him, our noses just inches apart. "But you have your office in Manhattan. You're a partner at your firm. You couldn't possibly leave your practice."

"I only have one client," he says, frowning at me. "I can do my work from anywhere. My practice will stay exactly the same."

I panic, afraid to believe that there's any hope of this working out between us. "But what about all of your stuff?"

"What stuff?"

I panic. *What stuff?* What does he have that could possibly destroy our chances of being together? There must be something. I blurt out the first things I can think of. "Your officey stuff. Veronica. Your copy machines. The gym where you work out. Linny . . ."

He smiles. "I can put a copy machine in wherever I am, and I certainly don't need Veronica in my life. And you have a gym in town. It's only twenty minutes away. It takes me twice that long to get to the one I use in the city."

"Really?"

"During rush hour, sure. Easy."

"But what about Linny?"

His expression darkens and he sighs. "That is an issue. I have to be there for her, there's no question. And her mother lives in the city."

"Oh." I reach out from the covers and play with the edge of his shirt. The Linny issue is not the only one we have to deal with. "I had a conversation with Red today."

He blinks, maybe in shock at the sudden subject change. "You did? About what?"

"About the past. About his history with my mothers. About what the band went through. About the settlement."

"Oh." Greg takes my hand to still my movements, backing away a little. "Did you discuss anything specific? Come to any conclusions about anything?"

He looks worried, and I have to smile at that; the lawyer in him never sleeps. "I don't know. Maybe. He said some things that were very compelling."

"Compelling in what way?"

He's so serious with his responses, it's actually a little bit annoying. "Why? What does it matter?"

"I thought you told me you weren't going to take that settlement."

I pull my hand from his and gather the blankets so I can push them off me and sit up. I glare at him. "So what if I change my mind?"

"You can't just change your mind." He sounds offended.

"Says who? It sure seemed like Red was suggesting I could today. Was he wrong about that? Is there some kind of legal problem involved? Did I sign something?"

"No . . . because . . . ," he sputters, "once you make a decision, you should stick to it."

I frown at him. "That doesn't sound very lawyerly."

"What do you mean?" He sits up and pulls back, stopping near the edge of the bed with one leg hanging to the floor.

"You said I can't change my mind, but you aren't giving me a legal reason for saying that, are you?"

"I'm giving you a commonsense reason. You've made your decision. It was a good decision, and you should stick to it."

I really want to slap somebody right now. "What *is* it with you and that settlement, Greg? Do you want the money for yourself or something?"

He looks at me like I'm crazy. "What? No! I have no entitlement to those funds whatsoever."

"Then what's the big deal?"

He looks away and hisses, running his hands through his hair. He punches the bed, causing me to jump in shock.

"What the hell is your problem?" I grab the pillow next to me, prepared to knock his block off with it if he gives me even a hint that physical violence is in my future.

He looks at me with the most horrible expression on his face. It looks downright scary, it's so serious. "You can't take that settlement."

I'm two seconds from kicking him out of my bedroom. "Give me one good reason why not."

"Because. You're not entitled to it." He stands and walks to the door.

I jump out of bed and run after him, grabbing the back of his shirt before he can reach the door handle. "Not so fast. You're not going anywhere until you tell me what the hell you're talking about."

He stops, still facing the door. He says nothing but lifts his hands to run them through his hair. His elbows stick out to the sides and he bends over backward slightly, making a loud noise that sounds like a growl. When he straightens, he pulls his hands from his hair and turns around to face me, his arms folding over his chest. "We have a problem. We have a legal problem, and you are right in the middle of it."

I stare at him in shock. "What are you talking about?"

He shakes his head. "This is not the time to discuss it." Lawyer-Greg is back.

"This is the perfect time to talk about it. And you'd better start talking now, or I'm going to start yelling." I lift an eyebrow at him, daring him to test me. *Go ahead . . . make my day.*

He shifts his weight slightly. Lawyer-Greg looks like he might be a little bit scared. He unfolds his arms. "Yelling? No. No yelling. Please."

I nod, feeling very, very sure of my decision. "Oh, yes I will. I will yell the roof off this house if you don't start talking. I am not kidding."

An epic stare-down commences. I try to express through narrowed eyes and violently flared nostrils that I'm not joking, but Greg just juts his jaw out and looks like he's not going to say anything, so I open my lips and get ready to scream.

He slaps his hand over my mouth and leans in, whispering, "Okay, okay! Please don't scream. I'll talk."

I nod and he removes his hand. We slowly back away from each other. I cross my arms over my chest. "Well? I'm waiting."

CHAPTER THIRTY-SEVEN

Greg is just opening his mouth to spill the beans—whatever those beans are I have no idea—when the unholy sound of Banana going berserk stops him in his tracks.

Greg cocks his ear toward the door. "What's that?"

I hurry to pull my robe on. "That is Banana losing his shit. Something's going on outside." I wrap the belt of my robe around me and push Greg out of the way. "Watch out." I run out into the hallway, but I'm not the only one there. Amber's on the landing below me and so is Barbara.

"Is that Banana?" Barbara asks.

"Yes. Something's going on." I race past them down the stairs and find Banana digging at the door trying to get out. His doggy door is locked and he's stuck inside. "Banana! Come *here*!"

He totally ignores me, barking and growling and scratching at the door. Something is out there and he wants at it. And frankly, I want him to resolve whatever issue he's having before he wakes the entire household. I run over without a second thought and unlock the door, throwing it open. He takes off, racing toward the clinic, telling me there's something really wrong down there. My heart feels like it's going to explode with the stress and worry. *The animals!*

I pull on the boots closest to the door, throw on my long jacket, and run out after him.

"Where are you going?" Amber shouts from the doorway.

"To the clinic!"

Pounding footfalls come from behind me, followed by heavy breathing. Greg is suddenly at my side. "What are you doing?" he says, putting his hand on my arm.

I push him away and keep going, jogging in boots that are too big. "Something's happening at the clinic. I have to get there."

"I'll meet you up there," Greg says, racing ahead and leaving me in his dust. His form disappears, swallowed up by the darkness. I'm left with the sound of my heavy breathing and my feet pounding on the road.

It's the longest trip to the clinic I've ever made. I'm moving as fast as I possibly can, but it's taking too long. I smell smoke and, as I draw nearer, see fire. Panic seizes me. "Oh my god. *No!*" I'm running as hard as I can, my blood pumping, my limbs practically a blur. I'm crying as I try to breathe. "No! No, no, no!"

By the time I get there, Greg is already inside. I race in after him as fire climbs two of the walls in the lobby. "Greg!" I scream. "Where are you?!"

"I'm in the back! Help me with the kennels!"

I race in there and find him standing in front of the wall of animal cages with Banana barking at his heels, trying to figure out how to rescue my patients.

"The latches!" I yell, pointing to the wall. All of the kennels are affixed to the wall so they won't tip over. Metal buckles hold them in place, making it impossible for the cages to fall over by accident but able to be detached for repair or replacement.

Greg grabs a chair and jumps up onto it, reaching on tiptoes to get to the first latch. It's easily released, but there are so many . . . I can barely breathe with the panic that's consuming me. *The animals are going to die. WE are going to die!*

Greg moves to the next one and I grab the first cage, yanking it off the stack. "I'm sorry, baby," I say to the animal inside who's being jostled around. I regret causing him discomfort, but there's no time to be gentle. I set the kennel down on the ground and start shoving it toward the door; there's no way I can carry it out, it's too heavy. *It's not going to be enough! We'll never make it!* I could never choose which animals should survive and which ones shouldn't. I'm going to keep working until I collapse on this floor; there's no other way . . .

Suddenly, there are more hands there. Ty is standing in front of me.

"We gotta get these out!" I scream, very near the edge of insanity. My eyes are starting to sting from the smoke.

"Go, go, go!" he yells, waving me away. "I got this one!"

I go back and get the next kennel. Greg helps to put it on the ground, and then Sam is at my side taking it from me. He lifts it like it's made of cardboard. Hope soars inside me. Two down, ten to go!

The next kennel comes down, and then the next, and the next. As soon as I get one to the ground, someone is there taking it away. I see Sam and Ty, Amber and Emerald. Then Red, Mooch, Paul, and Cash show up, each of them grabbing cages without a word and rushing out. My moms are last, working two at a time to help me lift cages down and hand them off. A task that would have been impossible alone has been made possible through the teamwork of my family.

We have all of the animals out in the grass within ten minutes, with no one suffering anything worse than a little smoke inhalation. Thankfully, none of us are bad enough off that we need oxygen. Everyone made it. It's a miracle.

I feel light-headed, not from the ordeal but from the idea that one of us could have died. How did this fire start? Was it faulty wiring or something more sinister? The last thing burning is the front door, and I can see the paint—B-I-T-C-H—bubbling as it melts away.

We all stand in a circle and watch the last several years of my life and my hopes for the future go up in flames. The distant sound of fire engines comes, but they're too late. All four walls and the roof are now aflame. We have to move back, dragging the cages with us because the heat is so intense. We're a full fifty yards away when we hear glass breaking and things popping inside.

My sisters are on either side of me hugging me. "I'm so sorry, sweetie," Emerald says. "This is so awful."

"We'll rebuild," Amber says matter-of-factly. "End of story. It's already done. And this time we're putting a bedroom in it so when you have to sleep there, you won't have to put your head on the desk."

What's the point of rebuilding if someone's just going to burn it to the ground again? "Somebody did this," I say, my chin trembling as I stare at the destruction. I no longer believe it's faulty wiring. I was just fooling myself; we had the electrical totally redone five years ago. "Whoever was calling me and whoever painted on the door, they did this."

"Do you really think so?" Emerald asks.

I nod, no question in my mind anymore. The stink of hatred is all over this mess.

The fire fighters arrive, and soon the place is a hive of activity. Several men are hosing the place down using the reservoir on a water truck, but they're not going to get it under control until the entire building is destroyed. The barn is old and the wood is as dry as a bone. It was the perfect place to start a bonfire, actually. I look behind me at the kennels and the stressed-out animals inside them. I'm relieved and thankful that we got them out, but what the heck am I going to do with them now?

"We need to get the animals out of the cold," I say.

"Put them in my studio," Em says. "I'll go start moving stuff out of the way right now." She leans in and kisses me on the cheek and then she's gone. She and Sam leave in a hurry.

Red comes over and pulls me into a hug, kissing me on the head. "We can fix this. Don't you worry."

"It's not fixable." He's talking about the building, but it was just a place. A place you can fix. A broken dream you can't.

He pulls away and looks at me. "Everything's fixable. All you need is determination and money."

"Determination I have. Money I don't."

He gives me a scolding look. "You've got all the money you need. Don't be silly."

I look over at Greg. He's busy talking to somebody from the fire department. I can't comment on this money issue until I talk to him again. He has something to tell me, and I'm dying to know what it is.

Red is distracted by one of the band members calling him over, so he leaves me. Amber comes into my view and I turn to face her.

"What's going on?" she asks.

I shake my head. "I don't want to get into it right now."

Her voice softens. "What can I do to help?"

"You can help me transport the animals for now. If I need anything else later, I'll let you know."

She leans in and kisses me on the cheek. "You got it. I'm going to start loading them into the truck." Somebody brought the truck down, and Amber starts recruiting people to help her in her mission. I stand there as tears stream down my face; seeing my family loading my patients into the back of the pickup touches me so deeply. They don't question anything. They don't complain. They do what needs to be done, and they do it with heart. I am the luckiest girl in the world, and I don't say it with reservation anymore. I don't say, *But I never had a father growing up.* Everything that has happened to me has happened for a reason . . . a *good* reason. I can't regret how my life turned out without regretting what I have today . . . and I'm nothing but absolutely grateful.

Greg comes over and stands next to me. "What a tragedy," he says softly.

"That's one way to describe it."

"We're going to find out who did this, and I'm going to use every contact I have to make sure they're prosecuted for it."

"Okay." I don't care about the fire right now, and I don't care about the evil person who set it either; there will be plenty of time for me to fret over that stuff. The animals are okay and they're going to be fine, so they don't worry me either. Right now, all I want to know is what Greg was going to tell me before the emergency pulled us out of my bedroom. I won't be able to sleep until I hear the words come out of his mouth.

He turns and looks at me, as if he's read my mind, and I stare back at him.

"We have a lot to talk about," he says.

I nod. "Yes, we do."

"Can it wait?"

I shake my head. "Not really."

He looks off into the distance and reaches behind his head to scratch himself on the neck. "Fine. If you need to know now, you need to know now. Might as well get it over with." He takes a deep breath and huffs it out, his explanation coming from the man I know as Lawyer-Greg.

CHAPTER THIRTY-EIGHT

I know you're thinking about taking the settlement." He looks over his shoulder for a second at Red before shifting his attention back to me. "And I know after this fire it's going to be more tempting than ever to do that, but you can't."

I fold my arms over my chest to keep the cold at bay. "So you said. Now you're supposed to tell me why."

"Because . . . ," he sighs heavily and looks at the ground, "you're not a daughter of anybody in the band."

It takes a few seconds for his words to sink in. "What?"

He looks up at me, his gaze cold and hard. "That settlement money has been put aside into an irrevocable trust for the daughters of the members of Red Hot. You, however, are not a daughter of any of the current members of Red Hot, and therefore you are not legally entitled to the funds in that trust. Not the way it was written. Their accountants advised them to set it up this way for tax purposes, and there's nothing I can do about that. It's impossible to change what's already been done."

"What are you talking about?"

"I have good reason to believe that your father is not in the band."

"How could you possibly know that?"

"My knowledge is based on information that I have access to."

"I'd really like to know what that information is, and if you're not willing to share it, then I have to wonder why. And I also will have a very hard time believing you unless I see proof." If he tells me he somehow took a DNA sample from me and had it analyzed, I'm not only going to sue him, I'm going to sue the entire band. My earlier warm feelings toward them are starting to cool really quickly.

"I'm not at liberty to share that information with you. Client confidentiality rules forbid it." He pauses. "I want to . . . but I can't."

"Then I'm not at liberty to believe you or listen to anything you say." I turn away from him to stare at the fire that's still busy destroying my building. It feels like my entire future is turning into ashes before my eyes.

"You need to listen to me. I'm not kidding."

"I know you're not kidding, but that doesn't mean I have to listen to you." How could he be so cruel? I thought Greg was kind, but now he looks and sounds like a monster.

His voice drops. "I have reason to believe Darrell is your father. And as you know, he was officially kicked out of the band and paid a sum for that departure over twenty years ago. The language used in the trust only applies to the children of Red, Keith, Mooch, or Cash . . . not Darrell. If you walk away from the settlement, I never have to say anything to anyone, and you and your family can continue on as usual. But if you try to take part of the settlement, I will have to tell them the truth of what I know. There's no way around it. I'm just trying to protect you."

I whip my head around at him, instantly furious that he felt it was okay to reveal something to me that I'm not prepared to discuss. My voice comes out as a growl. "How *dare* you." How could he do that after he touched my body, after we were so intimate? I should have known after I made that phone call to him and he was so cold toward me that deep down inside he was a heartless jerk. He was probably just sleeping with me so he could keep tabs on my thoughts toward the settlement!

He doesn't respond to my ire. I can see his jaw twitching in the light of the fire, but he's holding back. He's not going to say anything in his defense, which only confirms my suspicions that he used me. I'm so angry, I want to slap a response out of him. He's not going to just stand there and ignore me this time.

"You had *no* right to keep that information from me." I wipe away a tear. I'm so mad at my body right now for being weak, for showing him that he's hurt me.

"Maybe not," he says.

"What about my sisters? Are you going to force them to take DNA tests if they want the money?"

"No. I'm not required to do that."

I want to scream with frustration. "I don't get it! You can't prove they're not Darrell's kids without that!"

He sighs. "Listen, I know this is confusing. Let me try to explain it better." He pauses, running his hand through his hair before continuing. "According to the language in the trust, I'm allowed to identify daughters of the band—the band without Darrell on the roster—using simple methods, like I did. I found the almost-twenty-five-year-old daughters of the mothers who were with the band, and I was allowed to assume they were entitled to the funds in the trust. We set it up that way so that this messy stuff with Darrell wouldn't even come into question. No one wanted to cause bad blood between you girls or your moms by getting into the nitty-gritty of your parentage. It was supposed to be simple."

"That worked out *so* well." It's impossible to keep the bitterness from my voice. *Simple, my ass.*

"Yeah. Right. Anyway, the problem arose when Darrell got into the mix. He's how we found you in the first place, but then when he realized his revelations of your existence weren't going to help his situation, and he was going to continue to be cut out of the band's business, he upped the ante and told me what he knew about you."

"That thing you can't share with me." I'm trying so hard not to walk away. I really am, but my feet are getting seriously itchy.

"Exactly. And once I knew that information and saw it with my own eyes, I knew you weren't legally entitled to the trust's funds, and I could no longer just go along and pretend I didn't know it and let you take the money. It would be unethical." He looks angry as he delivers his last line. "In other words, I know too much."

"You know what, Greg? You're a really good lawyer."

"What do you mean by that?" He looks directly at me, but his expression is impossible to read now. I'd like to believe I see regret there, but I'd be fooling myself. His feelings for me were entirely manufactured; he proved that to me tonight.

"You've shown that you'll go to the ends of the earth to do your job. You made that perfectly clear today. I'm sure your clients will be very happy with your performance, so good for you."

"I don't know what you're talking about." His jaw tenses. I've made him mad, and I'm glad for it.

I throw my hands up, gesturing around me. "This whole thing! Pretending to be interested in what I do . . . in my animals. In me! Cleaning out kennels, for God's sake! And sleeping with me? Wow. That was really above and beyond." I laugh bitterly. "Bravo, Greg. You found a way to work a bonus for yourself into the deal. You can check 'sleeping with a hippie chick' off your bucket list. Well done."

He grabs my hand as I try to walk away. "Don't you dare," he says.

I yank my hand away from him. "Don't I dare what? Throw the truth back in your face?"

"No!" he yells. Then he lowers his voice. "No. Don't accuse me of doing those horrible things. I would never do that *to* anyone *for* anyone. Not a client or anyone else."

"Oh, yeah? Then explain yourself. Explain to me how you could know these things about me—about my heritage—and not share them with me . . . and yet go ahead and *sleep* with me? Please. I really want to know." At this point I'm starting to think all men are total shits and I will never understand their gender, even if I had a million years to try.

His voice goes even lower as he steps closer. He's still angry. "I slept with you because I *like* you. I'm attracted to you, and I think I could have a future with you. There's no ulterior motive involved in that *at all.*"

"Yeah, right," I scoff, rolling my eyes. He is so full of crap. He's probably worried I'm going to tell Amber, and then she'll tell the band and he'll get fired. Surely they didn't ask him to sleep with me or to tell me not to take the settlement . . . Red himself asked me to do it just today!

"I didn't want to have to tell you anything about that ridiculous settlement. I was glad when you turned it down. You walking away from it would solve all of our problems."

"All of *our* problems. You mean all of *your* problems."

"These are your problems too, in case you haven't noticed. This whole thing your family has going on is predicated on the idea that you children were fathered by the guys in the band."

"No, it isn't," I say. Red and the rest of the band know that Darrell *could* be my father, yet they've always acted like it doesn't matter. Why is Greg acting like it does? I just don't understand.

"Darrell was kicked out of the band for a reason. He's kind of a dick, and I'm sorry to say that about a man you're related to, but the truth is what it is. He's the reason your mothers left without saying anything to anybody. He was very involved in that whole cover-up. He knew your mothers were pregnant, and he didn't care. Unlike the other band members, he *chose* not to be a father to you, and he was intimately involved in ruining your sisters' chances at a relationship with their fathers. You know there's no love lost between him and Red. You think it won't matter to them that you're Darrell's daughter?"

"No." At the same time I'm declaring this, I'm doubting it. They all either hate him or have no respect for him. He ruined lives, for God's sake.

"How do you think everybody's going to react when they find out?"

"Find out what?" I'm playing dumb as my heart is hammering away painfully in my chest. I don't want to think about this now—or ever, for that matter—but he keeps pushing and I can't seem to walk away.

"That he's your father." Greg actually has the gall to look concerned over the idea.

"They already know!" I yell, the strongest piece of me clinging to the idea that my family would love me no matter what. "He publicly claimed me, as you well know."

Although . . . my mother made it perfectly clear at that same meeting that Darrell was not the only band member she was sleeping with. Did she do this in front of everyone that day because she realized that my family might reject me if they thought I was his daughter?

Sickness fills my gut. I suddenly feel excluded from the group made up of my mothers and sisters again, same as I did when Darrell first made his grand statement. They despise him. What will they think of me if it turns out I'm his daughter? And how does Greg know for sure that I am?

I'm furious at Greg for even bringing this up. I would've been happy to live in ignorance for the rest of my life. "So what do you expect me to do?" I ask. "Walk away, even though you supposedly can't tell me how it is you know that I'm related to him?"

"No, don't be ridiculous." He tries to reach out and take my hand, but I pull away. "Nothing has to change," he continues. "Just keep doing what you've always done."

"What? Pretending like I belong?"

"You *do* belong. You belong in every single way that counts. I just can't let the money go to you if you're not legally entitled to it, and I have information that leads me to believe you're not. I can't just ignore what I know; it's a violation of ethics rules. My mandate from the very beginning was to identify the children of the band members, find them, and make them the offer. I went on this journey assuming they were correct in believing you were related to them, but after I spoke extensively with Darrell and consulted with a doctor who specializes in genetics, I found out differently. I'm just doing my job."

"Always the lawyer, huh?" I hate him at the same time as I respect him. As angry as I am, I know that he's telling the truth. If he's the only one besides Darrell who knows the facts and not just the rumors of my parentage, it wouldn't hurt him to let me take the money. When would anyone ever find out? Darrell's been trying to get at them for years with no luck. Greg could have kept on sleeping with me and getting whatever he wanted. But he didn't. He told me this awful secret about who my father is and risked everything we had going by doing it.

"I am what I am, Rose. I'm not going to apologize for being that person. I've worked my entire adult life for these men, and I have always put their needs first. I'm going to do the right thing by them before I do the right thing by myself or you, because *that is my job*. I can't lie to them by keeping information to myself that's relevant. I have a fiduciary duty to them according to the law, and I have a duty to be loyal."

"Loyalty is the law too?"

"No. That's just me. I'm loyal to people who have taken care of me like they have. Without them, I'm not sure how I could be the guardian that I am to Linny, and that's very important to me."

I'm not going to argue with him about his loyalties. I'd lose the debate because I actually admire that about him. Instead, I switch to another part of his statement. "'If it becomes relevant,' you said to me before. That was an interesting choice of words."

"Exactly. I used them for a reason. If you don't take the settlement, the conversation between the band and me never needs to happen. But if you bring it up, I have to tell them what I know and how I know it."

"Are you trying to blackmail me? Are you telling me that I need to keep my mouth shut or you're going to cause trouble for me?" *The gall of this guy!*

He drops into a squatting position and rests his head in his hands and his elbows on his knees. "No, God, no. Please, don't say that. You make it sound so awful."

I look down at him . . . angry, distant, disgusted, sad, and desperately lonely. "How else am I supposed to say it? According to you, I either need to stop talking about taking the settlement, or you're going to go to the men in the band and tell them I'm not their daughter . . . that I'm the daughter of the one man they can't stand to even look at."

He just shakes his head, not saying anything.

The truck rolls up and the window goes down. Amber sticks her head out. "Are you coming with us?"

"I'll be right there," I say.

I look down at Greg still squatting nearby. "I don't ever want to talk to you again." I walk away, leaving my heart on the ground behind me.

CHAPTER THIRTY-NINE

This is the second time my heart has been broken, only this time it's much worse. In my first big relationship, I was a young girl with stars in her eyes who fell for a guy because she was in love with the idea of love; but with Greg I was a grown woman falling in love with a real man who I admired and respected, who made my body catch fire and my imagination soar. I had such high hopes for our future together, but now that hope is gone and all I have left is regret.

Regret sucks. It sucks big, rotten eggs. And all the work I've been doing cleaning up what used to be my former clinic is not helping to take my mind off it. All I can think of is Greg . . . how he touched me, spoke to me with kindness, laughed with me, cared about my life. I can't believe all of it was a ruse to keep track of my thoughts on that damn settlement. There had to be some truth in there somewhere, but it doesn't matter now. He's gone, and my life has literally been turned into ashes.

A truck pulls up behind me, so I stop, standing and wiping the sweat off my forehead. It's freezing cold outside, but I'm not feeling it. I've been working for hours, trying to break my back and forget the fact that I feel like I'm dying inside.

Smitty gets out of his truck and comes sauntering over, carrying a thermos. "You look like you could use a cup of coffee," he says.

I go over and stand in front of him, pulling my gloves out of my coat pocket and sliding them on to my hands. "Sounds like a good idea to me." I sure wish he had some whiskey to add to it. About a pint would do me just fine.

He pours me a cup and hands it to me. "What are you doing out here?"

"Just trying to clean up a little bit."

"You should use a bulldozer to do this cleanup." He looks sad as he surveys the damage.

"Probably. But I need to do something to keep my mind busy, so I'm using these." I raise my hand and wiggle my fingers.

"What's going on with all your patients?"

"They've all been farmed out to different clinics. I don't have any left." I can't believe how sad this makes me. It's been years since I've been able to say there are no animals in my care. My chin trembles, and I turn away so Smitty won't see it.

He comes closer and wraps his arm around my shoulders. "It's going to be okay. You'll see."

"There's no fixing this, Smitty. It's over."

"Please don't say that."

He sounds way more upset than it seems like he should be, and I don't think it's because he wants to date me. "What's going on, Smitty?"

He uses his free arm to wipe his face with his jacket, scrubbing at his forehead. It knocks his hat off-kilter, and it takes him a second to fix it. "Nothing. I'm just worried about you." He's staring at the building with such intensity it's almost freaky. He's taking this almost as hard as I am.

"I'm managing . . . one day at a time. I haven't decided anything yet about where I'll go from here."

He nods silently, staring off into the distance. I get the sense that his mind is far away.

I jab him in the ribs. "What have you been up to?" I need to move the subject away from my sadness so I don't start bawling and force Smitty to awkwardly comfort me.

"Oh, nothing." He looks down at me and smiles sadly. "Just trying to corral my brother. The never-ending task."

"Really? I figured Brian would be busy with school." Smitty's brother has been a hell-raiser from the word *go* . . . a born troublemaker and the exact opposite of Smitty. He's ten years younger than his older brother, so he's still in high school. Because their parents have huge problems of their own, the boys have been left to their own devices, with Smitty overseeing his younger brother as much as he can while working here on the farm and at other places in town. We never see Brian at Glenhollow because he considers us lame and goofy, or so Smitty confessed to us years ago. Brian thinks smoking and sleeping around are better ways to spend his time.

"I'm having trouble with him." Smitty rolls his eyes and hisses out a sigh of annoyance. "He's getting messed up in drugs now. I swear, I feel like it's an uphill battle with him that I'm never gonna win."

"I don't understand why it's on your shoulders to take care of everything. Why aren't your parents involved?" I don't know a lot about them, other than the fact that they never supervised Smitty and are gone most of the time. He spent more time at our house than he did at his own growing up.

"My parents . . . Don't even get me started on them."

"I'm sorry you're having to deal with all that. You don't deserve it." I look up at him to assure him with a smile, but his expression isn't what I expect to see after giving him my support; he looks furious. My attempt at good humor falls away. He's kind of worrying me.

He moves away and goes over to the stack of wood I was just working on. "Maybe I can give you a hand over here." He starts moving pieces around, taking the heavier ones I couldn't manage and putting them on top.

I sip more of my coffee, watching him work. He's always helped with chores around our place in exchange for meals or money, even as a kid. On one hand, he's the same old Smitty . . . pitching in and lending a hand; but on the other, not really. I thought I knew him pretty well, but he's been acting so strange lately. "I think it's another one of those never-ending tasks," I say, hoping the small talk will help ease us past this uncomfortable moment. "I don't know why I'm even bothering."

"It gives you something to do. Helps keep your mind away from things it shouldn't be on. I get it." He strips off his jacket and tosses it onto a nearby bush. After throwing around some more wood, he stops to roll up his sleeves.

Something on his arm catches my eye. *What the heck . . . ?* I put the coffee cup on the hood of his truck and go over to help him with the stacking. I pretend to be interested in the task, but I'm more focused on his injury than anything else.

"What did you say happened to your arm again?" I ask casually.

Smitty looks up at me. "What'd you say?"

I point. "Your arm."

He looks down and quickly shoves his sleeve over it. "Oh. That? Cut myself. Working on my car."

He moves more wood as I stand up, searching my memory for an earlier conversation. "I thought you said you cut your arm gardening."

His smile falters. "Oh, yeah. It was gardening. Caught it with the clippers."

I reach down and grab for the same piece of wood that he's reaching for. We both stand up with it in our hands. We're face-to-face and he looks nervous as hell. Something is definitely not adding up here. "How did you cut your arm with a pair of two-handed clippers?"

He tries to smile, but it comes off as awkward. "They slipped. Slipped and cut me. No big deal." His face is beet red.

I drop the wood and grab his wrist, shoving his sleeve up to his elbow. I have time to examine the fresh, pink scar before he yanks his arm away. He steps back two paces, staring at me. "What's wrong with you?"

I feel so sick to my stomach I'm ready to vomit. I've seen wounds like that before, many times. Hell, I've got scars from one myself. My voice comes out shaking. "Smitty, that is *not* an injury from clippers or from fixing your car, is it?" I glare at him, growing angrier by the second.

"Yes, it is." He's clearly nervous, trying to move away, but I'm not letting him. For every step he takes backward, I take one forward.

"Tell me the truth." I move closer to him, anger fueling my movements.

"Listen, I know you're upset about what happened with the barn, but I don't think you should be taking it out on me." He looks left and right, seeking an escape.

I pull the phone my sisters and I bought when Amber went to New York out of my back pocket and start dialing. Thank goodness I thought to shove it in there when I left the house. "I'm calling the police. I know very well you didn't hurt yourself on your car or while you were gardening. That is a *dog bite* on your arm." And there's only one reason why he'd lie about that . . . it's a bite from *my* dog. Now Banana's behavior toward him makes all the sense in the world. I'm so furious, I can't cry. I can't even think straight. *He stole my computer! He ran over Banana! He burned down my business and almost killed my patients!*

Smitty grabs the phone out of my hand and holds it above his head.

I stand there frozen in place and stare up at him in shock. A man I've known almost my entire life as the cool guy who lives up the road has revealed his true self to me today—he's a monster. My heart feels like it's collapsing in on itself, and my face crumples into tears. "Oh, Smitty. How *could* you?"

He holds the phone out at me like a stop sign. "No, no, no! Rose, it's *not* what you're thinking."

279

I'm full-on bawling now. I can't help it. All the sadness and depression that I was feeling over Greg and the animals comes right to the forefront, and I lose it. I start keening with the pain. My whole world is falling apart around me, figuratively and literally.

"Please don't cry. It's really not what you think, I swear to God."

"What else could it be?" I scream at him. "*You* did this!" My arm sweeps out to include the burned-out husk of my career.

His eyes bug out. "I didn't! Rose, I swear to God *I didn't.*"

"Give me back my phone." I hold my hand out. My fingers are trembling. I've never been afraid of Smitty before, but I am now. I cannot let him know that, though, or he'll use it against me. Who knows what he's capable of? If he'll burn down a barn full of innocent animals, the sky is probably the limit . . . and we're out here on an empty road that no one has any reason to be traveling right now. I need to get my phone back.

"I don't want you to call the police," he says.

"Too bad. You broke the law. You destroyed *everything* that means anything to me." I should probably shine him on, tell him this can stay between us, but he knows me too well for that to work. No way am I going to let this slide. I can't even fake that I could.

His face scrunches up as he moves into begging mode. "I swear I didn't break any laws. Not really. Just hear me out. I'll tell you the truth. Honestly, I'll tell you everything."

Greg's words come back to me. *Everything is negotiable.* I work to calm my voice. "Give me back my phone, and I will give you two minutes to explain yourself."

"You promise?" He starts to move the phone toward my hand.

"I promise." I'm not telling the whole truth. If he says anything weird or comes at me, I'm hitting 9-1-1 and letting the chips fall where they may. I'll go down fighting, that's for sure.

"I'm trusting you. And I want you to trust me because you've known me your whole life and you know I'm not a bad guy."

I speak through gritted teeth. "Give me . . . my freaking . . . phone."

He hands it over and then seems to cave in on himself. He loses inches off his height and his chin drops to his chest. "Everything got so screwed up. It got so out of control. I didn't mean for it to get so bad." He stops and looks up at me, the most pitiful expression I've ever seen on his face.

"I'm listening. But the first thing you have to do is admit that *that* is a dog bite on your arm. If you try to lie to me again, I'm out of here."

He nods. "It's a dog bite. Banana did it."

I take several steps away, stricken. It's one thing to think I know and another to have it confirmed. "You hit Banana with your car?"

He looks up suddenly. "No! I did *not* do that." He puts his hands out and places them in prayer position. "Please, just *listen* to me . . . let me *explain*."

I hold my phone up at him so he can see it. "I am dialing 9-1-1, but I'm not going to hit the Send button right now; I'm going to let you talk . . . But if you say *anything* I don't like, I'm hitting the Send button, and the cops are going to come."

He nods rapidly. "That's fair. That's totally fair. I'm cool with that."

I point. "Go stand over there. You're too close."

Tears rush to his eyes. "You don't trust me? You think I'd actually hurt you?"

"No, I don't trust you. You hurt my dog."

He takes several steps back. "I did not hurt your dog. Let me explain."

"Go ahead." I dial the three numbers that could send this family friend to jail for a really long time and let my finger hover over the Send button. "You have two minutes."

CHAPTER FORTY

S mitty takes a big breath and begins his explanation. "I told you I was having a problem with Brian. It's true. I'm having a *lot* of trouble with him. I have been for a while. I don't tell you guys about what goes on at my house because it's so ugly. Whenever I come here, everything is so great, and I just want it to stay that way." He looks up the road toward the house. "I guess you could say this is my safe place."

"That doesn't explain anything." What he's saying is twanging my heartstrings, and it's probably true, but I don't care. It doesn't make hurting my dog or destroying my work-life okay. I've heard plenty of rumors in town about his deadbeat parents and his delinquent brother, and I've certainly seen things with my own eyes over the years with his brother acting out and causing Smitty strife, but it doesn't explain to me how my dog ended up with a broken leg and my building ended up burned to the ground.

"When Em got into that relationship with her new boyfriend, I gave up on the idea of going out with her. And then there was you . . ." He says it like I just appeared out of nowhere once Sam came on the scene. "I've always admired you, and you're beautiful and funny and kind . . . and the more I thought about it, the more I thought I'd like to see if there was something between us that's mutual . . . that maybe you might want to go out with me. I said something about it at home to my mother, and my brother overheard it."

Smitty's voice and expression go dark. "He got this asinine idea to come out here and mess with you, because he was pissed at me for telling our parents something he'd done that got him in trouble. He's the one who stole your laptop."

"Why would he do that?" It certainly explains why Smitty bought me a new one; I guess he felt guilty.

"Because. He's a punk. He's got a drug problem. He's got a bone to pick with me for being a goody-two-shoes—that's what he calls me."

"But he doesn't even know me."

Smitty looks ashamed. "He asked me some questions about your clinic, acting like he was interested in you and what you do, but all he was doing was fishing for information. When you told me that your laptop had been stolen, I had a feeling it was him, and then I found it in his room."

I cannot believe I was robbed by a neighbor. Smitty's brother, no less! "I'm sorry, but your brother is a little shit." And when I get my hands on him, he's going to be one sorry little shit, too.

Smitty looks so sad. "He's a good kid, but he hooked up with the wrong people and got in with a bad crowd. I feel responsible for him, so when he did what he did, I tried to fix it."

"But he stole it from *me*, Smitty. We're practically family. Buying me a replacement computer doesn't undo what he did, nor does it undo the fact that you kept that information from me."

"I know. But your family is so much better off than mine is. You guys all love each other and now you've got Red Hot here probably pouring money all over you. My brother and I have nothing but our freedom. If he goes to jail, he could end up in there for the rest of his life, and he's just a kid."

I'm not totally immune to what Smitty is saying, so I'm going to let him continue beyond his two minutes. My finger is still hovering over the green button of my telephone, though.

"I yelled at him for stealing your laptop, and I took it away from him. I still have it, so don't worry. But I couldn't give it back to you without telling you about Brian, and I felt terrible that you weren't able to run your business without it, so I bought you a new one."

"That doesn't make this okay, Smitty." I look over at the burned building, and he follows my gaze.

"I had no idea he would go this far."

My heart lurches. "It was your brother who did this?"

"I don't know. Maybe." He looks at the ground. "I know he's the one who spray-painted your door. I saw the color from the paint can on his hands. I asked him directly if he did it, and he admitted it. He was really proud of himself. I almost decked him, I swear to God."

Now my heart is burning with rage. That little shit, Brian. If I could get my hands on him right now, I'd wring his stupid neck. "Maybe you should've."

He nods sadly. "You're right. Maybe I should've. But I'm not a violent person."

He takes a step toward me, but I move back and hold up the phone. "Stay right where you are."

He puts his hand on his chest. "You still think I'm a bad guy, don't you?"

"You were bitten by Banana the night he got hurt. That means you were here when my laptop was stolen. Explain that to me."

"One of Brian's old friends told me where he was going, worried he was going to make trouble. He still has one or two buddies who haven't totally deserted him. So I drove out here to stop him, but I was too late. I caught up with him at the main road, and I knew he'd done something he shouldn't have, but I didn't want him to get caught. I figured I'd make it right with you all later if he'd done something bad here. I was wrestling him into my car when Banana came out of nowhere and attacked me. So I just shoved my brother and his backpack into the truck and drove away. But I swear to God, Banana was totally fine when I left."

I feel so sick. "And you expect me to believe you." My ears are hot, but the rest of me is chilled to the bone.

Smitty's eyes are filled with tears. "Please, you *have* to believe me. I would never in a million years hurt one of your animals. I know how much they mean to you. I care about you, Rose. I care about your entire family. You guys have been a second family to me. I consider your moms *my* moms too. They've done everything for me."

I throw my hands up. "We *have* been like family to you, which is why I don't understand how any of this could have happened!"

"I can't explain it in a way that makes sense, I'm sorry. All I can tell you is my brother is a messed-up kid, and I'm trying to help him, but I'm failing. And you guys got dragged into it because he knows I care about you. He's angry and jealous. He doesn't have another family in his life like I do. I'm all he's got, and apparently I'm not good enough, and he knows I'd rather spend my time out here with you guys than with my own family."

Smitty is breaking my heart down into little pieces. I can only guess how sad and lonely his home life has been, but I still don't have the whole story from him, so he's not off the hook with me by a long shot. "I don't understand how Banana ended up on the side of the road."

"When I drove away, I looked in my rearview mirror and he was running behind my truck. I didn't stop, though, I kept on going, and there's no way he could've caught up to me. I was going, like, sixty miles an hour, and I left him way behind me in the dust."

"So your story is—somebody else on the road hit him."

"It has to be that, because it wasn't me. I will swear on my life, on my brother's life, my parents' life, on the Bible . . . I will swear on anything you want me to. It wasn't me. If I'd hit Banana, I would've stopped and I would've come and confessed everything at the time."

"But you found out later that Banana got hit by a car. Why didn't you confess then?"

"I don't know." He sounds tortured. "I want to say it's because I knew I wasn't the one who hit him, but I know my brother is the reason Banana was out on the road that night. If Brian hadn't come and done that to you, and if I hadn't come after him, Banana would've never been out there. So it *is* my fault. I should've told you sooner."

I don't know whether to rage at him or cry over how cruel the universe can be sometimes. "If you had told me sooner, maybe my clinic would still be standing."

He nods. "It probably *would* still be standing, because there's nobody else in the world who'd want to hurt you besides Brian. And the only reason *he* wanted to hurt you was because I cared about you so much. I do think he did it . . . lit the fire . . . but he's been denying it." Smitty's voice drops to a near-whisper. "I found the clothes he was wearing that night; they smell like smoke and diesel fuel. I hid them, in case you need them for evidence."

This is such a horrible situation, I really don't know how to handle it. Nothing in my life has prepared me for this level of sadness, betrayal, pity, and disillusionment. I want to hate Smitty for being a part of it and for allowing some of it to happen, but I can't. He's just a sad guy who's trying to do the right thing and who wants to be loved like everybody else. He's been dealt a hand that would have been impossible for many to manage. At least no one was hurt in the fire. I have no more emotion left in me except sadness. There's no room for forgiveness right now, but maybe in the future there will be. I just can't say at the moment.

"Smitty, you need to go." I clear the number off my phone and slide it into my back pocket.

He nods, tears running down his cheeks. "I am so sorry. I am so, so sorry."

"I understand. Please go."

He shuffles away, grabbing his jacket and the coffee cup from the hood of his car, throwing them into the truck. He leaves, not speeding away like I expect him to, but driving slowly and carefully over the road. His truck disappears in the distance, and I wonder if I'll ever see him again. I'm not sure whether I care. I look over at the burned remnants of my building and imagine that it matches what I feel like inside. I have been burned to the ground. There's nothing left for me here and nothing left to hope for. I lower myself to the earth and cry.

CHAPTER FORTY-ONE

Some experts say that crying is great therapy. I say it's a great way to wear a person down to the point where she doesn't even want to breathe anymore. After I cry for a full hour on the ground in front of my burned-down clinic, I find my way home and into my bed. I crawl under the covers fully dressed and pull the quilt up to my head, promptly falling asleep.

I wake up sometime in the middle of the night. I don't bother looking at my clock, but it's dark out; it could be early morning or late at night. I use the bathroom, shuffle down to the kitchen, and take a piece of bread out of the cupboard. After I'm in my room again, I take two bites of it and put the rest on my bedside table before I strip down and go back to sleep. My breath is stale and rank, my eyes are swollen from crying, and my body could use a shower, but I don't care. All I want to do is make the days go by faster, and the best way to do that is to sleep, sleep, sleep . . .

I don't know how much more time passes before somebody wakes me. The covers are pulled off my face and a bright light hits me, pressing against my eyeballs. I pry one eyelid open and look at the face before me.

"Hey, there, sleepyhead. It's time for you to get up and stop feeling sorry for yourself." It's Amber, of course, and she has a very annoying smile on her face.

I pull the covers back over my face, partially to block the sun and partially to shield my well-intentioned sister from my toxic dragon breath. "Go away."

"Nice try, but I'm not going anywhere." She yanks the covers back even farther this time.

Cold air hits, and makes me cringe. I curl up in a ball and slap a pillow over my head. "I'm not in the mood, Amber."

"What's wrong with you? I know your building burned to the ground and your boyfriend's not here, but there's got to be something else going on with you. The Rose I know wouldn't let these things get her down. Not for this long, anyway."

"Go *away*," I say more forcefully, grinding out the words through gritted teeth. I'm so close to reaching out and slapping her.

Wonder of wonders, Amber actually listens. I hear her footfalls going from my bed to the door, and I'm left alone to wallow in my sadness. I put the covers back where they belong and sigh long and hard. Then I have to move the covers away so I can actually breathe because—damn—my breath is something else.

Just as I start to fall back to sleep, Amber returns. My quilt disappears, and the pillow I was using to shield my eyes is whipped off my head.

"Hey! What the hell?" I open my eyes to find not just Amber but Emerald standing there in front of me.

I snort in disgust and close my eyes, pulling another pillow over my face. "No way. This is not happening. Go away."

"You see?" Amber says. "I told you; it's serious."

"Rose, honey, what's going on?" Emerald asks. It's her kind and sensitive tone that gets to me. The tears start coming again, and I know they're not going to stop anytime soon.

The bed dips down as my sisters climb in next to me. They fight and argue over who gets to be next to me, and then Amber is at the side of my bed again, nudging me. "Move over. You have to be in the middle."

I refuse to listen, but does that stop them? No, of course not. The two of them drag and push me until they get what they want. I am now the baloney in a sister sandwich.

Amber and Em put their arms around me and hold me close. Somebody smells like garlic. "Ugh. You guys stink."

"I just had some toast, leave me alone," Emerald says. I can tell from her tone she's pouting.

"She might be talking about the garlic croutons I had in my salad," Amber says.

"I'm talking about both of you. You both smell. Get away from me."

My sisters quiet down and snuggle in. I start to get very warm. Too warm. I'm still crying, and I really wish they'd leave me alone. Their love is suffocating me.

"Did I mention that I went online and looked at veterinary colleges?" Amber asks.

"You did mention that," Emerald says. "That's very exciting. What did you find?"

"Shut up!" I yell. I don't want to hear this. Not now and not ever. My dreams are ashes, and there will be no phoenix rising up from them.

Amber continues. "Did you know there's a veterinary college in New York City?"

It feels like my sister just stabbed me in the heart with a knife. I can't even speak I'm so upset. What does she hope to accomplish with this?

"You don't say?" Emerald exclaims. "Is it expensive?"

"I'm sure it is, but that's not really a problem, is it?" I can hear Amber's smile in her voice.

"No, not at all. Because I'm looking for ways to invest my money in something worthwhile, and I think sending one of the most talented animal people I know to school is *very* worthwhile." Em sounds very proud of herself.

I shove the pillow off my face and glare at each of them in turn. "Both of you need to shut up and get out of my room *right* now."

Amber smiles at me and pats me on the cheek. "Not gonna happen, sweetie. We don't do the pity party thing here."

I look over at Em, the only one I have a chance of intimidating. "Get out."

"I'm with her." She points at Amber and gives me a shy smile.

I close my eyes and breathe through my nose, slowly and calmly. I need to get control of my emotions, because I really feel like slapping somebody right now, and I have two very deserving candidates in close range.

"Today's the first day of the rest of your life," Amber says. "What are you gonna do with it?"

"I'm going to stay in bed. I'm going to stay in bed today and tomorrow and the next day. I'm going to stay here until I die." I try to pull the quilt over my head, but my sisters' big, stupid bodies are lying on top of my covers and won't let me. I sigh in frustration.

"I know you're really sad and you're really angry," Emerald says. "We are too. But it's time to pick up the pieces and move on."

I glare at her, ready to let her have it . . . ready to tell her that the boy we grew up with is the reason my building burned down, but I stop myself. I can't do it. Not only will Smitty's brother go to jail, because I know my sisters will tell the cops, Smitty would no longer be welcome in our home, and I know what this place means to him. It means the same thing to him that it means to me, and I'd die if my family rejected me.

"What is it that's making you so sad?" Em asks. "Is it the clinic?"

"Or is it Greg?" Amber adds. "He took off yesterday really upset. I know you said something to him."

"It's over between us," I say. I stare up at the ceiling as the tears fall out of my eyes and drip down to my ears.

"It's over? What do you mean?" Em asks. "You just got started."

"It's over." I shrug. "I don't know what else you want me to say."

"What happened? Just tell us," Amber prompts, nudging me.

"I'd rather not. I'd rather just leave it alone."

"I guess there's only one thing for me to do," Amber says, sighing. I look at her. "Don't talk to Greg."

"You're not leaving me with much of a choice if you won't talk to me."

I can picture her doing exactly what she's threatening, and it makes me instantly furious. "You don't need to know every detail of my life!" I yell at her.

"Since when?!" she yells back.

Since I found out I'm probably not your biological sister. Surely if I were, Darrell would have spoken up about it and Greg would have cut her out of the irrevocable trust too. And knowing now what I do about our parentage, it changes things. I don't know why, but it does. Of course I don't say this out loud. But I feel it. My heart is breaking all over again, and I thought the damn thing was already completely broken. How many times can a heart break before it's totally shattered?

Amber stares at me, her eyes narrowed. "There is something really big going on here, and if you don't tell me what it is, I am going to pull everything in this house apart until I figure it out . . . and then you're going to be in really big trouble for making me go to all that effort."

Her energy and willfulness exhaust me. "Don't threaten me. It's not going to work." She'll never find out, because I know Greg won't tell her anything and neither will Smitty, but I still don't want her digging. I just want her to let it go so the hurt can scar over.

"Oh, yes, it is going to work. I am *very* scary when I want to be."

Her offense at my statement almost makes me laugh. She actually enjoys being a tyrant. And I always thought it was just a personality quirk.

I sigh in defeat. "Can't you see I'm tired and want to be left alone?"

Amber puts both hands on my cheeks and touches noses with me. All I can see now is one giant eye in the middle of her forehead. "I look at you and I see sad and brokenhearted. I see exhausted. I see years of working eighty-hour weeks finally catching up with you. And I see one other thing that really, *really* scares me."

"What's that?" I ask, trying to inhale around her garlic breath.

"I see defeat. Your giving up is scaring the shit out of me."

I turn away and face Emerald. "Would you please tell Amber that I'm fine? I'm not going to kill myself. I just need a break."

She looks sad as she shakes her head. "I see it too. Please talk to us."

I sit straight up and punch the covers next to me. "Jesus, you guys are *suffocating* me."

"Suffocation . . . love . . . Is there really a difference?" Amber asks, her voice sounding dreamy.

"Not when you're involved," Em says, giggling.

Amber loses her dreamy tone. "Hey, watch it, lady."

Their easy teasing brings back memories. I love my sisters so much. More than anything. More than the clinic and my patients, more than Smitty, more than this house and farm. We couldn't be closer if we were triplets. I don't care if any of us share a father. We've grown up together since birth, and our moms are always going to be best friends. Most people will never find the closeness I share with these women.

Despite my recent losses, it's a relief to know that there are some things in my life that will never change, no matter what. What my sisters are doing right now is really annoying, but I know it's coming from a place of love, and I really could use some of that right now. I put my face in my hands and take a few deep breaths, trying to calm myself. I need to talk to my sisters. I can't carry this burden alone anymore. "So much shit has happened, I don't know where to start."

"Why don't you start at the beginning," Amber suggests.

"How do I know which part is the beginning?" It's all jumbled in my head—Greg, the barn, Smitty, my laptop, the settlement . . . They're all part of the same confusing web of lies and deceit.

"How about if you start with the thing that's hurting the most?" Emerald says gently. "And then we can work backward from there."

I nod and turn around so I can face my sisters, adjusting myself on the bed so I'm comfortable. "I hope you guys have a couple hours, because this is going to take a while."

Em and Amber sit up and put their backs against the headboard. "We've got all day," Amber says.

Em nods. "All day long and all night too, if necessary."

I nod and reach for their hands. Leaning together, we make a circle, filled with love. "How about if I start by telling you who my father is."

CHAPTER FORTY-TWO

It is such a relief to get all that off my chest. And now I feel like I'm full of helium as I watch my two sisters pace across my bedroom floor, working themselves up into a lather.

"How dare he. How *dare* he say that to you!" Amber is shaking her fist at the ceiling. "I'm going to get you, Greg Lister. You are going to be *so* sorry you opened your big, fat mouth! And you're also going to tell me how you know this stuff about my sister, too!" She mutters something and then speaks up again. "Genetic specialist? Really? What in the hell does that even mean?"

"Don't be mad at him. He was just doing his job." Telling my sisters the story did help put a few things into perspective. It reminded me that I admire a lot of things about Greg, like how much integrity he has, how good a lawyer he is, and how he dedicates himself to his one client. The problem came up for us when there was a conflict between me and that client. Of course he picked his client over me; it's his job. It's what keeps food on the table and a roof over his and Linny's heads. He took an oath to be an ethical person, and that's what he's being. It's not like he's in love with me; we just started our relationship. To expect him to put us over them would be unfair and unreasonable.

The problem for me, however, is that he knew about the conflict all along. He should've told me as soon as we started contemplating being intimate and let me decide if I wanted to go forward or not. I'm still mad at him about that. He ruined what could have been a really great thing by being too much of a lawyer. I wish it didn't hurt so much.

"I don't know what makes me more upset," Em says. "The stuff that Greg said or the thing that Smitty did."

I look at her in a panic. "Please, you promised; you can't tell *anyone*. You can't tell anyone outside this bedroom ever."

"I know." She frowns at me. "I'm not going to say anything to anyone. But still . . . I told you there was something wrong with him."

"You never actually told us what it was that made you think that about him," Amber says. "Since we're telling stories here, maybe it'd be a good time for you to confess."

Em's eyes go wide. "No, that's okay. Some secrets are better left unsaid."

I shake my head at her. "Shame on you . . . after giving me such a guilt trip."

She sags, dropping her shoulders forward and hanging her head. "Please don't make me tell you."

"Don't even try it," Amber says. "Straighten up and 'fess up, or I'm going to come over there and put you in a headlock."

She looks up and sticks her tongue out at Amber. "Fine. You really want to know? I'll tell you. He wanted to sixty-nine me."

I burst out laughing. "What?" That is not at all what I was expecting to hear.

Amber rolls her eyes. "Oh my god, you are such a prude."

"I am *not* a prude. I do all kinds of crazy things in the bedroom; you can ask Sam."

"No, thank you," I say, still giggling. "Like you said, some secrets should be left unsaid."

She puts her hands on her hips. "You don't ask a girl to do sixty-nine with you when you're sleeping with her for the first time. Sixty-nining is for more *mature* relationships."

"If you say so," I tease. I love my sister so much. She's especially cute when her hair is sticking out all over the place like it is right now. We've totally got her flustered.

"Speak for yourself," Amber says, wiggling her eyebrows.

"Are you saying you'd sixty-nine on the first date?" Emerald demands.

"I think you could if you really wanted to." She looks over at me. "What do you think?"

"I think that I do not need to picture my sister and Smitty doing *that* together, if that's okay with you."

Amber gets a disgusted look on her face. "Yeah. You have a point there." She pats Em on the shoulder. "I get it. I understand why there was no second date."

Em folds her arms over her chest. "Thank you. Thank you for backing me up. *Finally.*"

We all start giggling, and eventually Em lets go of her defensive stance. "What are we going to do with this mess?"

Amber holds up her hand before I can respond. "I have all the answers if you want to hear them."

I sit on the bed cross-legged. "By all means. Write the script; I'll just follow it." For once I'm glad my sister is so bossy. I really have no idea how to handle any of this, and I would love for her to just tell me what to do so I don't have to think anymore.

"First of all, we are *not* going to tell anybody about Smitty. I do think we should tattle on his brother, though, because he's a little shit and he deserves to go to jail."

"Maybe we can talk to Smitty about getting his brother some help," Em says. "Something a little less drastic that might keep them out of trouble."

Amber waves her hand. "Fine. We can try that first." She looks at me. "And as far as the daddy issue goes, I say we talk to the band. Let's see what they want to do. If they want to do DNA tests, fine. We'll do them. I don't care at this point, but I'd rather know for sure than go off some genetic specialist's theory."

"Me too," Em says. She looks at me. "And any settlement that I get is half yours anyway."

"Mine too," Amber says. "I'm sharing it." She looks over at Em. "Let's just put it in one big pool and we'll divide it by three."

I shake my head, overwhelmed by their generosity. "You guys can't do that."

"Like hell we can't. It's our money." Amber frowns at me. "Don't be a mule. You know that you'd do the same thing for us."

She's right about that. I shrug. "I would."

"Good. That's resolved. And finally, here's how we're going to deal with Greg," Amber says, rubbing her hands together. "First, I'm going to put itching powder in his underwear . . ."

"Are we getting our revenge schemes from *Mad* magazine now?" Em asks.

"Shush, I was just getting started . . ."

I raise my hands to stop both of them. "Can you just leave the Greg thing to me? I think that would be a better idea."

Amber looks at me with her eyebrows raised. "Are you going to make him pay for what he did? Because if you're not, I'm going to have to take over."

"I'm going to handle things in a diplomatic and responsible way so that there aren't any hard feelings between him and the band. He does a good job for them, and I know you respect him; I don't want to cause problems with any of that."

Amber thinks it over for a few seconds and nods. "I could live with that. And if some itching powder happens to make its way into his underwear after, well, that's how life goes sometimes."

I have to laugh at her persistence and loyalty. I wouldn't change Amber or Emerald for the world. They are my world.

Em holds her arms out. "How about a hug?"

298

Amber and I move into her embrace without stopping and our heads accidentally clunk together. We giggle as we rub our foreheads.

"Thank you for pulling me out of my funk," I say, exhausted but relieved.

"That's what sisters are for," says Em.

"Yeah. And I really miss seeing your face at the table," Amber says.

"Speaking of dinner, I'm kinda starving," I say. My appetite comes back with a vengeance as I imagine the dining room table and all my family sitting around it.

"I think dinner is going to be on the table in about an hour," Amber says, pulling away to look at her watch.

It gives me just enough time to call Greg at his office. I step back from my sisters and look around the room. "I need to hop in the shower and get dressed. See you guys down there?"

They make their way to the door. Em goes out first and Amber follows. She stops just before she shuts the door and looks straight at me. "Don't put up with any of his shit," she says.

"Whose shit?"

"Greg's. I know you're going to call him as soon as I close this door. Don't let him get away with anything. He's a good guy, but sometimes he puts his head super far up his ass, and you have to pull it out for him." She shrugs. "Head-from-ass-removal is part of my official job description, so I should know."

"Thanks for the tip." I grin at her silliness.

She winks at me. "Anytime."

When she's gone, I move over to the telephone extension in my room and pick it up. I don't know his number, but I can certainly find it by calling directory assistance. My heart starts beating wildly and I feel sick to my stomach. I hope I'm doing the right thing.

CHAPTER FORTY-THREE

The phone rings several times before it's picked up at his extension. "This is Greg Lister."

All I can do is breathe. I can't talk and I can't hang up. Just hearing his voice stuns me.

"This is Lister."

I can't talk! What's wrong with me? I'm the creepy stalker. I'm just like Smitty's brother. I know it was him on the line all those times.

"Rose?"

Hearing my name breaks me out of my trance. "Yes. It's me."

His voice softens. "How are you?"

"I've been better." It feels good to admit it, but at the same time, it's scary. My admission that I'm not Superwoman with a heart of steel makes me vulnerable.

"I can imagine."

The conversation dies. I don't know what to say. If I were Amber, I'd start yelling at him, but I'm not her.

"How is your family?" he asks.

"They're fine."

This could not be any more awkward than it is. I don't know why I called him. I should've just let sleeping dogs lie. *It's over, it's over, it's over.* I just need to keep drumming that into my head until I believe and accept it.

"I'm sorry, Rose. I'm really sorry."

I start to cry silently. This is the official end of the relationship, and he's apologizing. Where were his regrets weeks ago? Why couldn't he have told me the truth back then? "It's okay. Shit happens, right?"

"I don't know." He sounds sad. "It doesn't have to happen, does it?"

"What do you mean?"

His voice turns angry. "I didn't have to say anything. I could've just kept my damn mouth shut and let things play out."

I can't tell who he's angry at—himself, the band, Darrell, or me. "About what? About me? Darrell?"

"Yes, about Darrell. I could have just let things play out with him. I should have."

"No, you shouldn't have." The reality sinks in. He's telling me he had a choice, but I know he didn't. I'm seeing as clearly now as he was the night he told me. "You did the right thing."

"No, I didn't. I hurt you. I hurt you very badly."

"You did, but not for the reasons you think."

"What do you mean?"

"You think you hurt me because you told me something I didn't want to hear: that I wasn't going to get a settlement."

"That, yes, but also because I told you who your father is, which was something you wanted to find out on your own terms. You didn't want some asshole blurting it out in the middle of what was already a horrible moment for you."

I like that he's calling himself an asshole now. It makes it easier to have the rest of the conversation, because we at least agree on one point. "That wasn't so great either, you're right, but that's not what hurts me now." As I'm explaining this to him, I'm finally understanding it for myself.

"I think I know what you're saying." He's back to being sad again.

"Why don't you tell me what it is, then, if you know." Maybe his explanation will help clarify it for me.

"The first time I met you, you talked about how honesty was important to you. You said I needed to be honest about everything."

"That's true."

"And I wasn't being honest with you. There were things that I wasn't telling you. Things that were relevant to different conversations we had. I kept those things to myself rather than sharing them with you."

"Yes, you did." My heart feels like it has a cramp in it.

"I've been a lawyer for a long time now, and I've never had a problem with my morals or my ethics. The direction I should take when a conflict arises has always been very clear and straightforward for me. I don't share my clients' secrets, and I don't give out information where it's not needed. I have this very strict line that I follow all the time."

"I understand."

"I don't think you do. My interactions with you never fit the program."

"What you mean?"

"There was no bright line with you. Not for me, anyway. There were things I felt you should know, but I knew I couldn't tell you or I shouldn't tell you what they were. And then I did. I feel terrible about it. I've never felt even the slightest twinge of regret about any decision I've made in my career, outside of this one." He sighs loudly, and I can picture him running his hands through his hair. "Things are the way they are, and me being a lawyer isn't going to change that, but I didn't want to be the one delivering *that* news to you. I didn't want to be the one bringing you pain. The other night, the last night we were together, was the worst day of my career. Maybe of my whole life. I didn't want to be a lawyer in that moment."

"But you were."

"Yes, I was. And it almost makes me wish I had never had Red Hot as a client. Then I could've avoided doing that to you."

"But then you would've had a completely different career. You would have missed out on all the fun of working with them."

"Fun?" He laughs bitterly. "I don't know if I'd characterize my work with them as fun, but I understand what you're saying." There's a long silence before he speaks again. "What are you going to do?"

"About what?"

"About the settlement."

I let out a long, frustrated sigh. "I can't believe you're asking me about that again."

"I'm sorry. I'm not asking you as a lawyer now; I'm asking you as a guy who cares about you."

"I don't know. I really don't know."

"Do you want some advice?"

"From you?"

"Yes."

"Legal advice?"

"No. I can't give you legal advice, but I can give you advice from a friend."

"Is that what we are now? Friends?"

"I'd love to have more than that with you, but I can't imagine that you do."

I start to answer, but then I don't. The angry words that leap to mind won't come out of my mouth. He said something that was painful to hear, but was he being heartless? Was he being cruel? No. He may have been careless, but he was also doing his job. He was stuck in the middle and he tried to minimize the damage to my family. How can I hate him for that?

"I miss you," I say, risking the words and the heartache that goes with them.

"I miss you too. A lot. I had such a great time with you and such high hopes for a potential future together."

"What future?" I ask, sad that even if we find some sort of common ground, we're still miles and miles apart. "There is no future for us. I think we both knew that, and we just reached the logical conclusion faster than we expected."

His voice picks up tempo. "No, I didn't know that. I knew it would be an uphill climb, but I didn't *know* it was doomed from the start. I had hope."

"Not very realistic hope."

"Who's to say what's realistic and what's not? The universe throws people into our paths that we never expected to meet, we're given opportunities that we never thought would come our way. Life takes twists and turns that we never see coming. I think anything is possible."

"You and my sister Emerald," I say, echoes of her voice whispering in my mind.

"Do you think there's any chance in the world that you'd want to see me again?" he asks.

I feel like crying again, but this time it's not entirely because of sadness. "Of course. I want to see you right now, but that's not the problem."

"What's the problem, then? Please let me try to solve it."

"I don't know if you can." I'm afraid to hope. Afraid to believe he's as dedicated and serious as he sounds.

"I can't if you don't tell me what it is."

"I know that if it's a question of choosing between the band and me, you're going to choose the band. They're your clients, and they're owed your first loyalty; I understand that. My family is so precious to me, and what we have going on here right now is really delicate, with the band and our mothers figuring out what their relationships are, and my sisters taking their settlements . . . I couldn't handle going through the heartache I've been suffering a second time, but I know if push comes to shove, and you're forced to choose between them and me, you'll reveal what you know about Darrell and our shared genetics or whatever to the band. And that could destroy everything we've been working to rebuild. I just don't see how this can be resolved, because eventually, if you're here all the time walking the line between lover and lawyer, the secrets will come out."

There's a long silence before he answers. "Would you let me work on it? Would you let me try to come up with a solution?"

"I guess. But I think you're dealing with something that's pretty impossible."

"Nothing is impossible. You need to believe your sister and me."

I smile. A tiny flicker of hope comes to light inside my heart. "You are pretty smart people."

I can hear a smile in his voice when he answers. "We are, that's true. Especially your sister."

"How is Tinkerbell doing?" I ask, hoping the change of conversation will help me breathe better.

"Are we done talking about you and me?" he asks, impressing me with his tenacity. Any other man I know would have jumped on the opportunity to move on.

"I think so. It just really hurts me to think about not being with you anymore, so I'd rather not talk about it now."

"I understand. Tinkerbell is doing great, thanks to you."

"I'm happy to hear that. She's a sweet dog."

"She really misses Banana and Oscar Mayer, though."

"Really? How do you know?"

"Because I have pictures of them on my phone, and whenever she starts whining at me, I show her the pictures and she sits down and wags her tail."

"You show her pictures? That's so cute."

"Yes. And I have a couple of you on here that I stare at and wag my tail over, too."

I stifle a giggle at that image. "When did you get pictures of me?"

"I didn't take them; your sister sent them to me."

"My sister? Which one?"

"Amber . . . who else?" He says it like he's annoyed.

"What's she doing sending you pictures of me?"

"Oh, believe me, it hasn't stopped since I left."

"Are you serious?" I don't know whether to be mad or embarrassed. I think I'm both.

"Here, I'll read you her latest email." I hear some clicking on his computer and then he starts to recite her letter:

"Dear Greg. Would you please get your head out of your ass? Today would be great if you could manage it. My sister is crying and miserable, all because of you. You are a dick if you don't fix this. Here is a picture of the girl who I know you love. Now get your ass out here and fix this. Love, Amber. PS: Seriously, you are a dick if you don't fix this."

"Oh my god. I am *very* sorry." My ears are so hot they feel like they're about to burst into flames.

He chuckles. "Don't worry about it. This is classic Amber."

"No wonder you hate working with her." I can't believe she's so unprofessional.

"Truth be told," he lowers his voice, "I actually *like* working with her. But don't ever tell her I said that, or she'll never let me forget it."

Hearing him say this makes my heart soar. How can I possibly hold on to hurt feelings for a guy who puts up with my sister like such a champ? "I can't believe you. Just when I think you can't surprise me again, you do."

"What? You believed her when she said I was a stick-in-the-mud?"

"I thought Lawyer-Greg was a stick-in-the-mud, yes."

"Who's Lawyer-Greg?" His voice carries a smile.

"I don't know. I really *don't* know." The two men, Lawyer-Greg and Lover-Greg, are starting to blend together. My heart feels so much lighter than it did at the beginning of this conversation. I'm so glad I took the risk and called him.

"Listen," Greg says, "I've gotta get going because I've got about five people standing outside my door wanting to talk to me, but I want to continue this conversation."

"So do I." I mean it, too. I can't believe how much I've missed him and how much happier I am knowing that maybe there is a chance we could continue this relationship. Where there's a will, there's a way, and he seems to have a very strong will.

"How about I get in touch with you tomorrow sometime?"

"Sounds good." I move over to the receiver to hang the phone up. "I'll be here at the house all day."

There's a long pause and then, "Rose?"

"Yes?"

"I'm going to be thinking about you constantly until I see you again."

"You are?" My whole body goes warm.

"I am. And if you think of me, I hope they'll be good thoughts."

"They will be. Mostly."

"Next time I see you I'm going to get rid of all those bad thoughts. I promise."

"I sure hope so."

CHAPTER FORTY-FOUR

I don't hear from Greg for five days. Five whole days. I'm starting to wonder if we even had that conversation where he said he's going to come and make everything better between us. I don't want to call him a stupid guy, but I'm definitely on the verge of thinking it. He wanted me to only have good thoughts about him, but he's not making it easy.

I'm in the living room filing my nails when there's a knock at the front door. When I answer it there's a teenager standing outside. She smiles at me and waves. "Hi. I'm Linny." She looks over her shoulder and then back at me. "I ran ahead."

I stand there blinking at her and then pull the door open wider to look past her and down the driveway. There's an SUV parked about ten yards away, and Greg is unpacking suitcases and a dog carrier from the back of it.

I bring my attention back to my more immediate visitor. "Hi, Linny. I've heard all about you. Welcome to the farm." I reach my hand out to give her a handshake, but she comes at me with a hug. I happily accept it and squeeze her to me. She's tiny and warm, full of bubbly enthusiasm that's already brightening my day.

"Is Amber here? I made some photocopies for her."

"Photocopies?" I can't believe they make a teenager bring her work with her. "Of what?"

"My butt."

Okay, that makes a lot more sense. I point over my shoulder. "She's upstairs."

"Thanks." She takes off running, papers in her hand flapping in the breeze.

I look out the front door, unable to wipe the smile from my face.

Greg looks up. When he sees me, he drops a suitcase on the ground and gently places the dog kennel next to it. I walk down the stairs, and he walks over to meet me halfway, stopping when I'm in front of him. "Aren't you a sight for sore eyes?" he says, leaning down and kissing me on the cheek.

The smell of him gives me a head rush. "I just met your niece," I say, trying to stay on track. "She's pretty special."

"She is, isn't she? Did she show you the photocopies?"

"I did not see the photocopies, but I did hear about them." I have to restrain my laughter.

"That's Amber's influence, I hope you know. Our copy machines are being defiled on a regular basis now, thanks to her."

"I'm not one bit surprised. I have apologized more than once for my sister."

"Don't." He reaches out and puts his hands on my upper arms, rubbing them a little. "She's not causing any real trouble." He frowns when he notices what I'm wearing. "You need to get back inside. You're going freeze to death out here."

I step forward and wrap my arms around his waist, letting his warmth seep into me. "Just hug me and I'll be fine."

He holds me so tight it takes my breath away. His mouth rests near my ear. "God, you don't know how badly I've wanted to do this."

"You're right, I don't. Because you haven't called me for five days, you big jerk." I slap him playfully on the butt.

He leans down and kisses my neck. "I had some things I had to take care of, and I didn't trust myself to get it all done in time. Talking to you would have tempted me to come sooner."

"You're here now; that's all that matters."

He kisses my neck some more and then moves his lips to my mouth. Suddenly, his tongue is there, and all the passion that we had before is back, full force. I feel the muscles across his back tighten as he slides his hands over me.

"Hey, watch the PDA; I'm only a child," comes a voice from the porch.

We release each other and I turn around. Linny is running back down the stairs, now without the photocopies in hand.

"Amber loved my pictures. She says she's going to hang them on the refrigerator."

"No, she is not. Help me with these two cases." Greg tries to sound stern, but I hear the love in his voice.

"You're so bossy," Linny says as she picks up the purple suitcase and disappears into the house.

"Let me give you a hand with this," I say, picking up the dog kennel. I peer inside and see Tinkerbell's little face. She has a pink bow on. "Oh my goodness, she is so cute. Banana and Oscar Mayer are going to go crazy when they see her."

"Where are they?" Greg asks. "I expected to at least hear them by now."

"They're out taking a walk with my sister. They'll be back soon."

We make it into the house with all of his stuff. I look at the pile of his belongings, surprised to see so many of them. "You thinking about staying for a while?" I'm trying not to get too excited over the idea. I could be reading this wrong. Maybe he's just stopping here on the way to somewhere else.

"We decided to take a little vacation. We're hoping the farm can host us for a little while."

I walk over and take his hands. "We can host you for as long as you want to stay."

He gives me a funny look . . . part smile, part grimace. "That's good, because I'm kind of out of a job right now."

I stare up at him in shock. "What?"

"I told you I was going to solve the problem, didn't I?"

I back away, letting go of his hands. I feel light-headed. "What are you saying?"

"I'm saying I took care of the conflict-of-interest problem. I can't represent Red Hot and be with you, so I no longer represent Red Hot."

My voice comes out as a whisper. "Do they know that?"

"Yes, they do."

I look around us at the empty house. "What? How?"

"Two days ago. We made it official."

"But . . . nobody told me."

"They wanted me to tell you. This is between you and me."

"But you've worked with them for *years*." I'm blown away. I can't believe I'm hearing this.

"Yes, I have. And we know each other really well, and we agree on the fact that the most important thing here is your happiness. They can always find another lawyer, but no one can replace you in their hearts."

My legs hit the chair behind me and I fall into it. I sit down, staring up at him. "You did all that for me?"

He comes over and pulls the chair out so he can sit down next to me. He takes my hand and strokes it, hoping to calm me down, I think. *Good luck with that.* "I don't want you to freak out about this. I know it seems like a really huge commitment, and it might be, but it's more than that. Something more important."

I blink a few times, some of the surprise wearing off. "Explain it to me."

"I told you that I spend a lot of time with Linny. Well, I've talked to her mother, and she has agreed to let me take full-time guardianship of her."

"Guardianship? You're going to be her parent?"

"I will always be her uncle, but right now I'm going to be her primary guardian, so yes, like a parent. Her mother is no longer in a position to take care of her like she needs to be cared for, and she knows that. This is not an acrimonious thing at all. I'm very close to my sister, and I'm doing this because it's what Linny needs right now."

"Does she know you're unemployed?"

He smiles. "She knows I'm unemployed, and she also knows I made a lot of wise investments over the years and I've lived frugally."

"But that car we saw you driving when you came here . . ."

"A company car. Not my car, not my loan, not my problem."

"Oh."

"I don't need to work to earn a living. I could retire today if I wanted to, and I'd be perfectly fine."

"Oh. Well. That makes it easier."

"It does, doesn't it?" He reaches up and moves some hair off my face. "Like I said to you a minute ago; we're here for vacation. If things get weird, Linny and I can move on. I'm homeschooling her for now, so we can explore things for a little while. She's never really been out of the city, and I haven't been out in a long time either, outside of work duties, so I thought maybe we'd take in some world culture while we have the chance."

"Oh, that's really cool. Are you going to travel around the world?"

He shrugs. "We're going to play it by ear. We'll start here at Glenhollow and see where it takes us."

"So, you'll be leaving. Eventually."

"Yes. But we'll come back. As long as somebody here wants us to come back, anyway." He looks vulnerable for the first time since he arrived.

"That's so cool. Really, I'm happy for you." I shake my head, in awe at his bravery. "This is just so big. It's so wild. I didn't know you were that spontaneous."

"Neither did I." He reaches up and places his hand on my cheek, tracing my bottom lip with his thumb. "You and I don't know each other that well, and we didn't get the chance to spend a lot of time together when I was here before, but I'd like to. I'd like to get to know you better. I'd like to spend every moment with you for days and days until I know everything there is to know about you and your body."

My face flushes and I look down. "You're being very forward with me, sir."

"I am, I know. I'm tired of hiding how I feel. I'm tired of being professional and stiff all the time. I want to open up and be real for a change."

I grin at him and his newfound freedom. "I think the hippie around here is starting to wear off on you."

"Maybe it is, but is that such a bad thing?" His touch falls away, and he searches my eyes for my answer.

I take his hand and hold it in mine. "It's not a bad thing at all. It's a great thing. I wish more people were open to the idea of being free with their lives like that. Life is meant to be an adventure, not a chore."

"I thought you'd understand." He reaches into his coat pocket and pulls out a box. He holds it out between us and looks down at it for a couple seconds before he looks up at me. "I don't want this to freak you out."

I stare at what looks distinctively like a ring box. "Okaaay."

"There's something inside this box, and it's for you. I don't want you to look at it until I talk to you about it first, though."

My heart is beating so hard, it almost hurts. I feel like I'm going to throw up. I pull my hands back and fold them in my lap. "Okay. Start explaining yourself." I hope I don't have a heart attack right here in the dining room, because it sure feels like I might.

"After I left here and thought things were falling apart between us, I tried to go back to work, but I just couldn't do it. I couldn't concentrate on anything. All I kept thinking about was your face, the things you said to me, cleaning out those kennels . . ."

"The possum made a big impression on you, I see."

"That's not it," he says, moving past his smile. "You know what I'm saying. Or maybe you don't. Maybe it's not the same for you."

"It is," I assure him, putting my hand on his. "It is the same for me." I don't want him to think that he's alone in this crazy thing we have. I don't even know what to call it—a relationship? Mutual madness? A crazy adventure?

"I took a real hard look at my life, and then I got a phone call from Linny. She was crying and miserable. I've gotten phone calls like this from her before, and I've always managed to calm her down and move on with my life. But this time I couldn't do it. After spending time with you and seeing all of your compassion and your love for the animals who are struggling and need you, I realized that I was in the same position, kind of. I mean, Linny's not a possum, but I was being given an opportunity to do the right thing for a human being who I love, who needs me . . . who is struggling."

He takes me by the hand and looks at me, desperately seeking my understanding. "I'd been lacking the compassion that I needed in order to do the right thing by her and to make the right decisions for my life. I couldn't even see what was right in front of me. When she called me that night, I knew instantly what the right thing to do was. It just came to me in a flash: I need to focus on her and help her get over these issues that she's struggling with."

He lets my hand go and sits up straight. "And so I did. I had the best conversation with Linny that I've ever had, and I talked to my sister and it was the same thing. It was like my heart had been opened when before it was locked up tight." He reaches out to stroke my fingers. "I don't want to go back to being that other person. And I don't want to live in the city. I want to be with you."

My heart stops beating for long enough that it hurts before it starts again. Talk about taking a risk! Greg is jumping off that cliff he told me about once, and he doesn't have ropes or a parachute.

"I don't have a crystal ball," he says. "I can't tell myself or you how long this thing between us could last. But in my hopes and in my dreams, it lasts forever." He reaches down and opens up the box.

Inside is a beautiful diamond ring. "I went to the jewelry store on a whim. I told myself I was just going to look, but then I saw this. It's not the biggest one in the store; I could've bought you something that would've had people talking whenever you walked into a room, but then I thought . . . this woman is going be a veterinarian someday, and she's going to need something that she can wear when she's working."

My heart feels lighter when I envision him thinking of me while he was doing something that was probably freaking him out the whole time. He's also painted a pretty alluring picture of me as a veterinarian wearing his ring.

He holds the box up closer. "So this is the one I picked out. If it's not something you like, we can change it. And if you don't want to be with me in that way, I'll close this thing up, put it in my pocket, and you'll never see it again . . . no harm, no foul." His voice wavers as he loses confidence. He closes the box and continues. "I know it's crazy for me to propose to you when we've only been with each other for a short while, and most of the time with no real defined relationship. But I feel like I already know you so well, and I can't imagine my life without you in it anymore. Believe me, I've tried. It's not going to work to try to push you out of my mind and heart."

He's describing me like I'm the love of his life. How can this be possible? I thought I was the only one falling in love here . . .

"I figured if I don't take a risk, I'm not going to gain anything. I took a risk with you before, and it worked out, so I thought, What the hell . . . I'll try it one more time and see if my luck holds out." He looks down, his face flushed. "It's nuts. I know it's crazy. You can just tell me to put my bags back out in the car and I'll totally understand."

I use my finger to lift his chin so that we can see each other eye to eye. "You are so very brave." He doesn't say anything. He just stares at me, waiting for what I'm going to say next.

My heart is swirling and spinning and flipping. My stomach is doing the same. I have never in my life felt about somebody the way I feel about him. I've dated a few men, and I've been around countless numbers of them as friends, and none of them, not even the ones I've slept with, not even the one I thought I loved, have even come close to making me feel how Greg does.

This man rocks my world. I knew he was a good guy in the months before this moment, but that's nothing compared to what I'm seeing now. He's changed his entire life to help a niece who needs him. He's sacrificing everything so that she can be happy and so that he and I can have a chance at a relationship. And he's asking me to join him in the adventure of a lifetime. I think. He hasn't actually said the words, but I think he means to.

I believe that the universe puts people in my path who need to be there. And I also believe that forces I don't understand push me in the direction I need to go. Someone out there saw fit to have Brian burn my clinic to the ground and take away everything that tethers me to this farm. And now there's a man standing in front of me, a man who's proven himself to have integrity and dedication, offering me the world as my oyster. How stupid would I have to be to say no to that? Nothing ventured, nothing gained, right?

I reach down and open the box. "Can I just take another look at that?"

He pulls it up toward his chest and holds it tight in his fist. "Let's do this the right way." He slowly slides off his chair and goes down on one knee. He lifts the box and opens it, moving it toward me. "Rose Lancaster . . . will you do me the honor of marrying me, for better or for worse, for richer or for poorer, in sickness and health, but mostly for love, happiness, and adventure?"

I nod, unable to say the word. Tears flow out of me.

He sighs and shakes his head slowly. "I gotta hear you say it, babe. I am a lawyer, after all."

"Yes," I say, laughing and crying at the same time. "Yes, I'll marry you, Adventure-Greg."

EPILOGUE

Rose stares at herself in the full-length mirror. "I don't mean to sound vain, but I *really* love this dress." She turns left slightly and right, enjoying the sparkles coming off the sequins sewn into the bodice.

"Me too," Amber says, standing next to her sister while holding out the side of her own gown. "This one's not too shabby either." She tries not to grin but fails, her smile practically glowing.

"It'd better not be, considering what you paid for it," Emerald adds, nudging both of them out of the way with her hip to get a better view of her own fancy garb.

Amber steps between her sisters and wraps her arms around their shoulders, drawing them in close so they can stare at their reflections together. She sighs with happiness. "We look delicious. Like a giant pile of vanilla frosting."

"*You* look like frosting," Rose says. "I look like a mermaid." She smooths down the white satin material that hugs her every curve. The months of vacation she's spent with Greg, traveling the world, hiking up mountains and through forests, relaxing by the beach and sightseeing in cities, have both firmed up her physique and cleared her mind, preparing her for what's ahead.

Amber rolls her eyes. "Stop bragging about your hot bod, would ya? Some people just had babies around here. We can't all look like savagely tanned supermodels."

"Yeah," Em adds. "Fluffy dresses are better at hiding this stubborn baby weight." She pats her tiny belly, hardly visible through the layers of embroidered white organza.

"And it's good for showing off your ginormous boobs, too," Amber says, poking at her sister's cleavage.

"Hey, hands off the merchandise," Em says, turning away. "I just got them all tucked in and now they're falling out again." She lifts out the top of her dress, checking to make sure there won't be any wardrobe malfunctions at the big event.

"How much time do we have?" Rose asks, turning away from the mirror to find her makeup. "Should I put on my mascara now?"

"I don't know," Amber answers. "Are you done crying yet?"

Rose rolls her eyes and sighs, walking over to the window and pushing the curtain aside. "I want to say yes, but then *this* happens." She gestures out at the view.

Amber and Em join her, looking beyond the glass to the front yard of their childhood home below. "Can you believe it?" Rose asks. "They're all here for us." More than two hundred brightly dressed guests mill about, sipping drinks and eating hors d'oeuvres.

"Look," Amber says, pointing to a man wearing a tuxedo. "There's my guy. Is he hot or what?"

"Yep. Almost as hot as my guy," Em says, pointing to the tuxedoed man standing next to her sister's fiancé. The girls can't see their tattoos from up here, but Ty's unkempt hairdo and Sam's beard make them both easy to spot.

Greg's more sedate look sets him apart, sending Rose's heart hammering again. She never gets tired of looking at him and still can't believe he's all hers.

Amber pushes Em's finger down. "Please. Don't embarrass yourself. We both know who bagged the hotter babe in the Stanz family."

Rose reaches between them and points. "Talk about babes . . . look at *those* adorable baby cakes."

The three sisters gaze down at Amber's and Emerald's children all dressed in white. The tiny ones are in strollers being watched over by their three grandmothers—Carol, Barbara, and Sally. Emerald's older daughter, Sadie, and Greg's niece Linny are standing watchfully nearby, the two of them fulfilling the dual roles of flower girls and babysitters.

"Beautiful," Emerald says. "Dammit, now I'm crying again." She wipes away the happy tear that escapes, sniffing loudly.

"I thought our hormones were supposed to calm the hell down once the babies were born," Amber says, dabbing at her eyes with a lace handkerchief.

"Look at our moms," Rose says. "Can you believe it? They're all in dresses and heels."

"Better take a bunch of pictures, because this is probably the last time it'll ever happen," Amber says, chuckling.

"Maybe we should have spread our weddings out," Em says. "Had three parties instead of one?"

Rose and Amber shake their heads together. "No, thanks," they say in tandem.

Em grins and lifts her voice. "You're right. One giant party to rule them all."

Amber throws out her arms. "And then off into the wild blue yonder we go!"

Rose loses a bit of her good cheer at her sister's words, backing up to sit on the edge of her bed. "Aren't you guys at all worried about our futures?"

"What's to worry about?" Amber asks, turning to face her. "You're starting vet school an hour away, and Greg is going to be by your side the entire time working from the home office of that giant house he bought for you guys . . ." Amber shifts her focus to her other sister. "Em is getting her new home built a hundred yards from here that includes a studio so Sam can work at home; and Ty and I are going to run the Red Hot empire from our gorgeous condo in the city. But we'll be back all the time . . . every holiday and long weekends too, I promise. Our futures are so bright we're going to have to wear shades, babe."

"Yeah, but . . . marriage? Are we crazy?" Rose looks at her sisters as a sliver of panic slips in. "I mean, think of all the years we've lived with women who never wanted to be tied down by men. Are we doing the right thing? Is it worth the risk, giving our hearts away like this?"

Amber sits on Rose's left and Em sits at her right. Em is the first to speak. "I'm one hundred percent sure we are doing the right thing, and I haven't even been on a vacation with Sam yet. You've traveled with Greg and Linny for *six months*. You know them almost as well as you know us, and vice versa." Her voice softens. "And even after all that time, you still love them to pieces."

"Seven," corrects Amber. "Seven months. Don't forget the month in the cabin." She wiggles her eyebrows at Rose.

"Yeah, talk about putting the cart before the horse," Em says, snorting with suppressed laughter.

"What's that supposed to mean?" Rose asks, fighting the smile that memories of that trip always bring.

"If that wasn't a honeymoon, I don't know what was. All alone up in the mountains for an entire month, no kids, no responsibilities, a case of champagne . . ."

"Who told you about the champagne?" Rose asks, trying to sound indignant.

"Red. He said he gave you and Greg an early wedding gift—full access to his wine cellar—and an entire case of his best stuff was missing."

Rose shrugs. "What can I say? We wanted to splurge a little."

"Well, now you can splurge all you want, since you've got ten million bucks in the bank," Amber says.

Rose frowns. "So do you and Emerald. But you know I'm not spending that money on champagne."

Amber rubs her back. "I know, I know. I'm just yanking your chain. I know you have tuition to pay for and a future vet clinic to build."

"And don't forget about Brian," Em adds. "We're all chipping in to help him out with that therapy program."

"I still feel terrible that he was having such a hard time and we never really bothered to get to know him," Rose says. "The poor kid was in crisis just down the road from us."

"That's pretty generous, considering he burned your clinic to the ground and called you the b-word." Amber snorts.

Rose gives her sister a scolding look. "We're way past that at this point, aren't we?"

"I know, I know. Yes we are." Amber sighs. "I'm glad we're helping Brian. He's a good kid. Confused, but good down deep, thanks to Smitty being there for him all those years. I just wish Smitty hadn't left, though, you know? I feel like we drove him away."

"No we didn't, don't be silly," Em says. "I got an email from him this morning. He loves being in the air force. He's bummed he couldn't be here for our big day, but he's having a ball. He said he's found his true calling as an aircraft mechanic. And it was good for him to get away from all the stuff at his house. It was high time his parents started taking care of Brian for a change, and the only way they were going to do that was if Smitty left."

"I miss him, though," Rose says. "He's been a part of our lives forever, and now he's not here. Everything is changing so much."

"He'll be back. Everyone always comes back here," Em says, walking over to look out the window again. "This place is special."

"More than special," Amber adds, going over to join her sister. "It's heaven on earth. I love the big city, but I'll never be fully away from here. This is where we grew up. It's our one true family home. Our mothers *and* our fathers live here now and will always welcome us back no matter what." She sighs with happiness. "It doesn't matter how busy I get or how successful Ty and I become, there's a lot to be said for unconditional family love. I'm never going to take it for granted again."

Rose walks over to be with her fellow brides. "You're right. No matter where we go, no matter how much our lives change, we always have Glenhollow Farms, the people who live here, and all the wonderful memories we made together." She dries her last tear. "I think I'm ready to put on my mascara."

Amber and Em turn, the three sisters facing each other in a circle. Amber speaks first. "A year ago, Red Hot walked into our lives and turned everything upside down. But I don't regret it one single iota. I found the love of my life, started a family with him, and began a career that makes me feel amazingly accomplished and fulfilled." She looks at Em and then Rose. "We all found these things. We've all started down paths to our adult lives, to our new futures. And we're doing this together, just like we've done everything else. The miles that separate us won't make a bit of difference."

Rose nods. "Agreed."

"Yes," Em adds, lifting her chin.

Amber continues. "We were wrong to think Red, Cash, or Mooch had done something purposely to hurt our mothers all those years ago, and I'm glad we finally got to the bottom of everything." She looks at Rose. "It doesn't matter to me that some genetics expert doctor can tell from a photograph that you're related to Darrell; like Red said, it doesn't matter who donated the DNA that makes us who we are. The only thing that matters is that we all love each other equally, and that we want nothing more than to love and support one another."

Rose nods. "And that's exactly why those three men and Paul will be walking us down the aisle today, regardless of the fact that we will never have DNA tests done."

"Exactly," Em says. "They're our family. And you're my sisters." She holds out her arms and the other two happily join her in a group hug.

"Damn. I'm glad I didn't put any mascara on yet," Rose says, pulling out of the hug and wiping at her eyes again.

Amber fans her face with her hand, looking up at the ceiling. "Me too. Holy moly, talk about emotional moments."

"Did you hear that?" Em asks, her ear cocked to the window. "The music; it's started."

Rose rushes over to the dresser, grabbing the mascara. "Just give me five seconds."

Amber checks her hair one last time and then lifts her bouquet from the large box by the bedroom door.

Emerald makes sure her bosom is completely contained within the confines of her bodice and looks up to grin at her sisters. "My boobs and I are ready!"

A knock comes at the door. "Come in!" sings Amber.

Red sticks his head in the room. His hair is neatly combed and slicked back. "Fathers of the brides here, checking to see if they're ready." The door pushes open farther and Mooch steps in past Red. "Better get down there quick before all the champagne is gone." Cash is the last one to enter the room. He stares at the girls and smiles. "Well, I'll be a monkey's uncle. Would you look at you three pretty girls . . . Angels in white." He lifts a hand to wipe a tear away, his chin quivering.

Red's voice is gruff as he elbows his bandmate. "That's enough of that. Come on, ladies." He waves his hand to hurry them along, the silver rings on his fingers glinting in the light. "There are three anxious guys downstairs worried someone might be changing her mind."

Amber walks over first, pausing to kiss each of the three men on the cheek as she passes. "See you downstairs." Her dress makes swishing sounds as she maneuvers around them.

Emerald is next. "If any of you see my boobs trying to escape, warn me before anyone else sees." She kisses them on the cheeks as she passes.

Red holds his hand out to Rose. "Last but not least." She slides her palm into his.

"Not by a long shot," Mooch adds, putting his hand at her back as she walks by.

Rose stops, staring at the three men who are not her fathers but who love her as a daughter just the same. "Thank you."

"For what?" Red asks.

"For being who you are. For being here for us today. For loving our mothers enough to forgive them."

Red kisses the back of her hand. Cash leans in and kisses her on one cheek as Mooch kisses the other.

"There was nothing to forgive," Mooch says. "Love like ours happens once in a lifetime, and it comes with bucket loads of understanding. We were young. Careless." He touches her shoulder gently. "Just do us a favor and learn from our mistakes. Never walk away from something as good as what you have with the people you love."

Rose pats him on the cheek as the warmth of his wisdom and caring flow through her. "I won't. I'm ready." She looks at each man in turn. "Walk me down the aisle?"

Mooch holds out one arm and Red holds out another while Cash opens the door wider. He grins and gestures out into the hallway. "Come on, family . . . it's showtime."

ABOUT THE AUTHOR

Elle Casey, a former attorney and teacher, is a prolific *New York Times* and *USA Today* bestselling American author who lives in southwest France with her husband, the youngest of her three children, and a bunch of cats, dogs, and horses. She writes in several genres, including romance, suspense, urban fantasy, paranormal, science fiction, dystopian, and action/adventure.

28143565R00200

Printed in Poland
by Amazon Fulfillment
Poland Sp. z o.o., Wrocław